The Botanist's Daughter

Also by Kayte Nunn

Rose's Vintage

Angel's Share

KAYTE NUNN

The Botanist's Daughter

hachette
AUSTRALIA

First published in Australia and New Zealand in 2018
by Hachette Australia
(an imprint of Hachette Australia Pty Limited)
Level 17, 207 Kent Street, Sydney NSW 2000
www.hachette.com.au

This edition published in 2019

10 9 8 7 6 5 4 3 2 1

A catalogue record for this book is available from the National Library of Australia

ISBN 978 0 7336 4233 3

Cover design by Christabella Designs
Cover photographs courtesy of Shutterstock
Text design by Christabella Designs
Typeset in Minion Pro by Bookhouse, Sydney
Printed and bound in Australia by McPherson's Printing Group

The paper this book is printed on is certified against the Forest Stewardship Council® Standards. McPherson's Printing Group holds FSC® chain of custody certification SA-COC-005379. FSC® promotes environmentally responsible, socially beneficial and economically viable management of the world's forests.

For Sheila, who loved lilies and reading

I love you as the plant that never blooms
but carries in itself the light of hidden flowers

– *Sonnet XVII*, Pablo Neruda

Chapter One

Sydney, Autumn 2017

Anna opened the door to see three men standing there. The one closest to her was a lumbering, Neanderthal-browed hulk; the next a middling, middle-aged figure in overalls; and just behind him, there was a shorter, thinner, younger one with tattoos running down the sinewy muscles of his forearms.

'The three bears,' she said under her breath, noticing as she did that the paint on the jamb had begun to flake. It was a deep mulberry shade called 'Grand Poobah', the name of which had made her grandmother honk with laughter in the middle of the hardware store. It had been a few months after Anna's granddad died, and Gussie had wanted to cheer herself up.

Shifting her gaze from the men, Anna pressed the tongues of loose paint against the bare wood in a futile attempt to reaffix them.

'What's that you say?' asked the lumbering one, who, with his rough halo of golden hair and a belly that strained the weave of his shirt, reminded her distinctly of Papa Bear. 'Have we got the right place?' He consulted a notebook, running a stubby forefinger down the page, and then looked across at her. 'Jenkins, is it?'

'Sorry,' replied Anna, suddenly flustered at the thought that he might have overheard her. 'Come in.'

She stood back and ushered them through the door, and the men looked around, sizing up the place, their heavy boots echoing in the empty house. Anna held her breath as she led them into the kitchen, a tiny space in the middle of the long, narrow terrace that hadn't seen an update in decades. She gazed at the lemon Formica, the timber cupboards and the orange-and-brown linoleum, its patterned surface worn to a blur by a million steps. She remembered the excitement of coming to stay as a child, being driven across the bridge from her leafy suburban home to what seemed like another world, one of endless, twisting narrow streets and slivers of houses fronted by lacy wrought-iron balconies. Of sitting at the kitchen table eating jam sandwiches washed down with frosted glasses of icy pink Nesquik. Of her granddad taking her and her sister up the street to the corner store, skipping ahead of them over the cracks in the pavement, eager for the Redskins and Violet Crumbles that were stacked on the shop's narrow shelves. In summer there were sweet and sticky Icy Poles or Paddle Pops. A Monaco Bar if they were really lucky.

Sweet memories, all.

Papa Bear spoke. 'All right then, love, we'll go and get our gear and make a start. Shouldn't take us too long,' he said as he led the others away.

They returned a few minutes later, armed with crowbars and hammers, and Anna left them to it, going up the stairs and into her grandparents' old bedroom at the front of the house. The flowered yellow wallpaper was mottled with faded patches where the afternoon sun caught it and the carpet was worn. As she reached the centre of the room she caught a faint whiff of Gussie's perfume – Youth Dew. Applied with a generous hand and worn without a hint of irony. She half-expected Gussie to come bustling out at her, grey hair neatly curled, drying her hands on a towel and scolding her for the lack of warning, a ready smile dimpling her cheeks nonetheless. Granddad had died when Anna was a teen, but it was the loss of Gussie she felt the most.

Of course, in recent years, more often than not when Anna would call round her grandmother would mistake her for her mother, or worse, not recognise her at all. Now, the sombre tick of the clock on the mantel was the only welcome.

Anna ran a finger along the dusty windowsills, then opened the French doors onto the balcony that faced the street, letting in the breeze. The house had been shut up for a few months, and the smell of damp couldn't be ignored; it had been an insufferably humid summer.

Her grandparents had favoured dark, heavy furniture with sturdy turned legs that weighed an absolute ton; the house had been crammed with it, every last bit of wall space taken up with sideboards and dressers, their surfaces laden with floral china, crocheted doilies, dusty glass ornaments, collectors' dolls dressed in native costume from countries they would never visit. But the clearance firm had been the week before and now the place was emptier than Anna had ever known it, almost all trace of its former occupants erased. Sudden grief overwhelmed her and brought a rush of wet heat behind her eyes.

It's only stuff, she told herself sternly. *None of it will bring Gussie back*. Her grandmother had left this house, the Paddington terrace she'd been born in, raised a family in and died in, solely to Anna. That had been a surprise. Almost as shocking as the fact of her grandmother's death. Despite her fading memory, the old lady had been spry, insisting on living by herself. 'What would I want with a load of old strangers dribbling into their tea and cacking their undies?' she'd asked when Anna's mum had tentatively suggested several times over recent years that she might want to think about moving to a retirement home, especially after her Alzheimer's diagnosis.

Anna felt suddenly overwhelmed. Was she doing the right thing? Should she have waited? Did she have the strength to do this on her own?

Don't be ridiculous, she scolded herself. The decision had been made. She would see this through.

She walked down the stairs, stepping over the one that had always creaked, cast a swift look at the builders, who had begun the demolition of the front room – the 'good room', she remembered with a faint smile – then turned towards the back of the house. She passed through the draughty sleep-out where she and her sister used to stay when they were kids, and opened the back door.

She let out a long sigh.

She shouldn't have been surprised as she'd not been out the back for months, but she was disheartened nonetheless. The garden, for so long her grandmother's pride and joy, was in a complete state. Overgrown wasn't a strong enough word for it: great choking weeds had sprung up, overwhelming the once carefully tended plantings. Anna, who as a girl had loved to potter about in the postage-stamp-sized space equipped with her own little trowel and fork, helping her grandmother weed and water, had been too concerned with the life ebbing away inside the house to do so much as even peer outside; and then, after Gus's death she hadn't wanted to linger in the house. She spent her days looking after other people's gardens and had left this one untended.

The east fence was an unkempt hedge of murraya, its normally heady-scented bell-shaped flowers dried up and brown. The path had almost disappeared beneath a creeping mat of tradescantia. Ivy curled its strangling tendrils up the crepe myrtle. And the wisteria, trained over the back fence, had collapsed on itself. Under her breath, she recited the names of her grandmother's favourite plants as if they were a litany, searching for each among the tangle of weeds. She murmured their names under her breath as much to reassure herself as anything else . . . brilliant orange strelitzia – birds of paradise – purple aster, a deep magenta bougainvillea, hippeastrum, hellebores, camellia, pelargonium and delicate viola in the shade there . . . the familiar words a salve to her sorrow.

As she cleared a space to sit on the weathered Lutyens bench at the back of the garden, her gaze rested on a spider's web that billowed in the breeze like a parachute, its gossamer threads stretched almost to breaking point. Had it been nearly six months? Half a year already? For all that time she'd been an automaton, roused daily from heavy sleep by her alarm, going through the motions at work, barely remembering conversations with her clients, losing herself in the repetitive digging and weeding of garden beds and the mowing of summer lawns. She had avoided returning to this garden, a place she was once so fond of.

She squinted up at the sun, which had climbed higher in the sky and then across to the apple tree in the corner, last season's wizened fruit still hanging from its branches. Here in this garden was the proof: while some lives ended, the rest of the world marched relentlessly on. Trying to stop it was as futile as attempting to catch water in a web.

She sat, surveying the scene, when from inside the house suddenly came a louder thump than all the preceding ones, followed by a shout. She heard her name called and sprang up, hurrying back along the path.

As she entered the house, clouds of white dust filled the air, and what were once three small rooms on the ground floor was now an open space, bigger than she had imagined it might be. It had all come apart so quickly. The old carpet had been pulled up and rolled up and now lolled halfway out the front door. Bricks and crumbling mortar and plasterboard littered the floor.

'All right, love?' said the tall, lumbering one. 'We thought you might want to see this.' He pointed at the bookshelves, which the builders had begun to rip away from the far wall. 'Almost a shame to pull them out, really. You don't often see workmanship like that these days.'

'What?' Anna had left clear instructions to demolish the shelves, in order to widen the narrow room, so she wasn't sure what they were showing her.

'Look a bit closer, there,' he said, pointing to the wall that had been covered by the bookshelf furthest from the window. She did as she was asked and then she saw it – a hole at about waist height. As she stepped forward to get a better look, she noticed the smallest of the demolition men standing to her left. 'Here,' he piped up, his voice as reedy as his frame, and as she turned towards him he held out a battered notebook. It was completely grey, covered in dust and fine spider filaments. 'Not sure what this is, but you might like to take a gander at it.'

'Thanks.' She took the notebook and blew on its surface, sending a cloud of ash puffing into the air. She wiped at the book with one finger, revealing a dark blue cover. She opened it carefully and saw dense, spidery writing covering the yellowed pages. 'How odd. I wonder how something like this ended up in the brickwork?'

'Well, what is it?' he asked anxiously.

'I'm not sure. It must have got stuck behind there before the shelves were built. I'll take a better look at it later.'

She returned to the garden and, after placing the notebook on the bench beside her, was pondering where to start work, when there was another crash and a shout for her. *What this time?*

She retraced her steps and leant around the door: this time the middle-sized builder was holding a greyish box, about the size a pair of boots might come in.

'In *there*?' Anna asked, staring at the hole in the wall, which scarcely looked large enough to have contained the box. As if to convince herself, she stepped forward and peered into the space. She shuddered as she looked into the pitch blackness, imagining enormous spiders and the round, hard shells of dead woodlice.

'Take a look,' said the boss, picking up a torch and shining it upwards.

She stared up into the narrow opening: about half a metre up, the chute widened slightly to some kind of shelf.

'Yeah, up there,' he confirmed. 'I was having a bit of a sticky beak. I just about got my arm up there and tipped it over, and down it came. It got stuck, but I managed to wiggle it out.'

Anna turned back to the builder who was holding the box. Taking it from him, she was surprised at its weight and had to tense her biceps to avoid dropping it. It wasn't in fact grey, just covered in dust and cobwebs as the notebook had been. She rubbed her fingers across the top to reveal a tarnished metal surface. The edges of the box had been etched into shapes and as Anna brushed more of the dust away, she discovered three-dimensional bees and curlicues of plants and flowers. Four-leafed clovers were carved at each corner. 'Bloody hell,' she exclaimed. 'How bizarre.'

'If you say so, love,' said the boss, scratching his head. 'Lucky it didn't break Nathan's arm when it came down.'

'Yes, I guess it was,' she replied absently, still absorbed in the box. She put it down on the floor and tried the lid, but it wouldn't budge. Wiping away the dust from the sides with her hands, she discovered a small heart-shaped padlock keeping it shut tight. It must have once been brass, but it was now as tarnished and black as the rest of the box. 'I wonder what it is?'

'Want us to have a crack at it?' asked the boss, lifting his sledgehammer.

'No!' cried Anna, still bent down looking at it. 'No. I don't want it damaged.'

'I've got a crowbar,' Nathan added.

'I think I'd better take it to a locksmith actually,' she said, hating the primness in her voice. 'But thanks for the offer.'

'Okay, love, whatever you say. We'll crack on, then. I reckon we'll have most of the demolition in here done by the end of the day.'

Anna looked at the flimsy remains of the bookshelves and nodded. 'Okay, thanks.'

She picked up the box again, holding it away from her body to avoid covering herself in more dust as she headed for the stairs. She felt a shiver as a gust of wind blew through the open front door. How on earth had such a thing come to be hidden away in the wall cavity? Even through the grime she could see that it must have once been very beautiful. Probably valuable, certainly antique. What had possessed someone to hide it like that? Could Granny Gus have wedged it up there, hidden it somewhere it would almost certainly never be discovered? Anna reached for her phone. She had to speak to her mother.

Chapter Two

CORNWALL, 1886

The boots were newly arrived from London, ordered in happier times. There were twelve tricky buttons, each firmly hooked into the Moroccan leather, and Elizabeth wrestled with them, trying unsuccessfully to pull each boot from her swollen feet. The bootmaker was renowned as one of the county's finest, and the leather the softest money could buy, but after a mere hour's wear they had given her blisters. If she were at the house, Daisy would have been there to help, button hook at the ready, but as it was she had to make do with her own fumbling fingers, wondering whether the correct last had been used.

Several minutes later, her toes were finally free of their wretched encasement and she wiggled them luxuriously, pressing the tender red spots on her heels and assessing the damage.

'Oh Lord save us, who would wear such things if they had the choice?' Elizabeth said aloud.

Not that there was anyone to hear her complaint.

Earlier, she had escaped the torpor brought on by the late-afternoon heat that crept into every corner of the rambling Trebithick Hall. It had rendered its few occupants – with Elizabeth the sole exception – into a state of dozy insensibility. And so she was able to slip unnoticed into the gloom of the stables, where she commanded Banks, the stablemaster, to bring Achilles to her. 'With my father's saddle, if you please,' she said, daring him to contradict her. Now was not the time for a lady's sidesaddle.

Once he had led the black stallion up to the mounting block, she dismissed him. 'I can certainly manage from here.' She didn't want Banks to see her struggle with her dress, nor – heaven forfend – catch sight of her undergarments. Standards of propriety might have temporarily been eased at Trebithick Hall, but she didn't want to make Banks feel more uncomfortable than he doubtless already was. Hitching up the black bombazine of her skirts, she clambered awkwardly astride the sweating horse and kicked him on. She tried not to think about the fact that she had never ridden Achilles before, and certainly wouldn't have been granted permission when her father was alive, never mind to ride him astride. 'Sidesaddle is the only decorous way for ladies to comport themselves,' John Trebithick had always insisted. Though progressive in other ways – he had encouraged Elizabeth and her sister to study Latin and ancient

Greek, for example – he had been immovable on that particular point of decorum.

'Come on, boy, let's go!' she'd cried, wheeling the big horse around the yard and pointing him out of the hall's side gate and towards the bridleway that ran along the eastern boundary of the Trebithick estate. Achilles needed little encouragement and Elizabeth gripped the reins as he bucked at the unfamiliar weight on his back. Much like her, he had been cooped up for months, as her father became too frail to venture outdoors let alone ride his favourite mount. Although Banks had turned the horse out, letting him kick up his heels in the meadow with the rest of the stable the day before, he was still as fresh as new milk.

Achilles exploded into a gallop before she could rein him in and Elizabeth experienced terror and exhilaration in equal measure at the realisation that she had far less control than she had imagined over the solidly muscled beast. He took off like a skyrocket and with about as much accuracy of direction. 'Steady on there, mister! Whoa! Whoa, boy!' she shouted, her words carried away on the breeze, heeded by neither man nor beast. She curled her fingers into the horse's mane and hung on for dear life. Her bonnet flew off, caught by the wind as they sped onwards. She barely registered the bright purple of the corn-cockle weed, the sheaves of wheat gathered into stooks, leaning like drunkards at a wedding, nor the nettles, grown several feet high along the bridleway, her stockings at least offering some protection from their stinging leaves. It was more than a mile before Achilles seemed to hear her pleas, to feel her frantic sawing of reins on his mouth, and he slowed a fraction, allowing her to catch her breath and summon her scattered wits.

The bridleway led towards a tiny inlet, and, as if scenting the sea, Achilles sped up once more, hurtling towards the cliff edge at such a pace that Elizabeth feared the stallion wouldn't stop in time and they would both tumble onto the rocks below. She hauled on the reins again and squeezed her knees into Achilles' flanks with all her might until the horse came to an abrupt halt with less than a foot of ground to spare. He gave a snort and tossed his head arrogantly, jangling the bit between his teeth as if to say, *Satisfied?*

Grasping the pommel of the saddle with trembling hands, she leant forward and flung her leg over Achilles' rump, as she'd seen men do, and slid to the ground. She stumbled, muddying her skirts, but picked herself up and, seeing a nearby elm, tied the reins to a low-hanging branch. It took longer than it should have done; her hands would not stop trembling, nor her chest heaving from the effort of keeping Achilles under control.

The crystal blue water sparkled invitingly, a million diamonds strewn on its surface, the horizon a blurred navy line in the shimmer of the noonday heat. The Cornish coastline was renowned for its treachery, with shipwrecks a common occurrence, but Elizabeth knew this tiny inlet well. Ladylove Cove, better known as Lady Luck Cove.

She had spent much of her childhood scrambling over its rocks, pausing only to marvel at the tiny, tenacious plants that clung to its cliffside. The way down to the pebbled beach was steep, but stairs had been cut into the rocks – by long-dead contraband merchants, so the legend had it – and, happily, the going was dry. Recovered somewhat from the ordeal of her ride, she scampered down the rough steps with the grace of a sprite.

Elizabeth didn't stop to think what Georgiana might say if she knew where she was or what she was up to. Her older sister and her husband, Robert, had arrived from Plymouth three weeks before, too late for the end but in time for the tolling of the church bell that announced her dear papa's death – nine times for a man, and then a further fifty-seven for the years of his life. They were likely even now combing Trebithick Hall for bounty, earmarking paintings and furniture for their own ends. Not that Elizabeth cared. The only thing of value to her was her dear papa, and all the tea in China wouldn't bring him back. She stifled a sob. The time for weeping was over.

In the days after her father's death she had restlessly paced the gardens: going up and down the long walk in a daze, uncertain where or what her future might be. She had no patience for needlework or embroidery, and playing the pianoforte was out of the question. She found no solace in drawing, until then her favourite pastime. She was no longer able to help her father in the meticulous cataloguing of plants; an absorbing task that she had relished when he was alive.

After her sister and brother-in-law had arrived, there had followed a fortnight spent mostly in the stifling drawing room reading condolence cards from visitors; some were dear to her but most she was indifferent to, a few she privately detested, and several she had never met nor heard of. Though Elizabeth was grateful for the company of her sister, who had only returned home on a few occasions since her marriage six years previously, the need to escape, to fill her lungs with salt-laced air and to feel the breeze against her skin, had become almost overwhelming. Which was why, finding herself unexpectedly alone that afternoon, she had made her way to the stables.

For more than a month before her father's death she had been loath to leave the house for long, venturing only briefly to the gardens for herbs to make into a poultice to try to ease his suffering. She had gone back and forth to the kitchen, much to the annoyance of Cook, to supervise the making of calf's-foot jelly in an attempt to persuade her father to eat something nourishing. Once she had taken the carriage to Padstow, to the new pharmacist, clutching the receipt for a nostrum that her great-grandmother had sworn by, and that had cured Georgiana of a bout of illness when she was a child.

The doctor had made his daily call, purging her father with leeches until he lay back on his pillow, face drained of colour, wracked with a terrifying cough, scarlet blood soaking his handkerchief. But it was all to no avail. Papa had consumption, and there was faint hope of recovery.

Elizabeth struggled to reconcile the pale, weak invalid with the father she had known and loved, a man who was as strong as an ox but as gentle as a lamb with her and Georgiana. A man who chased adventure; a collector of plants who travelled the world and brought back not only exotic and unusual specimens, but also incredible stories of strange lands and peoples. She and her sister would listen, wide-eyed with wonder at his tales of ancient cities and crescent-shaped boats. They would beg him to tell them of the almond-eyed and dark-skinned women, of snake charmers, mystical healers, holy men and thieves. He would tantalise them with stories of riding on majestic elephants in the Himalayas, of Arum lilies that stank like salted fish and of juicy fruits that tasted sweeter than a kiss. And he would tickle them as he told of hissing snakes that rose up as tall as a man and hairy-legged spiders larger than dinner plates. He might have been absent for many months at a time, but when he was home he delighted in his daughters and paid them careful attention, doing his best to make up for their lack of a mother.

Elizabeth had reached the shore, her boots slipping on stones tumbled smooth by strong Atlantic tides, before reaching the surer footing of the fine golden sand that ringed the bay. She was almost certain of being undisturbed on this wild beach; few if any came along the path she had ridden to reach it. Taking a careful look around to be sure she was unseen, she sat upon a branch of driftwood and began to undress, beginning with the new boots. They were not the best choice of footwear for riding, but she had been so anxious to be free of the stifling house that she had given it little thought. She was forced to wrestle with the buttons on her gown as she had with the boots, but after some contortion was able to unfasten the topmost ones and slip her dress off her shoulders. She loosened the binding laces of her corset, releasing her stays, and was eventually free of its constriction too. She had frequently cast off all but her underclothes as a little girl while on this beach, but never as a young woman, and she felt a powerful thrill at such an illicit and daring pleasure.

Elizabeth cared as much for corsets as she did for convention, but she had little choice in the wearing of them, despite reading in *The Times* of the Rational Dress Society and silently applauding its endeavours in the big cities. 'If only women did not have to be so constricted in their garments!' she had railed to Mam'zelle Violette. 'Be thankful you are not subject to tight-lacing,' her governess had replied, unmoved.

Finally, she was stripped down to her chemise and bloomers, and the salty air whipped through the fine cotton, both cooling and rousing her. She stretched out her arms, noticing as she did the butterfly-shaped mark on her shoulder. *Café au lait*, Mam'zelle Violette had called it. For Elizabeth, it was an ever-present reminder of her mother, who had the exact same mark in the exact same place – she had seen it on the painting of her that hung in the morning room.

She felt dangerously free, as she hadn't since she was a girl rambling the shoreline with her father, searching for seashells and crabs, for tiny translucent school prawns and seaweed blisters to pop. She stood at the edge of the fizzing, hissing sea, feeling it suck back over her toes, beckoning her. She waded into the water as it frothed around her bare ankles like lace. Further out, it was darker, indigo blue and menacing, white caps indicating a strong offshore wind, but here, in this sheltered cove, on this sweltering summer afternoon, the water was as clear as gin. Elizabeth gasped as the cold reached her knees but she waded in undeterred. As it reached her chest and dragged her chemise down, swirling the fabric about her, the shock of the icy water forced the air from her lungs and froze her legs to a searing numbness. She could no longer feel her sore and swollen toes. With a determined set to her chin, she struck out until her feet lifted off solid ground and floated, suspended in the ocean's chilly embrace.

She lay back in the water, raised her face to the sky and closed her eyes, seeing red from the warm sun behind her eyelids.

For the first time since her father had died, she felt truly alive.

Chapter Three

Cornwall, 1886

'Where on heaven's earth have you been?' Georgiana demanded as Elizabeth crept back into the house by the servants' entrance. She had spent far longer at the little cove than she had intended, drying off on the beach and becoming lost in thought, trying to determine the best way to convince Georgiana and Robert to agree to her plan – the plan her father had requested she carry out.

She wondered if they might be considering a move back to Trebithick Hall. She wasn't hopeful; she rather imagined they might prefer the more cosmopolitan environs of Plymouth, for there was precious little society to be had in this Cornish backwater.

Her father had never cared much for entertaining, preferring, when he was home, to keep the quiet company of his daughters and the occasional visiting scientist or explorer. Oh, there were stories of great dances and house parties, with guests journeying from as far afield as London, but that had been when her mother, Augusta, was alive. Augusta's gay presence had touched every corner of the house, filling it with laughter and songs and music, so Georgiana had told her. Her sister, four years older, had a few precious memories of those times, and in later years would whisper stories to Elizabeth at night as they lay in the nursery; tales of a house garlanded with flowers, of serious-faced musicians performing in the great hall, and of ladies swirling in bright silks.

Elizabeth had only been a few days old when her mother died, and after that the parties had ceased. Her father had taken longer and longer journeys to far-off lands, leaving them in the care of Mam'zelle Violette, returning with plants, gathered in his vasculum – a metal case made to be slung over one shoulder – or pressed carefully between sheets of paper, or kept alive on deck in a glass-and-zinc Wardian case, together with seeds that he carefully tended, coaxing them to grow in the unfamiliar Cornish soil. The most successfully cultivated specimens were sold to collectors for vast sums. There was a ready market for exotic blooms and her father was richly compensated for his travels, though in truth he had chosen his occupation more for love than money.

Queen Victoria had become enamoured with the fruit of the Chilean guava that he had brought back from a journey to the Valdivian rainforest and successfully propagated at Trebithick Hall. She was said to love its strawberry-like aroma and sweet flesh, and when it was in season, parcels were routinely dispatched to the Royal household from Padstow by train. Cook made the leftover fruit into a jam that was Georgiana's favourite.

John Trebithick had instilled in his daughters a reverence for all growing things, and Elizabeth in particular was an avid student.

~

Their father's will had provided for both sisters, giving them equal rights to reside at Trebithick Hall as long as they should live. In the absence of male relatives, the house and the estate were to pass to Georgiana and Robert. Elizabeth was relieved that there was no distant male cousin to eject her from her childhood home, but nevertheless she was no longer sure of her place there.

Before his illness, John Trebithick had planned another journey, this time to South America, and Elizabeth had petitioned assiduously to be allowed to accompany him. 'Just think, Papa, how useful it will be to have drawings of the plants as well. Why, I'd say it's practically essential,' she had implored. 'I would not be a hindrance, I promise you that.'

She had dreamed of nothing else for months: how she would sketch and record the plants of the countries they visited, helping her father in his work to catalogue and examine the native flora of Chile and Argentina. But he was immovable. 'Your place is at home, Elizabeth my dearest. The exotic wilderness is no place for a lady. I have witnessed and endured things that would make a lesser man quail, let alone a slip of a thing like you.'

His passage, and that of his manservant, had been booked mere days before he took ill, with berths reserved on a steamship departing from Liverpool docks, its final destination Valparaiso, a port city on the west coast of Chile. Elizabeth had resigned herself to once again staying home, practising her drawing by copying those in William Hooker's *Botanical Illustrations* – 'You would do well to practise incessantly, and there is no one better to learn from,' her father had commanded – as well as sketching from real-life examples growing in the estate's bountiful gardens, and stitching hassocks for the parish church with churlish ill humour.

~

She had been tiptoeing up the grand staircase when her sister spotted her.

'Georgiana, I thought you had a headache and needed to lie down. Are you recovered?' Elizabeth said before her sister could enquire further of her disordered state. She had managed to remount Achilles by dragging him to a nearby stile and had made it back to the stables without mishap, but she hadn't been able to retrieve her bonnet, with the result that her long golden hair, the exact colour of ripe corn, had escaped from its upswept bun and now fell in damp disarray about her shoulders. The day had been a fine one, so she could not claim it was from a sudden shower.

'I am recovered now, thank you, sister, but that doesn't explain where you have been. We've been looking for you for hours.

Bingley said he believed you were out in the gardens, but I searched high and low and could find no trace of you.'

'Oh, but I was,' said Elizabeth, thankful for the butler's supposition. She wasn't *exactly* lying to her sister; she had, after all, passed through the gardens on the way to the stables. 'I was walking. We must have missed each other. Now, if you will excuse me, I really must go and ready myself for dinner. I don't want to be late.' Elizabeth hurried up the stairs before her sister had a chance to notice the sand clinging to the hem of her dress.

'You know better than to go outside without a hat, dear one. You will ruin your complexion and then what will become of you?' Georgiana called after her.

Elizabeth paid no heed to her sister's concern. She cared not a whit about preserving her porcelain skin. Indeed, as girls they had both spent much of the long Cornish summer outdoors, her father unmindful of the necessity of shading his daughters' fair visages, and Elizabeth now bore a telltale scattering of coffee-coloured freckles across her perfect tip-tilted nose.

Had her sister forgotten this so easily? It seemed that ever since she had been betrothed and then wed to Robert Deverell – 'the most dashing man in all of Cornwall' Georgiana had recounted breathlessly upon first being introduced to him – she had effected a *volte-face,* as her French governess would have said. No longer was her sister her carefree companion. Georgiana had become a paragon of respectability – and was fast becoming a pompous one at that, thought Elizabeth crossly.

She had only just entered her bedroom when there was a knock on the door. She immediately recognised the gentle tap-tap. 'Come in, do please,' she said. 'I'm going to be fearfully late!'

'Oh, miss!' Elizabeth's maid had entered the room and looked mournfully at the watermarked fabric of her dress.

'I know, but there's no use in getting upset over a silly gown, now is there, Daisy?' said Elizabeth, her annoyance at being caught out by Georgiana making her impatient. 'Besides, I'm sure that it can be fixed – Mrs Pascoe will doubtless have a remedy and it'll soon be good as new.'

'Were you out riding?' Daisy asked.

'Yes, I took Achilles down to Lady Luck Cove.'

Daisy gasped. 'Achilles?'

Elizabeth grinned broadly. 'I'm nearly as good a rider as you, Daisy.'

Before entering service at Trebithick Hall, Daisy had grown up on a farm on the estate and ridden bareback around the fields and along the Cornish sands that bordered the land. Elizabeth, who had sometimes ridden with her as a child, knew that Daisy was a more adept horsewoman than herself.

'If you says so miss, but Achilles? Weren't you scared? He is a powerful beast.'

'A little,' Elizabeth admitted airily. 'But it was worth it.'

'You're a braver soul than me, miss,' said Daisy as she began to unfasten the buttons at the back of Elizabeth's gown. 'I think I'll be able to fix your hair too, if you'll give me a minute.'

'It's only Georgiana and Robert,' Elizabeth complained. 'But I suppose we must, for appearances' sake.' She rolled her eyes at

Daisy. 'Lord knows why we have to go through this ridiculous charade of dressing for dinner. It's not as if any of us has much of an appetite lately. In fact, I don't know why I am so anxious to be on time; it's not as if it really matters, does it?' she asked with a heavy sigh. 'Does anything really matter any more?'

'Oh, miss,' Daisy soothed. 'It is a terrible business. We all feel the loss of Mr Trebithick, but you must do so more than anyone.'

'Oh, I do, Daisy. Oh, how I do,' she lamented.

The young maid was skilled at her job and soon had Elizabeth clothed in a new black gown with lace cascading down the bodice. Elizabeth's untidy ringlets had been brushed out and caught up in a plain bun at the nape of her neck. Daisy had also fastened a simple jet necklace about her mistress's throat. Once again Elizabeth looked like a respectable young woman from a good family, rather than a sand-encrusted gypsy.

'Thank you, Daisy,' said Elizabeth when she was done. 'I don't know what I would do without you.'

The dinner bell sounded, its sonorous gong echoing through the hallways of the house. The maid bobbed a curtsey and left the room.

As Elizabeth entered the drawing room she caught sight of herself in the looking glass that hung over the mantelpiece. Her cheeks were rosy from the afternoon sun and her blue eyes glittered defiantly back at her. She was flushed with the exhilaration of her decision; a decision she had spent weeks turning over and over in her mind, and had finally arrived at down at the cove as she floated in the icy water. It was a decision so bold that she felt as if she might have been stabbed in the stomach.

After weeks of lassitude, she was possessed with a fierce energy, ready to grasp her destiny with both hands. All she had to do was persuade her sister of her plan. And hold her nerve.

Chapter Four

Sydney, Autumn 2017

'You could always let it on Airbnb,' Vanessa said, a determinedly helpful expression on her face.

Anna had happily accepted her sister's invitation to dinner on Friday night – she wasn't exactly fending off more compelling social invitations, and she liked Vanessa's noisy menagerie. Anna was particularly fond of her youngest niece, Fleur, who with her retroussé nose, delightful dimples and a heart-shaped face looked like a throwback to a gentler age but had an attitude that was fiercely modern. Recently though, Anna had noticed that Ivy, the eldest – just turned thirteen – had begun to speak in a bizarre patois, completely inexplicable given that she was a North Shore private schoolgirl. Anna never quite knew what to say to her when greeted with a 'Wassup, girlfrien'?' or a 'Dass cool' and accompanying fist bump. Vanessa merely shook her head and shrugged her shoulders. Jasmine, the middle child, was the quietest of the trio, generally preferring the company of books to people. They were all growing up too fast; blonde and leggy, like seedlings after summer showers.

Anna had been astonished that neither her mother nor her sister had begrudged her the house. Their mother had been adamant that the girls should be the beneficiaries, insisting that she already had everything she needed. Vanessa had been left the holiday shack further down the coast, and some of her grandmother's jewellery including a diamond-and-emerald ring the size of a marble, but it didn't seem entirely fair that Anna had got the much better part of the estate, for the Paddington house was probably worth twice the one on the coast. She had tried to talk to her sister about it, but Vanessa had shut her down. 'Anna. If anyone deserves it, it's you,' Vanessa had said. 'Besides, you were the one who was there for her more than any of us, especially at the end.'

'But you had your own family to look after, and Mum . . . well, I was just closest,' Anna had insisted.

'Doesn't matter. Those were Granny's wishes, and that's that. The last thing I want is an argument over money to come between us.'

Harvey, Vanessa's husband, hadn't taken the news so well, of that Anna was certain. She could sense it in the little digs he made, pointing out how lucky she was, what good fortune had befallen her. Anna didn't feel particularly lucky or fortunate; she would far rather have had Granny Gus still with them, alive and kicking out at anyone who dared cross her.

'In the state it's in?' Anna scoffed at Vanessa's Airbnb suggestion. 'Yeah, right.'

'Well, obviously it's going to need some work. But nothing that a coat of paint and some newly varnished floorboards can't fix,' said Vanessa. 'It's got bags of character. And it's very central.'

'And the rest!' Harvey spluttered from behind his newspaper. 'Um, the fifties called – they'd like their bathroom back. Not to mention the place needs a decent kitchen. The stove alone is a liability.'

'Hm, I suppose you're right,' Vanessa agreed. She folded her arms over her 'Namaste in bed' T-shirt so that only the word 'Namaste' showed and flicked her blonde ponytail, so similar to Anna's, over her shoulder. 'How she ever cooked in there without everything ending up as charcoal I've no idea.'

Anna looked around the snowy expanse of Vanessa's kitchen, at the marble countertops and butcher's tiles, the deep drawers and the butler's pantry. Granted, it was a mess, sticky with the detritus of family life, but underneath the empty chip packets and half-drunk, lidless milk cartons, it was a beautiful room. Her sister had always had a sense of style.

'Mm,' Anna said noncommittally. Any criticism of her grandmother, however slight, made her uncomfortable.

'Do you know,' said Harvey looking up from the paper, 'in China, unmarried women over the age of twenty-seven are called *sheng nu* – "leftover women". Humph . . . how about that?'

Anna took a sip of wine from the glass that Vanessa had just handed her and did her best to ignore him.

'So, what are you going to do?' asked Harvey, rubbing the top of his prematurely balding head and looking at her over his reading glasses.

'About being over twenty-seven and unmarried, or about the house?' she bristled. She'd grown used to Harvey's lack of tact over the years, but really, he was being even more thoughtless than usual. She had wanted to wait before mentioning the box and the notebook that the builders had uncovered, at least until she'd found out more, and now she decided she'd rather not discuss them while Harvey was around either.

'Oh, don't be so sensitive. I meant about the house. I know you're not one to make a snap decision, Anna, but it's been a while now.'

'Well, I'm not going to sell it, if that's what you're thinking.'

Harvey folded up the newspaper, tossing it untidily onto the kitchen counter. 'Steady on there, no one's pressuring you.'

'Anyway, it's not like I have to make a decision straightaway.'

'Heaven forbid!' said Vanessa, raising her eyes to the ceiling.

Anna permitted herself a slight smile. She had always been the cautious one of the pair. It had taken her two months to decide whether or not to go to university – studying Plant Science after much deliberation – and three months to choose her first car. She'd moved out of home two-and-a-half years ago, but only after Vanessa had sat her down and told her that if she wasn't careful she would end up aged forty still living with their mother and the cats, and that she couldn't cut herself off from the world forever. She had reluctantly seen her sister's point, and even her mother had encouraged her to find a place of her own, 'Not that I don't love having you here, darling,' she had reassured her. 'But perhaps it's time you found something . . .'

Vanessa hoicked up the exercise pants she was wearing ('I'm lying on the sofa in my activewear,' she'd guffawed to Anna on the phone the night before when inviting her to dinner. 'Raising an eight-ounce glass rather than my heart rate.') and opened the fridge. 'I suppose I'd better feed the hungry hordes. Pasta all right for you?'

Thankfully the question of what Anna might do with the house had been superseded by the needs of three growing people with the appetites of locusts, and Vanessa hadn't quizzed Anna any further. Anna didn't want to tell her sister exactly what she was planning. She didn't want her bossing her around, second-guessing her choices and taking over the whole project: something Vanessa was highly likely to do, in the nicest possible way of course. Anna could imagine her saying, 'Leave it to me, I know *exactly* what needs to be done.' The truth was, she would, but for a change Anna wanted to do something on her own, even if it meant making mistakes.

Chapter Five

Cornwall, 1886

One afternoon, about a week before her father died, he had summoned Elizabeth to his bedside. Rushing into the sickroom, she had looked at him, worry creasing her normally smooth forehead. John Trebithick had always been robust, but the man who lay before her was already a ghost. She tried not to let her shock show as she reached over to squeeze his hand in hers. She felt a gentle pressure returned, and her father opened his eyes and fixed his gaze on her.

'Lizzie,' he whispered.

'Hush, Papa, save your strength. Know that I am here, praying for your recovery.'

He had waved away her concerns. 'Sit,' he whispered hoarsely. 'Sit. I must speak to you about a matter of the greatest importance.'

Elizabeth did as she was bid, and pulled a chair towards the head of his bed.

'Lizzie, my darling girl, I have to face the fact that I may not recover.'

Elizabeth looked away, willing her tears to remain unshed.

'I need you to be strong.'

She nodded, pressing a handkerchief to her reddened eyes.

'There is a man. Mr Chegwidden. As big a scoundrel and a cad as has ever walked this earth. I can scarce believe that he is a Cornishman; he doesn't deserve the honour. He has dogged me for some time now, always nipping at my heels, trying to out-do my finds. In fact . . .' Her father gestured to the sleeve of his nightshirt. 'I have come off the worse from him on a previous occasion. We encountered each other in the Himalayan mountains, both in search of a particular magnolia. He stabbed me, here.' Her father twisted his arm and showed her the thin red line of a scar. 'A glancing blow, and I was lucky to get away before he inflicted greater damage, but proof of his ruthlessness indeed. He has let it be known that he wants to be revered as the greatest plant-hunter in all of England.

'Now I have heard from friends of mine that he has been searching for one of the deadliest plants ever seen. They say he believes it will make his fortune, and he will stop at nothing to get what he wants.' Her father closed his eyes, worn out with the effort of speaking. Elizabeth waited in wonder as he gathered his strength; he had never before mentioned the dangers he had faced when he had entertained his daughters with the fantastical stories of his adventures.

'My next expedition,' he said, opening his eyes again. 'It is not merely to bring back samples for Messrs Greaves & Sons, and for our own splendid gardens. There is another purpose: to track down that plant. It is feared and revered as the world's most poisonous – ingest it in its raw form and death is certain, a long and excruciating demise, one that you would not wish upon the worst of your enemies . . .'

Elizabeth's eyes grew round with horror at the thought of such a plant. 'If it is so destructive, why would you want to bring something like that to England?' she cried.

'Because I have it on good authority that it also harbours one of the most powerful healing substances known to man; in the right hands it can cure almost any ill you could imagine.'

He paused, exhausted, and Elizabeth dipped a cloth in a basin of cold water that sat on the nightstand next to him, gently mopping his waxen skin. After a few moments he continued to speak. 'Mr Chegwidden intends to find it and bring it back to England, to sell it to the highest bidder – and there will be plenty of those who wish to get their hands on it with the hope of making their own fortunes. I cannot let him have this prize. My desire was to get there ahead of him, to bring it back for our finest scientists to study. They say it can even raise the dead. Imagine what that might mean—' He broke off, coughing into his handkerchief.

'Oh my goodness,' said Elizabeth, unsettled both by her father's words and the clear effort it took for him to speak them.

'My dear, I have come to the decision that you are the only one who can continue my work,' he gasped, the effort of speaking making him breathless. 'Although you are but a woman, I have seen a strength and determination within you in these past few weeks that has convinced me. You have more courage than most men I have encountered. I wish I did not have to ask this of you Lizzie, but there is no one else I can trust. But, I must warn you that it will likely be dangerous.'

Again he sank back on his pillow, and then, in a voice barely above a whisper, he told her all he knew about this rare and mysterious plant. 'Even the local people hardly speak of it, it is so fearsome. They have tried to destroy it, by fire mostly, so I am told. It is rumoured to grow in the alpine valleys somewhere between Valparaiso and Santiago. You will know it by its smell, for it is as sweet as a siren's call; and its flowers, which bloom only rarely, are the most exquisite in the world to behold.'

Elizabeth kept her expression neutral as her mind raced. Was he really entrusting her with such a perilous mission, when only weeks before he had been utterly opposed to the idea of her accompanying him on such a journey?

'Does it have a name?' she asked, caught up in the fantastical story.

'The native *chilenos* call it *Trompeta del Diablo* . . . Devil's Trumpet.'

'Devil's Trumpet,' Elizabeth repeated, feeling the name on her tongue like a curse. Despite the warmth of the room, gooseflesh rose on her arms at the sound of it.

Her father sighed. 'Would that I had a son whom I might have charged with this mission. But promise me you will search for it in my place? It is a daring and dangerous undertaking, especially for a young woman, and it is not something I ask of you lightly. My notebooks have all the information I have managed to gather. No one must know of this. If the *chilenos* were to find out, they would most likely hound you out of the country, or worse. They pretend that this plant does not exist, especially to foreigners. They guard its power like a jealous lover. But if you travel in the guise of an artist, you will be unlikely to rouse suspicion. In all probability,' he said, almost as if it had only just occurred to him, 'the very fact of you being a woman may be an advantage. No one will suspect a woman of daring to undertake such a task. You must, above all else, keep this a secret – no one can know, not even your sister.'

'Oh Papa,' cried Elizabeth, overwhelmed by his request.

Her father held up a hand, silencing her protests. 'I must also warn you to be very careful if you encounter Mr Chegwidden – and you almost certainly will, for society there is limited. He can charm the skin off a snake, but he has the scruples of the devil himself. Don't give him a single reason to suspect you, or you will be in fear for your life.'

'But surely you will be well enough in time to make this journey?' she asked, knowing the answer even as she uttered the question.

He looked at her with deep sadness in his eyes, and Elizabeth saw something more, something that broke her heart. 'No!' she cried. 'You must not give up! You will get better. You *will*. You *must*!'

'Elizabeth, my dear,' he replied. 'I know that I am not long for this world. Now, swear that you will do this.'

She took a deep breath to steady herself. 'Of course, Papa. You have my solemn vow.' She had no choice but to make the promise, though in that moment she scarcely believed she would have the courage to keep it. Travelling abroad with her father to protect her was one thing; going halfway across the world on her own was another altogether, especially on so hazardous a journey.

Thus it was no surprise that in the weeks that followed her father's death she had been able to think of little else but the perilous mission with which he had entrusted her.

~

'I will not be a caged bird!' Elizabeth protested over dinner as she, her sister and her brother-in-law sat at one end of the vast mahogany table. It was set with three different types of crystal glasses and an array of silverware, as it always had been when her father was alive. Three slim wax candles burned in an elaborate candelabra, casting a flickering light on their faces.

Elizabeth put down her spoon and glared at Robert, her chin set once again in stubborn defiance. The dessert course had been served, a confection of raspberries, sherry and cream, but it might as well have been ashes in her mouth. 'The passages are booked and we cannot cancel. And you know how much dear Papa abhorred waste of any kind. I must continue his work. I shall be going in his place.' It was essential that Georgiana and Robert did not oppose her plan.

'I don't think you have thought this through, dear sister,' said Georgiana, a gentle and slightly puzzled smile on her face.

'A lady, venturing in a foreign country all on her own? It's not seemly, nor is it safe. I have heard tell of female travellers being shot, or worse,' she shuddered dramatically. 'Papa would never have agreed to it, God rest his soul.'

It troubled Elizabeth that she could not tell her sister that it was their father who had made this journey his dying wish, but she had to put such concerns aside. She had sworn to tell no one, not even her family; not a word of her true mission must get out until she was safely returned. 'Oh don't be ridiculous!' she scoffed, bravado in her voice. 'The ship will be perfectly fine, and then I will be met once it docks. I have the letters of introduction. All will be well.'

'But, but . . .' Georgiana spluttered. 'Must you be so singular?'

'So headstrong!' Robert chimed in. 'It'll come to no good, mark my words.'

'It is obvious to me that I am unlikely to marry, and indeed I have no wish to be the chattel of any man,' Elizabeth said.

Her sister looked startled by Elizabeth's statement. It was the first time the delicate subject of Elizabeth's spinsterhood – for at the age of twenty-five she could rightly be considered one – had been openly referred to.

'And surely you can see that I must find something to do in this world aside from inflicting my poor needlework on the local parish and painting every flower in the gardens?' Elizabeth added, tempering her tone. She desired her sister's support in this matter and tact, however difficult it was for her to summon, was necessary.

'You cannot travel alone, and that is that,' said Robert.

Elizabeth wanted to glare at him, but restrained herself. 'Of course, you are right, dear Robert. Daisy shall accompany me.' She said this with certainty, not imagining it in the slightest bit necessary to check with Daisy before committing her to the journey.

Chapter Six

Sydney, Autumn 2017

The room was almost pitch-dark, the only colour coming from scattered irregular fluorescent shapes. A thumping bass reverberated through the space and the instructor had to shout over its thump-thump-thump to get the class's attention. Sweat beaded on Anna's forehead. Her legs, like everyone else's, spun in a blur of movement, trying to keep pace with the relentless beat of the electro-pop. She was consumed by the sound, her heart thudding as she gasped for breath.

She had come to this spin class every Saturday for nearly six years, only missing a session if she was too ill to get out of bed, and she could count on the fingers of one hand the number of times that had happened.

She always arrived early, securing her favourite spot – at the back, by the door, carefully selected for a quick getaway. She never stayed to chat, hadn't got to know any of the other regulars, none of whom had been coming as long as she had in any case. Instructors had also come and gone over the years, some better than others, not that she cared much about who took the class. For Anna, losing herself in the darkness and the sound was enough. If anyone ever noticed that the sweat dripping down her face and onto her towel was mingled with tears, they were tactful enough not to remark upon it. It was cheaper than therapy and it whipped her arse at the same time.

The gym was near her mother's house – she'd first started going there when she was living at home – and she hadn't wanted to change gyms once she'd moved, even though it meant a forty-minute drive there and back from her apartment.

She'd swapped a message with her mother the day before, arranging to meet later that morning. 'Of course darling.' Eleanor's voice had sounded concerned. 'I hope everything's okay.' Anna didn't often ring out of the blue and suggest coffee, even if she was in the area every weekend; Eleanor was always at yoga, or Spanish lessons, and more recently art classes, so they tended to catch up over dinner at Vanessa's house, where the melee of kids precluded anything other than superficial conversation.

The volume of the music increased and the instructor thrashed the class into a frenzy, whooping at them to give it ten out of ten for effort, that this was where it began if they wanted to see real change. Once again, tears sprang from Anna's eyes until they were indistinguishable from the sweat trickling saltily on her lips. She wasn't sure for whom she was crying – Granny

Gus . . . Simon . . . herself . . . possibly all three – but her legs, conditioned to respond, obediently complied with the instructor's demands, and they spun, ever-faster. Going nowhere.

~

By the time she reached the cafe Anna had done her best to wipe away the sweat from her workout, but her hair still clung to her forehead in damp sandy-blonde tendrils.

'Oh, hello darling. Gosh you look lovely! You're glowing!' Eleanor bustled up to Anna as she sat at an outdoor table, and placed a hand on her shoulder.

Anna rolled her eyes. Only a mother could think her progeny beautiful despite stringy hair, a beetroot-red face and suspiciously puffy eyes. She secretly resented and was reassured in equal measure to be the recipient of that much unconditional love.

'Nice leggings.'

Anna looked down at the swirled purple-and-green lycra covering her legs. They were a bit loud, not really her at all, but Vanessa had passed them on – 'Too small for me anyway' – and she had to admit they were very comfortable.

'Coffee, ladies?'

Anna was thankful for the interruption, diverting her mother's scrutiny away from her face to the menu, which the waitress had thrust in front of their noses. 'Or are you having breakfast?'

'Just coffee, thank you. Flat white. Anna, have you ordered?'

'Coffee for me too, please. Skinny latte, double shot.' She summoned a smile for the waitress, who relieved them of their menus and left to fill their order.

'Well, this is a nice surprise,' said her mother. 'How are things?' she asked with careful casualness. 'You must be busy at work. You know, now it's autumn. All those leaves to sweep up.' She trilled a laugh, as if aware of her banal statement.

Anna nodded. 'Lots to catch up on, that's for sure.' She took a deep breath. No more small talk. 'Actually Mum, I've been meaning to tell you. I've started some renovations on Granny's house.'

'You mean your new house,' her mother corrected her.

'Oh, I don't know if I'll think of it as my house for a long time. If ever. Doesn't it feel more like yours? After all, you grew up there.'

'A little, I suppose,' her mother admitted. 'But that was years ago, and I've had several homes since then, darling.'

'Well, anyway I contacted some builders – the ones who did the work on Vanessa's place a few years ago.'

'Oh, yes?'

'I should at least put in a decent kitchen and sort out the plumbing.'

Her mother laughed. 'I'm surprised that old hot-water system kept going for as long as it did. Well, good for you, Anna.'

Anna noticed a fleeting look that she could have sworn was relief mingled with concern in her mother's eyes.

'Do you need any help? It can't be cheap.'

'I'm perfectly capable of this,' she replied. 'Besides, I've got some money saved up.' It was true. Anna wasn't the type for designer handbags and new shoes; she couldn't see the point.

She spent most of her days in shorts and work boots, and never really went anywhere that required fancier footwear.

'Of course, darling, but is there anything I can do?'

Anna shook her head, a stubborn set to her chin. 'No it's fine, really. I'm perfectly able to handle it on my own.'

'I wasn't suggesting you weren't,' her mother said gently.

Their drinks were delivered to their table and they chatted idly about a cruise that Eleanor was thinking of taking. 'Imagine, darling. The Rhine in summer . . .' Her mother paused, the memory lingering unspoken between them of the European trip Anna had once planned. A trip she had never taken.

'Sounds lovely, Mum,' said Anna brightly in the face of her mother's hesitation. 'You should go.'

'Hm, well, we'll see. Vanessa needs me. With the girls. God knows Harvey's hopeless.'

Anna snorted. 'Honestly, Mum. Why on earth shouldn't you go away, if that's what you want to do? It's your life, you know. You did enough for us when we were growing up; it should be your time now. Let Vanessa cope without you. She'll be fine. They're *her* kids, after all.'

'Yes, but they're my grandkids.'

'Mu-um.' Anna's tone was testy.

'Oh, I know, I know. It's just that they have so many activities now. She can't get them all everywhere they need to be, especially with Fleur's ballet.'

Anna only just stopped herself from rolling her eyes. 'She's seven. I can't see why she needs to dance for eight hours a week.'

Her mother shrugged. 'Vanessa thinks she might be the next Darcey Bussell.'

Anna spluttered into the remains of her coffee. 'Really?' She loved her niece and admired her nascent talent, but she couldn't help but wonder when her sister had become so horrifyingly ambitious for her offspring. Why couldn't they be normal kids? Why set them up with grand expectations?

'Anyway, I didn't arrange to meet just to talk about Vanessa and the girls. There's something you might be able to help *me* with.' She took a sip of her coffee. 'The builders found something when they were pulling out the bookshelves in the living room. A box.'

'A box?' her mother echoed, a puzzled look on her face.

'Yes. A big, heavy metal box with engravings on it of flowers and bees and clover. And the letter E engraved in the centre. It was pretty filthy and it's absolutely ancient by the look of it.'

'Ooh, a mystery,' said her mother. 'How thrilling!'

'Perhaps someone hid it there for safekeeping and then forgot about it?' Anna was pragmatic. 'Anyway, I wondered if you remembered a box like that, from when you were little. Do you remember Granny Gus, or Granddad for that matter having such a thing?'

Her mother looked blank. 'No darling, I can't say I do. Did you open it? What was inside?'

'It's padlocked. I don't want to damage it, so I thought I'd take it to a locksmith later today.'

'Oh, good idea. Have you got it with you now – the box, I mean? Can I see it?'

'It's in the car.'

Her mother drained her cup, a look of anticipation on her face. 'Well, let's go and have a look, then.'

When they reached Anna's car, she opened the passenger door. She had folded an old towel around the box and now she carefully unwrapped it, standing back so her mother could see.

The night before, she had cleaned the worst of the grime from the box, making a paste with bicarb and water and using an old toothbrush to get into the crannies between the engraver's marks. It had come up surprisingly well. 'Oh gosh, darling,' Eleanor breathed. 'It's a bit special, isn't it?'

Anna nodded, feeling surprisingly protective and proud of the engraved box, as if by cleaning and polishing it back to life she had staked a small claim of ownership to it.

'Here, let me look at the lock.' Her mother bent down, holding it between two slender fingers. 'Hm,' she mused. 'I've got something here that might do the trick.' She scrabbled in her handbag, giving Anna a triumphant look as she found what she was looking for and raised it up for Anna to see.

'A hairpin? Really, Mum? You've been reading too many bad detective novels. I mean, the lock's probably rusted solid.'

'Well, there's no harm in trying, is there? Come on, don't give up so easily.'

Anna frowned and Eleanor scrambled to take back the comment. 'Oh sweetheart, you know I didn't mean it.'

Anna sighed. 'I think it might be easier to take it to the locksmith.'

'Nonsense. I'm sure this will work. Look, why don't you let me have a go?'

Anna held up her hands. 'Okay, be my guest.'

Eleanor leant in, a look of concentration on her face, and lifted the box to get at the lock. She slid the hairpin into the tiny keyhole and wiggled it a few times, twisting it one way and then another. 'It's not as easy as it looks,' she admitted, dropping the box with a thump and straightening up. She glanced at her watch. 'Heavens, is that the time? I've got to get on. I've got my book club coming over tonight and I've still got to pick up the wine. You know how they love a drink. I don't suppose you'd care to join us? We're discussing the new Liane Moriarty. Should be good.'

Anna didn't want to admit that she had no plans on a Saturday night, nor that her mum, a widow for more than twenty years, had a better social life than she did. She shook her head. 'Thanks, but I'm off to the movies later with, er, a friend.' She was hopeless at lying but her mother seemed to believe her, though her eyes widened as she read more into Anna's remark than Anna had intended. 'Not that kind of a friend,' she said, her tone warding off further questions.

'All right, but call me when you get home and tell me how you get on, won't you? I'm dying to know what's inside it.'

Anna scoffed. 'It might be nothing, you know. Just a pretty, empty box.'

'Don't be silly darling. It feels heavy enough to contain several gold ingots, I'm sure.'

'As if,' said Anna with a grimace as she closed the door. It wasn't until her mother had gone that she realised she had forgotten to mention the notebook, which Anna had left lying on a windowsill in Gus's house.

Chapter Seven

Cornwall, 1886

The smell of fried kippers assaulted Elizabeth as she came down to breakfast. The question of her travels remained unresolved and she had gone to bed simmering with the injustice of it all. Oh, the misfortune to have been born a girl. There would have been no doubt about her undertaking such a journey had she been a man, her father's son. Indeed, she would have been encouraged in the endeavour. Why should it be otherwise simply because of the accident of her sex?

She was, however, perspicacious enough to judge that her brother-in-law might want her out of the way so that he could have Trebithick Hall all to himself; a fact that might help her case. At dinner, he had asserted his intention to settle there with Georgiana 'and our future children, if it please God' and take on the management of the estate. 'I am willing to give up my practice in Plymouth,' he said with a magnanimous air, as if all three family members seated around the dining table were unaware that the Trebithick estate would prove more lucrative than a living as a country solicitor – if he were able to continue to supply the demand for their plants and pay careful attention to the business, that was. That she did not know him well enough to ascertain if he might be a prudent businessman was of concern, but she had other, more pressing worries on her mind. 'It has fallen to me to ensure the continued upkeep and future prosperity of Trebithick and I intend to take my charge with due seriousness and diligence,' he continued, oblivious to his own pomposity.

Elizabeth couldn't help but think sourly of the way he must be congratulating himself on having married so wisely and well – but then she chided herself for being ungenerous, for he and Georgiana were clearly besotted with each other. To Robert's face, she pretended to be pleased, and indeed part of her was. It meant that she need not worry about her sister or what would happen to the house while she was gone. And though she loved Trebithick Hall with all her heart, she couldn't deny her hunger to see the world, a hunger that had been burning in her since she was a little girl captivated by her father's wild and outlandish stories. Trebithick Hall would always be there when she returned.

Eschewing the kippers, she helped herself to eggs and devilled kidneys from the warming dish on the sideboard before ringing for Bingley to bring some tea. Of Georgiana and Robert there was no sign, though she was not overly surprised. Since their arrival they often slept in late, not appearing for breakfast much before eleven. Elizabeth, on the other hand, was generally early to rise, waking almost as soon as the sun began to show its face. She was much like her father in that regard, she reflected, feeling the pain of his loss as sharp as the scent of the box hedge that floated in through the open window.

Today she planned to make an excursion to Truro. The combination of the illicit swim and the confrontation with Georgiana and Robert had helped her shake off the ennui that had beset her since her father's funeral. She had no time to waste if she was to set her plans in motion, and she wanted to make an early start to the journey, for it would take the best part of the day.

After dinner the previous night, she had excused herself and retired to her father's study, where she opened her writing case and dipped her pen in the inkwell. She now had a letter to post, informing the Pacific Steam Navigation Company of the change of passengers (she had yet to broach the subject with Daisy), an appointment with her milliner and pharmacy supplies to order. Before coming down to breakfast, she had methodically surveyed her father's travelling medicine chest, finding a lancet, pestle and mortar, leech tubes and laudanum, but she needed to supplement it with, at the very least, fever powder, blistering plasters, sal volatile and ipecac. The lands to which she intended to travel harboured unknown sickness and precious little local medicine. And that was without considering the journey alone, the privations of which, she had heard, could fell even the strongest of men.

The *Corcovado* was scheduled to leave Liverpool docks in three weeks and Elizabeth's mind was in a whirl considering everything that had to be arranged beforehand, not least of which was her wardrobe – there were stockings, gloves, bonnets, stout boots and serviceable brown Holland gowns (for those times it would be unwise to draw attention to herself) as well as ones of silk, poplin and merino to order, not forgetting new chemises and bloomers. A new cloak too, to ward against cold weather, was a necessity. Her father had advised her to take supplies of tobacco and sugar, as gifts for those who might assist her with lodging and act as guides.

Most important of all, however, were her drawing materials to be ordered from Winsor & Newton – lead pencils, hard and soft; new watercolours, both cakes and in tubes; and an array of fine, perfectly flexible Russian sable brushes. She had a handsome mahogany-and-brass artist's case that contained porcelain pans for mixing colours, wash bowls and tins for chalks and charcoal, but several of the tubes of colour – notably her favourites burnt sienna, cadmium yellow, scarlet lake and Prussian blue – were in need of replacement. She must also place an order with Whatmans. Her father had been insistent that she take large sheets of their Griffin Antiquarian paper for her sketches and watercolours. 'It is the strongest you will find, and it will stand up to the voyage better than anything else.' She would need a plentiful supply of both paper and paints, because she could not be certain of getting anything of such quality on her travels. She also needed to arrange for a passport from the embassy for herself and Daisy, neither of them having been further than St Austell, some fifteen miles away, in their young lives.

In one of their last meetings, her father had pressed a bag of sovereigns and a sheaf of bank notes upon her, instructing her to sew them into the lining of her cloak. She would ask Daisy to help her, for her own skills as a seamstress were sadly lacking and she knew she could trust her maid's discretion in the matter. She only hoped her cloak would not crackle or clink too dreadfully when she wore it.

Elizabeth bolted down her breakfast, delighting in the fact that there was no one to chide her for slurping her tea – Mam'zelle Violette would have been horrified – and went to collect her things for the carriage ride to Truro.

Before departing, she slipped around to the back of the house. Her boots – she had reverted to an older, more comfortable pair, knowing she would be traipsing the town's cobbled streets – crunched on the gravel path that surrounded the rectangular green lawns. She made her way across the grass, which was bisected by the path and had a circle of gravel at its centre. In the middle of the clearing stood the new sundial. It had been commissioned more than a year earlier and installed in the last weeks of dear Papa's life. He had roused himself from his sickbed to see it and it was one of the last times she had seen a look of pleasure upon his craggy features. It was indeed a thing of beauty, cast in bronze with a raised relief of thirty-eight different herbs on a horizontal ring. She removed a pale kid glove and ran her bare hand along its cool surface, recognising mint for virtue, oregano for joy, lavender for devotion, hyssop to cleanse, lemon balm for wit, borage for courage, chamomile for comfort and bay for glory. Aside from the relief of herbs, the main feature of the sundial was a globe, which turned on an axis, the countries of the world etched onto it. Elizabeth traced the outline of Great Britain, and then ran a finger across the Atlantic Ocean to the Americas until it reached the southernmost tip. Her destination. It looked so far away, but the metal was cool and soothing to the touch and helped steady her resolve.

'Ma'am?'

She turned around, surprised to have been disturbed. 'Yes Daisy?' The maid stood in the shadows of the house, barely visible, but Elizabeth could make out the vibrant red of her hair.

'Ma'am, the carriage is ready,' her soft Cornish burr carried in the still morning air.

'Thank you, Daisy.'

She made as if to return to the house but Elizabeth called her closer. 'Daisy?'

'Yes, ma'am?'

'Come over here, will you? I have something to discuss with you.'

Elizabeth waited as the maid walked along the path to join her.

'Daisy. You know that my father had planned another journey . . .' She paused, taking in the display of scarlet pelargoniums, the topiary lion painstakingly created by Hoskins, the head gardener, and the tall monkey-puzzle tree that her father had planted on the occasion of her birth twenty-five years before. She noticed bees flitting from bloom to bloom, filling the air with the sound of their low hum, and over that the bright squawks of a pair of choughs. In the distance, the kitchen garden beckoned, sunlight reflecting off the panes of the glasshouse, where pineapples and tomatoes grew in the forced tropical heat. It was all so dear and familiar to her that, for a second, she hesitated, wondered if she was doing the right thing.

'Yes, ma'am.'

'Well,' Elizabeth forced her attention back to the maid. 'I intend to go on his behalf. To continue his work. And I am hopeful that you will accompany me.' She paused, waiting for her reaction.

Daisy's eyes widened in surprise, but she quickly recovered herself. 'Of, of course, Miss Elizabeth,' she stammered. 'It . . . it would be a great honour.'

'Not to mention a great adventure!' Elizabeth's eyes gleamed with excitement, her earlier trepidation forgotten as she relished the audaciousness of her plan.

'If you say so, ma'am.' The maid looked far less enthusiastic than her mistress.

Elizabeth had reckoned that Daisy, who like her had grown up in this wild part of Cornwall, would not find it easy to leave. She reached for her maid's hands and took them in hers, looking at her earnestly. 'We won't be gone forever, Daisy. I promise you that. A year at most.'

'Right you are, ma'am.' Daisy looked bewildered at the thought of such a long and uncertain journey, but when Elizabeth released her hands she gave a quick bob of a curtsey, saying only, 'The carriage, ma'am?'

'Tell Banks I'll be there shortly,' she replied.

Daisy made her way towards the stables as Elizabeth took a last look at the sundial and the sweeping lawns behind it, taking in the rhododendrons along the eastern border, the camellias and azaleas growing along the western edge, up against the red brick walls of the ladies' walk. The garden was where she felt her father's presence – or more accurately, his absence – most keenly. He had brought back many of the plants from his various travels and, lovingly raised and propagated, they had flourished over the years in this rich soil and temperate climate. Cornwall was a fertile place for growing exotic species, often from all parts of the southern hemisphere, the warm trade winds providing a kinder climate than anywhere else in Britain, with perhaps the exception of the Isles of Scilly. Such plants were highly prized by society gardeners and botanists alike, and her father had made a good deal of money supplying them with the most fashionable and rare plants.

Elizabeth's governess had been the one to encourage her artistic talents, steering her towards the study of plants, showing her how to document their structure and blooms with unerring accuracy. She had proved a prodigious pupil, earning the approbation of several of her father's regular guests, experts in the field of botanical study. One such visitor, the eminent botanist George Bentham, who was now sadly dead and buried these past few years, had seen her talent, even as a young girl, and encouraged her in it. She had swelled with pride as he singled her out, declaring that she should devote several hours of her day to the study and drawing of plants, in order to understand them all the better. Mam'zelle Violette was instructed to accommodate this, and, much to Elizabeth's delight, she was allowed to spend the most part of every afternoon with her sketchbooks, while Georgiana was schooled in the more conventional endeavours of needlepoint and playing the pianoforte. Elizabeth was much relieved to be excused from needlework in particular – she might be able to draw the most detailed pattern of veins on an oak leaf, but she could barely sew a straight seam.

As she gazed across the lush gardens, her heart thrilled with a mix of excitement and apprehension at what she might experience in the months ahead, what she might discover, document and perhaps bring back for all of England to marvel at. A chill ran through her as she recalled Papa's words about Mr Chegwidden. Her father had said that he had left aboard a ship some two months previously. What if he had already discovered the plant of which her father had spoken?

Chapter Eight

Sydney, Autumn 2017

After saying goodbye to her mother, Anna made a detour to Gussie's house.

Earlier in the week she had arranged for her assistant, Sally, to take over for a few days so Anna could spend some time sorting out the house, but she felt guilty – even though The Secret Garden *was* her company, she reminded herself, and she *was* her own boss – for neglecting her clients' gardens. She had taken enough time off to nurse Granny Gus as it was.

She had started The Secret Garden five years ago, not long after she graduated. Vanessa and Harvey had been her first clients, but now Anna had more work than she could cope with – it seemed the good people of the affluent North Shore spent more time adjusting their cufflinks on their bespoke

French-cuffed shirts than actually rolling them up and getting their hands dirty. She didn't mind – it kept her in business. If it meant she wasn't exactly making the best use of her degree, no one in the family had dared say so.

Anna had employed Sally in the weeks before Gussie died. It was a decision she had mulled over, but because she was spending so much time with her grandmother she had eventually seen the necessity of it. Sally was a bright and bubbly girl who made up for her lack of plant knowledge with an irrepressible enthusiasm for even the dirtiest of jobs. She also had the added advantage of being able to chat up the clients in an easy, carefree way that Anna had never quite managed. Anna grudgingly admitted to herself that hiring Sally had been a good decision, and it also meant that taking a few days off wasn't exactly the end of the world.

She had driven past the locksmith on her way to Gus's, pulling up outside it only to find that they were closed on Saturdays. As she drove on, she made a mental inventory of the tools in the back of her ute. A hedge trimmer and a couple of hoes, hacksaws, rakes and a shovel wouldn't be of any use, but the heavy-duty pruning shears might work.

As soon as she arrived at the house, she rummaged through the toolbox, found what she needed and hauled the box inside.

Late-afternoon sunlight angled through the kitchen windows, illuminating the downstairs level of the terrace. All traces of 1970s laminate were gone, and the only thing remaining was a thick layer of builders' dust. Anna set the box down on the scarred timber floorboards, not caring that her leggings might get dusty as she sat beside it. 'Now then, you little mystery,' she said, her voice echoing in the empty room, shears at the ready. 'Let's see if you'll give up your secrets.' She grasped the small lock and angled the blade to cut through the bolt. Nothing budged. She rattled the lock in frustration. It suddenly seemed terribly important that she find out what the box contained, right then and there. She was sitting glumly on the floor when she had a flash of inspiration. There was a hardware store up on the main road. Grabbing her wallet, she flew out of the door.

The owner was arranging a stand of paintbrushes and garden rakes that were on display outside the store when Anna rushed up, breathless.

'Steady on there, where's the fire?' he asked.

'Please . . .' She tried to catch her breath. 'I need something to break into a padlock. It's rusted over.'

He raised an eyebrow but didn't ask why. 'You'd better come in then and I'll see what we've got.'

Anna returned to Gus's house, at a somewhat slower pace than she'd left it, and let herself in. From her bag she pulled a small pair of bolt cutters and placed them in the middle of the lock, then gave them the hardest squeeze she could, her fingers white from the effort. Nothing. She took a deep breath and tried again. This time there was a loud crack and the lock split in two. *Sometimes you have to break a heart*, she told herself, her lips twisting at the irony of it.

'Bloody hell,' she breathed quietly as a small thrill at her handiwork surged through her. 'Anna, you did it.'

She slid the bar of the lock carefully through the lid of the box, placing it on the floor next to her. She pushed hard at the lid and it seemed for a moment as if it too might have rusted shut and she tore a nail trying to force it open. Grimacing at the exposed tender flesh, she sucked on her finger and reached for a paint-spattered chisel left behind by the builders on a windowsill.

Easing the end of the chisel into the seam between the box and its lid, she felt it loosen slightly. She wiggled it more forcefully and then gave it another shove with the heel of her hand. It moved a few millimetres. She shoved it again, and again, slamming her hand against the chisel until the lid finally popped off with a snap and clattered onto the floor. Anna wrinkled her nose. A mustiness, overlaid with a salty smell, wafted towards her, as if the box had been kept near the ocean and some of that briny air had become trapped inside it. She ran her fingers over the lining, a faded blue velvet that was darker in the corners. In the middle of the box was a large, leather-bound volume. It was as soft as a baby's cheek and about the same blush colour. On its surface was an embossed, curlicued letter E picked out in gold leaf, just as there had been on the lid of the box.

Scarcely daring to breathe, Anna gingerly lifted the hard cover of the album to reveal a sheet of pale tissue paper, darkened yellow at the edges. As she lifted it, it crumbled between her fingers, the edges disintegrating to dust. She wiped her hands on her leggings and caught her breath when she saw what lay beneath. Carefully, she lifted the album from its velvet casket.

Anna sat, absorbed in the album, turning the thick cottony pages slowly, astonished by what she saw before her. She barely felt the hard boards of the floor, nor cared that the sun was disappearing from the room.

It wasn't until her stomach gave a loud growl that she looked at her watch. It was nearly three and she'd not had anything since the coffee with her mother that morning. The album – a sketchbook, really – contained exquisite botanical illustrations that boasted intricate detail, breathtaking precision and colours as bright as if they were painted only yesterday. Her botanist's heart thrilled at the sight of such artistry and accuracy, but her stomach rumbled again and she reluctantly closed the book, replaced it and leant on the lid to close it completely.

Her head swirled with questions as she got awkwardly to her feet, shaking out her stiff legs and wincing at the pins and needles that invaded her toes.

Who was the mysterious E to whom this had belonged? How had it survived? And how had such a thing ended up behind the bookshelves of her grandmother's house?

Anna locked up the house and trudged westward towards bustling Oxford Street, where she was forced to weave her way past slow-strolling couples, a group of girls laden with shiny shopping bags, and an old man slumped in a doorway and clutching a bottle in a brown paper bag. Saturday afternoon in the city. She reached the cafe she'd had in mind and was shown to a small table at the back. It was filled with family groups and a couple clearly on a first date, the girl laughing and flicking her hair as they chatted, toying with the piece of cake in front of them, the man fiddling nervously with the cutlery, grinning with relief every time the girl laughed at something he said.

She studied the menu, unsure whether to have a late lunch or make it an early dinner, and surreptitiously watched the first-date couple. She'd forgotten what it was like to go out with someone you were interested in, the excitement of getting ready. The anticipation of what such a meeting might bring was a dim and distant memory. The couple might as well have been aliens from another planet. She shook her head. That kind of complication only led to trouble. It wasn't for her.

Chapter Nine

Cornwall, 1886

'Lizzie dear, I trust you had a successful journey?' Georgiana enquired as Elizabeth alighted from the carriage upon her return from Truro. She was tired and dusty and looking forward to a glass of cool lemonade, perhaps a sandwich and some of Cook's damson preserves made from last year's orchard fruit.

'Quite, thank you. Though I have a terrible thirst.'

'Why don't we take some tea? Mrs Pascoe can see to your purchases.'

Once Elizabeth had removed her hat and gloves and the two sisters were sitting comfortably in the parlour, Elizabeth began to speak. 'I hope you have had some time to think over our conversation of last night,' she began.

'Indeed,' said Georgiana, 'it has been preying on my mind. But you must not think I am about to commence lecturing, for I do not desire to quarrel with you.'

'Good,' said Elizabeth, relieved. 'Because I am not to be persuaded out of it.'

Georgiana looked her sister square in the eye, her gaze steady. 'I was rather afraid of that. You always were the stronger of the two of us.'

'Then you understand that I must go?'

Georgiana nodded sadly. 'I do.'

'And do you think you can convince Robert of it? A blessing from both of you would mean the world to me,' Elizabeth pleaded.

'I will try,' Georgiana said. 'I need to pick a time when he is likely to be most amenable.'

'Of course.'

'But I will miss you so,' she wailed. 'It has been hard to be separated since my marriage. We were so close as girls. Do you remember how we used to give Mam'zelle the slip and hide in the potting shed, or take the horses for gallops along the cliff edge?'

'Egging each other on to see who could go the fastest,' said Elizabeth, reminiscing. 'I'm surprised we were never caught.'

'I will worry terribly for you, my dearest sister,' said Georgiana, her smile fading.

'I know you will, but I have steadfast faith that no ills will befall me. I am young and strong and quick-witted. In any case, you have Robert and your life with him. When do you plan to return to Plymouth?'

'Next week, I believe. But we will move our household here before long. Robert has decided it, and I shall be happy to return home.' She sighed. 'Even if it will be a quieter and more sombre place without you in it.'

'I shall not be away forever.' Elizabeth placed a reassuring hand on her sister's arm. 'The time shall fly by.'

'I imagine you shall find things quite changed on your return.'

'What do you mean? Does Robert already have plans afoot?' Elizabeth looked at her with concern. 'Will he alter the house? Or the gardens?' The thought of the fabric of the house, most especially the gardens, changing without her knowledge, though she had little control over such matters, set her stomach churning.

'No, nothing like that,' Georgiana replied with a smile. 'In fact, it is I who shall be most changed.'

'Why, sister dear?' Elizabeth took a sip of her tea.

Georgiana glanced coyly down at her lap. 'I am with child.'

'What?' Elizabeth hastily put down her cup, inadvertently slopping hot liquid into the saucer and narrowly missing staining her skirts. 'Are you sure?'

'Quite sure,' Georgiana replied. 'Though I must confess, we had hardly dared hope, not after so long . . .'

'Oh, but that is the first piece of good news we have had here in weeks!' Elizabeth exclaimed, before looking at her sister more carefully. 'You have been looking a little pale, but I thought that was due to Papa's passing. How are you feeling?' Elizabeth knew only the barest outline of what carrying a baby entailed; it was something only married women were privy to, and Mam'zelle's teachings on the matter had been vague.

'I'm perfectly fine,' said Georgiana. 'Though I have been a little tired, and somewhat delicate in the mornings.' She looked soberly at her sister. 'I am happy, but I am also terrified, dear sister.' They both glanced at the portrait of their mother, Augusta, which hung on the wall in front of them. Mr Rossetti had been commissioned to make her likeness and he had done a fine job. Her gown was of a blue that perfectly matched her eyes, with creamy lace at her sleeves and bodice. A dimple marked each of her cheeks, giving her a sweet countenance – both of her daughters had inherited these dimples – and her fair hair and cornflower blue eyes shone out from the painting, almost making her seem alive; as if she could step down and take tea with them on this sunny afternoon.

'Oh, now I do feel so terribly selfish to be going away and leaving you at such a time,' said Elizabeth, a sorrowful expression marring her features.

Georgiana shook her head. 'Do not worry yourself. Robert has promised me that I will receive the best possible care. If necessary, he says, we shall reside in London in the months before the birth, so as to be near the finest physicians. And in the meantime I shall be kept busy piously sewing for the poor and seeing to the running of this house,' she said with the barest of winks.

'It is true, Robert does look after you well. I am glad that you will be in safe hands,' replied Elizabeth. 'Now, if you can bear it, do you think you can help me begin to plan for my journey? I am overwhelmed by what I might need; the sheer amount of it. I don't quite know where to begin and I know you used to help father pack for his trips.'

'Of course. We might use several of his trunks. I will ask Bingley to have them brought up to your dressing room. What did you order in town today?'

Georgiana thought of everything that would be needed on a lengthy voyage, from parasols to keep the harsh South American sun off Elizabeth's fair complexion, to smelling salts and a small flask of brandy – 'Absolutely essential, according to Papa,' Georgiana insisted. They were disturbed in their planning by the entrance of Robert, who had arrived back at the house after a tour of the estate. He was still wearing his riding breeches and tall leather boots that reached to his knees. Elizabeth looked at them longingly – how much easier her ride of the previous day would have been had she been able to wear trousers and boots.

'You're back in time for tea, my dear,' said Georgiana. 'No doubt you are thirsty and hungry.'

''Tis hot work, that is true,' said Robert. 'And I shall be glad of a cup.' He looked at his wife, and Elizabeth felt almost an intruder seeing the tender glance that flew between them. 'How are you feeling this afternoon, my dear?'

'Much better, thank you. Now before you have time to disapprove, I have shared our good news with Elizabeth.'

He frowned.

'She is my sister, after all,' Georgiana continued, bestowing on him a persuasive smile.

'Yes, it is wonderful news,' added Elizabeth quickly.

'It is indeed,' he said. 'We are most blessed. But pray what else were you discussing so animatedly as I arrived? I am sure I heard talk of gowns and a new cloak?' he said teasingly, apparently appeased by his wife.

'Actually, my darling, Elizabeth and I were planning her wardrobe for the journey she is about to make,' said Georgiana.

Robert raised his eyebrows, a frown forming. 'I thought we had discussed that last night and there was no question of her undertaking such a perilous expedition. Am I to believe that my views are to be completely disregarded? I will not be outvoted, even by two sisters. I am the man of the house now, do not forget. I am responsible for you both.'

'Hush now, we'll talk more of this later,' said Georgiana, offering him a cup of tea. 'Do sit and tell us of your findings today.'

Robert's frown did not leave his face. 'I will not quarrel with you, dearest Georgiana, for I have no desire to upset you, especially in your delicate condition. But you,' he paused, looking at Elizabeth. 'You and I must discuss this matter further.'

'Really, Robert, there is nothing that you have to say to my sister that I cannot hear also. I am not *that* delicate,' insisted Georgiana.

'I have no wish to quarrel either, Robert,' said Elizabeth, 'But as I am of age, I am perfectly able to make up my own mind on the matter. And made up it is. I am afraid that I doubt anything you have to say to me will convince me otherwise, try as you might. I know you act purely out of concern, but do not fear. I am a capable woman.' She gave him a bold stare, daring him to disagree with her further.

Chapter Ten

Sydney, Autumn 2017

The sound of a frog's throaty croak woke Anna. That would be Vanessa, the ring tone courtesy of her niece Jasmine.

'Well, then?' her sister was impatient when Anna eventually answered the phone. 'Did it work? Did you manage to get it open?'

Anna lay back against her pillows, looking at her bedroom window and noting that the sun was barely lighting the sky. 'Vanessa!' she was indignant. 'It's Sunday morning! And it's the arse crack of dawn,' she grumbled as she checked the time, neatly avoiding answering her sister's question.

'Oh I know, but you're always up so early every other morning . . .' Her sister's voice was unapologetic. 'Anyway, I've been up since sparrow's with Fleur. No matter what I try I can't get her to sleep past five am. It's cruel. No, it's beyond cruel, it's a particular form of torture. Tell me again why I wanted kids?'

'Mm,' said Anna tiredly. There went her only chance of a lie-in for another seven days. Last night, after finishing her meal and driving back to her flat she had pottered on her small balcony, tending her plants, watering and weeding. She had stayed up to watch a late-night thriller and was then unable to get to sleep. Visions of the book she'd found and its extraordinary contents kept running through her mind like an old-fashioned zoetrope, insistently flickering. She'd had a dream of a triffid-like plant growing up around her flat, imprisoning her with its thick, green tentacles, and she had woken feeling unsettled. 'Anyway, who told you about the box?' Anna asked, knowing full well the answer.

'Mum did, of course. She rang me yesterday afternoon. Couldn't wait to tell me the whole story. I have to say, it sounds very mysterious, doesn't it? A bit like Pandora's box, if you ask me. Mum said something about it being heavy enough to be full of gold bars.'

Anna groaned inwardly at the inevitable interference that would come from her sister or, more likely, Harvey.

'So? Did you have to go to the locksmith?'

Anna was torn between telling her sister the truth, or lying and keeping her find to herself, for at least the time being. The fewer people involved the better. But Vanessa *was* her sister. She dithered. 'Um, not really . . . but a visit to the hardware store was successful.'

'Ooh! I knew you'd be able to open it. You always were the practical one. Come on then, spill. What was in it? Gold? Jewels? Love letters?' she asked, an excited note in her voice. 'Do you think Granny Gus had a secret lover?'

'No, nothing like that, I'm afraid. I think it predates Granny Gus by at least thirty years.'

'How do you know that?'

'There are dates,' said Anna, cryptically, enjoying keeping her sister on tenterhooks.

'Right.' Her sister's tone was firm. 'That's it. I'm coming over. Give me half an hour to sort out the rabble. *Harvey!*' she yelled and Anna was forced to hold the phone away from her ear. 'Harvey! Something's come up. With Anna.' There was a muffled sound and a pause. 'Yes, really.' Her sister hung up the phone.

Great, thought Anna, sinking back onto her pillow, *at least now I know how I'm going to spend my Sunday morning.*

Sunday was Anna's least favourite day of the week. On weekdays, as soon as she woke she did a mental run-through of her clients, deciding which needed attention and what was on her slate for the day. Then she was out of bed and in the shower before she knew it. On Saturdays she could keep busy, going to the gym, catching up on groceries and laundry and even doing a bit of bookkeeping. But Sundays were empty and endless. Interminable blank hours. More often than not on the day that most people looked forward to, she woke with dread like an ache in the pit of her stomach.

It had been a Sunday when she'd last seen Simon. In those days Sundays felt like they had been dusted with gold. Lazy mornings, breakfast out, a walk or a visit to a garden, a drive out of the city, the occasional weekend away, beachcombing or hiking. Glasses of red wine and log fires and the comfort of being in the arms of someone you loved and who loved you just as much.

Anna threw back the covers and resolved, for what seemed like the trillionth time, to stop wallowing. She shivered a little in the cool late autumn morning as the breeze from the open window tickled her bare legs. Without hesitating, she headed for the shower.

~

Vanessa arrived an hour later in a flurry, carrying a tray of coffee and a white paper bag in one hand, her keys in the other. 'The least I could do, given I woke you up,' she said waving the bag in front of Anna with an apologetic smile. The scent of warm bread filled the small flat.

'If it's bagels, you're forgiven,' Anna said grudgingly.

'With salmon and cream cheese,' Vanessa replied.

'There had better be dill. And onion.'

They took their breakfast out onto Anna's sunny balcony. The rear of her apartment looked out over a large park, which was the main reason Anna had bought it. She'd ignored the fact that it wasn't even big enough to swing a cat, and seen past the dated bathroom and the dodgy carpet to the green, green view and had known that it was perfect.

Vanessa looked around at the plants that tumbled over each other along the railing, and inhaled the scent of orange jessamine that perfumed the air. She glanced over to the far wall, which was entirely green, a vertical garden with thriving mint, thyme, parsley and chives. 'God, Anna,' she said enviously, 'I don't know how you do it. I can't even keep a cactus alive. I'm wanted for herbicide in three states.'

'It's not that hard, really,' Anna laughed. 'You just need a good fertiliser. The stables over at the park do me a deal on manure. Anyway, you're busy growing your own three flowers and not doing such a bad job there.'

Vanessa rolled her eyes at her sister's corny comment and wrinkled her nose, sniffing as if she could smell the manure, then sat at one end of the bench that faced the view. Anna sat beside her and leant back against the wall, placing the bagels between them.

'Remember when we used to spend every Sunday together? Before Harvey. Before Simon.' Vanessa lifted her face to the sun, closing her eyes against its glare. 'I kind of miss those days.'

'Yeah. How about that time we got the bus to Bondi Beach and then you nearly lost me in the rip?'

Vanessa laughed and looked shamefaced. 'You've never forgotten that, huh?'

'Nope. The look on your face as the lifeguard hauled me out of the water.' Anna chuckled. 'You were absolutely furious with me, but you couldn't yell at me, not with everyone watching, especially the lifeguard.'

'Well, he *was* pretty cute. We never told Mum, did we?'

'No sense in worrying her. Besides, she might not have let us go again.'

'True,' she smiled and turned to look at her sister. 'What happened, Anna?'

'Life happened, Ness.'

Her sister took a bite of the bagel. 'Are you going to let me in on the secret?'

Anna's heart stuttered. She gulped, then recovered herself. The box. That's what Vanessa meant. 'Well, it's all very strange. Fancy there being such a thing hidden away like that for so long? It's as if someone didn't want it found. It's beautiful.'

'Okay, let's see this mysterious beautiful box, then.'

'Can I finish my bagel first? We'll have to go back inside. I'd hate it if anything blew away out here,' Anna chewed hungrily. 'What's in it is pretty fragile.'

'Ooh, now I'm really curious. Come on. Where is it?' Vanessa crumpled up the empty paper bag and grabbed their coffee cups, heading inside to the kitchen. Anna followed, swallowing the last of her breakfast and detouring to her bedroom.

The sketchbook sat where she'd left it in the box on the floor, illuminated in a shaft of sunlight, and as Anna looked at it she had a sudden premonition, a feeling of apprehension. Exactly what had she discovered? What changes would this bring to her carefully ordered life?

'Bloody hell!' Vanessa was as entranced as Anna had been the night before. 'This is incredible. Look at the detail!' she exclaimed, marvelling at the intricate etching, tracing her finger over the box's surface. 'Extraordinary.'

Anna pushed off the lid and retrieved the sketchbook, placing it on the table in front of them. Vanessa slowly turned page after page of the drawings. 'Oh, look at the dates,' she said. 'April . . . May . . . June 1887. That's, what . . .'

'Nearly a hundred and thirty years ago.'

Vanessa exhaled a long, low whistle. 'And it's been hidden away this whole time, do you think?'

'Well, Granny Gus was born in 1918, so it predates her by thirty-odd years.'

'I wonder how it got there, and whose work it is? Do you reckon it's worth anything?'

That the sketchbook might be of value hadn't crossed Anna's mind. She'd been more interested in who the mysterious E was, and what the story behind it might be. 'Does that matter?'

'I suppose not,' said Vanessa. 'I guess it belongs to you now.'

'I'm not so sure . . .'

'Well, who else would it belong to?'

'I don't know, but I'm going to try to find out.'

'It's certainly stunning. Even the inside of the box is beautiful.' Vanessa stroked the worn velvet lining. 'Hang on a sec . . .' She ran her fingers over the lining again and Anna could see that she'd found a small loop of ribbon at one end on the bottom, something Anna hadn't noticed. Vanessa tugged on the ribbon and the base of the box came away, revealing a hidden compartment beneath.

The two sat in stunned silence as they contemplated what lay there.

Chapter Eleven

Liverpool Docks, 1886

Elizabeth couldn't help but let out a small squeal of excitement as she caught the first glimpse of four tall masts, their sails reefed, and a monstrous iron hull looming above the dock. It was a sight to behold. The ship was tethered to the land by means of thickly knotted ropes, but they looked flimsy in comparison to its huge size. 'Look, Daisy, there she is, the *Corcovado*, one of the finest windjammers to sail the high seas!'

The maid looked as nervous as Elizabeth was excited, her skin even paler than usual as they peered out the window of the hired brougham. 'Yes, ma'am,' she replied, clutching her valise tightly across her lap, 'a most impressive sight indeed.' All around them was a flurry of activity the like of which neither of them had ever encountered. Mountains of goods sat on the dockside waiting to be loaded into the ship's hold, and porters shouted instructions to each other as they wheeled handcarts about the dock, weaving in and out of the stacks of crates. Families bade tearful farewells to loved ones. It was so noisy and chaotic Elizabeth could barely take it all in: the very sight of so many people and things in one place made her giddy.

It had taken them several days to make the long journey from Cornwall to the northeast of the country, stopping in London for a night (where Elizabeth took advantage of their stay and arranged for a final delivery of paints and brushes). Travelling with Helyer, the footman who was also Daisy's eldest brother, as chaperone, they had departed Euston (Elizabeth in the First Class carriage) and then billeted overnight in the bustling port town. In her excitement to be away, she had barely slept a wink, and was up before dawn to reach the ship with plenty of time before their afternoon departure. This was the furthest Elizabeth had ever travelled in her life, and she hadn't even left England yet. She reminded herself that this was the least of what she was likely to experience in the months to come, but her excitement did not fade.

Now she could actually see the ship, at nearly four thousand tons one of the Pacific Steam Navigation Company's finest vessels, she could not wait to set sail.

'Steady there, miss,' said the footman as he helped her down from the carriage.

'Thank you, Helyer,' she replied, leaning against his arm as she was jostled by the press of people on the Prince's Landing Stage.

'I shall see to the trunks,' he said once she was safely on the dockside, 'while Daisy and yourself make your way to the terminal.' He pointed to a long, low building at the far end of the wooden wharf before climbing up to the roof of the carriage to retrieve the many trunks that Georgiana had deemed necessary for the voyage.

Packed carefully in one of the trunks was a metal box, similar in form to a jewellery casket, but rather larger in size. It had been presented to Elizabeth by her father shortly before he became ill and it was made by the same firm that had cast the sundial at Trebithick. It featured similar embossing work of curlicued herbs and flowers and in the centre of the lid was a stylised 'E' surrounded by flowers and birds. 'Oh!' cried Elizabeth when she had first seen it. 'Papa, it is beautiful!'

'Well, my dear, you should have somewhere safe to store your drawings.'

'Oh, I adore it!' she said, lifting a latch to reveal a lining of plush midnight blue velvet trimmed with dark sateen ribbon.

'There is a lock here, too,' he said fumbling on the credenza and presenting her with a small but solid-looking heart-shaped lock and key. 'And it is airtight. Seals completely. Best way to keep your materials free of damp.'

At the time Elizabeth had wondered why her drawings might need to be so secured, but all became clear once her father had entrusted her with his mission. He had also presented her with several thin glass plates. 'For the drying of seeds,' he had explained.

Elizabeth turned to look for Daisy, who had stepped down from the carriage and was gazing around in wonder at all the activity. The maid gave her a broad grin – it looked like she was beginning to be as caught up in the thrill just as Elizabeth was.

It was past midday; they had breakfasted simply and early on bread and tea, and now Elizabeth was starving. She was anxious to board and make her way to the dining saloon where, she had been informed, there would be refreshments waiting. 'Come on then Daisy. We'd best be getting on.'

'Yes, ma'am,' Daisy replied, looking suddenly bereft. Elizabeth, too, felt a pang of loss amid the anticipation. They were both leaving behind all that was familiar. Though Elizabeth had bade Georgiana and Robert farewell two mornings before, Daisy was now faced with a final goodbye to her eldest brother, and she hugged him fiercely, tears dampening his waistcoat. 'Now then, Daisy, don't carry on so,' he scolded her gently. 'You're off on a grand adventure – seeing the world! We'll be seeing your cheeky face afore long, don't ye worry. And hearing all your tall tales of life on the high seas.'

'I know. Forgive me, brother,' she sniffed, relinquishing her hold on him and squaring her shoulders. 'I shall be fine. And I shall try not to miss you all too much.'

'Come on now, Daisy,' said Elizabeth impatiently, hunger getting the better of her. 'Dry those tears and let's begin.'

'Godspeed,' Helyer called after them. Elizabeth could hear the envy in his words.

As they ascended the gangway, her stomach lurched. She was about to sail halfway around the world in search of a deathly poisonous plant. With Daisy following close behind, Elizabeth didn't allow her steps to falter. It was too late to back out now.

~

There were only a handful of passengers aboard the *Corcovado*, as she was predominantly a cargo ship, taking mail and china to Valparaiso via Bordeaux, Lisbon and Rio de Janiero and then returning with sugar, cocoa and textiles. The ship's saloon was low-ceilinged and compact, containing a long wooden table that ran the length of the room, flanked on both sides by a row of rounded chairs that were bolted to the floor. Elizabeth discovered this as she tried to pull one out to sit down. 'Oof!' she cried, unable to budge it.

'Here, ma'am. I think this might help.' Daisy had deftly twisted the chair to one side so Elizabeth was able to sit.

'Oh. Thank you, Daisy,' she said, red-faced as she realised her mistake.

A plate of buttered bread had been laid out on a sideboard, together with a fruitcake, and a large teapot stood next to it, resting on a metal trivet.

'Shall I pour, ma'am?'

'Yes please, Daisy. And for yourself. Now we are aboard, I think we might perhaps relax the normal rules, don't you agree?'

Daisy looked at her blankly.

'There are no separate servants' quarters and so we will eat together. You will also have plenty of time to yourself, as I will need little assistance while we are at sea.'

'Yes, ma'am,'

'And so I think we can dispense with "ma'am" and "miss", can't we, Daisy? When we were girls and played together, we were Daisy and Lizzie, and so I think for this journey we should be that to each other again. What do you say?'

'Yes ma— Of course, Miss Lizzie.'

'Come on, Daisy, you can do better than that,' Elizabeth commanded.

'Yes, Lizzie,' Daisy replied obediently, giving her mistress a tentative half-smile.

And with that small matter settled, they turned themselves to the important business of eating. Unfortunately for Elizabeth, it was to be the last meal for many a week that she was able to enjoy.

~

They had been at sea for less than twenty-four hours when she was struck down. The following day, she and Daisy had partaken of a solid luncheon of boiled beef stew – tolerable enough, thought Elizabeth, stirring the gravy with her spoon, though it could have done with more salt – and steamed plum duff. After the meal, Elizabeth had retired to her cabin. 'I didn't sleep at all well last night, and I think a nap might help me shake off this tiredness, Daisy,' she said.

'Of course,' replied Daisy. 'Do you need me to come and help you undress?'

Elizabeth waved her away. 'I think I might manage to loosen my own stays.'

'Of course. Then I think I shall remain on deck; the fresh air pleases me.'

Lulled by the thrum of the ship's engines – they were to run on steam while there was no wind, but sail otherwise – Elizabeth was asleep in an instant, despite the narrow bunk with its thin mattress that passed for a bed.

When she awoke the cabin was dim, very little light coming in from the small porthole, and the ship was rolling from side to side. Elizabeth's travelling bible, which she had placed by her bedside, had been flung across the room and her sunbonnet was on the floor beside it. Her stomach roiled, matching the swell of the ship and she clutched her hand over her mouth. 'Oh, heavens above,' she muttered to herself as she raised her head off the bed. There was a jug affixed to the nightstand and she only just managed to reach it in time as a violent stream of vomit heaved up from her stomach and splattered into it and onto the floor. After a series of lesser heaves that left her trembling all over, she wiped her mouth with the back of her hand and staggered to her feet.

When eventually she was certain that there was no more left in her to expel, she left the cabin, which now reeked of the sour stink of her stomach contents, and went in search of Daisy, clinging to the corridor as she staggered towards the open deck.

The maid's flame-coloured hair was like a beacon and Elizabeth spotted her at the far end of the ship. She hurried towards her, grasping the ship's railing for dear life as it lurched and rolled on the messy ocean. 'Oh Daisy!' she cried as she reached her. The wind whipped her hair about her face and carried her words away.

'Elizabeth, isn't it something! Look at the sea. It's so vast! There's no end to it!' She seemed positively exhilarated.

Daisy looked more closely at Elizabeth and noticed her green-tinged pallor.

'Oh, Miss, what is wrong? Is it the seasickness? They did warn us of it.'

Elizabeth nodded dumbly, feeling hopeless and feeble, too nauseous even to be disappointed in herself for succumbing to such a triviality. She was supposed to be an intrepid traveller and here she was falling at the first hurdle. She groaned aloud and Daisy took her arm. 'Stay out here for as long as you can bear it. Being below decks is the worst thing for seasickness, so Mr Williamson was telling me.'

'Mr Williamson?' Despite her fragile state, Elizabeth was curious.

'He and the other gentleman, Mr Windsor, were out here earlier.'

Elizabeth noticed a faint blush colour Daisy's cheeks.

'They had plenty of advice to impart about life aboard ship. This is their fourth such journey together.'

'So, they are old hands,' replied Elizabeth through gritted teeth. She had seen the two gentlemen at dinner the previous evening. There had been sixteen of them in total in the saloon: a family with three children who looked to be aged between twelve and four, together with their maid and manservant, who, in the absence of separate dining quarters, sat at the far end of the table; two other couples, and the two gentlemen, the captain, and Elizabeth and Daisy made up the rest of the party. In light of their new agreement, Elizabeth had insisted that Daisy sat next to her.

'Indeed. It seems that they have travelled quite extensively. The Sandwich Islands – wherever they are – Australia and the Americas. They export goods across the globe and have particular interest in the nitrate market in Chile, though I confess I am not certain exactly what nitrates are.'

'Impressive in any case,' Elizabeth muttered. 'But for now, Daisy, I worry that I shall be indisposed for the entire voyage.' Her heart sank at the thought of spending several months in such dire straits. She couldn't imagine ever feeling well again, her stomach churned so.

'There, there. Don't fret now,' said Daisy, comforting her. 'You'll get your sea legs soon enough.'

'I'm afraid my cabin is none too clean,' she apologised.

'Oh, of course,' said Daisy, catching her meaning. 'I will have it right as rain for you in no time. Though I think you should try to stay outside for as long as possible. At least until dinner is served.'

At the mention of dinner, Elizabeth's stomach gave another almighty heave and she hurled herself towards the railing, retching bile out into the choppy grey water.

Daisy placed a hand on her mistress's back and rubbed it gently in a circular motion. 'There, there,' she soothed again. ''T'will ease off soon.'

Elizabeth wanted desperately to believe her.

Chapter Twelve

Sydney, Autumn 2017

'It's like a time capsule!' Vanessa exclaimed.

She lifted out a jet necklace, almost small enough to be a choker, that was decorated with an intricate pattern of beads and droplets. Its facets twinkled as they caught the sunlight. 'Not especially valuable, but pretty nonetheless. Late Victorian, I'd say.' Before having kids Vanessa had worked for one of Sydney's foremost jewellers, specialising in estate pieces.

Then she found an elaborately decorated but tarnished silver-backed hand mirror. It rattled slightly as she raised it up to her face, the looking glass loose in its setting. She admired her reflection in the age-spotted surface and then turned it over to see the 'AT' entwined on the back.

'So, we have an AT from this, and an ET from the sketches,' mused Anna as she examined it.

Next was a small, grainy, black-and-white photograph.

'Ooh, now we're getting somewhere!' said Vanessa, holding it up to show Anna.

The photograph, mounted on stiff card, showed an outdoor scene with a man sitting in a spindly-wheeled old-fashioned wheelchair. Next to him stood a young woman, her fair hair drawn back from her face and a slight smile on her lips. The man was wearing a suit and collar and the woman a dress with long leg o'mutton sleeves, her waist cinched in to tiny proportions. In the background was an imposing house, with more than a dozen chimney pots atop its steeply pitched slate roof. A grand front door was flanked by a series of tall, rectangular windows, their panes divided into small squares. In front of them was a wide drive, and on the left, in the foreground, a series of large, bushy shrubs.

'It looks English, doesn't it?'

'Could be.' Vanessa turned the photo over. 'Look, there's something written on the back.'

'Well, what does it say? Can you make it out?' asked Anna impatiently. Excitement pulsed through her veins at their discovery. It was like discovering clues to a fascinating puzzle.

'*John Trebithick and his daughter.* There's a date too. *Spring 1886,*' Vanessa added.

'The same year as some of the drawings are dated,' said Anna. 'I wonder if ET is his daughter? Do you think she's the artist?'

'Or it could be AT,' Vanessa reminded her. 'Like the mirror. And anyway, the watercolours might be the work of a man.'

'To have been kept in such a box?' Anna was doubtful.

'Good point.'

'She's very pretty, isn't she?' said Anna, studying the image as Vanessa returned to the box.

'And what's this?'

Pressed between two pieces of thick paper was a pale, almost translucent flower. It crackled as Vanessa placed her finger on the petal. 'This is your area of expertise, sis,' Vanessa said, carefully handing it over to her. 'What do you reckon?'

'Some kind of lily, at a best guess,' she said, examining it gently. 'But not a type I've ever seen before.'

Vanessa, meanwhile, had returned her attention to the box's false-bottomed compartment. It seemed it had one more treasure to yield.

'Silk damask, I think,' she said, holding out a small drawstring bag, that once might have been a vibrant scarlet but was now mostly faded to a light red. Carefully, Vanessa loosened the ties at the top of the bag and peered inside. With a bemused expression she then emptied the contents onto Anna's dining table: small, brown, dried-up bean-shaped objects tumbled onto the table, some spilling on the floor.

Anna stopped her examination of the pressed flower and bent down to retrieve the wayward seeds. Gathering them in the palm of her hand, she pinched one between her thumb and forefinger and held it up, viewing it with the eye of an expert. 'Never seen anything like it,' she murmured to herself, before carefully returning all of the seeds to the bag. 'I wonder if I planted . . .'

'So,' Vanessa said, sitting back in her chair. 'What do you make of all this, then?'

Anna was still thinking. 'I'm not exactly sure.'

'How could it have survived for all these years?'

'Well, the box is pretty strong. It must have protected this stuff from anything that could have damaged it, like extremes of temperature or humidity. And the paper is quite thick; rag paper, I reckon, or something similar. I remember learning about it in history – they sometimes used to make paper with old cotton cloths way back when. Oh, just a minute!'

Anna reached over to the bookcase and retrieved the notebook she had brought back from the Paddington house. 'This was the first thing the builders found in the cavity. I forgot all about it.'

As she opened it, the binding cracked slightly and she saw that the front page was torn out. She turned the pages, which were densely covered in a spidery writing, the ink faded to sepia.

'It seems to be a diary,' she said. 'Look, there are dates at the top of some of the pages.'

'It's been kept away from light for a long time, too,' Vanessa added. 'That would have helped preserve it.'

'Do you know, it's really odd,' said Anna looking up from the notebook. 'But I could have sworn I smelled the ocean when I first opened the box.'

'Well, it might have come by sea?'

'Yeah, maybe. Or maybe it's just my imagination running away with me. But the drawings. They're not of plants native to England. Nor Australia, for that matter,' said Anna.

'Any idea where they might be from?'

'I was trying to figure that out last night. A lot of them look South American to me.'

'So, the mystery deepens,' said Vanessa. 'How thrilling! And what about the diary? Is there a name written inside it?'

Anna shook her head. 'It looks as if someone has torn out the first few pages. And the writing's really hard to read.'

'Can you make out any of it? Here, let me have a look.'

Anna had opened the diary at random and together they pored over it. 'There's something here about a ship. "The decks are iced . . ." Is that word "iced"?' Vanessa asked.

'I think so.'

'"The decks are iced over and we cannot leave our cabin . . ." Cool.'

'Literally,' said Anna, rolling her eyes.

'Looks like you were right about the box having come here by ship.'

'I guess. I'll have a proper look at it later today.'

'Oh, bloody hell!' Vanessa grumbled as her mobile began to ring. She pulled it from her jeans pocket and glanced at the screen. 'Harvey.'

Anna disappeared to the kitchen to clear up their breakfast mess, and to let Vanessa talk to Harvey.

Her sister soon appeared in the doorway. 'I'd better run – he's wondering where I've got to. Honestly, he can't cope with those kids for more than five minutes on his own. It was so worth coming over though, sis – that's quite a find. Any idea what you're going to do with it all?'

Anna blinked. She hadn't imagined that she needed to do anything with it. Then a thought occurred to her. 'Well, there's Jane, one of my old mates from university. She works at the Gardens now. I've kind of lost touch with her . . .' She paused as Vanessa raised her eyebrows. 'Yeah, I know,' Anna continued, 'but I could ask her. She might know, or know someone who could shed some light.'

'Sounds like a plan,' said Vanessa gathering her keys and handbag. 'Keep me posted – I'm dying to know more, and I'm sure Mum is too.'

Anna spent a few hours trying to decipher the diary entries, but with limited success – looking at the writing for too long gave her a headache. She couldn't guess at its connection to the sketchbook and box, for the handwriting was different, though the dates were similar, the diary entries just a year or so later.

She managed to work out that its author was called Marguerite, and that she was sailing to Australia. The first few pages were dated February 1888 and spoke of long days at sea, rats gnawing at her boots and a mysterious 'L' growing fretful and sick. Marguerite seemed to bear the arduous journey with fortitude, reminding herself to stay strong, though she mentioned growing tired of the continued suppers of greasy mutton soup, coarse bread and hard cheese. She also disapproved of the copious jugs of rum the male passengers downed, often retiring early to her tiny cabin with L, lying awake on their hard bunk while L slept. Anna hadn't yet figured out who 'L' was, other than a baby.

As she lay back on her infinitely softer bed, Anna was transported back in time, imagining the rolling ship and the endless weeks at sea, the waves twice the height of a man washing over the decks, trying to care for a sickly infant. Marguerite didn't mention a husband, so why would she have been at sea with a child? Was she widowed, travelling to make her home in a new land perhaps?

Anna could scarcely imagine the courage it had taken to embark on such a journey, into the complete unknown, and what's more with a baby to keep safe.

She read on . . . Marguerite seemed apprehensive, 'glad to be quit of the place' and the 'evil spirits' that pursued her. 'I can never return home,' she wrote. 'For surely he will find me, and the child and I would fear for our very lives. But soon I shall be a free woman, and for that I will be forever grateful.'

A chill went through Anna as she read this. How dreadful to have to flee your home, to travel for weeks and face the unknown. Marguerite must have been a stoic woman indeed.

Chapter Thirteen

At sea, 1886

Calmer waters did not alleviate Elizabeth's seasickness. The ship called at Bordeaux and then, later, at Tenerife, where she roused herself to view the island's spectacular peak. No one was allowed ashore.

'It is not safe,' warned the captain. 'I have word of Spanish hostilities.'

Daisy reported two stowaways who were found in the ship's hold. 'They were quickly put to work in the stokehouse, so I am told.' Several weeks later she came to Elizabeth with stories of vast pods of whales spouting to the starboard side of the ship, her eyes round with the excitement of it. The following morning, she said she had been out on deck at night, 'with the stars in the sky brighter than I could scarce believe'.

Elizabeth barely raised her head from the bunk. She was indisposed almost the whole way to Rio de Janiero, a journey of nearly a month, and survived only by nibbling thick, dry bread and taking mere sips of water. The drinking water became so slimy that they were forced to strain it through their teeth, and Elizabeth shuddered at the cockroaches that skittered over her bunk in the night. She constantly scratched at the louse bites that peppered her arms and legs. She felt as weak as a kitten. In fine weather, she was able to lounge outside on a deckchair, her knees covered by a warm woollen rug as if she were an invalid, but the feeling of wellbeing she had known all her young life was as elusive as the scent of spring bluebells in the woods behind Trebithick Hall. She was unable to leave her cabin at all on the last day of October, even though it was her birthday. She felt utterly wretched and began to wonder if she would even survive the journey to see out her twenty-sixth year.

Daisy, by contrast, thrived on the bracing sea air, and Elizabeth noticed that she became more confident and independent almost by the day. Their roles might as well have been reversed, she thought listlessly, noticing that Daisy had struck up a particular friendship with the younger of the two gentlemen on board. She had quizzed her maid, and it seemed that, without either of them formally declaring it, Daisy and Mr Williamson contrived to find themselves walking the length of the ship's deck every morning after breakfast. Daisy reported her conversations excitedly to Elizabeth, perhaps hoping to stir her interest in something, anything other than the terrible tedium of the voyage. 'He exports cocoa from Brazil and Peru all the way to the docks of England!' Daisy said. 'He says that there is a fortune to be made and that he and Mr Windsor stand to profit handsomely from their endeavours. At least those were the words I think he used. What does "endeavour" mean?'

'In this instance, work,' said Elizabeth. A sour note had crept into her voice after weeks of hearing Daisy's stories. 'It is clear that this impresses you, Daisy.'

'Why would a person not be impressed by such a thing?' replied Daisy, hurt.

Elizabeth was immediately contrite. 'Oh, I'm sorry, sweet Daisy. I am merely so sick of feeling sick, it makes everything most disagreeable.'

'And I am trying my best to take your mind off it,' said Daisy calmly. 'That is all.'

Thus Elizabeth was not the only one who was relieved when, a day's sail on from Montevideo, she awoke one morning feeling somewhat recovered. If Daisy was surprised to see her already out of bed when she came to help her dress, she said nothing.

'I think I shall take some breakfast this morning Daisy,' Elizabeth told her. On all previous mornings, she had waved away the offer of food, refusing to set foot in the dining saloon for fear of nausea overtaking her again.

'Yes, of course,' replied Daisy. 'You will be in luck. The ship's cook took on supplies. We have fresh fruit the likes of which I've never seen. Persimmons – they look like a tomato but taste more like an orange. And blueberries, oh, the blueberries, you must try them!' exclaimed Daisy. 'They are so sweet and flavoursome, like nothing I have ever encountered.'

Elizabeth's shrunken stomach, instead of flip-flopping as it had done at the thought of food all of the previous days at sea, gave a loud rumble. 'Come on then, Daisy, let me try these strange fruits. I do declare I am starving!' she cried in surprise.

The air was warm and soft, the sunlight hazy, and Elizabeth was glad of the parasol that Georgiana had insisted she bring with her. After breakfast Daisy had also fetched Elizabeth's sketchbook and pencils. Though everything else was damp and sticky with salt, her box, with its watertight seal, had kept them mercifully dry.

'I'm not sure there is much point in those,' Elizabeth said as she saw what Daisy had also brought with her. She looked out to the horizon; the sea was as still as molten glass. 'For there is precious little to see.'

She was surprised to notice Daisy looking anxiously at her, biting her lip as if she had something that she wanted to say but was afraid to.

'What is it, Daisy?'

'Well, Miss . . . er . . . Elizabeth.' The maid twisted the cotton fabric of her skirt. 'I was wondering if you might help me with my writing. I can read a bit – my dad taught my brothers and me when we were little. But I never learned to form my letters properly, and I should like to. That is, if you could spare the time?'

Elizabeth could not hide her astonishment. 'But you speak most eloquently. I had no idea you could not write nor read.'

'I confess I have made careful study of the way in which you converse, Miss Elizabeth, but the writing is a different thing. As for reading . . .'

'Well, Daisy. Time is one thing we both have plenty of at the moment, wouldn't you say? I should very much like to be your teacher, if only to thank you for looking after me so well the past several weeks.'

'T'was no more than my duty,' Daisy replied.

They smiled at each other almost as they had done when they were girls, and Elizabeth took up a diary that Daisy had also brought out. 'Here,' she said, carefully forming the letters of the alphabet. 'I'll write them out and then you can copy them underneath. If there was one thing Mam'zelle Violette insisted on, it was elegant penmanship, and so I shall teach you as she taught me.'

The warm air, diligent study and the fact that for the first time in weeks she had nourishing food in her belly brought colour back to Elizabeth's cheeks. She and Daisy were laughing together over Daisy's shaky script when the two gentlemen interrupted them.

'You appear to be in much improved spirits, Miss Bligh,' said Mr Williamson, inclining his head towards her. 'Allow us to introduce ourselves, since we have not yet had the pleasure. My esteemed companion, Mr Arnold Windsor, and myself, Daniel Williamson.'

Elizabeth could see why Daisy might be impressed by him, for he spoke well and had a kindly expression. His features were pleasing and his hair of a ruddy colour similar to her maid's.

'I am indeed, Mr Williamson, thank you,' Elizabeth replied after a pause. It had been her father's suggestion that Elizabeth travel under her mother's maiden name, to avoid anyone connecting her with Trebithick, and she hadn't yet become accustomed to the new moniker. 'It is a relief to be well again. It would seem that, at long last, I have the "sea legs" that Daisy has been telling me about.'

'And not before time,' he said. 'For we feared you might not survive the journey.'

Elizabeth saw him and Daisy exchange a look and Daisy's cheeks redden at his interest. Exactly how close had they become while she had been laid low?

'Oh, I am sure I am not the delicate flower you imagine me to be,' Elizabeth insisted.

'Just not a sailor perhaps, then?'

'Indeed,' Elizabeth admitted, picking up her travel guide, which Georgiana had pressed into her hands as they left. 'What say you to this, Mr Williamson? "The best travellers are those who can eat cats in China, frogs in France and macaroni in Italy; who can smoke meerschaum in Germany, ride an elephant in India, shoot partridges in England and wear a turban in Turkey . . ."?'

'I would have to agree, ma'am. 'Tis often a wise notion to adapt to the culture you find yourself in.' As if to prove his point, he indicated his linen shirt, which was unencumbered by an ascot or tie.

'Up to a point, though,' argued Elizabeth. 'For I cannot imagine losing all sense of England, no matter the circumstances.'

He tipped his hat to her, a smile playing about his lips. 'I would say you are in no danger of that, Miss Bligh.'

Elizabeth staved off ennui with her lessons for Daisy and the companionship of the other passengers. The journey was long, tedious and uncomfortable and, perhaps because of their mutually endured hardships – the rats, as they scrabbled unseen in her cabin at night, were the worst by Elizabeth's reckoning – they had become a close-knit band of travellers, forced together by the confines of the ship and finding camaraderie therein. Elizabeth became quite fond of the three children, especially the littlest, and engaged them in games of chasey, hopscotch and deck quoits when their parents tired of their company.

Christmas Day was celebrated on board, though the fare was not what any of the passengers would have recognised as a festive repast.

'There is a particular shortage of turkey in this part of the world,' Mr Windsor had joked.

'Nevertheless, we have a fine pudding, do we not?' Elizabeth remarked, spooning up the fruit-and-brandy concoction. She had begun to enjoy the avuncular company of Mr Windsor – he reminded her a little of Papa in his interest in all of the goings-on in the world, but she kept a careful eye on the blossoming friendship between Daisy and Mr Williamson. Despite the relaxed boundaries that shipboard life had necessitated, she had no wish for her maid to lose her head and her heart, nor abandon her as soon as they reached land. The journey had changed Daisy,

Elizabeth reflected. She had proved a keen scholar and their daily lessons meant that her reading and writing were much improved. But it was more than that. Daisy was no longer the shy Cornish country girl, but a capable and steadfast young woman who seemed afraid of very little.

From being struck low by the fierce heat of the Equator, Elizabeth was then once again confined to her cabin as the ship rounded Cape Horn in heavy seas, pitching and shuddering until she was afraid it would be rent in two. She was unable to find comfort even in the onion-skin pages of her bible. Shivering under a pile of blankets, she was barely able to stop her hands shaking enough to make out the words. The damp, icy chill had soaked through to her bones. If she were ever forced to sail through the Drake Passage again, it would be too soon, she decided. She could not wait to reach dry land.

Chapter Fourteen

Sydney, Autumn 2017

When Anna stepped from the Botanic Gardens into Flourish cafe, she was surprised to see not one but two people waiting at a table. Jane had hardly changed in the years since Anna had last seen her, but the other person was a complete stranger and Anna couldn't help but feel a little disconcerted by his presence. It was going to be hard enough seeing Jane again after so many years, and face her questions, let alone deal with an inquisitive onlooker.

'Anna! Hi! You look great,' Jane called out, standing up to envelop her in a hug. 'It's been too long, hey? I have to admit, I was surprised to get your message. I thought you'd dropped off the face of the earth, or at least ended up on the other side of it. That was your plan, wasn't it? After university?'

Anna dismissed her question with a tiny wave. 'No, still here.'

Jane looked at her in surprise and then seemed to suddenly remember that there was another person with them, someone who was contemplating Anna with amused interest. 'Anna, Noah. Noah, Anna,' she said.

Noah's handshake was solid, and Anna briefly noticed the pleasing dry warmth of his fingers and the calloused skin of his hand before he withdrew it and they all sat down.

'So, Anna, Jane tells me you've got some botanical art you'd like assessed,' he said.

'Well, I'm not sure about assessed really. But I thought Jane might be able to shed some light on it.'

'Noah's really the expert on this kind of thing,' Jane explained. 'That's why I asked him along. He's recently helped to curate an exhibition. Did you see it? The one at the Lion Gate Lodge a couple of months ago?'

Anna shook her head and Noah looked momentarily disappointed.

Their conversation was interrupted as they ordered sandwiches and drinks, but then Noah began to talk about the exhibition, the work involved in collating it. 'It showcased some of Australia's and New Zealand's finest botanical artists. They're under-appreciated really. I suppose because it's such a specialist area. The painstaking detail they achieve is quite extraordinary, better than a photograph in some instances.'

Anna nodded. She too appreciated the intricacy and scholarship of botanical art, and that included the examples in the sketchbook she had placed in the calico bag next to her chair. She was waiting to get it out, though – the last thing she wanted was for a careless hand to spill coffee on something that had survived so long in such fine condition.

'So, where did you come across your drawings?' Jane asked.

'My grandmother's house. In Paddington. The builders found an old box when they were taking apart some bookcases.'

Noah's eyes widened. 'Cool. Any idea how long they'd been there?'

'Well, Granny Gus was born in the house, in the early 1900s, but that doesn't really help, because she died recently, so I can't ask her. The bookcases have been up for as long as my mother can remember – she grew up there. But the drawings are dated.'

Noah and Jane looked at her expectantly.

'1887.'

Noah whistled and Jane looked impressed, but Anna didn't have the chance to elaborate any further as a waitress delivered their orders.

Noah and Jane fell upon their lunch, though Anna noticed him glance up at her from time to time. 'Being outdoors really stokes your appetite,' Jane mumbled through her food. 'Especially at this time of year – it's been bloody cold in the mornings. I'm gonna need gloves soon.'

'I thought you'd be sitting inside a cosy lab somewhere,' said Anna, swallowing a mouthful of her sandwich.

'Not a chance. We're propagating a range of heirloom seedlings, looking at how temperature affects germination and growth. They need more TLC than a newborn,' Jane joked. 'Though you're right, I'm here on a secondment for a few months. I'm usually over at the Australian PlantBank. We're doing a massive classification of native plants and their seeds. Plants are being placed on the endangered list almost every day – people would be astonished if they knew the extent of it. We're also discovering new plants – last year alone there were more than a thousand new strains discovered across the globe, including coffee, parsnips and roses, if you can believe that.'

Anna nodded.

'And then we're looking at ways of preserving seeds with cryogenics.'

'What, like they freeze embryos?'

'Exactly. Except a lot of our rainforest species don't appreciate being dried out and deep-frozen, so we've got to come up with some other way to preserve them.'

Anna's thoughts flickered to the small bag of seeds that she and Vanessa had found in the box, but caution held her back from bringing it up; she didn't want the whole thing taken out of her hands. She wanted to see what the drawings were first, she told herself, and decipher the rest of the diary before worrying about a small bag of desiccated seeds and a pressed flower.

As Jane talked more about her work at the seed bank, Anna finished her sandwich and sipped the scalding coffee. When they were all done and the table was cleared, Anna reached down for the bag containing the book of illustrations. Jane and Noah fell silent as she opened it to the first page, a vibrant watercolour of a forest-green shrub laden with dark purple fruits, with the fruits shown in detail in a separate drawing. '*Aristotelia chilensis* – maqui berries,' said Jane. 'Full of antioxidants and touted as a "superfood" now.'

There was a note in pencil at the bottom of the page. 'Leaves used for brewing *chicha*,' Noah read. 'Whatever that is. "Sore throats, heals wounds, painkiller",' he continued. 'Extraordinary. I can't believe the condition it's in. It's scarcely aged at all.'

He turned the page to find a painting of a tall, oak-like tree with dark brown bark, oval-shaped green leaves and dense white flowers. '*Quillaja saponaria* – soapbark,' he read. 'Native soap, for the lungs and good health.'

They continued to leaf through the sketchbook, which contained more than a hundred drawings, each of a different plant.

'Hey, you know these are all native to southern Chile, right?' said Jane. 'And most of them are medicinal plants, by the looks of things.'

'Hm . . .' Noah mused. 'It's odd.' He came to the end of the book and carefully closed it, handing it back to Anna, who returned it to the calico bag. 'It doesn't look like the work of any of the Australian artists from around that time, or I'm sure I would have recognised it. I suspect it might be English. It's certainly a remarkable find. The artistry and the condition it's in are astonishing.'

'What are you going to do with it?' asked Jane.

'I have no idea,' Anna admitted.

'The style isn't anything like I've seen before,' said Noah. 'And, as accurate as they are, botanical artists do tend to have a signature style, if you know what to look for, almost like a fingerprint.' As he said this he placed a finger on his lips thoughtfully. 'I do know someone who might be able to help.'

'Did you find anything else with it?' asked Jane. 'You said it was in a box.'

'Well, there was a photograph,' Anna admitted. 'It seems to have been taken earlier in the same year. It shows two people standing in front of an old house. There's what looks like a rhododendron in the foreground.'

'So, you've got an antique sketchbook full of extraordinary watercolours apparently done in Chile and an old photograph,' mused Jane. 'Hidden in the back of a bookcase. Curious indeed.'

As they gathered their things to leave, Jane hung back with Anna, letting Noah go ahead of them. 'Anna,' she began, 'I never got the chance to say how sorry I was about Simon.'

Anna raised a hand to stop her saying anything further. 'It's fine. Really. A long time ago now.'

Jane took the hint. The truth was, it was still far from fine, but Anna had no desire to dredge up the past, not with anyone.

When they caught up with Noah, he pressed a piece of paper into her hand. 'It's my email address.' Anna worried for a moment that he might be angling for a date. She'd noticed a speculative look in his eyes that indicated interest in not only the watercolours. 'Drop me a line and I'll dig out the details of the person I think might be able to shed some more light on this.'

'Oh, great,' she said. 'Um. Thanks.'

'I knew it was a good idea to bring him along.' Jane said slyly as they departed.

Anna walked back alone through the gardens, enjoying the peace and stillness away from the crowded city streets. She tried not to think about the times she and Simon had spent there, the lazy picnics in the shade of the enormous spreading Moreton Bay fig trees, strolling hand in hand across the gardens' hidden bridges, talking, debating and finally kissing to the backdrop of the lotus pond, but they almost seemed imprinted on the landscape. It had been one of their favourite places in Sydney, and she'd not been back in years. For good reason.

As if of their own accord, her steps took her through the rose garden, its flush of blooms now fading with the onset of cooler weather. Gussie had loved roses more than anything but had always struggled to grow them in her tiny backyard. Sydney just didn't offer the right climate for them.

She reached the bronze sundial at the centre of the herb garden and ran her fingers along its raised surface, noticing the faint line of dirt under her nails, dirt that she could never quite scrub away. She traced the engravings of oregano, mint, parsley and, of course, rosemary. 'For remembrance,' she whispered.

Chapter Fifteen

Valparaiso, 1887

'Oh Daisy!' said Elizabeth as the maid entered her cabin to help her pack on the morning of their arrival into Valparaiso. 'I feel as if a thousand butterflies are milling around in my stomach. Now we shall begin the exploration in earnest.'

'Yes, we shall,' replied her maid, though her voice bore none of the excitement of her mistress's.

Elizabeth looked carefully at her. 'You will miss this, won't you?' Elizabeth understood that for Daisy, leaving behind their friends on the ship would be a wrench.

Daisy nodded. 'Mr Williamson informs me that they shall be in Brazil and Argentina for several months, but that they will return to Valparaiso in due course.'

'Well, then I am sure this is not the last you shall see of him,' said Elizabeth brightly. Inwardly she was happy that they at least would be gone for some time and that Daisy's friendship with Mr Williamson was to be nipped in the bud.

Daisy said nothing as she busied herself folding and stowing away her mistress's garments.

Elizabeth smelled land as soon as she walked out of her cabin and onto the deck. It was the scent of vegetation, of earth and wood smoke and even the faint stench of sewage, but to her, after months at sea, it was as if the sweetest perfume was borne on the breeze towards her. She inhaled deeply, closing her eyes. At last! The real purpose of her journey could begin.

Peering into the distance, she could see the small port, and a mass of ships – there must have been three score or more – including what looked to be a navy frigate. There was a strong onshore wind and so Valparaiso soon hove more clearly into view. The port town sprawled at the foot of steep cliffs, with a number of long, low stone buildings with regularly spaced windows set on gently curving, wide cobbled streets above the shoreline and whitewashed houses with red-tiled roofs scattered on the plain above. As well as the ships already at anchor, there were numerous boats no bigger than rowboats closer in. 'Why, that part of it looks so like a Cornish fishing village!' Elizabeth exclaimed in surprise. After sailing nearly halfway around the world, she had been expecting something considerably more exotic.

'Land ahoy, eh, Miss Elizabeth?' The voice behind her was that of Mr Windsor. 'You'll be pleased to get back on dry land, I'd wager?'

'Oh yes. I have a letter of introduction to the Consul-General, a Mr Fraser, in Santiago. Though I confess, he will be expecting my father, not me. Are you by any chance acquainted with him?'

Mr Windsor shook his head. 'No, though his reputation has him as a fine man.'

'Oh, that is good to hear,' she replied. 'I think we shall stay awhile in Valparaiso first before continuing to Santiago.'

'A sensible plan, Miss Elizabeth. For just as it took you a while to become accustomed to the ship, so you will have to find your feet on land again.'

Several hours after anchoring, and as she had watched with fascination the throngs of people who arrived to greet the ship, Jose, a manservant of a Mr Campbell met Elizabeth on board. He had been expecting her father, but nonetheless informed her that he would be pleased to escort her to her lodging. Daisy stayed on board to organise their belongings and Elizabeth was rowed ashore in a small boat, then continued on foot along a dusty road. Elizabeth felt almost giddy at the feel of solid ground beneath her boots and her disappointment at being a poor sailor, which had haunted her throughout the long days at sea, soon disappeared as she eagerly drank in the unfamiliar sights and sounds of the town. The landscape formed a natural amphitheatre, like the ones she had seen in books about Roman times, with rectangular buildings, some with columns and colonnades, as well as gracious squares filled with fountains and flowers on the flat ground surrounding the bay, and then further up, smaller dwellings arranged up the narrow streets that snaked up the hillside and on the plain that sat above this. 'There you will see the *ascensor*, the Concepcion. It was completed barely three years ago,' explained the manservant, pointing to a box-like carriage above which stretched a ratcheted railway.

She looked up at its fearful steepness and then back towards the bay. In the distance she could see the *Corcovado*, its masts now bare of sail. The sudden realisation of how far she and Daisy had travelled hit her like a punch to the solar plexus and momentarily stole the breath from her lungs.

There was no time to dwell on such matters, however, as they soon reached the lodgings her father had arranged. The house was the home of an English merchant and his wife, the Campbells, who had settled in the port some ten years earlier. They were the proprietors of a general store, the town's largest, Elizabeth's father had told her, as well as taking in occasional lodgers.

As they arrived, Jose whispered in the ear of a broad, rose-cheeked woman who came to greet them. Elizabeth heard her father's name mentioned.

'Oh my dear!' Mrs Campbell favoured a similar bright plumage to the birds that Elizabeth had seen on her journey to the house and almost completely filled the narrow passageway. 'I must confess, we were expecting Mr Trebithick. But how delightful that his daughter – for he spoke of you and your sister often – has made the journey to visit this fair country.' She beamed at Elizabeth, who felt the warmth of her welcome and was immediately grateful for it. 'Come, come, you must be exhausted merely from the walk here. And you look as though you would blow away in the first gust of wind. Such a slip of a thing! And you've come all this way on your own, you say?'

'Well, there is my maid, who will travel up from the ship shortly,' replied Elizabeth.

'Yes, yes, our man will see her safely here, along with your trunks. But now – food!' Mrs Campbell clapped her hands together. 'We must eat,' she said as she led the way through to a courtyard. The home was a modest but clean mudbrick dwelling, with four sides facing the courtyard in which they now stood. Within it grew such a variety of plants as Elizabeth had ever seen: white roses, carnations, lobelias, mimosas, even sweet peas tumbling over each other in vigorous abandon. At one end was a herb garden, and Elizabeth recognised rue, fennel, caraway, sage, thyme and mint. Through a doorway at the rear of the courtyard she could see a grove of olive and lemon trees and on the short walk from the harbour to the house she had spotted tall, spiky thistle-like plants, palms and trees covered in white flowers. She was seized with an immediate desire to open her sketchbook and take out the magnifying glass from the pocket of her cloak, to capture the intricate detail of an almond blossom, its calyx and corolla, stamens and carpel, or perhaps to draw the curl of a vine tendril or a spiky aloe leaf, but her hostess insisted that she sit with her while food was prepared. It would have been rude to do anything else.

The dullness of the ship and the never-ending uniformity of the sea and sky had left her parched for such beauty and she thirstily drank it in. 'What a serene spot,' she said as they sat at a low table in the shade. 'And how lush everything is.'

'Everything grows so wonderfully here,' her hostess agreed. 'It is barely any effort at all to cultivate a plant from seed, but doubtless your father would have told you that. It seems like only yesterday that Mr Trebithick was here with us, leading us all on merry outings into the *cordillera*. I am most sorry for your loss, my dear, I know how very fond of you and your sister, Georgiana, he was.'

'Thank you, it means a great deal to me to hear that,' Elizabeth replied.

'You must think of me as a mother while you are here,' she insisted, though Elizabeth had not been in need of a mother for many years, nor, in fact, did she know what it felt like to have a mother. Mam'zelle Violette had been the closest she and Georgiana had come to such a relationship, but she nodded politely.

'You will meet Mr Campbell anon, but I have to say he spends most of his time at our business, down in the town,' said Mrs Campbell. 'So, I am afraid you will have to satisfy yourself with my company for much of the time.' She said this with a twinkle in her eye, as if she were sharing a private joke between the two of them, and Elizabeth warmed to her even more.

A young Chilean maid with thick dark hair fastened in a plait that hung down her back entered the courtyard. Carrying a tray, she moved gracefully across the bare earth, setting it down before them and smiling as she did so.

'Thank you, Mercedes,' said Mrs Campbell. The maid disappeared as noiselessly as she had arrived.

Elizabeth was surprised when she spied a large wooden cup with a wide bowl instead of the china pot and cups she had been expecting, but waited to see what her hostess would do. Mrs Campbell raised the cup and sucked on a thin silver straw that Elizabeth now noticed stuck out from the cup. 'Matté,' she said after taking a sip. 'I find it quite refreshing.' She passed the cup along to Elizabeth, who hesitated, staring uncertainly at the mashed green leaves and water in the cup. Was she expected to drink from the same straw as her hostess? Mrs Campbell nodded, encouraging her.

It appeared she was.

Elizabeth sucked on the straw and a warm, harsh liquid flooded her mouth. It was bitter and she gave an involuntary shudder.

Mrs Campbell laughed. 'Don't worry, my dear, you will get used to it. It's really quite nice once you do.'

Elizabeth was not so sure.

'Here, try one of these. The sweetness will help.' She proffered a plate upon which sat several small, half-moon-shaped golden pastries. '*Empanadas*. They are often filled with meat, but I like these, more usually in the afternoon – a little pick-me-up after siesta and before I go back to the shop,' she explained.

Elizabeth gratefully accepted one, and bit into it. Sweet ripe pears flavoured with cinnamon and cloves provided the filling to a slightly cheesy pastry. 'Delicious,' she said, when she had finished her mouthful.

Mrs Campbell nodded, approving. 'You look like you could use a little meat on your bones, girl.'

Mrs Campbell was outspoken in her observation, but Elizabeth paid it no mind. She was not offended – indeed, her gown hung off her, no matter how tightly Daisy had tried to lace her corset. 'I was quite unwell on the voyage,' Elizabeth confessed. 'I survived on bread and peppermints.'

'Well, here, you must have another,' Mrs Campbell offered, pushing the plate towards her again.

As she was doing so, the plate began to shake and several of the *empanadas* bounced onto the dirt floor. The leaves of the plants had begun to tremble, and the table jittered and danced, jostling the cup of matté and slopping green sludge everywhere. The seasickness that had dogged her on the ship returned.

'Wh . . . what is it? What's happening?' Elizabeth's eyes were wild with panic.

Chapter Sixteen

Sydney, Autumn 2017

Anna pulled on a pair of overalls, boots and heavy gloves from the back of her ute and spent the afternoon dead-heading flowers and pulling out the asparagus fern that had completely taken over her client's front garden. As she worked, sweating in the warm sun, her thoughts returned to the photograph. 'Of course,' she muttered to herself. Why hadn't she thought to Google the name on the back? Trebithick. It was worth a shot. She pulled her phone out of her pocket but cursed as she realised the battery was dead. She would have to wait until she got home. After that, the afternoon dragged as she hauled out yet more of the invasive weed, her imagination swirling with the possibilities of actually identifying the house in the photograph, and from there . . . well, who knew? She couldn't wait to get home and so, just before five, when the light was starting to fade to a glorious rose-gold-tinged sunset, she pulled off her gloves and loaded up her ute for a final drop-off at the rubbish tip.

It was dark by the time she got home to her flat, and she made straight for the shower. It took a good scrub to lift the dirt from her hair and skin, but eventually she was clean, dried and dressed warmly in her favourite fleecy jumper, leggings and a pair of fluffy socks. She turned on the heater – the nights were definitely cooling. The fridge revealed a couple of wizened apples, half a loaf of bread and a block of cheese. Starving, she made herself a toasted cheese sandwich and opened a bottle of red wine. It was Friday, after all. She only allowed herself one glass, though. She had to be up early for her spin class in the morning.

When she'd finished eating and wiped the crumbs off her hands, she sat back with her laptop. Typing the word 'Trebithick' into the browser, she held her breath as the page loaded.

Trebithick Hall was listed on an English Heritage website. Apparently a Grade II–listed building in England, whatever that meant. She searched for a photo, but couldn't see one. She then clicked on another link, 'Historic houses in Cornwall'.

Bingo!

She sat back suddenly, almost knocking over her glass in her excitement.

There it was. Just as it looked in the old photo. The same long windows, circular gravel path and wide front door. Even the rhododendron, though far larger, was still there.

Anna reached for her phone.

'I've got ten eight-year-olds here dancing to Taylor Swift and I can't even hear myself think,' her sister yelled when she picked up. 'What's going on with you?'

'Listen to this,' Anna began, 'I think I've found something.'

'Hang on a sec, let me go somewhere a bit quieter . . . *Ivy!*'

Anna held the phone away from her ear as her sister yelled at her teenage daughter to watch her younger siblings.

'Okay. That's better.'

The music had quieted and Anna cleared her throat and began to read from the website. 'Trebithick Hall was donated to the National Trust by Florence Deverell in 1970. Florence (b 1935) never married. She is the only child of George Deverell (1887–1960) and the great-granddaughter of John Trebithick, who gained considerable renown as a plant-hunter and adventurer in the late nineteenth century. Many of the exotic plants that he brought back from his travels still flourish in the gardens, which are now on display to the public,' she said, a note of triumph in her voice.

'So, if this Florence Deverell was born in 1935 she'd be . . . what?'

'Eighty-two,' said Anna. 'That's if she's still alive, of course.'

'Well, according to the National Trust she is,' said Vanessa.

'How do you know that?'

'They'd have put the date of her death there.'

'Oh,' said Anna, overcome by what she'd found out. 'I see.' It made the sketchbook of watercolours all the more real, gave it a vital, compelling connection to a place, and to the present. 'Do you think we should track this Florence Deverell down?'

'Yes, of course!' said Vanessa. 'She might know the story behind it all – perhaps even how it ended up in Sydney. You've got to at least try. All right, *I'm coming*!' she yelled.

'What?'

'Sorry, not you. The girls want me to go and judge their dance-off. I may never get my hearing back and I've no idea where Fleur's learned some of those moves,' said Vanessa. 'Certainly not at ballet class.'

'Well, perhaps you could stop her watching music videos in the early hours of Sunday morning,' replied Anna.

'How do you know about that?'

'Favourite aunts are privy to all kinds of secrets,' she said, chuckling as she put down the phone.

Anna stared at the webpage and then continued her search for information about John Trebithick. She was excited to find a couple of references to him being a celebrated botanist and plant-hunter, as well as a purveyor of exotic plants. It wasn't until much later, when she was owl-eyed from tiredness and getting nowhere, that she remembered the slip of paper that Noah had pressed on her after their lunch. She retrieved it from her jeans pocket, smoothed it out and typed in his email address – but then she paused, her fingers hovering over the keyboard, uncertain.

Finally she decided to keep it brief, merely reminding him of their meeting and asking him if he could indeed put her in touch with his friend who knew more about nineteenth-century English botanical illustrators. Pressing send, she turned the laptop off and fell into bed.

Anna woke early the next morning, and for the first time in years she didn't feel like driving across the city to the gym. It was a clear, bright day and she felt a yearning for the ocean. Throwing on her exercise gear, she headed down the stairs of her apartment building and climbed into her ute. Fifteen minutes later she was at the beach.

A big swell had blown in overnight on a strong southerly wind and only the hardiest – or possibly foolhardiest – surfers braved the water. Anna watched as the waves crashed and foamed on the shore, barely noticing the handful of joggers and walkers moving around her. She took her shoes and socks off and wiggled her toes in the sand, breathing out as the water washed over them. Even though it was autumn, the water had yet to completely lose its summer warmth and it soothed her feet and calmed her soul. It had been years since she had been to the beach, somewhere she loved as a girl, and yet it was only a few minutes' drive away. Why had she left it so long? Had she really been too caught up in work, or had she subconsciously denied herself the simple pleasure of a walk on the sand? She had been sleepwalking through her life for far too long.

Chapter Seventeen

Valparaiso, 1887

'Just a small tremor. We get them all the time. Nothing to worry about. Well, most of the time anyway.' Mrs Campbell waited the few seconds that it took for the shaking to stop and then clapped her hands together sharply. The maid who had brought the tea reappeared and began to clear up the mess with an enviable calmness.

Elizabeth took a deep breath and pretended to be at ease with it all. Her thoughts flickered briefly to Daisy, who was most likely on her way to the house. After their experience on the ship, she had no doubt that her maid was perfectly capable of looking after herself, but an earthquake was something that would unsettle even the most sanguine traveller.

Mrs Campbell stood. 'I must get back to the shop. I trust you have everything you need, but if not, call for Mercedes and she will look after you. I shall see you at dinner tonight. We eat at ten. Late, I know, but it is the custom here.'

Elizabeth was left sitting in the courtyard, contemplating how to spend the remainder of the afternoon. She was anxious to begin to explore, but after so long aboard ship she was unsure how far her legs would carry her. The sun shone brightly overhead but the breeze was cool and the weather ideal for a walk. Resolved, she gathered her skirts so they did not drag across the dirt floor and returned to the room that Mrs Campbell had shown her to earlier.

'Ah, there you are!' exclaimed Elizabeth as she opened the door to see Daisy in their bedroom, surrounded by a sea of trunks. 'Did you feel the tremors? Were you scared?'

'No. Mr Williamson forewarned me.'

'Lucky for you. I nearly leapt out of my skin,' said Elizabeth.

Daisy looked sympathetically at her. 'Well, no harm done by the looks of things.' She pointed to a dark wardrobe that took up almost all of one wall of the modest space. 'I've put away some of your gowns, but I did not want to unpack everything. There isn't enough room.'

'Thank you, Daisy.'

'Good,' the maid replied, bobbing a curtsey.

'Now, where is my sketchbook? My fingers are itching to begin. Have you seen the array of plant life here? It is more than I even dared to dream of, more than Papa described.'

'It would be a grave disappointment if there were not,' said Daisy with a wry grin.

'Will you accompany me on a short exploration of our surroundings?'

'To the town?'

'Oh no. I wish to see the landscape beyond the town. The fields, the olive groves and the almond gardens. I glimpsed them briefly as we came to the house.'

'We shouldn't stray too far. It would be most unfortunate to get ourselves lost on our first day here,' warned Daisy. 'And you are not fully recovered from the journey.'

'Oh pish!' replied Elizabeth. 'I have absolute confidence in my sense of direction.'

~

The two young women set out – Elizabeth carried her father's vasculum and knapsack slung over one shoulder and a small portable easel over the other, while Daisy toted a satchel containing the sketchbook and paints – but the going was hard, with a steep climb up a narrow, rough path. The land swayed beneath Elizabeth's feet as if they were still at sea, and she began to realise how weakened she had become on the ship. They were forced to take frequent stops to rest, and her lawn handkerchief, which she used to wipe the perspiration from her brow and the back of her neck, was soon soaked through.

As they had sipped the matté, Mrs Campbell mentioned an area of almond trees and Elizabeth was relieved when they eventually came across it, bounded by a freshwater stream that rilled prettily over a bed of pea-sized pebbles. She drew out a small silver cup from her father's knapsack and knelt to dunk it in the water, filling it to the brim. 'Here, help me up, Daisy,' she said, holding out the other hand.

Daisy hoisted her up from the bank and Elizabeth offered her the cup first. 'Drink,' she insisted.

'Oh, that is delicious!' cried Elizabeth as she took her turn. After months of drinking brackish water from the ship's tanks, this pure stream water was crisp and sweet.

Daisy nodded in agreement and then looked up. They had climbed one of the steep hills that surrounded the town and now the sharp-toothed *cordillera* loomed in the distance, its peaks capped brilliant white with snow. Hummingbirds flitted among the almond blossoms and Daisy exclaimed at the sight of a flash of dull green. 'Oh! Mr Williamson told me of this parrot. It is well known in these parts.'

'Rather an ugly-looking thing don't you think? But curious nonetheless,' replied Elizabeth. She was far more interested in documenting the exquisite flowers before her. She set up her easel and rested her sketchbook upon it. After selecting a brush, she moistened the cakes of watercolour in her travelling palette with some of the water from her cup and, with careful strokes, began to record the almond flowers in painstaking detail. Her father had successfully cultivated them at Trebithick, but she had never seen them growing in the wild before.

More often than not, Elizabeth would collect plant samples to study carefully indoors, and would sketch them out before taking up her brush, spending hours ensuring she captured each detail precisely. But recently she had begun to experiment with a more free-form style of painting. It wasn't strictly the style of illustration she had learned, nor did she think her father would approve, but she loved the immediacy of it. The trick was to get the lighting just right – a strong source helped to create shade and give the work a three-dimensional effect. The afternoon light was perfect, and she also used a dry brush, rubbed over the paint cakes, to add detail and depth to the watercolours.

Daisy wandered off to the shade of a wide-spreading tree a few yards away. 'It's a canela tree, I think,' Elizabeth called out, pausing for a moment from her work. 'False cinnamon,' she explained.

'I can smell it,' replied Daisy, sniffing appreciatively. 'Like Cook's apple pie.' She sat down and leant against the fragrant tree. 'I think I shall rest here while you draw.'

Daisy closed her eyes and was soon asleep, but Elizabeth continued to paint, absorbed in her work. She barely noticed the cooling air and the sun slipping slowly below the horizon. As was so often the case when she was immersed in her art, time ceased to register, and several hours might pass as if merely the blink of an eye. It was only when she started to squint at the plant in front of her – a particularly fine specimen of *ficus* – that she became aware of the fading light and her cramped muscles. She would have to finish. Assigning her signature – the initials ET drawn with a flourish – and the date, she gathered up her materials and hastened towards her maid. 'Daisy, Daisy!' she said, shaking her gently. 'We must leave at once, for it will soon be dark,' Elizabeth cried as she heard the clamour of church bells in the town far below.

Daisy sat bolt upright. 'Heavens! I had no notion of sleeping for so long. Oh Elizabeth, I am so sorry.'

'It is not your fault. I too lost all track of the hour.'

Daisy scrambled to her feet and together they set off in the direction from whence they had come. However, unfortunately for them, the Chilean sunset was a short-lived one and before barely twenty minutes had passed they were stumbling in near darkness with only the stars and the few lights from the port below to guide their footsteps. It was all Elizabeth could do not to think of the ravines they had passed on the way up. A few steps in the wrong direction and they might fall to their deaths.

Elizabeth could hear the noise of small nocturnal creatures emerging from their burrows. Aboard ship, Mr Windsor had told of packs of mountain lions prowling the hills, and she shuddered at the thought of encountering even one of those. She silently cursed herself for having become so absorbed in her work. Really, what kind of a traveller was she turning out to be? Lost, in the dark, barely twenty-four hours on a new continent on the other side of the globe. She felt very foolish, but pride would not let her admit such a thing to Daisy. 'Shall we perhaps sing?' she said. 'For it might take our minds off the journey back.' She began a favourite childhood tune, her clear soprano ringing out in the darkness.

They had been walking for what seemed like more than an hour when Elizabeth heard a cough in the distance and looked up to see a small light bobbing up and down. 'Who . . . who's there?' she asked uncertainly.

There was no response.

'I know I heard something,' she called out, bolder this time. 'Whoever you are, show yourself.' She slowed and slid open the flap of the knapsack, her fingers closing over her father's small knife. Heart pounding, she withdrew it and held it concealed in the folds of her skirt.

Another cough, followed by the rustling of the grasses that lined the path. The light came closer. '*Señorita.*' A man's dark face loomed before them. Elizabeth could see the whites of his eyes and his teeth glowing in the light from his lantern.

'*Hola*,' she replied, that being about the limit of her Spanish.

'*Señorita* Elizabeth?' The man now stood before her, holding up the lantern to his face.

While wondering how on earth he knew her name, she couldn't help but notice his smooth brown skin and disarming smile. He looked to be about her own age, perhaps a little older and he was taller than many of the *chilenos* she had seen on her journey through the town earlier that day, and his eyes, which were on a level with hers, were a startling blue, the exact colour of the hydrangeas that bloomed every spring at Trebithick. She breathed out a little but still held tightly onto her knife.

'*Señorita* Elizabeth?' he asked again.

'*Si, si.* That is me,' she answered.

'Mrs Campbell sent me,' he answered. 'Tomas Esteban Flores, at your service.' He gave a low, theatrical bow. 'She was worried when you did not return, especially as you are unfamiliar with the city. There are several *quebradas* – ravines – not far from here, and an unwary traveller might accidentally fall into one. It is also not safe to be out after dark, for anyone, but especially a lady such as yourself.'

Elizabeth's grip on her knife loosened a little at his words.

'She asked me to search for you,' he continued. 'I am very pleased to have found you and can now happily and safely bring you back to your lodging.'

'Oh, thank you!' Daisy exclaimed. 'For you are right, we were lost.'

'Not lost at all, merely a little late,' retorted Elizabeth. 'We lost track of time, but we had not lost our way.'

Tomas's lips curved. 'Of course, *señorita*. But allow me to escort you both back to the *hosteria*. I would be negligent in my duties if I did not. And Mrs Campbell is not a woman whose wishes are easily disobeyed.'

'I understand,' said Elizabeth. Annoyingly he was right. 'As you wish.'

There was not room for them to walk abreast, and so Tomas led the way along the narrow path, with Daisy and Elizabeth following behind in single file. In only a matter of minutes they found themselves at the back gate of the Campbells' home.

'See, we were not so far from home at all,' said Elizabeth unable to keep the note of defiance from her voice as she stepped into the courtyard.

'Indeed, *señorita*,' said Tomas.

She didn't know quite why she was so irritated. The poor man had only been doing as he was asked. But there was something in his manner, which was not quite arrogant but certainly self-assured, that rankled her. She had never come across a man quite like him. He moved as gracefully as a cat, treading softly in his strange sandals, which appeared to be bound to his feet by thick twine. In the light that shone through the open doorway she could make out his clothing: loose trousers of a rough linen-like material and an open-necked light-coloured smock topped by a thick poncho that reached past his hips. His hair, thick, dark and glossy, hung loose about his face, reaching past his shoulders. He was dressed as a native but had the demeanour and language of an educated man, overlaid with a charming Spanish accent. The overall effect was disconcerting, as if a veritable Adam had sprung, perfectly formed, from the hills above them. Elizabeth shook her head to clear it. Really, she was having the most fanciful imaginings. It must be the effect of such a tumultuous day, she told herself. What with leaving the ship, finding their lodgings, experiencing an earthquake and getting caught out in the dark – she wouldn't allow that they had been lost – it had been a more eventful day than she had lived in months, if not years. Though she longed for adventure, she began to wonder if every day was going to be as unpredictable as this one.

'I will leave you now to pay my regards to Mrs Campbell.' Tomas Esteban Flores bowed low again and left them standing in the courtyard.

Elizabeth supposed she should simply be relieved that they hadn't met with misfortune on their first day in Valparaiso and that he had been a friend not a foe. But there was something about the man that intrigued her, though exactly what she couldn't say. She found herself wishing she had spoken more with him on their walk back to the house. He had given very little clue as to who exactly he might be.

Chapter Eighteen

Sydney, Autumn 2017

Anna began to painstakingly decipher the diary, typing it into a document on her laptop. She had completed about a dozen pages, learning that Marguerite and her daughter – Lily – had arrived in Sydney by ship, and spent six weeks at the city's quarantine station, on an isolated headland near Manly. During that time Marguerite had grown friendly with another woman, Alice, whose husband had become sick and died on their journey from Ireland, leaving her to raise their young son. Anna discovered that Marguerite and Alice planned to find lodgings together and look for work once they had been cleared of any potentially infectious diseases. 'Perhaps a situation in a shop . . .' she had written. Worried about who would look after baby Lily, Marguerite continued, 'I have a little money but I owe a great debt, one that I have sworn to repay eventually, so I must support the two of us as soon as I am able.' She also wrote of an acquaintance with a man on board. 'Joseph Bailey has been most kind to Lily and me. We pass the time in quiet conversation or taking a turn about the deck, much to the amusement of Alice. He is a carpenter and anticipates good employment in Sydney town. I confess I have grown quite fond of him and I hope our friendship will continue after we leave the ship. He has assured me it will, but I am no longer certain of anything in this life, for it can be unbearably cruel. Loved ones are torn away from us without a moment's warning.'

It was just after seven when Anna parked at her sister's house, pulling up beside her mother's little hatchback and Vanessa's shiny white four-wheel drive.

The front door was ajar, and she pushed it open, calling out as she stepped over the threshold.

'We're out the back.' Her brother-in-law's voice boomed over the sound of music and little girls' laughter.

'Yo mama!' called Ivy, her eldest niece, looking up from an iPad with which she seemed to be recording herself.

'It's a video-mime app,' Vanessa explained, coming over to give her a hug. 'It's actually quite funny.'

'I'll take your word for it,' said Anna, bending down to greet her littlest niece, Fleur, who was wearing pyjamas covered in red sticky gloop.

'Mm . . . fruity,' said Anna, breathing her in. 'Delicious! Can I have some?'

Fleur looked at her and giggled. 'No, silly. You can't eat it. It's bath gel.'

'Oh, all right then,' said Anna seriously, before lifting her up over her head and blowing raspberries on her tummy, reducing Fleur to shrieks of delighted laughter. 'Oof, when did you get so big? Every time I see you girls, you've grown again!' she complained, putting her down.

'They're like weeds,' said Vanessa. 'Ivy's nearly as tall as me – exactly when did that happen?'

Yes, when did it happen, wondered Anna. Only five minutes ago it seemed that Ivy was the same height and age as Fleur was now, and Fleur a chubby-faced baby.

'Hey Jas,' she said to her middle niece.

Jasmine looked up from behind her book and uncurled her long skinny legs, wiggling her toes as if they'd been cramped from too long in the same position. ''Lo Auntie Anna,' she said before returning to her book and tucking her legs back under herself.

'Hello love,' said Eleanor, coming over to kiss Anna. 'How are you?'

'I'm good,' said Anna with a smile, realising that she actually was. She wasn't sure if it was the impromptu trip to the beach or an afternoon reading about someone going through tougher times than she was that had brought on a lighter mood, but it was as if she had cast off a rock she had been unaware of carrying. 'I've been reading the diary. It looks as though it's the story of a woman, Marguerite, and her daughter, Lily, who came to Sydney in the late 1880s. She's at the quarantine station at the moment; well, that's as far as I've got. It's pretty hard to make sense of the writing; it's so faint and spidery. The spelling's a bit challenging to say the least.'

'Cool,' said Ivy. 'We learned all about the quarantine station in, like, year five. Did you know there are, like, ghosts there? For like real? Woo-oo . . .'

Fleur hid behind Anna.

'Oh my goodness,' said Anna's mother. 'Did you say Lily?'

'Yes, why?'

'Lily was my grandmother's name. Your great-grandmother.'

'Are you sure?' asked Vanessa.

Her mother raised her eyebrows at her.

'Well, it has to be her, then,' said Anna, feeling an excited fluttering in her belly.

'What was Lily's last name, Mum?'

'Bailey, why?'

'So, Marguerite married the carpenter!' Anna exclaimed.

'The carpenter?'

'She mentions she met a man called Joseph Bailey on the ship, bound for Sydney.'

'Oh, heavens darling, that was your great-great-grandfather, then.'

'So, Marguerite was my great-great-grandmother – your great-grandmother.'

'How exciting, love. I still don't understand the connection to the sketchbook, though.'

'Neither do I,' admitted Anna. 'Yet.'

'Are you going to have them valued?' asked Harvey, coming over to join them. 'They might be worth a fair bit, you know. There's a bloke at work, I think his wife works for Sotheby's. I could ask him about it.'

Anna bristled. 'Even if they are, there's no way I'd ever think of selling them,' she replied.

'You? What about *we*?' asked Harvey. 'Don't they belong to the whole family?'

'Harvey!' chided Vanessa. 'Stop teasing her.'

Anna didn't think he was entirely teasing. But his words had her feeling unnerved. It hadn't even occurred to her the items found in the house might not be her responsibility. She'd been the one to find them, in the house that now belonged to her. She didn't care about their value, monetary or otherwise. She simply wanted to find out for herself who the artist was and how the box had ended up in her grandmother's house, as well as figure out the connection between the diary and the sketchbook – for there had to be one, she instinctively knew it. She half-thought that the E of the sketchbook might be the Marguerite of the diary; that she might have written under an alias or changed her name. But that didn't explain the different handwriting. There was still so much to puzzle out. She couldn't just leave them be; she *had* to know the story behind them, especially now she had discovered that the diary was written by her great-great-grandmother. *This* at least was a mystery she might have some chance of solving; answers she might be able to find. Then she would think about what to do with the drawings; perhaps donate them to a museum.

'Don't be ridiculous, Harvey,' said Anna's mother, her tone brooking no opposition. 'Granny left the house to Anna, and everything in it. And that's that.'

It wasn't strictly true, but Anna shot her mother a look of gratitude.

'And what about the photo?' asked Vanessa. 'Any more clues there? Anna's tracked down Trebithick Hall,' she explained to their mother. 'That's where the photo was taken, the one I told you about, the one in the diary.'

'Well, it's in Cornwall, in England,' said Anna. 'And definitely still there. It belongs to the National Trust. But,' she paused, making sure they were listening. 'The last of the family, a woman named Florence Deverell, is still alive. I searched up her name and found an FE Deverell living somewhere called Trevone Bay. So, then I looked on Google maps, and it's really close to Trebithick Hall. It *has* to be her, doesn't it? Doesn't it?' she looked hopefully at her mother and sister.

'Oh,' said her mother. 'That's wonderful sleuthing, darling. I think you might be right.'

'I tried calling, several times, but there was no answer. I sent a letter instead,' Anna added.

'Don't tell me you're going to go over there yourself with the photo?' asked Harvey.

Anna fell silent, her buoyant mood suddenly deflating. They all knew she had never so much as left the country, never mind travelled as far as England. There had been plans, of course. She'd even had the tickets, sitting on her dresser. A six-week tour of the great gardens of Europe – Kew, Giverny, Versailles, Chateau de Villandry, even the Lost Gardens of Heligan, in Cornwall itself. That was all before Simon . . . she stopped herself from remembering any more.

'Dinner's ready, guys.' Vanessa rounded up her girls, hustling them into the bathroom to wash their hands.

'Can I sit next to you, Auntie Anna?' Fleur asked.

'Of course, darling.' Anna pulled out the chair next to her.

After they'd eaten, and Anna had read Fleur a bedtime story, she went back in to the lounge, where her mother and Vanessa were having a whispered conversation. There was, happily, no sign of Harvey.

As Anna reached them they fell silent. 'I'd better make a move,' she said, getting the familiar feeling that she had been the subject of their discussion. It was something she had learned to ignore over the years. 'Thanks for dinner.' She hugged her sister and then her mother and made her way to the door.

'Keep us posted on the diary, won't you, darling?' her mother called.

'Will do. Thanks Mum,' said Anna as she left. 'Love you.'

'Love you too,' her mother replied.

'See ya, sis,' said Vanessa walking to the door with her. 'And sorry about Harvey earlier. He's completely lacking the sensitivity gene. But he means well.'

Anna held onto her snort of indignation until the door had shut firmly behind her. She would rather be single than put up with that kind of self-satisfied condescension in a partner. She found herself fuming at his assumption that she would never break the boundaries of her carefully controlled life. He didn't know it, but he had inadvertently planted the seed of an idea in her mind.

Chapter Nineteen

Valparaiso, 1887

Upon their safe return, Daisy was ushered to the kitchen and Elizabeth joined the Campbells for a late dinner. Mr Campbell, as rotund and ruddy as his wife, greeted Elizabeth warmly. 'My dear, you are most welcome in our home, as no doubt my good wife has informed you. Your father had become a close friend of ours and we feel his loss, though we are blessed to make your acquaintance.'

After travelling so far and for so long Elizabeth was heartened by the couple's extension of fellowship, and to be in the company of those who had known her father. She took a deep breath before speaking. 'I am afraid I must ask that you not reveal my identity, nor my connection to my father. I have been led to believe that there are some who might wish me ill, and I would prefer to remain incognito.'

Mrs Campbell gave a shocked intake of breath.

'My story is that I am travelling to sketch the unusual flora of the region, a lady artist if you will. No more than that,' Elizabeth continued.

'Incognito, eh?' Mr Campbell looked surprised, but agreed to Elizabeth's request. 'Of course, my dear,' said Mrs Campbell. 'As a mark of our respect for your father, we will breathe not a word.'

'You did not say anything to Mr Flores, did you?' Elizabeth asked.

'No, no indeed.'

Relieved, and hoping that she could trust them to keep her secret, Elizabeth picked up her fork, feeling a keen return of her appetite. They feasted on more fresh vegetables than she had seen in months, together with a delicious spicy beef stew; and after weeks of seasickness and poor victuals aboard ship, Elizabeth happily helped herself to seconds as soon as they were offered. It was not until near the end of the meal that she raised the subject of her rescuer again.

'That man – *Señor* Flores – the one who came to look for us . . .' She hesitated, taking a sip of the rich white wine in her glass.

'Ah yes,' said Mrs Campbell, giving her a knowing smile. 'He is quite an interesting man, I am sure you will agree.'

'Well, actually, we hardly spoke. He came upon us not twenty minutes from here.'

'He is the son of one of the region's most notable men, *Señor* Mateo Flores.' Mrs Campbell warmed to her subject. 'They say his mother was a *machi*, a Mapuche medicine woman, and those who are inclined towards spitefulness say that she bewitched *Señor* Flores, casting a spell to make him fall in love with her. Of course I'm inclined to consider that all nonsense, but there was apparently quite a scandal at the time. Though it was some thirty years ago now, people here have long memories.'

Elizabeth looked at her hostess with wide eyes. 'Do go on,' she urged, just as Mr Campbell coughed loudly and waved his napkin at his wife as if to stop her from speaking.

Mrs Campbell ignored him. 'If ever the *chilenos* get sick they call on a *machi*; they are women of great power and their healing talents are highly revered,' she said. 'But, sadly, Sayelita – his mother, that was – died when Tomas was about ten. They were raised on the family's *estancia* in the mountains, between Valparaiso and Santiago, though Tomas lives in Valparaiso most of the time. He sometimes works as an interpreter between the *chilenos* and the British and Spanish here, and as a guide, though he helps his father in their business too. He knows this area better than any man around, which is why, when he called by this evening, I sent him to look for you when you hadn't returned by nightfall.'

That explains his excellent English, thought Elizabeth. *And his self-assurance.*

'He is a young man of great charm,' said Mrs Campbell, winking at Elizabeth. 'So, do be careful, my dear.' There was mischief in her voice, but Elizabeth reminded herself that she had no wish to be distracted from her purpose, the task her father had set her. She was also anxious to catalogue and collect as many native plant species as possible; what she had seen so far had made the blood quicken in her veins.

The conversation moved on to the subject of the recent war between Chile, Bolivia and Peru and the meal finished with no further talk of *Señor* Flores.

Elizabeth slept heavily that night, though at first she was fearful she might not, because every time she closed her eyes the floor swayed beneath her as if she were in her cabin on board the *Corcovado* once more. So it was that when she woke the following morning, at first she didn't know where she was. She had become accustomed to a darkened cabin, with Daisy coming in to rouse her from what was often a broken night's sleep as the ship creaked and swayed around her. This morning, however, sunlight streamed through a small window, high up in the wall across from her bed. She could make out gentle birdsong, a repeated chirrup of exceptional sweetness, reminding her of the sound of linnets in the wheat fields that surrounded Trebithick.

As she remembered the events of the previous day she stretched languorously, enjoying the feeling of her skin against the fine linen sheets, of not being suffocated by damp salty air and a constantly pitching, narrow bunk.

The previous night, she had taken her first freshwater bath since leaving Trebithick Hall – saltwater had been their only lot on board ship – and Daisy had washed her long fair hair, giving it a final rinse with chamomile purloined from the courtyard garden. She felt it now, spread out and silky on the pillow, and her mind strayed to the memory of the dark, glossy locks of Tomas Flores. What would they feel like between her fingers? Tomas Esteban Flores . . . she rolled his name around on her tongue, liking the sound of it.

A knock on the door brought her back to her senses. What was wrong with her? She had never taken the slightest bit of interest in a man before. Well, aside from Tommy Pengelly, the pastor's son who sang like an angel in the church at Trebithick. That had been a brief fascination, ending when she saw him in the churchyard after a service one Sunday morning throwing conkers at the squirrels that lived in the horse chestnut trees.

It didn't occur to Elizabeth that it was perhaps precisely because she had been so isolated at Trebithick Hall, with only her governess and her sister for company, that she hadn't had the opportunity to find any member of the opposite sex of her own age appealing. It had been different for Georgiana. When she was nearly nineteen, she had been whisked away to Plymouth to join their great-aunt for a summer, where she caught the eye of Robert. Elizabeth had been considered too young and was left at home to ride her pony and play among the glasshouses. By the time she was of age and might have been afforded the same experience, Great-Aunt Isabel was unwell and visitors no longer welcome.

Now, Daisy appeared in the doorway, a bright smile on her face. 'Good morning Miss Elizabeth. I trust you slept well?'

'Better than in months actually. It is a blessed relief to be off the ship. Though I confess the ground still sways somewhat beneath me.'

'I certainly don't miss the smell of it. The fish guts and salt spray and other things t'were even worse,' Daisy said with a shudder.

'Today is Sunday, is it not?' asked Elizabeth.

'Yes. Mrs Campbell said to ask if you would like to accompany her to church this morning. She will be leaving at ten.'

'Of course. But what time is it now? It feels as if I have overslept.'

'Not to worry,' said Daisy, a laugh in her voice. ''Tis only early and we have plenty of time to get you ready.'

'Well, you must come too. You might like to see something of the town.'

'As you wish,' replied Daisy with a quick bob.

They made their way to the church in a mule-drawn cart. 'It's the easiest way to travel when there are a few of us,' explained Mrs Campbell as she ushered them up the steps to the open carriage.

The two young women gazed about in awe as they travelled the short distance to the town's main streets.

'Oh look,' said Daisy. 'That must be the church.'

Elizabeth, who had been paying attention to the plants alongside the track they travelled on, turned her gaze to where Daisy was pointing. They were now on the flat land not far from the docks and in front of them was a stone church topped by a pretty tiered bell tower.

'The Iglesia de San Francisco,' Mrs Campbell said. 'It also serves as a lighthouse. I thought you might like to see a traditional service. Catholic, of course.' She murmured the last sentence under her breath. 'Here,' she said, handing them both folded lengths of black lace. 'Wrap these about you; it is traditional to cover your head and shoulders here.'

As they entered the church, Elizabeth saw that it was packed with families, and by their differing dress, of both Chilean and European nationality. They found a place towards the back and Elizabeth let the words of the service – in Spanish, which was incomprehensible to her – spill over her as she gazed at the barrel-vaulted ceiling. Lost in a daydream, she wondered if the opportunity might arise to be reacquainted with *Señor* Flores, not least – so she told herself firmly – because she was intrigued by the story of his mother. Sayelita would have known of the most efficacious Chilean plants, those to control fever, to banish evil spirits or to quell a delirium. She would surely have also known about the plant her father sought. Indeed, Elizabeth mused, perhaps Sayelita might have passed on some of that knowledge to her son? It was all well and good to sketch the almond groves and the fig trees, but she really wanted to find the medicinal plants native to Chile, the herbals and the curatives, the weeds with mysterious properties, with the power to heal or to harm depending on their preparation and dose, not to mention the one plant her father had charged her to discover: the Devil's Trumpet. She was, of course, there to fulfil the promise she had made him, the promise that had kept her from collapsing with uncontrollable grief when he died, and had sustained her throughout the long and terrible voyage to Valparaiso. Even though she had been through the worst of the journey, she was well aware that her true test was now upon her.

Chapter Twenty

Sydney, Autumn 2017

On Monday night a message from Noah popped into her inbox, and Anna eagerly clicked on it.

'A pleasure to meet you last week, Anna. The person who might be able to shed some light on your beautiful sketchbook is Dr Edwin Hammett-Jones. He's a taxonomist at Kew, specialises in South American flora, and he has a side interest in British botanical illustrators. You can reach him at . . .' she read, her eyes flicking quickly over the email.

She was about to close it when she read the PS. 'Let me know if you'd like a drink sometime, or maybe a movie?'

Even though she was alone at home she felt her cheeks redden. Was she being asked out on a date? Oh God. She didn't know how to reply, so she decided to ignore it for the time being. She closed the email and began to compose one to the very posh-sounding Dr Edwin Hammett-Jones instead.

'Dear Dr Hammett-Jones,' she began. She explained where she'd found the sketchbook and then uploaded a photo of a couple of the drawings that she'd taken on her phone. 'If you are able in any way to assist in identifying the artist, I should be most grateful,' she finished, pressing send and then shutting the laptop.

Anna's eyes lit on the silk bag of seeds that had also been hidden in the box. The thought she'd had when she first saw the bag resurfaced. She'd heard stories of seeds that were hundreds of years old being coaxed into life. Turning on her laptop again, she began to research. Yes, she'd been correct – there were even 1200-year-old lotus seeds found in a marsh in China that had been successfully germinated. Anticipation sparked through her. Maybe . . . just maybe.

An hour or so later, having read all she could find on the subject, she closed the laptop. Taking a dozen or so seeds, she gave them a light scuff with a piece of sandpaper, and then placed them in a dilute solution she made up from a little compost and water, and left them to soak overnight. She resolved to think about Noah's invitation in the morning.

Anna woke the following day with the feeling of hope rising within her once more. As she lay pondering this unusual emotion, another thought suddenly interrupted the others, and she sprang out of bed, flicked the kettle on and then opened up her laptop.

Two new messages. Another from Noah and – there it was – one from Dr Hammett-Jones. She imagined a stooped old man with half-moon glasses – short-sighted from peering at old watercolours – and thinning hair, sitting in dusty archives somewhere halfway across the world.

She clicked on the email from Noah first. 'Sorry,' it said. 'I hope you don't think I was being forward. Er, that is, asking you out. For all I know, you might be married, or engaged or with someone. Apologies if you are. But the offer's still there if you're interested.'

Anna certainly wasn't any of the above – married, engaged or with anyone, but was she interested? She didn't know. A voice inside her head warned of getting involved with anyone, but another voice, one that was growing stronger by the day, urged her to lighten up, live a little. *It's only a movie or a meal, for God's sake*, she scolded herself. Still undecided, she left the email open on her desktop and switched to the one from Dr Hammett-Jones.

'Dear Miss Jenkins. I am in receipt of your material. I have an idea as to its provenance, but I would, however, require the original artwork to be fully apprised of its authorship. I should be most pleased to receive you and conduct a proper assessment at your earliest convenience. Sincerely, E Hammett-Jones.'

Well, thought Anna with disappointment, *thanks for nothing*. He sounded as pompous as his name, and not in the least bit helpful. Did he really think she would just pop over to England?

Later, however, when she mentioned it to her sister, Vanessa persuaded her that he hadn't dismissed her email completely out of hand. 'He said he would be pleased to receive you,' she said, 'and would conduct a proper assessment. That's not exactly negative.'

'Yes, but I've got to go all the way to England for it,' replied Anna. 'And who's got time for that?'

'Is there no one else here, in Sydney, who can help?'

'No, according to Noah, the Pom is *it* when it comes to late nineteenth-century botanical watercolours.'

'Noah?'

'He works with my friend Jane, at the Botanic Gardens. He knows a bit about botanical illustration, but mainly Australian artists. He's the one who referred me to Dr Hammett-Jones. He's been really helpful.'

'Oh yes?' Vanessa looked at her speculatively.

'Not like that,' she said, exasperated, though she did avoid Vanessa's eyes. How did her sister manage to have a sixth sense about these things?

'Come on, sis, don't be like Mum,' she said gently.

'What do you mean?'

'She never got back out there, not after Dad . . .'

'That's not exactly fair. She had us to look after.'

'And your excuse is? Anna, sweetheart, you've got to let someone else in, give them a chance. You can't cut yourself off forever or you'll forget how to live.'

Anna didn't reply.

~

That morning she had also drained the seeds, wrapped them in kitchen paper dampened with water and put them in a ziplock bag, placing it on the kitchen windowsill to catch the autumn sun. She checked the soaked seeds every day that week, but each inspection revealed no change. She'd known it was a long shot, but had nevertheless allowed herself to hope.

On the fifth morning, however, when she removed the damp wrapping, there was a tiny nub of green poking out from one of the seeds. 'Unbelievable!' she called out loudly, dancing around her flat. 'Un-freaking-believable!'

She carefully removed all of the seeds and discovered that three showed definite signs of germination. She went out onto her balcony and retrieved a large terracotta pot. Shaking in some of the horse-manure compost and mixing it with a bag of potting soil she kept out there, she filled the pot almost to the brim. Then, using the end of a pencil to make shallow divots, she carefully placed a seed in each one until she'd planted half a dozen, covering them up with more soil. She sprinkled water over the whole pot, watering her other plants as well, and then placed it where it would catch the sun. Only time would tell if those tiny germinating seeds would flourish or founder.

A week or so after receiving the email from Dr Hammett-Jones, Anna had spent a chilly but sunny Sunday weeding the tiny pocket square of her grandmother's back garden, hard pruning the apple tree, cutting back the shrubs and generally creating order from the overgrown chaos. It was a bit of a busman's holiday, but she loved watching the garden re-emerge, to see it as she remembered when Gus was well enough to tend to it.

In the far corner of the garden was a tiny shed, little more than a cupboard really, that had once been the old dunny but was now fitted with shelves for storing old pots and gardening tools. Anna had cleared the overgrown passionfruit vine that had curled its way around the door, lifted the latch and peered inside. A pair of gloves, still moulded into the shape of Gussie's gnarled arthritic fingers, caused tears to prick at the back of her eyes. She moved them out of the way, spotting some old seed catalogues and a notebook at the back of a shelf. Gus had been an inveterate note-taker of all the goings-on and growings in her garden from season to season, and Anna felt a professional and a personal curiosity about what she might have recorded, so she stuck the notebook under her arm.

She was heading back to the house when her mobile rang. Fishing it out of her pocket, she glanced at the unfamiliar caller ID.

'Hello?'

'Anna? It's Noah.'

Anna stopped in her tracks, suddenly unable to summon a single sensible reply.

'Look, I'm sorry to bother you . . .'

'That's okay, you're not bothering me at all,' she finally managed, surprised that her voice sounded almost normal and inwardly cursing herself for not getting back to him.

'Well, er . . . I just wanted to know how you got on with my contact at Kew – Edwin. Was he able to shed any light on who the artist might be?'

'Not really, unfortunately,' Anna sighed. 'He said there wasn't much he could do unless he saw them himself.'

'Oh,' said Noah. 'What a shame. Sorry.'

'It's not your fault. But I'm not about to parcel them up and send them off to the other side of the world. Who knows what could happen to them? I'd never forgive myself if they got lost or damaged.'

'No, quite. I see your point.' Noah agreed.

'Look, thanks for trying. I appreciate it. Really. Perhaps we'll never find out who they once belonged to.'

'Oh come on, you can't give up that easily,' he said. 'This could be the key that unlocks a fascinating story. I don't know about you, but I'm certainly intrigued.'

Anna could hear the curator in him speaking and knew he was right.

'Look, it's your choice, obviously, but now that you've discovered it, don't you want to find out more?' he continued. 'Perhaps I can buy you dinner and we can brainstorm what to do next?'

Anna froze. Seconds passed.

'Anna. Are you still there?' he asked. 'It's only dinner,' he said gently.

'All right,' she said quickly. 'How about next Saturday?'

'Uh, sure,' he said sounding surprised but pleased. 'Okay. I mean, er . . . good. Chiswick – the restaurant not the suburb – seven-thirty? A mate of mine's the maitre'd. He should be able to swing us a decent table.'

'That'd be nice. See you then.' Anna rang off before she could change her mind.

Chapter Twenty-one

Valparaiso, 1887

On their return from church, Mrs Campbell proposed an outing, having invited several of her acquaintances to join them. 'You do ride, don't you, my dear?' she asked Elizabeth.

'Of course,' she replied, 'and Daisy too. You could not have made a more welcome suggestion.'

The party – made up of Elizabeth, Daisy, Mrs Campbell (Mr Campbell was busy with his accounts and had waved away any suggestion that he might join them) and a Mr and Mrs Gordon and their daughter, Sibyl – set off in the late morning. The Gordons were fine company, and Elizabeth chatted easily with them. The trio – 'Our people are the Wiltshire Gordons,'

Mrs Gordon said, 'from Salisbury. You have doubtless heard of them.' Elizabeth had not, but refrained from saying so – had lived in Valparaiso for some years, with business interests in the region, according to Mrs Campbell. Sibyl, who Elizabeth judged to be of a similar age to herself, was a dainty young woman, almost childlike with small hands and a tiny waist laced so tightly that Elizabeth wondered how she might breathe. Elizabeth felt almost gargantuan beside her, though she noticed that Sibyl handled her horse, an excitable chestnut mare, as well as someone twice her strength and size.

They were on their way to Lagunilla, a freshwater lake not far from the ocean. The going was steep at first, and once or twice Elizabeth's horse stumbled on the uneven ground. It was quite a challenge to stay in the saddle, but her mount appeared to be placid and Elizabeth was happy not to have been assigned one with a trickier nature. She thought fleetingly of Achilles and who at home might be riding him. Georgiana wouldn't be, of that she was certain, but Robert was a competent horseman and might have been inclined to keep him exercised. She sighed. England, and Cornwall and Trebithick Hall seemed like another lifetime ago. It was hard to believe that her sister would likely be great with child now.

Before long they reached the plateau and rode on companionably in the warm sunshine. Elizabeth was struck once again by the beauty of the landscape, with the coast and harbour on one side of them, and the distant snow-capped peaks of the Andes on the other. 'What a beautiful country this is,' she exclaimed to Sibyl. 'So wild and green.'

'Oh, but this is the growing season. It is not always so verdant. The end of summer can see it all quite bleached and dry,' Sibyl replied. 'Then, in winter, it is even more barren.'

They came upon a small stream, which pooled in between the thick grasses in places, and at others leapt along a stony riverbed. The horses forded the stream at a low point and continued on, traversing laurel and myrtle shrubs that gave off a sweet, pungent scent in the afternoon sun.

~

Elizabeth was surprised when, upon arriving at their picnic spot, she spied a smouldering fire set among several large granite rocks. A blanket had been laid on the ground not far from the fire, under the shade of a few spindly fruit trees.

Before they had a chance to dismount, three men, wearing wide-brimmed flat straw hats and tall leather boots emerged over the hill in front of them. Carrying shotguns. She gasped.

'I sent Jose on ahead,' Mrs Campbell explained. '*Señor* Flores, too, offered to accompany him,' she added, explaining the presence of the second man and the cause of Elizabeth's gasp of surprise. The third man was unknown to her.

As they came closer, Elizabeth could see that Tomas also looked to be carrying a brace of birds. Partridges, if she wasn't mistaken. He waved to the party, raising the birds in a triumphant gesture.

'*Hola!* We will have quite a feast!' he called, his teeth flashing white in the sunlight.

Elizabeth, whose horse walked next to Sibyl's, could not help but sense the young woman's intense interest, and she glanced quickly at her. Yes, her cheeks were flushed and her eyes bright, and it wasn't just from the warmth of the day or the dust of the trail. Sibyl Gordon was interested in *Señor* Tomas Flores. True, he was a disturbingly attractive man, if you cared to notice that sort of thing – but Elizabeth firmly directed her thoughts away from such frivolity.

She wanted to speak more with him, but not for the obvious reasons of his exotic good looks. She had been intrigued by Mrs Campbell's stories of his mother, and it had occurred to her that he might be able to help her in her search for the Devil's Trumpet, but she knew she must tread carefully.

The party dismounted and tied up their horses a short distance from the picnic spot as Jose brought buckets of water, drawn from the lake, for their mounts. Daisy went to see if any help was required to ready the picnic fare and the others found comfortable places to sit on the lush grass.

Tomas had retreated to a flat-topped boulder a short distance from the picnic, and Elizabeth watched as he expertly plucked the game birds and then retrieved a sharp-bladed knife from his pack. As he slit them down the middle the guts spilled out onto the rock, steaming and bloody, and Elizabeth turned away. She wasn't particularly squeamish, having grown up watching exactly this kind of activity, but she didn't care to see the livid blood on Tomas's smooth brown hands.

The third man was as fair as Tomas was dark, with almost white-blond hair. Elizabeth didn't have to wonder for long who he might be, for as Mrs Campbell bustled around making sure the picnic was organised to her satisfaction, she suddenly stopped and hurried towards the women. 'Oh, I do beg your pardon. Miss Elizabeth Bligh, Miss Sibyl Gordon, may I introduce you to Mr Damien Chegwidden. Arrived from England these few months past. Mr Chegwidden has an interest in plants, not unlike yourself, Elizabeth.'

As Elizabeth looked into a pair of coal-dark eyes, she did her best to keep her face immobile even as she swallowed a lump that rose in her throat. He appeared to be much removed from the monster she had conjured in her mind, being far younger than she had imagined and quite striking with his fair hair and lightly tanned skin. He was dressed most fashionably, with a scarlet ascot fastened by an amber pin and a suit of cream linen, but his eyes pierced her like two pieces of polished obsidian.

So, it was true – the man her father had so strongly warned her about *was* here. She found herself completely unprepared to meet him so soon, and she silently cursed Mrs Campbell for her loose words about their mutual interest.

Elizabeth's heart pounded painfully in her chest, but she masked her dismay with a laugh, pretending a gaiety that was far from her true feelings. 'Oh, really, I merely like to draw plants and flowers. Ephemera,' she said, 'that is all.'

Mr Chegwidden bowed low to the women. 'A pleasure to make your acquaintance, ladies,' he said. 'I sketch a little myself, as it happens.'

He seemed completely innocuous, a gentleman even, but Elizabeth knew better. Her father had warned her of the underhand methods he employed to get what he wanted. Her heart continued to pound and her hands grew clammy: if everything Papa had told her was correct then she would be in mortal danger were he to guess her true identity. Could Mrs Campbell be trusted to keep her promise?

With shaking hands, Elizabeth retrieved her sketchbook and watercolours from the saddlebag she had brought with her. She remembered seeing a particularly unusual shrub as they dismounted and decided that this might be an opportune time not only to record it but to remove herself from the presence of Damien Chegwidden and marshal her thoughts. Her father had told her that she might make his acquaintance at some point, but to be caught unawares was most unnerving. Balancing on a rock close to the plant, she set up her easel and picked up her brush. The hum of conversation from the others soon faded into the background as she became absorbed in her painting. Her fingers ceased their trembling as she began to paint, even though her mind was still swirling.

'You are very good, no?'

His voice was as warm and silky as honey, in her ear. He had crept up on her so silently that she had been caught completely unawares. The hair on the back of her neck stood on end and she shivered involuntarily at his nearness.

'Mrs Campbell told me that you are an illustrator, of plants.'

She nodded. 'Perhaps you can tell me what this one is,' she indicated the shrub that had been the subject of her work.

'Ah, yes, now that is quillaja.' Tomas reached to the plant and broke off a small section of the bark. 'It is our soap – for washing, you know?'

Elizabeth looked at him, disbelieving. She couldn't see how some dried-up piece of bark would clean anything, but clearly he had far greater knowledge than she did.

A light sparkled in his bright blue eyes. 'I can see you do not have faith in me!' he laughed. He strode away, and Elizabeth just had time to feel briefly bereft at his absence before he returned with a leather pail filled with water from the lake. Tomas broke off some more of the bark and plunged his hands into the water. He brought them up and rubbed them together, the bark caught between his palms. Sure enough, before long, small suds began to bubble up between his fingers.

'You would like to try?' he asked.

Elizabeth shook her head. 'My hands are perfectly clean and I do not wish to dampen my sketchbook, but thank you for the demonstration,' she said primly, hoping the smile on her face took the sting out of her words. 'But can you tell me how to spell qui . . . ? What did you say it was called?'

'Quillaja,' he repeated, before spelling it out to her letter by letter.

'You seem to know a good deal about the flora of this region?'

He inclined his head. 'A little,' he said modestly. 'We are fortunate to have a number of plants of great interest to collectors such as Mr Chegwidden, though I confess I admire them for their beauty –' he paused to pluck a deep-blue flower from a clump at arm's length from where they sat – 'as much as their rarity.' He presented her with it. 'A blue crocus.'

Elizabeth inclined her head, accepting the bloom and raising it to her face. He reminded her of her father in his enthusiasm for growing things, and she felt a bittersweet pang at the memory. 'It is indeed astonishingly beautiful,' she admitted. 'I have found that it is not until you properly look at things with the care of a botanist, or an artist, that you really see their true nature.'

'Indeed,' said Tomas, keeping his gaze on her.

Elizabeth felt as if she were a specimen under a microscope, so closely did he examine her. As she raised her eyes to meet his, time seemed to stand still. She was wondering how best to frame a question about his mother when they were disturbed.

'What can be so fascinating to both of you?' Sibyl enquired as she approached. 'Pray, do include me,' she said coquettishly, her eyes on Tomas.

He favoured her with his warm, ready smile. 'Of course, Miss Gordon. Miss Bligh did not believe me that you can use a plant to get clean, see?' He showed her his hands, which had been previously bloodstained from gutting the partridges and were now pink-palmed and pristine.

'Oh yes, quillaja,' trilled Sibyl. 'Our maid showed me this. But of course you are so new here, Elizabeth, and there is much to learn,' she said.

'Indeed, and I am very much looking forward to you both teaching me,' Elizabeth replied sweetly and was rewarded with a look of surprise on Sibyl's face.

Elizabeth hoped that Tomas would be able to provide a clue to her quest for the Devil's Trumpet, but she would have to work up to the question, to gain his trust, to get to know him. That would take time, but if this conversation was an indication, the prospect would not be too great a chore. She did not wish to rush the matter, and she could not allow Mr Chegwidden, or indeed anyone, to suspect her true intent in Valparaiso. It also occurred to her that she could safely assume that Mr Chegwidden had not yet discovered the Devil's Trumpet, for if he had he would surely have left with it on the first available sailing. That knowledge boosted her resolve and gave her hope that she had time on her side.

'I must go and see to the partridges, if we are to have luncheon soon,' said Tomas, interrupting her thoughts. 'Excuse me, ladies.'

Sibyl glanced at Elizabeth's sketchbook. 'Oh, you are so lucky to have such a talent. I swear I feel quite unaccomplished when I look at this.' There was grudging admiration in her voice.

Mr Chegwidden joined them and Elizabeth did her best to keep her expression pleasant. 'I concur with Miss Gordon,' he said. 'You are indeed most accomplished, Miss Bligh. I should be fascinated to know where you developed such skill. Who instructed you?'

Stick to the truth, but only insofar as it does not incriminate you, her father had advised. 'It was my governess who first encouraged me. But I have had little formal training, save for the study of *Curtis's Botanical Magazine*.' She refrained from adding that it was her father who had introduced her to the publication.

'Ah, yes,' he said. 'I know it well, a fine publication indeed.'

'Oh,' sighed Sibyl again. 'How I would love to be able to draw.'

'Now then, modesty doesn't become you, Sibyl,' said Mrs Gordon who caught the end of the conversation as she joined them. 'We can't all be good at everything, and we have only to hear your singing voice to know what a God-given blessing that is.'

Sibyl coloured at her mother's boastfulness. 'Oh mother, please!'

Elizabeth put down her sketchbook. Her hopes of being left in peace were not to be fulfilled, and in any case, she reasoned, it would be poor manners to ignore the rest of the party for too long. 'Shall we join the others?' she asked, looking in the direction of Mrs Campbell and Mr Gordon, who had settled near a boulder as Daisy unpacked the provisions they had brought with them. 'I am nearly finished here in any case.'

While they ate, Sibyl and her mother gossiped with Mrs Campbell about an American family who had settled in Valparaiso earlier the previous year. Elizabeth paid little attention to the chatter, not knowing the family in question.

As she sucked on a grilled partridge leg, which was surprisingly succulent and a hundred times better than anything she'd had aboard ship, Elizabeth turned her thoughts to the matter of exactly how she would discover the whereabouts of the mysterious Devil's Trumpet.

Would Tomas be the right person to confide in? Or was he close to Mr Chegwidden? She had yet to determine the exact nature of their relationship. Elizabeth sat and mused on her dilemma, her fingers curled in the lush green grass, as if to anchor herself to the ground. She looked up and caught Tomas's eye. He was gazing at her as if she were a fascinating artefact, one worthy of intense study, and his regard brought warmth to her cheeks. She glanced around at the rest of the party, but they were all, including Mr Chegwidden, caught up in the continuing saga being related by Mrs Campbell. Elizabeth stood, stretching out her legs, which had become stiff from sitting on the ground. 'It is rather hot,' she said quietly to Daisy. 'I think I will go down to the lake awhile.'

Tomas leapt to his feet. 'I shall escort you, Miss Elizabeth. I should hate for you to lose your way.' He said this with a knowing grin and Elizabeth bit back the ready retort that she could hardly lose her way on a walk to the lake that was at most three hundred yards away.

'Why, thank you *Señor* Flores, that would be most gracious of you,' she replied, taking the crook of his elbow as he came to stand beside her. She held her breath, hoping that none of the others would decide to join them, but they all seemed content to stay where they were, so she collected her skirts with her other hand and they stepped out in the direction of the water.

As they came to a halt, she had decided to plunge right in. 'Forgive me for any impertinence, but Mrs Campbell spoke to me of your upbringing,' she said.

'Oh yes? What of it?' he looked confused.

'Oh, I don't mean any disrespect. Rather, that it must have been a fascinating life. I understand your mother was a highly regarded healer.'

His expression cleared. 'Yes, yes she was. Many people came to her for remedies and her skills. She was an extremely learned woman. Not in the conventional way perhaps, but there was little she did not know about the power of plants. Plants that grow all around us, those that most pay no heed to. She knew exactly how to prepare them, to blend them, and how to cure ills that other doctors had no answer for. She also knew where to find the rarest and most sacred of them all.'

'And she obviously passed on this knowledge to you,' said Elizabeth.

'Well, some of it, yes, but only the simplest. I was still quite young when she died. In any case, she believed that only women should be party to the most sacred knowledge. Rather different from the ways of your country, so I am told.'

'I see,' said Elizabeth, doing her best to hide her disappointment. Perhaps he wouldn't be the best person to ask about the Devil's Trumpet after all. She regarded the lakeshore, which was clogged with reeds, but noticed a clearing a little further along where a small, pebbled shoal afforded easy access to the water and she could be sure of keeping her boots dry. 'Still, perhaps I might beg your indulgence to help me identify some of the plants native to Valparaiso? I do, of course, recognise the acacia, and the anemone, the geranium and the fuchsia, and we rode through laurel I am certain, but there are so many others that are completely foreign to me. I would welcome your assistance, and I can of course recompense you for your time.'

Tomas lit a small clay pipe and drew on it heavily. 'Let us not talk of money on such a beautiful day, *Señorita* Elizabeth.

I should be glad to be at your service.' He gave a mock bow. 'Not for nothing is it called the "Valley of Paradise",' he said, his low tone almost caressing her ears.

Elizabeth thrilled to the rich sound of his voice so close to her face, but heard a note of caution from her conscience. She hoped she had made a judicious call in enlisting his help, but she worried that he might be too close to Mr Chegwidden. She had much to find out and she must tread carefully.

Later that evening, as Daisy helped Elizabeth dress for dinner, Elizabeth noticed that her maid looked troubled. 'Daisy, are you quite all right?' she asked.

'Yes, miss,' the maid said, but her tone did not reassure Elizabeth. She turned to face Daisy and looked carefully at her face. 'What is it? Have you been crying?'

The maid gave a sniff but shook her head.

'Are you missing your family? I know we are such a long way from home . . . but I thought you had been enjoying the adventure so far.'

'No, miss, it's not that.'

'Well, come on then, do tell me. I am not happy to find you so upset.'

Daisy's voice shook. 'It was Mr Chegwidden . . .'

'What about him?' Elizabeth asked, her mouth set in a grim line.

'T'weren't much really. While you were walking by the

lake with *Señor* Flores, he came over to me and started to ask questions.'

'What kind of questions?' A shiver ran through her.

'Where I was from, how I came to find myself so far from home. He hails from Cornwall too, did you know?'

'As a matter of fact I did,' said Elizabeth. 'But that is a story for another time. What exactly did you tell him?'

'Only that I was from Trevone, and that I had been your maid for quite some years.'

'Anything else? You remember that we are here in a disguise of sorts.'

'No, nothing else, I promise you.'

'Good. And what did he do to upset you so?'

'Well, everyone else was far away by then. I think they had gone further along the lake from where you were. He . . . he tried to . . . Well, he tried to kiss me, and more. I did not invite it I swear!' Elizabeth could see that Daisy had flushed beet red with embarrassment. 'He tore my apron and a . . . a button from my dress. I didn't want to scream and make a fuss but I struggled against him as best I could.'

'Oh Daisy!' cried Elizabeth, roused to fury on her maid's behalf. 'What a foul, despicable man. How dare he! I've a good mind to tell Mrs Campbell straightaway.'

'Oh no, please don't,' said Daisy. 'I shall be mortified.'

'Did he do anything else?' Elizabeth asked.

'No, no, that was all. Miss Gordon came back before he could take advantage of me further.'

'Oh, thank goodness for that. Now listen to me, Daisy,' she said, holding her maid by the shoulders. 'I will make it my business to ensure that you are never left alone with that frightful man ever again, do you understand?'

'Yes, Miss Elizabeth.'

Chapter Twenty-two

Sydney, Autumn 2017

When she wasn't working, Anna had been busy transcribing Marguerite's diary, though her progress was still painfully slow. Marguerite had found lodgings in Surry Hills – 'They are tolerable,' she had written. 'Though the cold 'tis terrible and the wind does whistle through the doors and windows.' – with Alice, her friend from the quarantine station, and a job cleaning at a big house in Potts Point. 'There is a lady in our street who minds the child. She seems kind enough, but I do worry.' Lily, it seemed, had developed a terrible cough and Marguerite feared for her health. Marguerite also wrote often of a mysterious past, though she never mentioned from where she had come before arriving in Sydney. 'I must never go back. He must never find me,' she had written. Who had she run away from, Anna wondered. Her husband, perhaps?

'He's a good guy, you know. You should give him a chance.' Jane's voice interrupted her thoughts.

'Hm?' Anna looked up, startled.

'Honestly. You need to get back in the real world again, Anna. I know you've had it tough, but you can't hide away from life forever, you know. Noah's all right. Solid.'

They were standing in her grandmother's house, where Anna had spent the whole day cleaning up the builders' mess and scrubbing the place from top to bottom. After careful deliberation she had decided to have the façade painted a cool green, the colour of a new leaf. The mulberry paint had begun to flake in any case, and although it had been Gussie's taste, it wasn't really Anna's. Thanks to several days' effort on Anna's part, Gus's gorgeous garden had been restored to its former self, and now the house looked as good on the inside as it did on the outside. The builders had installed a kitchen, white cabinets and a pale granite benchtop, and the floorboards had been sanded back and stained a dark mahogany. The walls were now a bright white, and Anna had padded through the house in socks, sniffing the aroma of paint appreciatively. It smelled clean, and fresh. Comfortingly, Gussie's clock still ticked away on the mantel. Even though there was only the occasional piece of old furniture to soften it, the bigger living area looked welcoming. Ready for a new start.

A bit like you, a small voice in her head insisted.

As the house had taken shape and Anna began to wonder more seriously what to do with it, she'd had an idea. She wanted someone with a green thumb who would look after the garden, and she would far rather have someone she knew live there.

'Actually . . .' Anna began, a tiny smile playing about her face.

'You've said yes, haven't you?' cried Jane excitedly. 'Ooh, where are you going and when?'

'We might be going somewhere tonight,' said Anna coyly. 'But come on,' she said changing the subject, 'let's have a look outside.'

'Oh, how divine!' said Jane as Anna opened the back door. They walked along the path to the bench at the end of the garden. 'I've been looking for a new place. My flat is being sold, and everything I've seen is a soulless concrete box,' she said.

Anna nodded. 'I know. You mentioned it at lunch a few weeks ago. Have you had any luck?'

She shook her head. 'It's impossible. There's nothing. Well, nothing that I can afford, anyway. What I wouldn't give for somewhere with a bit of a garden. But they're as rare as hen's teeth in this part of town. Or if they do have any green space at all, they cost an absolute fortune. You don't know how lucky you are . . .' She stopped, aware that Anna hadn't, in fact, been particularly lucky in past years. 'Well, you know what I mean . . .'

Anna motioned her to sit down, taking a seat at the other end of the bench and turning to face her friend. 'Oh, I'm not moving in,' she said.

'Why not? This,' she said, spreading her arms wide, 'is gorgeous. Are you mad?'

'No. I'm perfectly happy in my little place in Queens Park.'

'So, you're going to let it out?' Jane said, interest plain on her face. 'Though I don't suppose I could afford it.'

'Would you like it?' offered Anna.

Jane looked at her. 'Anna! Are you serious?'

Anna nodded, a broad grin now on her face. 'I'd really like someone to look after it; someone who would care for the garden.'

Jane stood up and flung her arms exuberantly around Anna. 'Oh, I'd love it! It's the perfect little house, and the most gorgeous garden. Oh, thank you, Anna, thank you. But how much do you want a week?' she asked doubtfully. 'My budget isn't that big.'

'Mates' rates,' Anna reassured her. 'Whatever you're paying at the moment. I just want the place taken care of.'

'Oh, I'll cherish it. Truly I will. But are you sure about this? You could get much more if you let it through an agent.' Jane looked worried and excited at the same time.

'Of course I am. I've got the plumber coming to do a few final checks next week, but apart from that it's good to go.'

'Are you for real?'

'I think so,' laughed Anna, enjoying the feeling of being able to make someone else happy for a change.

Before she left, Jane extracted a promise from Anna to ring her and tell her how the date with Noah went. 'I'm so pleased we're in touch again,' she said. 'I missed you, you know.'

Because Anna had skipped her usual Saturday cycle class (the third week in a row – she didn't know whether to be annoyed or pleased with herself) to meet Jane at the house, she needed to get out and let off some steam. By offering the house to Jane she had put the first part of her plan into place, but the result of actually doing something to steer the course of her life for the first time in years had left her feeling off-balance.

Anna strolled through the winding streets of Paddington, down to New South Head Road and then across to the grassy park that fringed the water's edge at Rushcutters Bay. The calm blue harbour came into view, its glassy surface crowded with boats, their masts like needles piercing the clear autumn sky. As she kicked through drifts of fallen leaves, Anna heard the familiar hollow jangle of halyards coming from the marina overlaid by the yapping of several small dogs being walked by their heavily muscled owners. She'd brought a bag with her, and as she reached the water's edge, she found a bench to sit on and took out the notebook she'd found in the shed at the bottom of Granny Gus's garden. Anna wriggled on the bench to get comfortable and began to read, but the words swam before her as she recognised the familiar handwriting on the pages. Handwriting that she'd seen on numerous birthday cards, always with a ten-dollar note slipped inside, no matter what number she was turning. She blinked and turned the page. There were headings with the month and year, followed by cryptic notes: 'January. Stinking. Basil infested with thrips. New stakes.'

Anna sat and read, her surroundings fading as she became absorbed by her grandmother's jottings. It was almost as if Gussie was sitting next to her, bellyaching about a lack of rain and damned buggeration that she couldn't manage the weeding on her own any more. The book was a thread that connected them, and Anna would cherish it always.

The hard seat beneath her made sitting for too long uncomfortable, so she stood up, stretched and placed the notebook back in her bag. Without thinking about where she was headed she began to walk along the foreshore and up into the winding streets of Darling Point, through to Double Bay, with its coiffed old ladies and lycra-clad mothers drinking coffee in the afternoon sun, and then on to the wide stretch of Rose Bay, and up the steep part of New South Head Road – Heartbreak Hill as it was known to the runners who pounded up there in their tens of thousands every August on a run from the city to the surf of Bondi. Her footsteps took her to Nielsen Park. It had been one of Simon's favourite beaches and on summer days they had bunked off lectures to come and cool off in its balmy waters, gazing back at the far-off city.

It was where his ashes had been scattered, in a borrowed launch a few hundred metres off the shore. Anna had felt like a fraud being part of it, but she couldn't bear to hurt his parents by refusing to be there. Months later, she'd gone back with a small seedling, its roots wrapped in damp kitchen paper, tucked away in her bag.

She knew exactly where she had planted it, at the rear of the park, in a spot that got the morning sun, with dappled shade in the afternoon. She caught her breath as she came upon it now: *acacia spectabilis*, or Mudgee wattle as it was more commonly known. Although it was early for it to be flowering, its massed yellow blooms glowed golden, lighting up the sombre landscape.

Far from foundering as she had feared, the tiny seedling had thrived in the years since she'd planted it. She sniffed its dusty perfume, noting the flower's colour: it was what she imagined bittersweet would look like, if indeed an emotion could have a colour. Simon would surely have appreciated its beauty, she thought wistfully.

Eventually she turned back, retracing her steps, and her thoughts slowly shifted from Simon to Marguerite. She imagined a line of women, stretching back in time, beginning with the mysterious Marguerite arriving from who knew where on a pitching ship on the wild southern ocean, through to Anna's grandmother and finishing with Anna. Was it possible that this diary too might be a connection to her past, that it was a voice that also had a message for her, albeit at a far greater distance than that of her grandmother's garden notebook? In that moment, she was decided. There was only one way to find out.

Chapter Twenty-three

Valparaiso, 1887

One morning a week later, as Elizabeth was finishing her breakfast at a small table in the courtyard, Tomas called on her.

Before departing from their picnic, and while they found themselves alone at the riverbank, he had suggested this day to begin their plant identification. Elizabeth had spent the intervening time in a state of growing anticipation. Even Daisy had noticed her distracted demeanour, giving her a curious look as she went about her duties, helping her to dress and brushing out her long, fair hair before winding and pinning it at the nape of her neck. Elizabeth had struggled to stay still under Daisy's ministrations that morning, fidgety with the knowledge that she was to see Tomas within the hour. He had haunted her thoughts since the excursion, and she had found herself remembering the way he had held her gaze, the deepness of his blue eyes and the gentle way he spoke to her.

'Ah, Miss Bligh!' he called out. 'No, do not rise. Please, finish your breakfast. Mercedes is bringing some coffee, and so I would join you, if you permit?'

She found herself to be uncharacteristically tongue-tied, and was forced to remark on the weather, which had, according to Mrs Campbell, been unseasonably warm.

'It will mean that we may find more plants in flower than is usual at this time of year,' Tomas said. He too, seemed rather quieter than at their last meeting.

'Why yes, of course,' she replied. 'That had not occurred to me. Where is it that you suggest we go? The same direction as last week's picnic?'

'No, I think we should head east, towards the sierra, by the Santiago road. There is a valley not far from there, the Caxon de Las Palmas, the "Valley of the Palms", that I think you would very much like to see.'

They rode for several hours, chaperoned by Daisy, though she rode a discreet distance from them, allowing them to speak privately. Society's rules might be more relaxed on this side of the globe, but Elizabeth had her reputation to consider and would never have dreamed of taking off into the wilderness with a strange gentleman, no matter how charming his manners.

They followed a stream through the thick grassland, before arriving at a narrow mountain pass that was completely shaded from the sun. As the horses picked their way along, Elizabeth shivered at the delicious, crisp coolness of the air and marvelled to see that the shrubs along the way were still wet with dew.

Elizabeth looked up above them, to the mountain peaks gleaming with snow that clung to their steep, rocky sides. There, in the Andean mountains or in the valleys below, her father had said, was her best chance of discovering the Devil's Trumpet. But how was she to undertake a journey to such a forbidding place? 'It is an elusive plant,' Papa had whispered on his deathbed. 'Some mistake it for the more common Angel's Trumpet. They do so at their peril.' She shivered, remembering his words.

'Everything all right?' said Tomas, watching her closely. 'Would you like to rest?'

'No, no I am fine, just remembering something,' she replied.

Tomas continued to look quizzically at her.

'My father. I was thinking about what he said to me before he . . . before he died.'

'I am sorry. Mrs Campbell mentioned that you had suffered the loss of both your parents. I think you are extremely brave to undertake such a journey on your own. Was your father also a lover of plants?'

Elizabeth shook her head. 'No,' she lied. 'He was concerned with less ephemeral matters. I do miss him terribly, but then he was often away, so I suppose I am used to that. And as for being brave; I wonder sometimes if I am more foolish than brave.'

They rode on, passing through a gully between two steep hillsides and into a valley of exceptional beauty. Bees flitted between the flowers of myriad colours that bloomed amid the thick grass on the valley floor. Tall, spiky-leaved palm trees lined the edges of the valley, which was at least half a mile across by Elizabeth's reckoning. The only sounds were the thud of the horses' hooves on the narrow trail, the occasional swish of their tails as they swiped at a fly, the rustle of the wind in the trees and the drone of the bees. Though they had passed peons working in the fields as they began their journey, here there was not another soul to be seen.

After a while Tomas pulled up his horse and dismounted, his silver spurs gleaming in the sun that now reached the valley floor. 'The Caxon de Las Palmas. As promised, *señorita*,' he said with a flourish. 'We should stop awhile, let the horses rest.'

'What a beautiful place you have brought us to, *señor*,' Elizabeth said.

The valley lay before them, lush with thick green grass, and bisected by a lazily meandering stream. 'Why, it is as I would imagine the Garden of Eden!' she exclaimed.

'I am glad you think so,' he said. 'It is one of my favourite places. I am happy to share it with you.'

'Have you shared this with Mr Chegwidden also?' Elizabeth could not help herself asking.

'Why would you mention his name?' Tomas asked.

'Oh, I had heard he was keen to explore the area,' she said airily.

'It is true, he has engaged me in the past to guide him on his explorations.'

Elizabeth's heart sank.

'But not here, no,' he added.

'So, you are friends?' she enquired.

'We were introduced by Mrs Gordon, and have spent several days together, but he has not been in Valparaiso long enough for me to call him my friend, though he seems a pleasant enough gentleman.'

'I see,' replied Elizabeth.

'Like you, he is a lover of plants. But he tells me that he intends to collect a number of species and take them back to England. There is quite a demand; more and more plant-hunters arrive on every ship it seems.'

'Indeed, I have heard of this practice,' she said. 'And your countrymen do not mind this?'

'Look around,' he laughed, spreading his arms wide. 'A few cuttings will not make any difference.'

'I suppose not.' She smiled. 'Well, I am anxious to paint,' she said, dismounting and handing her reins to him.

'But of course,' he replied. 'There is much here for you to discover.'

She made her way towards the palms, leaving Daisy to rest not far from the horses. The trees towered over her, their brown trunks ridged in a circular pattern, atop which grew a spray of dark-green spiky leaves. Bunches of large, round, green pods hung below the fronds of leaves. 'Now this certainly does not look like Cornwall,' she murmured to herself.

She sat in a patch of sunlight, arranging her skirts around her until she was comfortable, and opened her sketchbook. Once again she lost herself in her work, barely noticing the sweat that had begun to trickle between her shoulder blades and make a sticky path down her back. She had brought with her several light cotton day dresses, but even the fine weave of the fabric felt like an overcoat now she was no longer cooled by the breeze.

'We take the older palm trees and burn them. The juice that comes out is a delicacy among the native *chilenos*,' said Tomas, who had joined her, offering a flask of water. 'Sweeter than any honey.'

Elizabeth drank thirstily, grateful for his thoughtfulness.

'Are there any other plants here that I should learn of? Any with any special qualities?' she asked.

'Oh, but there are many. There is *culen*.' He pointed to a yellow-flowered plant not unlike a buttercup, which grew nearby. 'My mother used the fresh leaves mashed into a poultice with lard to heal wounds, or dried and brewed them in a tea to calm a fever. The stalks give off a gum that can be used by our shoemakers . . . If you know where to look, there is medicine and more all around,' he said, indicating the valley.

'I see,' said Elizabeth. 'And what of plants that harm?'

'Oh, there are plenty of those too,' he replied. 'Of course there are some that look like healing plants but would fool the uninitiated, and those that if prepared incorrectly are deadly poisonous.'

Elizabeth shuddered theatrically. 'Oh, do tell me more of those,' she entreated, pretending naivety. 'I should hate to make a mistake.'

'Never fear. I have appointed myself your personal guardian when it comes to plant identification.'

Elizabeth laughed. 'And what did I do to deserve such attention?'

'*Señorita* Bligh, your beauty is my reward,' he said as he reached out and lightly touched her golden hair with his fingertips.

Elizabeth blushed and looked away. She was not used to the advances of a man and was suddenly lost for words.

'You flatter me, *Señor* Flores. There is surely no shortage of beauty in Valparaiso. I have seen it for my own eyes. Miss Gordon, for example.'

'Yes, but none so intriguing as you,' he said. 'I'd wager there is more to you than meets the eye. I sense you are holding much back. And that, of course, makes you quite fascinating.' His tone was playful but his eyes were serious.

'Well, fascinating or not, the only thing I am holding back right now is a fearsome hunger. Shall we?' she asked, holding out her hand to be helped to her feet.

Tomas laughed, throwing his head back and showing his white teeth. 'But of course, *señorita*. I would not wish to come between you and your repast!'

~

After lunch Elizabeth returned to her art as Daisy cleared away their leftovers. Tomas, completely unselfconscious, stretched out under a palm tree, tipped his hat over his head and proceeded to sleep. Elizabeth looked enviously at him. She was tired from their ride and would have liked to have copied him, but she wanted to finish her palm study and then spend some time exploring.

~

'Atención!'

The voice was far away but Elizabeth recognised it immediately.

'Over here!' she called back. She paused from her study of a tiny plant with white star-shaped, five-pointed flowers to wave at Tomas. She had nearly finished; a few more brush strokes were needed and she would have recorded it, but he was beckoning to her.

'You should not have wandered so far away,' he said, reaching her at last, an edge of annoyance in his voice.

'Now, really,' Elizabeth rebuffed him. 'I was in plain sight. Perhaps you might tell me of this plant?' She indicated the subject of her sketching.

'Oh that, that is a kind of potato. The tubers are quite delicious.'

Laughter bubbled up inside of her. 'I see I shall certainly never starve with you on hand!'

'Of that you may be certain,' he said, smiling at her, his annoyance evaporated.

'And these?' She pointed to a bush with intensely purple bell-shaped flowers that were nodding their heads in the breeze.

'Ah-ha, that is the *Palo de Bruja*. It cures many aches and pains, but it can also make you mad. It was one of my mother's favourite plants.' He paused and plucked some of the flowers and leaves, carefully avoiding the thorns that studded its stems. 'It is rare to see this,' he said, by way of explanation. 'My sister will be glad of it. Now come,' he said brusque once more. 'I am afraid we must depart. I should not want us to get caught out in the darkness.'

As he said the words, Elizabeth couldn't help but remember the occasion of their first meeting. Really, she did not know what to make of *Señor* Tomas Flores. One minute he was utterly charming and delightful and she could imagine herself as a special friend of his, the next he was abrupt almost to the point of rudeness, treating her like a naive schoolgirl.

~

It was as they were loading up the saddlebags that she noticed it. Actually, she didn't see it at first; what caught her eye was the brilliant aquamarine flash of a hummingbird's wing as it glinted in the sunlight. She moved towards it, captivated by its iridescent beauty, and stumbled in her haste, the toe of her boot catching a raised root in the grass.

And there it was.

Low to the ground, with rounded forest-green leaves that appeared thick and juicy. The plant bore pendulous white flowers that were closed up tight like a pelican's beak. Tell-tale black–purple stripes marked the outside of the creamy petals. Had those not been there, she could have been sure that it was the more common, and perfectly harmless, Angel's Trumpet.

Her heart stopped and then began to beat almost out of her chest, and her mind raced to keep up. Could it be? Really? Could she simply have stumbled over it? Was it going to be that easy? It looked exactly as her father had described. He had told her that it was most likely to be found in the mountains, but she was almost certain this was it. She had no time to gather a specimen, nor anywhere to conceal it. And in any case, her father had warned her to exercise the utmost care in handling it, lest she get any of the highly toxic pollen or sap on her skin.

Not wanting to draw the attention of Tomas or Daisy, she righted herself and returned to them. They had both been on the other side of the horses, occupied in readying them and so had not seen her stumble, nor the excitement that must have surely shown on her face at her discovery.

Frustrated, Elizabeth knew her only hope of collecting the samples she required was to return to the valley at another time. Was that really possible? She looked carefully about her, memorising the landscape, noticing two sentinel palm trees, much taller than the others, to the west of their position. To the south was a large boulder that looked like the hooked beak of an eagle. She moved a few steps away and opened her book, quickly sketching the view of the valley with these two landmarks. This rough map would be her best hope of finding the plant again.

'Still drawing?' asked Tomas, his voice breaking her concentration. 'Elizabeth, I am afraid that we must be off.' He sounded stern once again.

'It is so beautiful a place that I had to make a quick likeness of it, to remember it by,' she said, her words tumbling over themselves.

'You know, we can return any time you desire,' Tomas promised her.

Yes, she smiled at him, she would return, and next time she would be prepared to retrieve the Devil's Trumpet.

Chapter Twenty-four

Sydney, Autumn 2017

Anna scuffed through the thick carpet of leaves on the lawn as she approached the restaurant, enjoying the sound they made as they crunched and crackled under the soles of her boots, resisting the childish temptation to kick them high in the air.

Darkness had fallen as she walked the short distance from her flat in Queens Park, and by the time she arrived the air was chilly. She'd let her hair down from its usual messy topknot and even applied the tiniest amount of make-up for the occasion, though her cheeks were pink from the cold, and her skin, which tanned easily, was tawny from days spent working outdoors. She'd dug out a pair of slim trousers and a silk shirt from the depths of her wardrobe and slipped on tall, flat leather boots and a dark navy overcoat. It made a change from jeans and a muddy sweatshirt and she felt different from her workaday self.

Opening the door of the restaurant, she was assailed by a hum of conversation and the tantalising aroma of dinner being prepared. She took a deep breath as the scent of rosemary and garlic wafted towards her. The effect, amplified by the heaters that were blasting warm air onto the glass-paned room, was one of enveloping welcome.

Noah was waiting for her, at a table at the front of the glass-house that looked out onto the garden, and he stood up as she arrived, kissing her cheek. 'Hello Anna,' he said. 'You look lovely.'

She smiled at him, suddenly shy, very aware that this was the first date she had been on in more than five years. How was one supposed to behave? She had no clue. 'Thanks, Noah. Not so shabby yourself,' she replied, faking an ease she didn't feel as she noticed his crisply ironed shirt and irrepressibly curly hair.

No sooner had Anna taken the seat opposite him than the waiter kept them busy, unfurling napkins and proffering a menu, pouring water. 'Jane tells me you have your own garden business,' Noah began.

'It's pretty low-key. Mainly maintenance, weeding and mowing, that sort of thing. Occasionally I get let loose on a bit of garden design. That's the fun part.'

Noah nodded seriously. 'It must be so nice to be outdoors all day, though not perhaps so much in winter,' he raised his glass to the night outside the windows.

'It is,' said Anna, casting around for something more to add. God, she really had no idea how to make the kind of small talk she supposed was called for on such an occasion. As she was grasping for a subject suitable for conversation, the waiter came to take their order.

'So,' she began once they were alone again, inspiration having struck, 'how did you come to be so interested in botanical illustration?'

That was it; Noah was off, describing the history of botanical drawing. 'Did you know that the earliest surviving illustrated botanical work dates from AD512? The Codex Vindobonensis,' he said. He continued with a rundown of major botanical treatises up to the present day, and then told her of his own introduction to the subject. 'There's been a resurgence of interest in botanical art actually. I think it's because of our increasing awareness of the role of plants in keeping our ecosystems healthy.'

Anna nodded in agreement.

'Botanical illustration, because it is so painstakingly accurate, is a way of recording today's plant life and preserving it for the future. Illustrators are working with scientists and conservationists. There's even a degree course in it now,' he finished.

Anna had listened with interest until their entrees arrived.

'Looks good, huh?' said Noah with a smile. 'I love this place.'

'Do you bring all your dates here?' Anna risked a cheeky question.

'Only the pretty ones.'

'Oh, well of course!' she smiled back at him as she picked up her fork and speared her gnocchi.

They ate and drank and talked their way through the meal, Noah even making Anna laugh once or twice. When they were finished and he had settled the bill, they retrieved their coats and headed out into the cold night. 'I didn't drive, I'm afraid,' said Noah. 'Can I see you home in a taxi?'

Anna shook her head. 'I think I'd prefer to walk – I'm not so far away.'

'Then I'll accompany you home,' he said gallantly, offering her his arm before she had a chance to put him off.

They strolled up Queen Street, peering in the windows of antique shops. 'I'm thinking of taking the sketchbook to your friend, Dr Hammett-Jones, in Kew,' she blurted out.

'Oh wow. So, you *are* going to England? I know most people would wonder why you'd go all that way for a sketchbook full of pretty flowers, but for what it's worth, I think it's a great idea.'

'Well, I'm not just going for that,' she said. 'I'd like to see some of the great gardens while I'm there, maybe even get the Eurostar over to France . . . Giverny . . .' she said.

'Oh, now I'm really jealous,' he said. 'I went years ago and have never forgotten it. You'll love it.'

'Yes, well I was supposed to go a long time ago, but . . .' she shrugged. 'It didn't happen. I've got a passport that's never been used; in fact, I think it's only got a year left on it, so I really should go before it runs out and I have to go through all the palaver of getting another one,' she added.

He gently took her hand in his as he looked at her. 'Jane told me . . .' he said. 'About Simon.'

'Oh.' Anna didn't know whether to feel annoyed with her friend or thankful for having been spared the need to explain it. 'Well. It was a long time ago.'

'Yes, but you don't get over something like that in a hurry.'

'No, I don't suppose you do.'

They had reached her apartment and she halted outside the entrance. 'This is me, just here.' She pointed up to the lit window on the second floor. 'Thanks for dinner. I had fun.' They weren't empty words. For the first time in a long time, she had spent an evening in the company of an attractive – very attractive, actually – man who was interesting and made her laugh. He might even have restored a tiny bit of her faith in the world.

'Any time, Anna. Really, any time.' Noah leant towards her. At the last minute she turned her head to the side and his lips brushed her cheek. 'Just so you know, I had a good time too,' he said quietly.

'Thanks again, Noah,' she said, giving him a quick hug and slipping into the foyer of her building. She wasn't sure if she was ready to answer the question she'd glimpsed in his eyes.

Chapter Twenty-five

Valparaiso, 1887

Elizabeth had no opportunity to slip away unnoticed for several weeks after her excursion with Tomas. Mrs Gordon and Sibyl made it their business to introduce her to what passed for society in Valparaiso, and so she found herself a guest at an endless parade of luncheons and dinners held in her honour. The food was better than she could have imagined and certainly made up for the privations of being at sea. There was plenty of meat, often cooked over coals – *asado* – and an array of vegetables, including tender young corn and tomatoes. Fish, too, was plentiful, though not always of a kind Elizabeth recognised. She became particularly fond of *sopaipillas*, fried flatbreads made from pumpkin and flour, as well as the *empanadas* that Mrs Campbell's cook made almost daily.

She encountered Mr Chegwidden at one luncheon, and was alarmed to find herself seated next to him. By the time she noticed, it was too late to ask her hostess to reseat her. In any case, she didn't want to draw attention to herself, so she deliberately played the part of an ingénue, but didn't have to pretend to be impressed by his stories of his travels to India and Ceylon, Singapore and China. She explained that her parents were long dead, and that, with benefit of a small inheritance, she was anxious to advance her botanical studies.

Mr Chegwidden, for his part, seemed to enjoy the role of patron, and despite knowing of his perfidy in regard to both Daisy and her father, Elizabeth was surprised to find him engaging company. He had the dangerous charm of someone who knew himself to be of great appeal to the fairer sex and was most amusing, disarming her with his outlandish observations of the rest of the party.

'You see Captain Chapman over there?' he said, whispering in her ear so that only she could hear.

'What of him?' Elizabeth had been introduced to the British naval captain as she arrived at the luncheon, and had been intimidated by his stern countenance.

'They say that he keeps a monkey in his cabin. As a pet! And what's more, he croons to it as if it were a baby. Feeds it the choicest sweetmeats from his table and even allows it to sip from his flagon of rum.'

'No!' Elizabeth was shocked and didn't know whether to believe him. Fabricated or not, it made for an amusing anecdote.

Despite his intriguing stories, Elizabeth reminded herself sternly of her father's warning and Mr Chegwidden's reprehensible treatment of Daisy. She would not be fooled by this wolf in sheep's clothing.

'I shall have to introduce you to the gentlemen of Kew upon our eventual return to England,' he insisted as the meal drew to a close. 'They will be most interested in your work.'

'Oh, I doubt that, sir, but you are most kind to think of it. I am content to make my little drawings and watercolours,' she said modestly before turning the subject back to him and risking a question. 'So, tell me, pray, have you found any plants of interest since your arrival?'

He gave a brief nod. 'I might have, Miss Bligh,' he teased. 'But I am certain that the mountains have greater glories to offer up.'

She knew, without having to ask, what he referred to.

The days Elizabeth thought she might have the chance to escape, the weather turned inclement and she was confined to her lodgings, where she passed the time cataloguing the sketches and paintings she had made thus far, and beginning on a series of watercolours of the plants that surrounded the Campbells' villa.

One morning, when the rain finally appeared to have ceased, Mrs Campbell invited Elizabeth to the markets. 'You might find it of interest – it is quite astonishing the produce that is grown hereabout,' she said as they took their breakfast in the courtyard.

'Cook usually purchases our provisions,' said Mrs Campbell. 'But I like to go when I can and see what's in season. And check that she isn't cheating me,' she added with a good-natured laugh.

The town square, in which the market was held, was thick with activity when they arrived an hour or so later. Stalls piled high with bright green apples, oranges, limes, pumpkins and melons vied for their attention with those selling cabbages, beans, cauliflower and a kind of thin asparagus. All gleamed with freshness and were beautifully displayed in plaited leather baskets. The two women moved happily among the native *chilenos*, the men wearing breeches and waistcoats over linen shirts, coloured kerchiefs and straw hats atop their heads, the women with brightly coloured shawls and long dark skirts; all bargained with the sellers, exchanging a few copper coins or tattered paper notes once a price had been struck.

Elizabeth gazed in wonder and delight at the scene, almost losing Mrs Campbell as she lingered at a stall selling all manner of green leafy vegetables, the likes of which she had never before seen and wished she had the means to sketch.

After more than an hour, and having watched Mrs Campbell make her purchases, they were readying to leave when Elizabeth spotted him. Her breath caught as she recognised Tomas's tall figure in the distance. She had not spoken to him since their outing several weeks before and she was taken aback once again by his handsomeness. How could she have forgotten the broad shoulders, eyes the blue of the water on a summer's afternoon at Lady Luck Cove? She had an inexplicable longing to run her fingers through his hair, dark and shining in the sunlight, to test its softness, its strength. She sensed the vital energy that surrounded him, separating him from other men around him, most of whom he stood head and shoulders above. She went to call out, but the words died in her throat when she saw the beautiful dark-skinned young woman beside him; her hair hung down her back in two thick plaits and there were spots of colour on her high cheekbones. Elizabeth watched as he leant down to whisper in her ear, his arm protectively around the woman's shoulders. It was an intimate gesture, of that she had no doubt. The woman was wearing the traditional dress, as so many of the patrons of the market were, but she seemed to lend a special elegance to the shirred white blouse and cerise shawl wrapped about her slim figure. Elizabeth found she could not look away from either of them.

As they moved off, not noticing Elizabeth, she felt suddenly downcast and foolish for not having known that Tomas had a sweetheart – perhaps even a wife, though he had made no mention of either. Unaccountably irritated that Mrs Campbell had not brought it up, Elizabeth took a deep breath and sternly reminded herself that it really was of no consequence. She had not come all this way on a wretched ship and endured weeks of seasickness to fall for the first handsome man she stumbled across. She had been charged with a task, one that was far more important and far-reaching than mere matters of the heart. If she could find the plant she sought and return to England with it, to deliver it safely to the men of science at Kew, then not only would she have fulfilled her father's promise, but she would also have made a difference to the lives of many. The scientists would be able to propagate it, study it and make it available to those who needed it. That, surely, was a noble endeavour and one from which she would not waver. It was far more important than the favour of a young man, no matter how handsome and agreeable.

'Look at these,' said Mrs Campbell, who had bustled towards her brandishing several jute bags filled to the brim with leafy vegetables and bright oranges. 'Cook shall make us a feast tonight!'

Elizabeth nodded, trying to share her enthusiasm, but she could not get the image of Tomas and the beautiful young *chilena* out of her mind.

If Mrs Campbell noticed that she was quiet on their journey back to the house, she did not remark upon it. As soon as they had returned, Elizabeth went in search of Daisy, seeking to refresh herself after the dusty trek and then continue with her sketching. She was growing frustrated at the lack of opportunity to retrace her steps to the Valley of the Palms, and at the knowledge that Damien Chegwidden might get there before her. But, she argued with herself, could she really have stumbled over the Devil's Trumpet within mere weeks of her arrival? When she had consulted the sketches given to her by her father and compared them to her memory, she found many similarities – the size and shape of the leaves were identical, but in Papa's drawing the flowers were open, not closed tight like a purse, so it was impossible to be certain.

'Miss Elizabeth,' said Daisy, interrupting her ponderings. 'There was a message delivered for you. The Campbells' manservant brought it up earlier.'

'Thank you, Daisy. Where is it?'

'He left it in the morning room. Shall I bring you some matté? You look rather tired. Were the markets enjoyable?'

'Quite fascinating, actually. It is surprising the variety and freshness of the vegetables. They put our Cornish potatoes and carrots quite to shame! I'm perfectly fine, but yes, thank you Daisy, some matté would be nice.' She had grown used to the bitter green drink; indeed, she had become rather fond of it.

Daisy returned with the drink and handed her the message, which turned out to be a letter. From Tomas.

She turned it over in her hands, noticing the red seal that depicted a tree, its branches spreading out towards the edge of the wax.

'*Señorita* Elizabeth . . .' the flowing script began. 'I should be honoured if you would be a guest at a fiesta to be held a week on Saturday.'

Elizabeth read on. Both she and Daisy were invited to a party at Tomas's family's home, the *Estancia Copihue*, nearly a day's ride from Valparaiso. According to the letter, the festivities would carry on until late into the night and they were invited to lodge there.

Elizabeth didn't know what to think. On the one hand she wanted to stay as far away from Tomas's disturbing presence as possible, especially now that she had discovered he was most likely promised, if not married, to another; but on the other hand, it would be poor manners to refuse without a reasonable excuse for doing so – and one did not immediately spring to mind. She couldn't help but wonder why Tomas was taking such an interest in her, why he had bothered to take her to the Valley of the Palms and had now invited her to meet his family. Was it simply that she was a new arrival to the city and he felt obliged to take her under his wing?

Elizabeth traced the inked letters with her finger, pondering her decision.

Chapter Twenty-six

Sydney, Winter 2017

Anna gripped the armrests of her seat as the plane took off, her knuckles white against the dark leather. She looked down at the backpack that she had stowed underneath the seat in front of her. It contained the sketchbook, the diary and the photograph; she hadn't trusted any of them to her checked suitcase. She had never travelled in such a big plane or for such a long way, and so she wasn't sure if the queasiness was from nerves or the lift of the plane as it left the ground. Either way, she was astonished at how quickly everything had come about, and that she now found herself on her way to the other side of the world.

'Well, that's a bold decision, sis,' had been Vanessa's response. 'But why not? Make it a bit of a holiday, see some sights.'

'Oh yes,' her mum encouraged. 'I think it's an excellent idea.'

They had both looked at her like they'd swallowed something delicious and wanted her to try it too.

'Now,' said Eleanor. 'I've got some news of my own, as it happens. I thought I'd do a bit of digging. Try to find out something of our family tree, see if I couldn't connect the dots. I've been online. There's a family-history site, and—'

'Oh,' interrupted Anna. 'I was going to do that. Noah mentioned it.'

Vanessa gave her sister a questioning look, which Anna determinedly ignored.

'Well, I'm one step ahead of you,' her mother countered, pulling a folded sheet of paper from her handbag. Eleanor had drawn up a chart showing her side of the family's previous generations, starting with Anna and Vanessa, back to herself, to Granny Gus, then to Lily (who died in 1960), then with a dotted line to Marguerite and the word 'mother' queried. 'Lily's surname was Bailey.'

'Well, they came here by sea,' said Vanessa. 'I don't suppose the diary mentions which ship they were on?'

Anna shook her head. 'But there has to be a way to find out. And there may be more clues at Trebithick Hall or with Florence Deverell – I'm sure there's a connection between the diary and the things in the box.'

'Ooh, you *have* to go!' Vanessa said. 'I wish I could come too, but Harvey would have a pink fit if I left him to cope on his own.'

'What about your business?' her mum asked.

'It's actually a pretty good time of year to be away. Things get quieter in winter anyway, and Sally can manage without me for a few weeks.'

'Okaaay,' said Vanessa, a new look of respect on her face. 'You really have got it all sorted out.'

'It seems like there's nothing holding you back,' her mother added.

'I guess not,' said Anna, feeling nevertheless as if the ground had given way beneath her.

~

So, a week later and there she was, suspended in mid-air and caught between two worlds, excited for the adventure to begin.

She was feeling considerably less enthusiastic when, five movies, half a novel and a scant couple of hours' sleep later, she stumbled through customs, collected her bags and joined the line for taxis. She brightened a bit when she saw the reassuring trail of black cabs – so British, she thought with a grin. They looked just like they did in the movies. As her turn in the queue arrived, she climbed aboard, greedily taking in her surroundings as they flashed before her. It was early in the morning, but traffic was quicker than she'd expected and before she knew it the driver was pulling up at the address she'd given him. 'This is it, love,' he said.

'Richmond?' she asked.

The driver nodded. 'Larkfield Road, as requested.'

She looked out of the cab's window at the neat brick terraces with their gleaming white paintwork and black iron railings that failed to contain exuberantly blooming front gardens. So far, so good.

Her Airbnb host answered the bell almost immediately. 'Hello, there. You must be Anna,' she smiled a welcome. 'Come on in. You must be exhausted, flying all that way. I've only made the trip once, to see my son when he was out there. Not sure I'd ever do it again, though I did love Australia. Did you say it was Sydney you were from?' The woman talked at ninety miles an hour, not giving Anna a chance to answer, as she ushered her up a narrow staircase to the top of the house. The attic room was small but neat and the window looked out towards the river. Anna couldn't wait to collapse on the bed, which, given her jet-lagged state, looked like possibly the most inviting thing she'd ever seen.

'Now, you should have everything you want here. There's a bathroom next door and you're welcome to use the kitchen. I'll be downstairs if you need me.'

Anna dropped her bags on the floor with a thunk and, as the door closed behind the woman, fell on the bed. All she wanted to do was sleep.

Two hours later, staring wide-eyed at the steeply angled ceiling and listening to the burble of a radio and underneath that, the buzz of a lawnmower somewhere outside, she still couldn't drop off. She was bone-tired but her brain felt like it was on speed, with too many disjointed thoughts flashing through it. Eventually she sighed and got up, determined that a shower would help.

She nearly burst out laughing when she opened the bathroom door. It looked as if a lavender bush had vomited up purple everywhere, from the sprigged wallpaper to the matching shower curtain to the purple carpet. There was even a vase of the dried spears on the windowsill. Anna loved the fragrant plant, but not necessarily floor-to-ceiling. Standing in the shower – the tiles were lavender too – only added to her sense of dislocation.

Later, feeling slightly more awake after her lavender-hued shower, Anna headed out, armed with directions from her voluble host. The clouds had parted and a warm breeze lifted her hair. She reached the Thames – a wide stretch of the river where slim boats glided across the surface, their occupants rowing in perfect synchronicity, ripples spreading out behind them – and followed the narrow leafy path that ran alongside it.

She looked at her watch. Only twenty-five hours until her appointment with Dr Hammett-Jones.

Chapter Twenty-seven

Valparaiso, 1887

Elizabeth and Daisy arrived at the *Estancia Copihue* in the late afternoon on the appointed date, having travelled since dawn from Valparaiso with the Campbells in a *galera* – a small carriage that jounced over the rutted road, leaving them shaken to their bones. Mrs Campbell had eventually convinced her to attend, regaling her with stories of dancing and feasting at previous fiestas. Sibyl and Mrs Gordon were also to arrive later in the day, as well as several others from the town, many of whom Elizabeth had become acquainted with since her arrival.

The residence was situated at the base of a steep hill and surrounded by flat grasslands. Snow-capped mountain peaks rose in the distance behind the house, which although it was large, appeared dwarfed by the majestic landscape. A low stone wall stretched the length of the long adobe building, and a woman – a housekeeper, Elizabeth surmised – stood in the doorway, ready to welcome the hot and dusty travellers. They were ushered to their rooms, the woman speaking rapid Spanish that Elizabeth found hard to follow. She had picked up a few words and phrases over the previous weeks, but the woman's accent and delivery was too tricky to make much sense of. Nevertheless, her meaning was clear as she pointed in the direction of a small stone-floored whitewashed room that contained a timber bed made up with a brilliantly hued, scarlet and ochre thick wool blanket, a chair and a woven rug on the floor of similar colours to the blanket. Elizabeth sank onto the bed, surprised by its softness; she had expected something far more unforgiving from such a rustic setting. 'I should like to rest awhile,' she said to Daisy, who had lingered by the doorway to make sure of her mistress's comfort.

'Of course,' said Daisy. 'I shall endeavour to find out what time the festivities are expected to start and wake you at least an hour before. Would you like me to help you with your boots?'

'That will be most agreeable, thank you, Daisy,' replied Elizabeth, raising her feet off the floor and offering them to her maid.

~

She was woken from a deep slumber several hours later by Daisy shaking her shoulder. 'Miss Elizabeth,' Daisy called. (Daisy had tried but often failed to continue the practice that they had adopted on the ship of calling her mistress by her Christian name only.) 'Wake up! Wake up or we shall be late.'

Elizabeth blinked and looked groggily about her, not recognising the unfamiliar room at first.

'I have your gown ready,' said Daisy. 'It was a little creased from being packed away in the trunk, but I have been able to air it and the fabric looks almost as fine as it did when it was first delivered.'

Elizabeth gazed at the dress. It was one of her favourites, cut from pale-pink silk damask, with a tight-fitting bodice that sat low on her shoulders, designed to show her creamy décolletage to its best advantage. Silk-covered buttons fastened at the back and a sumptuous bustled skirt was caught up in a bow to reveal ivory satin beneath. Ostrich feathers, dyed to match the damask, waved at each capped sleeve.

'You have put on some of the weight you lost on the voyage, I am pleased to see,' said Daisy. 'I was worried that this would be too loose.'

'No, it fits perfectly again,' said Elizabeth once the dress was buttoned up. She smoothed the bodice beneath her palms. 'Thanks in no small part to the skills of Mrs Campbell's cook!' she laughed.

To complete the outfit, Daisy fastened around Elizabeth's neck a seed-pearl choker with a cameo portrait that had belonged to Elizabeth's mother. Elizabeth raised a silver hand mirror to her reflection. The light in the room was dim, there only being a small window set high up in the wall, but she knew that she had never looked better. Her hair, dressed expertly by Daisy, shone, and her fair skin was luminous. 'You look beautiful,' exclaimed Daisy as she stepped back to look.

'Thank you, Daisy. It is as much the result of your handiwork as anything God-given,' she said modestly as the two exchanged a warm smile. 'Now, don't let me hold you up any more, for you have yourself to get ready as well.'

'Yes, thank you. And I am so fortunate that we are of a similar size.' Daisy had only brought plain day dresses with her, never expecting to be part of any such grand festivities, but Elizabeth had insisted that she join her at the fiesta.

'It is a shame that Messrs Williamson and Windsor are not included in the party,' said Elizabeth.

'They are due back in Santiago at the end of the month, I believe,' said Daisy, colouring slightly. 'Mr Williamson sent a letter a few weeks ago.'

'I see,' said Elizabeth smiling at her. 'I was not aware you were corresponding. You must be fond of him.'

'A little,' Daisy admitted. 'I do enjoy being able to write to him, thanks to your lessons.'

'Well, be careful you do not catch the eye of any other gentlemen tonight, for in my gown you will look quite striking, I do believe.'

'Oh, miss, I am but a maid,' Daisy demurred.

'Nevertheless ...'

Elizabeth had lent her an aquamarine dress, originally made for Georgiana, with elbow-length sleeves and intricate embroidery of butterflies and bees. It set Daisy's red hair ablaze.

'Fire on the water,' Elizabeth had declared with pleasure when her maid had first tried it on.

Elizabeth gathered her fan, for it was a warm night, and made her way to the main hall. Butterflies massed in her belly, for she had not seen Tomas since her arrival, and she was nervous at the prospect. The guests were to assemble in the hall before being escorted across to the *estancia*'s main barn, which had been commandeered for the fiesta. As she stepped into the hall she noticed Mrs Gordon and Sibyl and several other of her new acquaintances milling around, chatter filling the air. It seemed that no matter where one was in the world, the excitement brought on by the prospect of a party was universal.

'You look quite splendid,' said Elizabeth to Sibyl, who did indeed look very pretty in a russet-coloured taffeta gown that matched her rich, conker-brown hair and emphasised her delicate shoulders and tiny waist.

'As do you, dear Elizabeth,' she replied.

Elizabeth was not surprised to see Damien Chegwidden among the guests, looking as immaculate as the last time she'd seen him, in a starched collar and dark frock coat, slim trousers and highly polished shoes. Society in Valparaiso was small, and this gathering was a large one. He was also acquainted with Tomas, so his inclusion was an obvious one. He smiled at her, looking as smug as a cat that had caught a rat. She fluttered her fan, giving him the barest nod of acknowledgement.

'I see that your maid is in attendance tonight,' he said, coming over to where she stood.

'She is more companion than maid these days,' said Elizabeth.

'And where does a maid come by such a sumptuous gown, I wonder? It looks as if it were fitted especially for her.'

Elizabeth did not like his tone. 'It was my sister's, if you must know,' she said, snapping her fan in annoyance. She would need to keep a careful watch on him that night, for Daisy's sake especially.

Just then, a hush came over the guests and Elizabeth turned to see Tomas making his way towards them. She couldn't help it; her heart beat faster at the sight of him. Unlike previous occasions where he had been clad in informal, traditional clothes, for the fiesta he had donned European dress, with dark trousers and a fitted tailcoat over a waistcoat that was as white as the breast of a gull. His hair was slicked back and the effect was, to Elizabeth at least, mesmerising.

With him was the beautiful girl from the market.

'Oh my,' breathed Sibyl in Elizabeth's ear.

Elizabeth pretended to be unaffected by Tomas's attire and indeed his very presence, though she did not know how the whole room could not hear the beat of her treacherous heart. She fanned herself, feeling the temperature in the room rise markedly.

'*Señora* Gordon, *Señorita* Bligh, *Señorita* Gordon,' he said, coming over to them and bowing low. 'I am so pleased that you could come to our little party. I trust you have rested from your journey?'

Elizabeth could do no more than nod.

The girl from the market greeted them with a wide smile. 'Welcome, welcome. Tomas has told me so much about you.

You must be *Señorita* Bligh,' she said. 'I have heard tell of your hair like spun gold and your talent at drawing. And *Señorita* Gordon, perhaps we might persuade you to play the pianoforte tomorrow before you leave? It is in sore need of tuning, I fear, but you might find it sufficiently mellow of tone.'

Damn it. Not only was she even more beautiful close up, but she was charming too.

'Sofia,' laughed Tomas, 'I see I have no introductions to make. How clever you are to identify our guests so easily.'

Pure jealousy stabbed Elizabeth as she noticed the fond smile Tomas bestowed upon Sofia. Damnation! How had she not known he was married, and to such a lovely woman?

'It is my pleasure to make your acquaintance,' said Sofia. 'Tomas speaks very highly of you.'

Elizabeth could do no more than give a curt nod of greeting and force her lips into a smile.

'Well, shall we make our way to the barn?' said Tomas to the assembled guests. 'I think you will find everything is ready.'

As she walked outside, Elizabeth could see that darkness had fallen, but that the inky sky was bright with stars. Her father had loved to point them out to her and Georgiana on clear summer nights, but as she surveyed these heavens she couldn't make out any of her favourite constellations. She felt suddenly homesick for the first time since she'd left Cornwall, and longed for the comfort of her sister, and the familiarity of Trebithick Hall.

'Are you quite well, *señorita*?' Tomas's voice was warm in her ear. She had been so absorbed in her stargazing that she hadn't noticed that the rest of the party had gone on ahead of her. She collected herself and blinked back a wayward tear that threatened to spill over. 'Yes, yes, thank you. I was merely looking for a few familiar faces.'

'In the stars? What an interesting thing to do. You are a most intriguing woman, *señorita*. Of course you would know that the stars you see here are quite different from the ones in the northern hemisphere.'

'Oh yes,' she said, feeling foolish once more. Of course they were. 'But that doesn't stop one looking, does it?'

'I suppose not. Come now, we have a wonderful fiesta ahead of us. I think you shall enjoy it.'

Elizabeth allowed herself to be escorted along the brazier-lit path to the barn, where the sounds of revelry streamed out the door, infecting everyone within earshot with exuberance. She caught the mouth-watering aroma of roasting meats and as they drew closer could make out the shapes of men turning great sides of beef over hot coals.

The barn was a cavernous space, with a few rough-hewn tables set at the edges and long benches for seating. At one end was a group of musicians – violinists and a harpist playing a rousing tune that had even Elizabeth's feet tapping. Several of the Chilean guests were dancing, doing a kind of heel and toe shuffle, stamping, kicking and hopping on the hard-packed dirt floor beneath their feet. They each held a bright handkerchief in one hand, waving it above their head with a flourish as they moved. Those watching clapped and pounded their feet in time to the music. 'It is called the *cueca*,' Tomas explained, leaning in so that she could hear him over the hum of the music and the crowd. 'Our traditional dance.'

'It's certainly very lively,' she said, caught up in the spectacle.

He left her side briefly, returning with two glasses. 'You must be thirsty,' he said, handing her a large goblet filled with a pale cloudy liquid. 'I hope you like it.'

She took a tentative sip. It was sweet and refreshing.

'It's made from fermented apples,' he explained.

'Oh! Cider!' she smiled.

He smiled back at her and their eyes met. Elizabeth tried to drag her gaze away from their piercing blueness, but she failed. 'I should not keep you. Surely your wife desires your company?' she said.

Tomas looked confused. 'My wife?'

'Yes, Sofia. Your wife.'

Tomas threw back his head and laughed. 'Sofia?' He laughed again. '*Señorita*, Sofia is not my wife.'

'She isn't?'

'No. Sofia is my sister. This is her home too.'

Realisation dawned on Elizabeth. 'Oh,' she said, embarrassed. 'I assumed she was your wife. You know you failed to mention earlier that she was your sister,' she snapped, annoyed with him.

'If that is the case, then you have my humble apologies. An oversight. Our manners are perhaps not as refined as those of the English? But let us not dwell on that this evening. Would you care to try this dance?'

Opportunities for dancing at Trebithick Hall had been scarce, but her governess had nonetheless schooled her in the quadrille and the waltz until she was proficient, if not expert – but this, this *cueca* was something entirely different. 'I am uncertain . . .' she began.

Tomas ignored her protest and whisked her towards the centre of the room. Thankfully a different tune started, and the dancers began to turn about in a kind of polka. Elizabeth recognised the movements and was soon twirling around in Tomas's arms, her heart growing lighter with every step.

So, he was not married. She did not know why that should cause her such joy, but it did.

The fiesta continued well into the early hours, with Elizabeth pausing from dancing only to refresh herself with the cold cider that Tomas offered and, when there was a break in the music, to feast on *empanadas* containing a flavoursome meat, rather like her favourite pasties from home, and then chunks of skewered beef and lamb served with a spicy sauce, a salad of tomatoes and onions, all washed down with red wine or more cider. Tomas stuck by her side almost the entire evening, only leaving her for a single dance with Sibyl, and one with Daisy, whose flame-red hair sparked in the candlelight and earned her several admirers.

In a brief interlude from the dancing, Sofia and Elizabeth had discovered a mutual love of plants, Sofia revealing that her mother had passed on much of her herbal knowledge before she died. Elizabeth was thrilled – this was the news she had been hoping for – especially when Sofia offered to teach her the very next day the names and healing properties of some of the plants that grew on the *estancia*.

Elizabeth noticed her maid keep her distance from Mr Chegwidden, and she tried her best to keep a watchful eye on him, anxious that he should not trouble Daisy again. For his part, Damien Chegwidden stood on the sidelines, refusing to take part in the dancing, but not taking his eyes off Elizabeth for a moment. He wore a faintly curious expression, his brows knitted together, as if she were a puzzle he could not figure out.

Chapter Twenty-eight

London, Summer 2017

Anna waited by the Elizabeth Gate at eleven the next morning, too anxious to admire the golden laburnum in bloom in front of her. She'd woken at stupid o'clock, thinking for a moment that she was back in her apartment in Sydney. Then she heard the gentle tweets of unfamiliar birds, and everything clicked into place. London. Kew. Dr Hammett-Jones. A thrill of excitement zinged through her. This was really happening.

She had spent the previous day wandering along the river until finally giving in to tiredness in the early afternoon and returning to her lodgings, falling into a deep, almost drugged sleep. She'd woken in time for dinner and then crashed again, sleeping through until morning.

She'd headed out early, walking the short distance to Kew Gardens and arriving as it opened, taking an hour to explore the grounds before her meeting. The huge expanses of green immediately soothed her as she wandered. She barely scratched the surface of what the great gardens had to offer, but gazed in awe at the spectacular Alpine House, the elegant Nash Conservatory, and sweltered in the giant Victorian glasshouse. She stopped to admire the succulent garden and the giant lilies in the Waterlily House, some of the pads of the *Victoria amazonica* more than a metre across, before wandering into the Rose Pergola, through a tunnel of blooms, rambling roses – including the 'Danse Des Sylphes' and the pink-blossomed 'Mary Wallace', she read – trained to climb in an arch over her head. Granny Gus would have loved it. So would have Simon.

Finally, she found herself at a gallery tucked away in a far corner of the gardens, where she spent a long time marvelling at the hundreds upon hundreds of paintings of Marianne North, an adventurous artist who, it turned out, had been alive at the same time as Anna's own mysterious illustrator. Perhaps they had known of each other? Marianne was certainly well travelled, with paintings depicting flora from countries as far flung as the Sandwich Isles, New Zealand and Africa crowding the gallery walls. Anna looked fondly at a vibrant oil of a scarlet banksia with the backdrop of Sydney Harbour. Home seemed a long way away right now.

She became so absorbed in the paintings that she only just made it back to her meeting place in time, dashing the last few hundred metres so as not to keep Dr Hammett-Jones waiting.

She hugged the bag containing the sketchbook to her chest, casting around for someone who looked like they were looking for her. A tall, attractive man wearing shorts and a polo shirt was approaching her – but no, that couldn't be him; he looked like he was on holiday, not a taxonomist at such a venerable institution.

Behind him was an older man with wispy greying hair and wire-rimmed glasses. Now, *he* looked more likely. She was looking at him expectantly when holiday man spoke to her. 'Miss Jenkins?'

He held out his hand as the older man passed them both, narrowly missing Anna. She shook his hand and looked at him in surprise. His eyes crinkled appealingly and she took in freckles sprinkled like nutmeg across a strong nose, broad shoulders, blond hair lit by the sun and curling into his collar. She was vaguely aware of people walking around them, but she could only focus on the man now standing in front of her. Dr Hammett-Jones. Edwin. He didn't look like any Edwin she had ever imagined. Not that she had met a great many. None in fact, until just now.

'That is you, isn't it?' he looked suddenly doubtful.

'Oh yes. Yes, it is me. That is, I am Miss Jenkins. Anna.' Her cheeks reddened and she found herself uncharacteristically flustered. She wasn't used to being called Miss Jenkins, she told herself.

'Oh jolly good!' he said, grinning at her and pumping her hand, pushing back his hair, which had flopped over his forehead, with his other hand. 'Ed. Hammett-Jones, that is.' The overall effect was of an extremely friendly Labrador.

'How did you know it was me?' Anna asked with a glance at the other women milling around them.

'You're the only one in the vicinity carrying what surely looks like a sketchbook. So, I took a chance.'

'Oh, yes . . .' She flushed, looking down at the package in her hands.

'Come on then, let me show you to my office. It's this way, past the south arboretum.'

Anna followed close behind him, hurrying to keep up with his long-legged stride.

'So, you're an Aussie,' he said.

'I suppose that must be obvious as well?' she said lightly.

'The accent kind of gives it away.'

'I'm still a little jet-lagged, I have to admit.'

Edwin stopped in his tracks and looked at her closely. 'You mean you flew all the way from Down Under to meet with me? You don't live here?'

'In your email you said that you'd take a look at the sketches if I brought them in.'

'But I thought you said you found them in a house in Paddington. Oh dear, Miss Jenkins, I do hope you haven't come all this way just for me to look at your sketches.' He looked both apologetic and bemused.

Her hand flew to her forehead. 'Of course! When I said Paddington, I meant Paddington, Sydney. Not Paddington, London. In any case, no of course I didn't come all this way just for our meeting,' she said unable to keep a note of huffiness out of her voice. 'I've got some more investigating to do, and it's also a bit of a holiday. I'm off to Europe in a few weeks . . . Giverny, Versailles . . . you know.'

It was true, she had planned to spend a few days in London and then get the train down to Cornwall to try to track down Florence Deverell. Then, depending on what she found out, she was going to book a ticket on the Eurostar and gorge herself on *pain au chocolat*, *pomme frites* and *gelato*, as well as the great palaces and gardens of France and Italy. But her meeting with him *was* the driving force behind her trip, even if she wasn't going to admit that to him.

'Oh, so you're in the business? Or an enthusiast?'

'The business?'

'A fellow plantsperson.'

'Well, only in a very small way. But I did study plant science at university.'

'Jolly good,' he said with a look of approval on his face. 'Let me show you around, then.' He checked his watch. 'Give you a personal tour. Especially as you've come so far.' With that, he strode off again in the direction of the great glass greenhouse. Anna didn't have the heart to tell him she'd already explored the gardens on her own before their meeting.

'You might recognise this one,' Edwin said, stopping in front of an evergreen. '*Wollemia*, of course.'

'Just about everyone in Australia knows that story,' she replied with a grin. 'Rediscovered in the Blue Mountains only a few years ago. Still on the critically endangered list.'

He nodded. 'It amazes me that we are still discovering and rediscovering plants in this day and age.' They marched on and he pointed to another, its delicate white flowers looking like five-pointed stars. '*Ramosmania rodriguesi* – native to a tiny island in the Indian Ocean. Thought to be extinct but rediscovered by a school student in 1980. And, this . . .' he said, stopping for a moment in front of a small plant with pale yellow flowers. '*Menodora linoides.* Only member of the olive family native to Chile. Highly endangered. Thanks to a partnership with the Chilean Agricultural Research Agency and our Millennium Seed Bank, we've been able to germinate seeds and successfully propagate it. We've provided seeds back to the Botanic Gardens in Chile, where they are looking at conservation options for it. It's one of our success stories,' he said proudly.

'Oh. Right,' said Anna, impressed, thinking how well he would get on with Jane.

'You might be able to guess that one of my specialist areas is endangered species. We've successfully banked around ten per cent of the world's wild plant species. We're aiming for twenty per cent by 2020.'

Anna opened her mouth to reply, but he continued, 'Every day another four plant species face extinction.' He stopped, realising he had interrupted her. 'Sorry. If you don't stop me I'll be on about it for hours. My daughter, Ella, is constantly telling me off about it. Says I could bore for England on the subject. What were you going to say?'

'It's just that I think I recognise that plant. There's a drawing of it, or something very similar, in the sketchbook.'

'Oh!' He looked like an over-eager schoolboy. 'Shall we go and take a look now? I can always show you more of the gardens later. Though you might, of course, prefer to explore on your own.'

'It's far more interesting to have someone who is so passionate and knowledgeable as my guide. Really.'

He beamed at her again and Anna's heart did a ridiculous flip-flop. She groaned inwardly at herself. Was this the effect of the time difference and too little sleep? He'd mentioned a daughter, so he was probably married.

By rights she should have been tucked up in bed on the other side of the world, but how miraculous that she was standing here in one of the most beautiful and fascinating gardens she'd ever been in, with a wonderfully interesting and attractive man who seemed, unless she was reading the signs wrongly, to find her appealing? It was almost too much to take in all at once, and not at all what she had been expecting.

'And here we have the Chilean blue crocus,' he said. '*Tecophilaea cyanocrocus*. It grows on the slopes of the Andes and was thought to be extinct in the wild until 2001, though it's a popular cultivated plant.'

Anna bent down to examine the iridescent blue flowers. She marvelled at the perfectly formed blooms. Anna didn't believe in God as such, but she couldn't deny the hand of a divine creator in the natural world.

'The genus *Tecophilaea* was named after Tecofila Billiotti. She was a botanical artist and the daughter of a botanist, Luigi Aloysius Colla of Turin,' he went on.

'You really do know your stuff,' she said. 'Now, *this* definitely looks like one of the drawings in the sketchbook.'

Edwin raised his eyebrows. 'Really?'

'Really.' She was solemn, but she couldn't help the twinkle in her eyes. Talking to him brought out her lighter side, one she'd almost forgotten she had.

'Then I absolutely can't wait to take a look. Onwards to my office, Jenkins!' He strode off again, leaving Anna to hurry along in his wake.

They came to a building at the back of the gardens, near the perimeter wall, and inside they made their way to a tiny, very untidy office. He cleared a space for her on a chair, heaving a stack of books and papers onto the floor. 'Sorry about this. It's more organised than it looks.'

'I'm sure,' she said politely, sitting down.

He faced her across his desk, which was also covered in papers. 'Now. Let's see what we've got.'

Anna took the sketchbook out of her bag and placed it reverently on the desk in front of him before relocating a half-full cup of coffee to a nearby bookcase.

There was silence as he turned the first page.

Chapter Twenty-nine

Valparaiso, 1887

Elizabeth hadn't meant to fall in love.

She knew it as soon as she woke. As she listened to what sounded like a linnet in the tree outside the window singing a sweet song as if only for her, as she hummed to herself while fastening the bodice of her dress, as she cursed her poor bruised feet (her dancing slippers had been no match for the hard ground of the barn) . . . she knew. She knew that her heart now belonged irrevocably to Tomas. Every part of her being sang it, every pore on her skin radiated it, her eyes were alight with it. Even as she thrilled to the knowledge, she cursed its inconvenience: it would complicate everything.

But she believed that he felt the same way, for even while he had danced with others, his gaze had never strayed far from her. He had been solicitous of her comfort all evening, had kept his arm at her back and talked easily to her of his upbringing and family, of his thoughts and interests. But words were the least of it: she shivered as she remembered the feel of his hand in hers, for there were no gloves worn in this part of the world.

Despite her joy, she was utterly confused. She'd had no experience of love, aside from being privy to her sister's courtship, and never seen evidence of love between a man and a woman at home, her father having never taken another wife after the death of her mother. She had no idea what happened next.

Breakfast had finished by the time Elizabeth reached the *estancia*'s large dining room, and the whole house was quiet, save for an occasional burst of song or giggling as the maids went about their chores. As she wondered where everyone might be, one of the maids entered and placed a silver pot on the sideboard, gesturing to her.

'*Si, si*,' said Elizabeth.

The coffee was strong and bitter, but served to chase away the dusty feeling in her head caused by the cider of the night before. She sat and sipped, wondering when she might see Tomas again, for her whole being longed for the sight of him, for his touch. She drifted away on the sea of her thoughts, remembering the feel of being encircled in his arms and twirled until she was dizzy, and so she didn't see Sibyl enter the room, only noticing her as she sat down on the chair opposite.

'Did you sleep well, my dear?' Sibyl asked, interrupting her musings.

'Oh, quite well, thank you. I confess I am still rather tired though and my feet are so sore I fear they shall never be the same again.' Elizabeth winced as she rolled her ankle to and fro in demonstration.

'I am not surprised. *Señor* Flores certainly made sure you scarcely left the dance floor.'

Elizabeth looked up from contemplation of her foot, surprised by Sibyl's aggrieved tone.

'Have I done anything to upset you, Sibyl?' she asked.

'Why, pray, would you think that, Elizabeth?'

'I know that you are fond of Tomas and I certainly did not intend for him to monopolise me. I should hate to cause you the slightest unhappiness. I have few friends here, and would hope to count you as one of them.'

Sibyl sighed. 'No, Elizabeth, you have done nothing to upset me. Well, nothing that is of your making. It is as clear as day that *Señor* Flores is much taken with you.'

'Oh, Sibyl, I fear I am also taken with him,' Elizabeth confessed. 'But I feel awful admitting that to you.'

'Truth be told I am glad you have,' Sibyl said. 'For I don't think I could bear it if you did not care for him as he obviously does for you. It would only serve to twist the knife in the wound.'

'You are most gracious, and I am sure I do not deserve such understanding. But I did not come here to fall in love,' she continued. 'I came to sketch and paint plants, and to return to England and share my discoveries.'

'Oh, dear Elizabeth, the heart chooses its own path and rides roughshod over everything else. Love does not respect intentions, nor boundaries, nor continents, nor wishes. Unhappily it has not found me yet.' She sighed again. 'For it must be the most glorious thing to love and be loved in return.'

'Of course love will find you, Sibyl. I am certain of it,' Elizabeth reassured her.

'You may be right,' she replied. 'But it is taking its time. I shall be quite grey if it does not hurry along.' She smiled, to Elizabeth's relief.

'Where is everyone? There is neither sight nor sound of Daisy, nor of anyone else, for that matter.'

'Mother was up early and said that Tomas was taking a party of guests out riding, those who have not already departed, that is. We are to leave after luncheon.'

'Oh,' said Elizabeth, deflated. She had been anxious to see Tomas again, but she did, however, have another plan for the day, but for that she needed to locate his sister.

'Did Sofia go with them?'

'No, I don't believe so. Perhaps we can ask one of the maids if they have seen her.'

~

'*Hola señoritas*,' Sofia greeted them warmly as she entered the room just as the women were finishing their coffee. 'I trust you slept well and are rested?'

'I am, thank you. And thank you for a wonderful evening. I cannot recall the last time I enjoyed myself so much. Though my feet are suffering this morning,' Elizabeth replied with a rueful smile.

'Oh dear, does that mean we must postpone our walk? I was so hoping to show you the plants we spoke of last night.'

'Oh no, not at all,' replied Elizabeth. 'I should very much like to walk with you. My feet will surely survive a few more steps.'

'*Señorita* Sibyl, would you care to join us?' asked Sofia.

'Thank you but I think I shall remain here. I might practise on the piano while it is quiet,' Sibyl replied.

'By all means,' said Sofia. 'We shall only be gone an hour or so.'

~

The two women, one so dark and the other so fair, one wearing a bustled gown in green bombazine that reached the floor, the other in a simple black shift topped by a brightly coloured woven poncho, left the house by the front door. They followed a path to the right of the barn where the fiesta had been held, and then through a gate and into a kind of meadow, beyond which rose steep hills. Lush grass sprang up around their feet and there were numerous wild flowers among the green like so many brightly coloured dots, extending as far as the eye could see.

'Our home is named after a flower, the *copihue* – see, here it is,' Sofia said, pointing to a scarlet, trumpet-shaped flower. And then she pointed out plant after plant, most of which Elizabeth had never seen before. She explained how one was used for curing eruptions of the skin, another for headaches, and another for dispelling evil spirits from a person. 'Oh how I wish I had thought to bring my sketchbook on our walk,' said Elizabeth, fascinated by all that Sofia was showing her.

'Do not worry. I am sure you will have many other opportunities to make likenesses of them,' she said.

'Well, I do hope I shall be invited again, though in truth I am not certain how long I intend to stay in Valparaiso.'

Sofia looked confused. 'But I thought you and my brother . . . Did you not know that he is absolutely smitten with you?' She clapped her hand over her mouth. '*Ay dios mio!* I have spoken out of turn. It is none of my business and he will never forgive me for interfering.'

Elizabeth smiled at her, thrilling inwardly to Sofia's disclosure. 'Do not worry,' she whispered. 'I shall not breathe a word.'

They walked in the meadow, and despite the fact that Tomas had been very much on her mind since she had first woken that morning, Elizabeth had but one question for his sister. She turned the conversation once more towards botany, and, after a while, spoke up.

'Tell me, Sofia, do you know of a plant called the Devil's Trumpet?' she asked. 'The shape of the *copihue* we saw reminds me of it a little.'

'*Demonios trompeta*.' Sofia's eyes grew wide and she crossed herself, muttering under her breath. 'How is it that you know of it?'

'I read its name somewhere, when I was researching this journey,' she bluffed, feeling a pang of guilt at deceiving Sofia.

'It is an extremely dangerous plant,' Sofia explained darkly. 'It is also now very rare, which may be a blessing. My mother and other *machi* like her did their best to keep its location secret whenever they came across it. In the wrong hands it can destroy a whole village, more even. And it can kill the one who tries to harvest it.'

'But I read that it can also heal. Is that possible?'

Sofia looked at her suspiciously. 'Only if you know what you are doing. And there are few left who do. My mother was one of the last.'

'What a great shame that she did not pass on that knowledge to you. For surely it is an invaluable gift. In the right hands, of course.'

Sofia paused before answering carefully. 'You think she did not?'

Chapter Thirty

London, Summer 2017

Anna held her breath. She could almost hear the seconds tick by and had to sit on her hands to keep from jumping up to point out particular details to him. She wanted him to evaluate it without any influence from her.

Ed slowly turned the pages, reaching for a pair of glasses and flicking on an anglepoise lamp to see the drawings better. 'Extraordinary,' he eventually muttered under his breath. He gave a long, satisfied sigh and looked up at Anna, his eyes shining.

'They are rather beautiful,' he said. 'Exceptional even.'

'I know,' she replied, feeling a quiet thrill that her intuition had been correct. 'How on earth did they manage such intricate detail?' she asked.

'Well, if they were in the field they would have had a small magnifying glass, but if they brought specimens indoors, then there was something called a *camera lucida* – a microscope with mirrors that allows you to trace the object you're drawing. Sometimes these illustrations capture more detail than an actual camera.' He went back to examining the drawings. 'Quillaja,' he muttered. 'A foaming plant. Used for bathing.' He turned the page to reveal a watercolour of a yellow-flowered buttercup-like plant. 'Culen,' he said, almost to himself. Eventually he reached the last page.

'That one's my favourite,' said Anna, unable to help herself.

He drew in a sharp breath, still muttering to himself. He turned towards his computer, tapped a few keys, then drummed his fingers on the desk as he waited for whatever he was searching for to load. He went back to the drawing, then picked up the phone on his desk and punched in a four-digit number. 'Hal? Got a minute?'

There was a pause.

'Okay, after lunch. See you then.' He put down the phone and looked at Anna. 'If it's all right with you, I'd like my colleague, Hal Graham, to come and take a look. He's head of identification and naming here at Kew, as well as being a plant historian. I've a suspicion about some of the watercolours, but he knows more about the subject than I do.'

'Okay, yes, that would be great,' said Anna, not knowing what to make of it.

He stood up abruptly, flicking off the light with one hand and taking off his glasses with the other, throwing them down on a pile of papers. 'He's not free until this afternoon. I don't suppose you've had lunch, have you? If my experience with jet-lag is anything to go by, you're probably starving.'

She was.

'Come on. Let's grab a sandwich while we wait for him and take it outside. It's a beautiful day and we should make the most of it. I know you probably take good weather for granted but us poor Englishmen have to take it when we find it.'

Ed led her out of his office, reaching behind his door where a checked woollen blanket was hanging. He rolled it up and shoved it under his arm as they walked.

They eventually emerged into the sunshine and strolled over to an expanse of lush green lawn, where he unfurled the blanket and motioned for her to sit down. 'Be right back. Chicken okay? Or are you vegetarian?'

'Chicken would be fine, and thanks.' Anna started to pull out her wallet to give him some money, but he refused her. 'Least I can do seeing as you've come all this way and brought me quite the most beautiful and fascinating thing I've seen in ages.'

Anna stretched her legs out in front of her, crossing them at the ankles before leaning back on her elbows. She watched Ed lope across the lawn, headed for a cafe she could just make out in the distance. She wasn't sure if it was his boyish enthusiasm or his charming dishevelment that was so appealing. She raised her face and closed her eyes, enjoying the sun's warmth on her cheeks. In that moment she felt as light as a feather and positively fizzing with excitement. Her instinct about the sketchbook had been correct – it *was* an important find.

Minutes later Ed returned juggling sandwiches and drinks. 'Elderflower cordial?' he said, offering one to her.

'How very English,' she said and felt a warm glow of pleasure as he gave a bark of laughter.

'Wouldn't dream of disappointing,' he replied, sitting next to her.

'So tell me about Sydney. I confess I have never been, but would love to go – that harbour, and the Opera House.'

'Actually,' said Anna, 'my favourite spot is on the harbour, apart from the Botanic Gardens obviously. It's a little park right on the water called Nielsen Park. In fact the beach is called Shark Beach, but don't let that put you off, it's a lovely place to swim.'

Ed raised his eyebrows in alarm.

'There's a long, semi-circular bench seat and if you sit at one end you can whisper to a person sitting at the other, and the sound will carry along the curve of the stone.'

'How charming,' said Ed sincerely. 'I shall have to remember that. And about the sharks.'

When they had finished their lunch, Ed stretched out on the grass, his arms folded behind his head. 'Sorry. Late night last night. I'm developing an app and it's taken all of my free time for the past six months.'

'Oh yes?' said Anna, idly plucking at the grass with her hands and acutely aware of the tall, leonine man stretched out only inches away from her.

'It's a plant-identification tool – take a snap of a plant and the app will tell you what it is. Well, that's the idea anyway. It's proving a bit trickier than I originally thought, though most of my side of the job will be done soon.'

'What a great idea,' said Anna. 'I often have clients asking me for a particular plant but they don't know the name of it.'

'Clients?'

As Ed lay back, Anna told him about her gardening business, and then the story of inheriting her grandmother's house and the discovery of the box hidden in the wall.

'How extraordinary, Jenkins. I wonder how it came to be in Sydney?' he mused.

'I've no idea. There was also a photograph, which we think was taken in Cornwall. Somewhere called Trebithick Hall. The date on it is 1886, the year before most of the watercolours were done.'

'Cornwall?' Ed looked interested. 'That's where I grew up. On the Atlantic side. Trebithick Hall . . .' he pondered. 'Rings a vague bell. Certainly sounds Cornish enough.'

He glanced at his watch and got to his feet with a groan. 'I could sit and chat to you all day, but Hal should be free now. Let's go and see what he says.'

He offered Anna his hand and she took it, feeling a shock go through her at his touch. He held it a moment longer than she thought was probably necessary, then relinquished it and began to fold up the blanket while Anna gathered their sandwich wrappings and empty bottles.

'Well, this is quite something, isn't it?' The man speaking to Anna was the one she'd nearly mistaken for Ed, and he looked if anything even more rumpled than he had that morning.

Anna nodded.

'Magnificent. So lush and vivid. A refined sense of composition and such a delicate hand. I'd like to hold onto it for a while, if I may.' It was more a statement than a question.

'Is there a reason?' Anna asked, alarmed. She wasn't sure she wanted to relinquish her precious find quite so readily.

'Oh . . .' He stopped when he came to the last page.

'There's no note on it,' she pointed out. Where each of the preceding plants had appended comments on their medicinal qualities, this final one was left unremarked upon.

'*Datura*,' he said almost to himself, rubbing at the bristles on his chin with his hand. 'But not any variety of *datura* that I've ever seen.' He looked up at Anna again. 'This is most unusual. It might even be one that's undocumented. I've certainly never seen anything like it alive . . . in the archives possibly . . . look, Ed, the petiole, the stripes on the petals.' He pointed to the illustration. 'That's not a typical *datura*. Not a *datura stramonium*, or *datura inoxia*.'

'Yes,' agreed Ed. 'Not jimsonweed – or thornapple as it's also known,' he said to Anna.

'That's one of the so-called witches' weeds,' Hal explained, though she knew them well enough. 'Closely related to belladonna, henbane and mandrake. Highly toxic, though also thought by some to have aphrodisiac properties. It's illegal to grow it in some countries.'

Anna looked at him uncertainly. 'You really think it's a totally new plant? An undiscovered varietal?'

'Do you know, I rather think it might be a new species of *datura*,' he said, eyes gleaming behind smeared glasses. 'Or possibly a long-extinct one; I'd have to do some more research. Ed says you're on holiday, Miss Jenkins. How long are you here for? I'd only need it for a few days, say until after the weekend? I'd like to consult a colleague, but he's not back until Tuesday.'

Anna wasn't entirely happy about leaving the sketchbook in the possession of this rumpled academic – what if he spilled his tea on it, or worse, misplaced it?

'Don't worry; I'll take very good care of it,' he reassured her as if reading her thoughts.

'Okay, then,' she said finally. 'I'm not due to go to Paris until the end of next week in any case.'

'Splendid!' he said, closing the sketchbook. 'Now, you're coming to the Gardens' summer party tomorrow evening?'

Anna looked doubtfully at him. Was he inviting her? She didn't really do parties. Had given them up, after Simon. She was about to politely decline when Hal got in ahead of her.

'Do say you will. You'll liven it up no end – it'll be full of crusty old botanists. Present company excepted, of course.'

'Well, as you've given it such a rap, how can I refuse?' she replied with a smile.

'Good. Ed here can escort you.'

Anna looked at him and a traitorous blush began to creep up her neck. The last thing she wanted was for him to feel obliged to look after her. 'No, really, I'll be fine on my own,' she insisted, not believing she was saying those words; she hadn't been to a party in years, let alone on her own.

'Nonsense, Jenkins,' Ed jumped in. 'They feed unchaperoned young women to the flesh-eating plants in the tropical house, didn't you know?'

'Oh well, then . . .' She grinned at him.

It was all settled. Anna left the sketchbook with Hal and arranged to meet Ed the following evening at seven in a pub on Kew Green.

'It's called The Botanist,' he'd said rolling his eyes as he said the name. 'Yes, I know.'

The following afternoon, after a day of sightseeing, Anna arrived back in Richmond with barely enough time to shower and change, thanking her sister's foresight in recommending that she pack at least one dress. It had thin straps and a fitted, square bodice, with a gathered skirt that fell to her knees and its periwinkle blue cotton set off her blonde hair. It was in total contrast to her normal jeans-and-T-shirt attire and she felt uncharacteristically girlish, as if she should swish her skirts about her and break into song in the manner of a 1940s movie star. She left her hair to fall loose about her shoulders and applied a sheer gloss to her lips. Her skin was tinted gold from her day's wanderings in the sun, and her eyes sparkled with anticipation. As she looked in the mirror, she almost didn't recognise herself.

Chapter Thirty-one

Valparaiso, 1887

'Señorita Elizabeth!' Tomas's pleasure at seeing her was evident as a huge smile spread across his face.

Elizabeth coloured as she remembered their leave-taking at the end of the fiesta. He had escorted her back to the house, under the canopy of stars, boldly taking her hand. 'Elizabeth, *mi amor* . . .' he had said, bending at the waist and raising her hand to his lips. Lips that she had found herself wishing would press upon her own.

'Tomas,' she greeted him, suddenly shy.

'I trust you are rested?'

'Yes, thank you. My feet are a little sore however, I must admit.'

He looked suddenly concerned.

'Merely from too much unaccustomed dancing,' she explained.

'Oh well, you shall have plenty of opportunity to rest them. I cannot hear of you returning to Valparaiso until they are quite better. You must of course stay here for as long as you wish. We will have a quiet family dinner tonight and we should be delighted if you and Daisy would continue to be our guests for as long as you desire. Is that not so, Sofia?'

His sister nodded enthusiastically, and Elizabeth smiled in return. 'Well, I should be glad to. Sofia has shown me so many fascinating new plants this morning and I am most anxious to paint them. They are quite unlike those I have seen closer to the town.'

'Then stay for two more nights,' Tomas said, as if it were a simple decision. 'Or longer.'

~

As it happened, Elizabeth and Daisy continued to enjoy the Flores's generous hospitality for a week. Mrs Gordon and Sibyl promised to send word back to Mrs Campbell of their extended absence. Elizabeth spent the cool of the mornings sketching and painting the various plants that grew in abundance around the *estancia*, occasionally sitting with Sofia. Once, Elizabeth casually brought up the subject of the Devil's Trumpet again, but, frustratingly, Sofia would not be drawn to answer, other than to emphasise how difficult it was to find for those who did not know exactly where to look.

In the afternoons, after a siesta, Elizabeth accompanied Tomas on horseback, exploring the hillsides as they climbed towards the high Andes. She kept a careful watch for signs of the Devil's Trumpet, but was not rewarded with even a single sighting, which emphasised to her how extraordinarily fortunate she must have been to stumble over it in the Valley of the Palms.

Either Daisy or Sofia usually accompanied them on their wanderings, but one afternoon Sofia had left for a nearby village and Daisy begged off with a headache.

'It is just the two of us, Elizabeth,' said Tomas as they walked to the stables, adopting his usual habit of dropping the *señorita* when they were alone.

She flashed him a teasing smile in response. 'Let us hope no one in Valparaiso should discover this.'

'Indeed, that would be most unfortunate. I doubt your reputation would survive it,' he said pretending seriousness.

The path leading from the *estancia* was wide enough for the two horses to ride side by side and Elizabeth became conscious of the occasional brush of Tomas's leg against her own as the horses jostled each other. Her heart fluttered foolishly at his nearness. As the week had progressed they had shared many conversations, and she had become even more fascinated by this man who straddled the traditional and the European worlds so effortlessly. If she had imagined herself in love with him on the morning after the fiesta, by the end of a week in his company she was certain of it.

Tomas was the first to raise the subject. They had paused to water the horses at a stream and sat upon the bank, drinking from a wineskin and picnicking on sheep's cheese and apples. 'Elizabeth,' he said, looking intently at her. 'You must know . . .' He seemed discomfited, and looked away, clearing his throat. 'You must know by now of my feelings for you. I am unable to keep them to myself any longer. I am not certain if this is the way things should be done.' He paused and Elizabeth noticed a faint sheen of sweat on his brow. She wanted to reach out and place a finger to it, to taste it, she realised, shocked at her brazen desires.

She looked at him, unafraid now, a smile of encouragement on her face.

'Tell me now: do you feel anything of the same?'

'I might,' she said, teasing him.

'*Mi amor*,' he groaned, pulling her towards him. She went willingly into his arms and lifted her lips to his. For an agonising moment he did not move, their breath mingling but their lips still not meeting, then he drew her closer and there was the roughness of his skin against hers, the intimacy of his touch, a touch she had never before known. Her arms moved of their own volition and she was powerless to stop her fingers becoming entwined in his silky dark hair, her own golden locks tumbling down as he caressed her.

After a while they pulled apart, both gasping from the joy of discovering each other, of knowing that their feelings were given and returned in full. He drew her forehead to his. '*Mi corazon*, beat of my own heart, how you have teased me, tested my patience these past few days,' he whispered to her.

'*Señor*, if I have teased, then it has only been in the gentlest fun. I have no wish to ever torment you,' she said earnestly.

As they sat, each whispering sweet words to the other, Elizabeth's horse, which had been tethered nearby, shied up, letting out a panicked whinny. Tomas sprang to his feet and began to calm the mare, normally a docile and gentle mount. Elizabeth looked towards the mountains, which towered in the distance, their jagged peaks hazy with snowy spindrift. She gave a quick glance to the sky, which was now coloured purple. 'Do those look like storm clouds to you?' she said.

'*Si*. We will not likely make it back to the *estancia* before it breaks. We should seek shelter. Come,' he said decisively, reaching for her hand to help her up, 'we must make haste.'

Elizabeth packed their things into a saddlebag and gave Tomas her boot so he could boost her up onto the saddle. Once he too was mounted, they kicked their horses into a gallop and she followed his lead across the valley floor.

After several minutes of hard riding Tomas pulled up his horse, indicating that Elizabeth should do the same. The sky had turned so dark it seemed as if it were twilight, but she could see a small stone hut built at the foot of the slope in front of them. Before they had time to reach the peculiar little shack, a flash of lightning illuminated the dark sky and then came an almighty crack of thunder that reverberated through her body. Jagged chunks of ice pelted them, bouncing as they hit the ground. 'Ow!' cried Elizabeth as they stung her body, seeming to cut through her cotton riding habit right to her tender skin. The temperature, which minutes before had been pleasantly warm, had plummeted and Elizabeth began to shiver.

'Quick, inside!' Tomas shouted over the noise of the hail-storm. He fastened the horses to a railing at the front of the hut, taking off their saddles and blankets and then, still holding the blankets, pulled her inside.

There was no door – 'likely burned as firewood a long time ago,' explained Tomas – merely a worn animal hide to block the worst of the weather. As they went inside, the sound of the storm lessened and Elizabeth shook the water out of her eyes and looked around the dim space. It was a wretched place, but at least it offered some respite. She could make out a narrow ledge on one side of the small room that looked like it was for sleeping, and at the other a large fire pit, with a deep pile of ash but no wood.

'It is a *casucha*,' Tomas explained. 'For shelter in times like this.'

Elizabeth could only nod as she shivered in her wet clothes.

'Here,' he said, handing her one of the horse blankets. 'You had better wrap yourself in this.'

Elizabeth, unwilling to admit she had been frightened by the intensity of the storm, the likes of which she had never before encountered, could not stop her teeth chattering.

'I think you might have to remove your dress,' Tomas said. 'You will never get warm if you stay wet. I shall look away. Please do not fear for your modesty.'

Elizabeth's fingers were stiff and clumsy with cold and trembled as she tried to undo the buttons of her bodice. Tomas, true to his word, had turned away and was busy shaking out the other blanket and laying it on the shelf.

She cleared her throat. 'Actually, I wonder if you might help me with this,' she said. 'My fingers will not do my bidding.'

Their eyes met, and from being freezing mere moments ago, heat began to rise up from deep within her. She held his gaze with a bold look.

'Anything you desire, *mi corazon*.' Tomas's blue eyes darkened as he unbuttoned her, his fingers lingering on the chemise beneath. 'I think this will have to be removed as well,' he said.

Elizabeth looked down, seeing that the fine linen lawn was soaked sheer to her skin. 'I think it will,' she said, swallowing, for her throat was suddenly parched. 'Perhaps,' she said, shocked at her boldness, 'you might help with that too?'

'*Si, señorita*,' he murmured, easing the fabric of the chemise over her shoulders. He then bent down and picked her up, taking her by surprise, before placing her on the sleeping shelf. Her legs dangled uselessly in mid-air. 'Your stockings . . .' he gestured, unlacing her boots and pulling them gently from her feet.

'Indeed. They are wet too,' she gasped.

It was Tomas's turn for trembling hands, and Elizabeth could see them shake as he reached up through her skirts, his fingers encountering the tender flesh at the top of her stockings. He gently unrolled the sodden silk, revealing first a pale kneecap and then a slim ankle and then repeated his actions with the other stocking. He bent his head and began to trail kisses from her instep to her knee. Her head spun. Had she taken leave of her senses?

Tomas suddenly ceased his worship of her legs and, placing his hands firmly about her waist, pulled her down from the shelf. She stood, facing him, her eyes searching his face. He lifted one hand to caress her cheek. Elizabeth ached for the feel of his lips, and raised her chin, yearning. As he bent and kissed her, she fancied she could smell the scent of a pine forest in summer, warm and sweet and richly resinous. Time seemed to stand still as they drank each other in, tasting, marvelling at the softness . . .

After a while, Tomas unfastened her skirts, letting them puddle on the ground, before fumbling with his boots and breeches and letting them drop too. Wearing only his shirt, he picked her up and settled her on the shelf again, then climbed up to join her. The storm continued its thunderous fury as they lay on the blanket, chest to chest, each feeling the beat of the other's heart. Slowly, gently, he began to caress her, starting with her shoulders and then tracing a line down over her breasts and down to the core of her. Elizabeth felt released. Released from shame or self-consciousness. Released from the moral strictures of society, from those who would seek to judge her. All that mattered was that she was here, in this dark shepherd's hut with Tomas, whom she loved like no other. She surrendered herself completely to him, no thought of anything other than that moment.

Chapter Thirty-two

London, Summer 2017

Anna noticed Ed as soon as she stepped into the small paved courtyard of the beer garden. He was waiting at a wooden picnic table that backed onto a wall overgrown with trailing *campanula* – bellflowers – that needed a trim, she thought absent-mindedly. He stood up as he noticed her.

'Anna!' He seemed extremely happy to see her; with nothing of the standoffishness of British men that she'd been led to expect was the norm. 'So pleased you could make it. What would you like to drink? Pimm's perhaps?'

'That sounds nice.' She had a vague idea what Pimm's was, though she'd never actually tried it. It sounded appealing.

He was wearing a crisp, pale-blue shirt and faded jeans, and even Anna, who had almost given up noticing such things, thought how well they matched his eyes. She moved closer to greet him and inhaled his aftershave: wintergreen and spice. Delicious.

'So, your daughter . . .' she said, sitting opposite him.

'At home with a babysitter.'

'And your wife? Is she coming too?'

There was a pause.

'She's dead.'

'Oh my goodness, I'm so sorry.' Her hand flew to her mouth. 'How stupid of me.'

'You weren't to know,' he said, reassuring her. 'And don't be sorry. She left me with Ella, and she's absolutely the best thing that ever happened to me.' He gave her a wry grin. 'As Matisse said, "There are always flowers for those that want to see them."'

'What a lovely sentiment. But you must have been a child bridegroom,' she replied, trying to lighten the situation.

He grinned. 'We met at the beginning of my final year at Cambridge; Ella was on the way by the end of it. Sometimes you just know and that's all there is to it. Now, let's sort you out with a drink.'

Ed went to the bar and Anna watched the other customers in the pub. Almost all of them seemed to have recently knocked off from work. Ties were loosened, jackets hung off the back of chairs. Large glasses of ale were being chugged. The air was filled with the sound of voices relieved to have put the grind of the day behind them.

'Here you are.' Ed put a tall, fruity-looking drink, filled with cucumber and mint, down in front of her and placed a pint on the table for himself. 'I hope you didn't feel steamrollered into this. Hal can be quite imperious when he wants to. He's always trying to set me up . . . Not that I mind in your case at all, of course,' he added hurriedly.

So, Dr Graham *had* persuaded him into bringing her. Her spirits tumbled.

'Oh golly, now it's my turn to put my foot in it? That didn't come out sounding right, it wasn't what I meant at all. How could I possibly mind being accompanied by a beautiful Aussie girl? Forget I said anything. Anyway, how was your day?'

He looked so contrite that Anna couldn't help but smile. 'I can't believe how many people there were out and about today,' she said. 'Pall Mall was absolutely heaving. And I barely even got close to the palace railings. But Green Park was lovely, though it was odd to see deckchairs on the lawns – I thought they were only for beaches. They were very popular with sunbathers, though.'

'Tourist season. Don't worry, it goes back to a manageable crush by September.'

'I feel like a country hick. It was exhausting.' She smiled to let him know she wasn't complaining too much.

'Speaking of the country, what are your plans for visiting Cornwall?'

'Well, I thought I'd get the train down tomorrow and spend the weekend there. Did I mention there's someone I'm trying to track down?' Anna took a sip of her drink. 'Oh, that's delicious!' she exclaimed.

'Good!' he beamed. 'Now, carry on. Who are you looking for?'

'There's a woman – Florence Deverell. She's the last surviving relative of the Trebithicks. I reckon there's a connection between the sketchbook and Trebithick Hall, because of the photo.'

'Yes, yes of course. How fascinating. Do you know where she lives?'

'If the telephone directory is correct, there's an FE Deverell living in Trevone – is that how you pronounce it? It's pretty close to Trebithick Hall, I think; well, according to Google Maps, anyway. I'm pretty sure it's her. I can't reach her on the phone, but I wrote to her before I left.'

'I know Trevone, and yes, that's exactly how you say it. A lovely bay. Great walks. We went there on a geography field trip when I was at prep school, if I remember correctly. I'll mention it to Hal when I see him; it might help him shed more light on the sketchbook.'

'Thanks, that would be great.'

They talked some more about Cornwall, and then Ed drained his glass and looked at his watch. 'I think we should probably get over there before all the food's gone; botanists are a hungry lot, not to mention the ground staff.'

The sounds of a string quartet floated on the air and the scent of flowers was borne on the breeze towards them as they approached a large marquee set up adjoining The Orangery. A crowd of people, the women looking like butterflies in pale-coloured, fluttering summer dresses, the men in blazers or pastel shirt sleeves, had gathered on the lawn, the twilight casting long shadows on the grass. There was even a straw boater or two.

It looked to Anna like a quintessentially English garden party. Which of course it was. She tried not to be too intimidated.

There was more Pimm's, and Champagne, and elderflower cordial. Anna found another glass of Pimm's – with what seemed like half a fruit bowl added to it – pressed into her hand as Ed, a guiding hand at her back, escorted her into the melee.

'This is my colleague, Nigel. Dr Nigel Hawking, Miss Anna Jenkins.'

A professorial-looking man wearing a striped bow tie and a waistcoat gave Anna a small bow and took her hand. 'Delighted,' he said to her. 'What an attractive couple you make. Ed, where did you find such a charming young woman?'

Anna blushed furiously. She wasn't used to being complimented; it must be the dress, she decided. The sooner she was back in trousers, the better.

'She's visiting us from Down Under.'

Nigel raised his eyebrows.

'And has brought with her rather a fascinating collection of botanical illustrations.'

'How wonderful,' he said, looking at her with possibly even more interest than he had before.

'Nigel's a keeper at the Economic Botany Collection,' Ed explained.

'We've been collecting medicinal plants at Kew since the 1820s – there are over twenty thousand specimens. Did you know that it was Kew that helped pioneer research into antimalarial medicine? All from various species of cinchona bark.'

'How interesting,' said Anna, a little put off by his intense stare, but then realised he was looking beyond her to an approaching waitress with a tray of canapés.

'Oh delicious, quail's eggs,' he said, snaffling several before continuing, spraying crumbs of food at Anna as he spoke. 'Botanical medicine is where it's at. There's a wealth of material out there and we don't know the half of it. We're at the forefront of identifying plant compounds that can help treat any number of diseases, from cancers to heart conditions. Alkaloids are particularly fascinating. It's not all just pretty flowers here, you know.'

'Apologies, Nigel, but we shouldn't monopolise you,' Ed interrupted. 'I think the Director is over there . . .'

Nigel's bushy eyebrows beetled up as he looked in the direction Ed was pointing. 'Oh quite, quite,' he said and scurried over to where the head of the Gardens was standing.

'Sorry about that, he gets a bit carried away. The man could go on for hours,' Ed apologised.

'Not at all,' said Anna. 'But thanks anyway.'

'Hello there!' A tall man with a stoop and wildly dishevelled hair nearly tripped over as he approached them. His pinstriped suit looked rumpled and smelled vaguely musty, as if it spent most of its time balled up in a cupboard.

'Anna, this is my colleague, Dr Thomas.'

'Oh, Albert, please.' The man grinned at her as he pushed his hair out of his eyes and focused on her.

Anna smiled back.

'Work in the city, do you?' he asked Anna.

'Er . . .' Anna looked at him in confusion.

'No, she's visiting from Australia,' said Ed. 'Not one of your plant-loving bankers I'm afraid, Albert.'

'Oh. Pity. I'd heard there were a few coming. They're all plant collectors these days – it's the new art, or wine, or . . . something,' he said in a confiding tone. 'Mad about *galanthus* – snowdrops, that is. And saguaro cactus. Some of them even have security guards and insurance, can you imagine? Thought I might be able to talk one of them into some sponsorship. If I can find them, that is.'

'Good luck with that,' said Ed, as he steered Anna towards the centre of the tent. It was a warm night and as Anna finished her glass she suddenly felt light-headed. 'Do you think we might sit for a bit?' she asked. 'Those Pimm's are stronger than they look.'

'Of course,' Edwin was solicitous. 'Why don't I find us some food? Sit here,' he said guiding her to a bench, 'and I'll be right back.'

Anna sank onto the seat. The air was still balmy, despite the sun lowering in the sky. Twilight in England seemed to go on for hours, like a guest reluctant to leave a party. She loved the day's slow drawing to a close, but as she glanced over towards the gates of the Gardens, she noticed thunderclouds gathering overhead.

'Jenkins?'

'Mm?' Anna looked up to see Edwin standing before her carrying two plates of food heaped with a variety of salads. 'I wasn't sure what you'd like, so I got a bit of everything.'

Anna was touched at how he was looking after her. 'Really, you are very kind, but you don't have to babysit me all evening.'

'But what if I want to?' he said, earnestly, the Labrador look back on his face. 'You can't get rid of me that easily,' he added.

'Oh, well in that case . . .' She gratefully took a plate from him and made space on the bench for him to sit beside her.

'Do you know, I've been thinking,' said Ed, between mouthfuls. 'You might want a car when you're down in Cornwall – I wouldn't chance trying to rely on the local bus system there; it's close to non-existent.'

'Oh,' said Anna, 'okay. I'll look into it. Do you think I should hire a car when I'm down there, or drive from London?'

'Well, actually . . . I'm not doing much this weekend. I could drive you down. Only if you want, that is,' he said tentatively.

Anna hadn't the heart to extinguish the look of hope in his eyes. Besides, she would be happy to have the chance to spend more time with him. Very happy, in fact.

'But what about Ella?'

'It's her cousin's birthday party this weekend. She'd have a pink fit if she missed that. My sister will be glad to have her – Ella and her cousins are more like siblings. I've had to rely on her a lot, since my wife . . . you know.'

'Well, only if you're sure.'

'Honestly? I'd welcome the chance to get out of the city on such a stifling weekend and see the place again – it's beautiful down there, there's a special magic. The coastline is so wild and unspoiled. The beaches even compare favourably with Australian ones, so I'm led to believe. And besides, there's clotted cream and pasties and real ale – what's not to like?'

'You've convinced me,' said Anna, laughter catching in her throat as a flash and a loud rumble sounded overhead.

'Oh heavens,' said Ed. 'Quick, we'd better get out of here before we get drenched.' They put down their nearly empty plates and fled in the direction of the marquee. The other guests had a similar idea and soon the open tent was a mass of people sheltering from the coming storm. Everyone carried on their conversations, shouting to be heard over each other, and the noise was soon deafening. Waiters did their best to thread their way through the crowd, but there was the inevitable smash of broken glass as someone backed into a full tray of drinks. Ed caught Anna's eye. 'Shall we get out of here?' he yelled.

'Okay,' she said, leaning in to him and, as she did so, catching again the scent of his cologne. 'Where to?'

'If we leg it now, we might be able to pick up a cab before the worst of it hits. Sorry, I didn't bring a brolly.' Ed grabbed her hand and pulled her towards the gates. 'Follow me.'

At that moment there was another huge clap of thunder and fat, heavy raindrops began to spatter the ground, lightly at first, then, within seconds, turning to a deluge, soaking Anna and Ed. Anna's blue dress stuck to her skin, plastering itself to her legs, and she gathered up her skirt to make it easier to run. Water streamed down her face, making star points of her eyelashes and dripping off her chin. She began to giggle at the absurdity of it and Ed joined in, his baritone ringing out over the sound of the rain. A cab, its light blinking orange, came around the bend and Ed hailed it.

'Look at you: wetter than an otter's pocket,' said Ed as they bundled in, which only made Anna laugh even more, and she shook the tendrils of damp hair from her eyes, hiccoughing with giggles.

'I'm what?'

'Soggy as a sandwich. Damp as a squib.'

Another giggle rose irrepressibly within her.

'There you are . . .' he said, tucking a wayward strand of hair from her ear and gazing into her eyes. 'I knew I'd find you eventually.'

Any formality that had been between them was washed away by the mutual soaking, and Anna's insides turned to liquid. She barely recognised the feeling. It was very much like happiness. How could she have forgotten that the world was capable of delivering such uncomplicated joy?

She looked down. Ed was still holding her hand.

Chapter Thirty-three

Valparaiso, 1887

'You can do your work here. There are enough plants to last a lifetime,' said Tomas, curling a lock of her hair about his finger. He looked so earnest; Elizabeth's heart went out to him. The storm still thundered outside the dank and dim hut, but they lay cosy and warm beneath their cover of rough blankets. She snuggled closer into his arms, still not quite believing that they lay, skin to skin, all boundaries crossed. She had never been this intimate with another person, never imagined such tenderness, such joy. She delighted in the silky feel of his skin against her own, the lean planes of his muscular body . . . it had been enough to make her lose her senses, but she was completely unrepentant. She finally felt like a woman, and hugged the mysterious discovery of such pleasure to herself. Another secret to be kept from the world.

And now, they were discussing her future. Tomas had declared that he could never live without her, would not live without her. Elizabeth readily agreed with him, but despite everything they had just shared, she held back from explaining her true purpose in Chile. Her father had been so insistent that she not tell a soul, and she didn't want to break a promise she'd made at his deathbed. It would be dishonouring his memory somehow.

'You will marry me,' he stated, as if it were already decided.

'Oh, will I just?' replied Elizabeth teasing him but at the same time a little piqued at his assumption that she would simply fall in with his plans. 'Well, that is a fine way to ask a woman to be your wife.'

He was instantly contrite. 'I apologise, *cariño*. I did not mean to sound so imperious, but you must know that this is our way in Chile. I will try again.' He looked tenderly into her eyes. 'Elizabeth, *mi amor*, would you honour me by becoming my wife?'

Elizabeth's eyes glittered as a sudden rush of emotion overtook her. Was it the right thing to do? She had never particularly wanted to find herself married, a man's wife, his possession, never desired it, but somehow this – Tomas – was different. He was no starch-fronted, pompous Englishman, but a beauteous being of sweet flesh and hot blood, a man who made her feel more alive than she'd ever imagined it possible to be. She hungered for him, his nakedness, even when he was no more than arm's reach from her and she could no more resist him than iron filings a magnet. She nodded in response as he gathered her into his arms and kissed her until they were both breathless once more.

Eventually they slept. The rain continued to drum on the roof, and they woke much later as the first fingers of dawn found their way through the cracks in the walls. Elizabeth stirred, not wanting the day to come, for the light to take away the intimacy of the night. She smiled to herself as she remembered Tomas's proposal. Heavens! What was she going to do? He was correct, in that there were enough plants in the region to keep her sketchbook filled for years to come, and though she missed home, it would never be the same there without her dear papa. She must write to her sister and tell her – Georgiana would be as shocked as Elizabeth herself was. She wondered if there was already a tiny niece or nephew sleeping in the family bassinet at Trebithick Hall. And Daisy: what would Daisy do? She could hardly expect her maid to stay on in Valparaiso indefinitely, but she would be devastated to lose her. And what of the Devil's Trumpet? Of her promise to unearth it and bring it back to Mr Ormond at the Royal Botanic Gardens in Kew? Perhaps she might persuade Daisy to stay a little longer, until she had time to return to the Valley of the Palms, and then give her the plant to transport safely to England. She could trust Daisy with the secret. Of course, it would mean having to say goodbye to her forever – she very much doubted she would be able to persuade her maid to make the journey back to Chile again – but she would thus fulfil her father's dying wish.

Resolved, she shook Tomas awake. 'My love.' She almost blushed at the unfamiliar words but liked the way they sounded.

'The storm is over. We must return to the *estancia*. Heaven only knows what your sister must think of me, staying out all night unchaperoned.'

Tomas stretched lazily. 'Do not be concerned. She will have seen the storm and guessed that we would seek shelter. Nevertheless, we should get back. For I have much to prepare.'

'Prepare?' asked Elizabeth.

'For the woman who is to become my wife. Do you think I want to wait a moment longer than is necessary?' he asked, gathering her to him and kissing her with renewed passion.

Dressed in clothes that were much the worse for wear, still damp and now smelling strongly of sheep, Elizabeth ventured outside. Trees had been blown to the ground, their bare roots extending skywards, but more worryingly, only one of the horses remained. Tomas was unperturbed. 'She will have bolted for home,' he said. 'Come, we can ride together on this one. We will have to be bareback; one saddle will not be comfortable for both of us. Are you up to it?'

Elizabeth grinned at him. 'Of course. I used to sneak out and ride the horses at home when I was little. Never bothered with a saddle.'

'May you continue to surprise me, *corazon*.'

Elizabeth loved the feeling of riding behind Tomas, her arms gripped tightly around his waist, and was almost sorry when they reached the path that led to the *estancia*. In the distance she could make out a tall, dark figure walking towards them.

'Father!' Tomas called out as they approached.

'Oh good lord,' muttered Elizabeth, aware of her dishevelment.

'I did not expect you back so soon,' said Tomas.

'I finished my business in Santiago earlier than I thought. I was lucky to miss the storm but it does not look as though you were so fortunate.'

Tomas laughed. 'Indeed. We sheltered in the old hut along the Valle de Casablanca.'

'Very good,' his father replied.

'But I am forgetting myself,' Tomas said as he dismounted and then helped Elizabeth down. 'May I present *Señorita* Elizabeth Bligh. She has been staying in Valparaiso, arrived on the *Corcovado* some several weeks ago. She is an artist of great talent. Elizabeth, this is my father, *Señor* Mateo Flores.'

Elizabeth noted that he did not introduce her as his intended bride, and for that she was thankful. One thing at a time.

'*Señor*,' she said, embarrassed, 'I must apologise for my bedraggled state.'

Tomas's father brushed away her concerns. 'It is a pleasure to meet you, my dear. I am happy that you are safe. Sofia informed me that the two of you had ventured out yesterday and not returned. Please, don't let me keep you, for I am sure you wish to put on some dry garments.' He turned to Tomas. 'Son, we have much to discuss. Not least of which is that you ventured out unaccompanied with a young lady. I hope you have not caused irreparable damage to her good reputation.'

Elizabeth didn't want to stay to hear any more and hurried towards the house, where Daisy was waiting for her.

'Oh, Elizabeth, I was so worried for you. What a terrible storm. You must have been sorely frightened.'

'I'm fine, Daisy,' Elizabeth reassured her. 'Look at me, no harm came to me.'

Daisy looked closely at her but did not comment on the sparkle in Elizabeth's eyes or the flush in her cheeks. 'Well, let me draw a hot bath for you and see if I can get the mud out of that gown. It will need a good brushing, that's for certain.'

'So will my hair, Daisy,' laughed Elizabeth, running her fingers through her tangled locks.

Once Elizabeth had bathed and dressed in clean clothes, Daisy brought her breakfast. She devoured the hot coffee and warm rolls, slathering the bread with a sweet, thick jam, before spooning up some of the *olla*, a type of meat stew that she had become quite accustomed to, even at breakfast time. 'No dinner last night,' she mumbled to Daisy through a mouthful.

As she ate every last crumb, she pondered her situation. She wished her sister were there to consult with, for she would have welcomed her wise counsel. She would write to her, but decided to wait until things were a little more settled. She still couldn't quite believe it herself – was she really to be married? Was this insanity brought on by a night spent out in the elements in a foreign land? Would Tomas's father agree to such a match?

Several months ago she would have vehemently denied she could ever fall in love, let alone so suddenly, but then several months ago she had not imagined a man like Tomas.

By dinner that evening, Elizabeth had begun to fret. She had not seen Tomas all day and feared that she might have imagined the events of the previous night. That he might have changed his mind or, quite possibly, that his father might have changed it for him. She almost confided in Daisy, but became suddenly superstitious about mentioning Tomas's proposal to anyone, at least until he had discussed the matter with his father, and once a suitable ring was on her finger. 'Keep still, please Miss Elizabeth,' Daisy pleaded as she fastened her bodice. The ivory dress was affixed with tiny seed pearls at the neck and sleeves and featured a row of pearl buttons down the back. The material itself was embroidered with several of the plants and flowers that grew in the gardens at Trebithick – wisteria and fern, passionflower and ivy. It had been made for her just before her father died and she had not yet had occasion to wear it.

'I'm sorry,' she apologised. 'I am unsettled and out of sorts. Are we nearly finished?'

'Yes, all done,' Daisy replied, standing back to look at her mistress.

'Thank you. I do not wish to keep Tomas's father waiting. I fear he got quite the poor impression of me this morning and I must do whatever I can to repair it.'

Elizabeth entered the dining room to see Sofia, Tomas and their father standing looking out over the valley, deep in conversation.

Mateo turned at the slight sound Elizabeth's shoes had made on the stone floor. 'My dear, there you are. My son was not mistaken, you are indeed a beauty!' he said, giving her a warm smile.

'Now I am cleaned up again, *Señor*,' Elizabeth replied.

He laughed in response. 'A little bit of dust and dirt never harmed anyone, but yes, in your case, I can see you all the better for the lack of it about your person.'

Tomas moved to her side, taking her hand. 'I have been speaking to my father about you,' he said, giving it a reassuring squeeze.

Elizabeth looked up at him, her heart skipping a beat as she gazed into his blue eyes. She hadn't imagined it, then – he really did love her with the same unquestioned devotion that she did him.

'It seems we should be congratulating you both,' said Sofia, coming over to embrace her. 'Tomas has told us that you intend to marry. While it is sudden indeed, I cannot think of anyone I should like more as a sister-in-law.'

'Oh,' Elizabeth gasped, 'he has shared the news already. I find it all a little hasty myself, but I could not be happier. That is most kind of you, Sofia. And yes,' she glanced sidelong at Tomas again, 'he has convinced me to stay in Chile and be his wife.' After a beat, she added, 'Of course, I am honoured to be welcomed into such a warm and highly respected family.'

'I am very pleased,' said Tomas's father. 'You both have my blessing. Tomas tells me that your father and mother are no longer living.'

'Yes, that is right. I have only a sister; she resides with her husband in the county of Cornwall.'

'Tomas also tells me that you both wish to be married as soon as possible, is that correct? Though I cannot understand the rush, he has convinced me of his intentions. I certainly have no wish to stand in your way.'

Elizabeth was confused. Though she and Tomas had discussed being married in very general terms, they had not talked about a ceremony or a date. 'Well . . .' she began, playing for time. 'If that is what Tomas wants, then who am I to tarry?'

'Good, good. We shall have the celebration in Valparaiso. In what, say a month from now? Will that give you enough time to make the appropriate arrangements?'

Elizabeth's head spun. Was she really to be married in four short weeks?

Chapter Thirty-four

London and Cornwall, Summer 2017

When she woke up, Anna just had time to call her mother – it was late evening in Sydney – 'Yes, I'm fine, Mum. No, I don't have any more information yet. I should know more by next week,' she reassured her. 'Sorry but I've got to rush. I'm on my mobile anyway and it costs a fortune from here. Don't forget to water my plants. Love you.' As she rang off – feeling only a brief pang of homesickness – a horn sounded outside. She opened the window and peered down to the street to see that a dark-green sports car had pulled up in the middle of the road. She hurried down the stairs, dragging her suitcase behind her, saying a quick goodbye to her host before tumbling out of the front door just as the horn sounded again. A long arm extended from the car window, waving on a car that had stopped behind him, and then saluted her as she appeared. Ed hopped out and lifted her suitcase into the boot. 'Jenkins! All set?'

'Yep, I reckon so.' A frisson of excitement ran through her as his eyes met hers.

'Good. An early start will see us miss most of the city traffic,' he said, confidently easing the car onto a main road. 'It's a bit of a hike to get down there, at least four hours, maybe five.'

Anna laughed. 'That's nothing,' she said. 'A day trip.'

'Yes, well I forgot that you're probably used to travelling further. I took the liberty of booking us into a pub down there, not far from Trevone. It's nothing flash, but it's got a few rooms and the grub's supposed to be not too bad either.'

Anna nodded in thanks. 'Gosh, you are organised; I was going to wing it and see where I ended up. I'm really very grateful. It makes the trip a lot less daunting, having some company. Was Ella okay with you going away?'

'She was so excited about spending the weekend with her cousins that me not being there hardly registered. I'll call her tonight, though. We've become a pretty tight team since her mum died.'

'Was it long ago?' Anna ventured, stealing a glance at him.

'Five years. An age, but then again no time at all.'

Anna knew exactly what he meant.

'Ella still talks about her a lot; she was seven when Lucy died. Cancer. Very sudden. Harder on us, but a release for Lucy. I hated seeing her suffer.' Ed fell silent.

'Shall we talk about something else?' said Anna gently.

'Like why you're wearing peacocks on your legs?' he asked, his lips twisting in an amused grin.

Anna looked down at her tights, which were indeed vibrant shades of blue and purple. 'My sister gave them to me. She's got a thing for activewear. I thought they'd be comfy for the drive,' she said, protesting at the incredulous look on his face.

'I'll have to warn you, you might give the natives heart failure, Jenkins. I don't think Cornishmen are used to activewear, whatever it is.'

'And you won't?' she said, indicating his khaki shorts, brogues and fawn ankle socks.

'Oh no, absolutely not. This is the national dress of the British male in summertime, if you don't mind.' He looked at her out of the corner of his eye, as if assessing how seriously she took his comments.

'I stand corrected,' she laughed again. 'And the British female?'

'Well, obviously not peacock leggings. No. A twinset. A twinset and pearls. Even with shorts,' he said teasing her further.

'Now I know you're pulling my leg.'

'Quite possibly. You'll have to find out for yourself.'

Ed continued to amuse her with his descriptions of the various types of Englishmen she was likely to encounter on her travels, and by the time they pulled up at a slate-roofed, whitewashed pub several hours later, Anna's sides ached from laughter. As they drove deeper into the countryside she'd noticed with alarm that the roads narrowed until they became barely wide enough for a single car to drive along, let alone pass another coming in the opposite direction. The first time they did meet a vehicle,

Ed good-naturedly backed up until he reached a passing place. She held her breath as the other car inched past.

At the pub, she climbed out of the car and stretched her legs. The sky was blue, the air warm on her face and clean-smelling, and birds chirruped softly from nearby hedgerows. It was pretty much a perfect summer's day.

'Are you hungry? Shall we see if they're still serving lunch?'

'You bet.'

They walked through the pub's front door, Ed ducking his head to avoid the low-set lintel. The pub was busy – it was a Saturday lunchtime, if a little late – but Anna found a table by a window and before long Ed returned with two pints. 'Doom Bar. Local. Named after a treacherous sandbank near here. I think you'll like it. The beer that is, not the sandbank.'

'Cheers,' she said, raising her glass.

'Here's to mysterious missions,' he replied.

'Indeed. How far away did you say Trebithick Hall was from here?' Anna's stomach flip-flopped at the thought of seeing the house from the photograph in person, of touching its walls and imagining the people in the photograph living there.

'Just past the next village. We'll check our bags and then head over after we've eaten.'

They both ordered pasties from the bar menu, and fell upon them as soon as they arrived. 'Did you know they originated as food for the miners to take to work with them in the tin mines of Cornwall?'

Anna shook her head, her mouth full of pastry.

'They say a good pasty can survive being dropped down a mine shaft.'

Anna gripped hers tightly. She was too hungry to risk dropping it anywhere. They ate quickly, neither of them leaving more than a few crumbs, and then Anna went to the bar to order them another drink while Ed spoke to the landlord. 'We're in the two rooms at the far end, up the stairs and along the corridor,' he said when she returned to the table. 'He's given me the keys – I'll take our bags up.'

'Thanks for organising all this,' Anna said.

'Stop thanking me. You've done me a favour too – I don't get out of London often enough. I'd almost forgotten how lovely it is down here. And I'm as intrigued as you to find out more about the photo and its connection to the sketchbook. Let's finish these and then we'll go.'

~

Less than an hour later they were standing outside the imposing façade of Trebithick Hall. 'It's *just* like in the photograph,' Anna said, fumbling in her bag for the picture.

'Absolutely!' he said as she handed it to him. 'Only the rhododendron is much larger. Quite a remarkable specimen.'

It was – towering over them at the front of the drive and wreathed in vibrant scarlet blossom. The house was high on a hill overlooking the fishing port of Padstow, which they'd driven through on their way to the house. Even from this distance Anna could hear the screech of seagulls as they wheeled over the stone harbour front, scavenging for scraps.

'Well, it's open to the public, so let's go and have a look then.'

As Anna and Ed joined several people wandering along the drive they heard an announcement that a tour would start in a few minutes' time.

'Good afternoon, ladies and gentlemen,' said a portly man who appeared from the gloom of the house. 'Today you are visiting one of the finest houses in Cornwall. Dating back to the 1750s, Trebithick Hall was home for many years to the Trebithick family, landowners of these parts. The estate originally spread over several hundred acres, stretching right down to the sea. Today a mere seventy-five acres make up the Trust's holdings,' he continued, in a sing-song rustic burr. 'Though the house dates back to Georgian times, the stables were constructed much later, in the nineteenth century.'

There was a murmur from the crowd standing around him.

'One of its most famous occupants was Sir John Trebithick, a Victorian plantsman who made many dangerous expeditions across the globe to collect the hundreds of specimens you see thriving here today in the gardens.'

Anna looked at Ed with wide eyes. It really was all true. She could scarcely believe it.

'The gardens are particularly fascinating, and a program to restore them to their original splendour is almost completed. Later, you can visit the formal garden, where there is a particularly fine example of a late-Victorian sundial in cast bronze.' He cleared his throat before continuing. 'I'm also very pleased to be able to tell you that the replanted woodland walk is now open to the public for the first time in fifty years.'

He ushered them inside. The air was several degrees colder than outside and Anna shivered. She found herself in a grand entrance hall, its oak-panelled walls hung with dark oil paintings.

'In the hallway you will see portraits of Sir John and his wife, Augusta, who, sadly, died shortly after childbirth. But we will not linger, for there is much to discover. Come with me and we will continue to the green sitting room . . .' Anna couldn't hide a gasp as she heard the name Augusta – the same as Granny Gus . . . Her mind began to spin. It was no coincidence, of that she was certain.

She looked closely at the portrait of Sir John. He was painted with a plant in his hand, a globe behind him and a gun dog, its ears pricked with alertness, at his feet. He looked like a formidable man. She then turned towards the portrait of Lady Augusta. A young woman gazed steadily back at her, blonde hair piled high and wearing a blue silk dress that dipped low over her shoulders before tapering to a tightly laced bodice. Apart from the costume, it was like looking into a mirror. Anna's heart thumped in her chest and she heard a roar in her ears. The painting began to swim before her eyes.

'Jenkins? Anna! Are you okay?'

She heard Ed's voice as if through a tunnel, and her knees buckled beneath her.

Chapter Thirty-five

Valparaiso, 1887

The wedding was a small one. Elizabeth had no family, and only a few friends in Valparaiso. Daisy, Mr and Mrs Campbell and Sibyl and Mrs Gordon were among the handful of guests from her side.

Before her nuptials, Elizabeth had written to Georgiana with her news. 'I know you will be most surprised, but I pray you will be happy for me, dear sister. I for my part pray that you are also well and happy.' She received a letter that must have crossed paths with her own, with Georgiana's news of a son, George John Trebithick Deverell, born healthy and named, in part, after their father. She was happy to hear of his safe arrival, and her sister's good health following the birth.

Mr Chegwidden had left for Santiago shortly after the fiesta and had not been seen since. Elizabeth was relieved that he was not to be on the list of attendees, but she couldn't help but wonder if he had yet discovered the Devil's Trumpet. It was surely only a matter of time before he did.

Tomas, too, had wanted little fuss, and managed to overcome the objections of his father, who had wished to invite all of his friends, acquaintances and business partners. Tomas agreed, however, to a party a week or so later at his father's home. By a stroke of good fortune, Mr Williamson and Mr Windsor had returned to Valparaiso from Santiago and were also invited to the short service in the Iglesia de San Francisco and the dinner, which was to be held afterwards.

Mrs Campbell had helped Elizabeth consult a dressmaker, who had been able to procure a bolt of white silk and had worked day and night to finish the gown, which had a boned bodice, puffed sleeves and a short train at the back. Sofia had lent her a lace mantilla.

Tomas favoured traditional dress, and as she entered the church on Mr Campbell's arm, with Daisy ahead of her as a bridesmaid, Elizabeth saw him, resplendent in tight-fitting black trousers and a short black jacket with a white silk shirt underneath. A brightly coloured poncho embroidered with scarlet roses sat across his shoulders. Atop his head was a broad-brimmed black hat with a bright-coloured trim. She had never seen him look so handsome and he fairly took her breath away as she walked towards the altar. She felt a brief pang of sadness that her sister could not be there to see her, but she was sure that her dear papa was looking down from heaven, smiling. Even as she planned to make vows to another man, she would not forget her promise to her father.

The service was in Spanish, but she had picked up enough since her arrival to understand most of what was being said, and knew when to say '*Si*' at the appropriate, important moments. It was also necessary for their union to be formally recognised by a judge, which they had done the previous day (she had signed her assumed surname with scarcely a pang of conscience), but for Elizabeth, it was only after the church ceremony that she felt truly married.

The service took place in the late afternoon and the sun was casting shadows across the plaza as they emerged. Elizabeth stood, arm in arm with Tomas. Her husband. Tomas's eyes searched hers as if to reassure himself of her happiness and she grinned broadly back at him. She could barely believe it; she was married. To a man she loved with all of her heart.

Her father-in-law was to host a dinner for the newlyweds and so the small party climbed aboard coaches for the short ride to his Valparaiso residence.

Later, as she and Tomas sat at the long dining table, the room lit by candles, Elizabeth looked around, seeing everyone laughing and talking, eating and drinking. She noticed Daisy, looking quite striking in a midnight-blue silk gown that Elizabeth had lent her, smiling at something Mr Williamson had said, and wondered if perhaps a romance might now augment their friendship. Though she cared for Daisy's happiness, she was not certain how she felt about such a prospect. Selfishly, she did not wish to lose her maid and companion, and certainly not before she had entrusted her to undertake her vital mission.

In between fittings for her gown and the almost continuous round of luncheons and dinners, Elizabeth had immersed herself in her sketching and painting. She barely had a moment to consider the consequences of committing to live in Chile for the rest of her days. Now, sudden homesickness curdled in her stomach and she put down the glass she had been holding, no longer caring for the sweet wine. It was unlikely that Tomas could be persuaded to make the voyage to England and she had little desire to make the long, awful journey again herself, certainly not for several years at least.

'Everything all right, *mi corazon*?' Tomas asked, noticing her falter and taking her hand.

'*Si*,' she said. 'I suppose I am feeling a little overawed. My life has changed forever.'

'You have second thoughts?' he asked.

Elizabeth looked into his eyes and her doubts disappeared. 'No, no, not at all,' she said smiling at her new husband.

~

Elizabeth had moved from the Campbells' lodgings to a home provided by Tomas's father in the town. Daisy, of course, came with her and Tomas engaged a cook and a housekeeper. When knowledge of her betrothal became known, Elizabeth had taken Daisy aside and asked her to stay, at least for a few months. 'I do not expect you to stay forever,' Elizabeth told her, 'but I would be so glad of your company a while longer, while I adjust to life as a married woman'. To Elizabeth's relief, Daisy had agreed.

The heat of summer abated and autumn came to the city, bringing cool mornings heavy with mist and shorter days. Elizabeth was free to wander and sketch to her heart's content. She kept close to home, not wanting to venture too far on her own, but she had not forgotten her sighting of the Devil's Trumpet and she plotted a way to return to the Valley of the Palms before winter took hold, when the route would become impassable.

One evening, barely three months after the wedding, Elizabeth winced as Daisy laced her into a gown for dinner.

'Careful, Daisy, I'll not be able to breathe,' she said.

'I'm sorry, but I cannot get the fabric to meet,' replied Daisy, who was hauling on her mistress's corset with both hands.

Elizabeth put her hands around her waist, not believing her maid. But the evidence was unmistakable . . . her waist, normally barely a handspan across, now bulged outwards. She also realised with a shock that it had been weeks, no probably months, since her last bleed. 'Oh Daisy,' she exclaimed. 'Do you think . . .'

Daisy looked at Elizabeth's flushed face and rounded breasts. 'Almost certainly,' she replied.

Elizabeth hugged the knowledge to herself all throughout dinner, waiting to tell Tomas when they were alone. When she broke the news in their bedchamber as they retired for the night, he was delighted, both with her and the fact that he was to become a father. '*Mi corazon*,' he said, caressing her belly under her chemise. 'I could not be a prouder man. Now you must make sure you rest. You have my son there.'

'Of course, Tomas. But I am not a china doll – women have babies all the time.' However, Elizabeth could not help but think of her mother, dying so soon after childbirth, and sent a swift prayer that it would not be her fate.

Elizabeth enjoyed an easy pregnancy, feeling the return of her energy after the early months, and she continued to ride, though never at more than a walking pace. She had not forgotten about the Devil's Trumpet, and made several visits to the Valley of the Palms, but failed to find the plant again. She hid her frustration from Tomas, but, as Damien Chegwidden had not been sighted for some time, with rumours that he had perhaps even left Chile altogether, the immediate threat caused by his presence seemed to have abated.

She was also able to continue her sketching, arranging for a portfolio of her drawings to be sent back to Trebithick on a mail ship that was due to dock at the port in late autumn.

However, her peaceful existence was shattered when, one afternoon, as Tomas joined her for a siesta he mentioned that he had run into Mr Chegwidden. 'He is recently returned from high in the Andes. Said he nearly froze to death; that the snows came much earlier this year.'

Elizabeth was immediately alert. 'Did he mention anything else? Did he discover any of the plants he sought?'

'Mm?'

'Any new plants?' Elizabeth repeated, careful not to let Tomas hear a note of alarm in her voice.

'I think so,' he replied. 'Though I am not certain which they might be.'

Elizabeth lay silently next to him, grinding her teeth in frustration. She had to get the Devil's Trumpet back to England before Mr Chegwidden. She owed it to her father. The following Sunday after church she persuaded Tomas to join her on one final ride to the Valley of the Palms.

'You are very fond of that place aren't you?' he said, an amused smile on his face. 'You know there are other valleys, equally as beautiful.'

'Oh please,' she entreated. 'I do so love it there. It would make me so happy to return before I am great with this child.'

Tomas, who rarely denied her anything, smiled. 'Of course, my darling, if you think you are able. But you are to take the gentlest mount in the stables. And no galloping for you.'

Elizabeth nodded. 'Of course. I wouldn't dream of doing anything else.'

~

The day of the ride was a sunny one, but a breeze blew down from the mountains, keeping them cool in the saddle.

After a couple of hours' slow riding they reached the valley, where Tomas kindled a small fire before boiling water to make matté. Elizabeth found that it revived her when she was weary and gladly accepted the cup when he passed it to her.

While Tomas was busy, she consulted her sketchbook, looking once more for the rough drawing she had made on their first visit; comparing her sketch with the valley before her she calculated that they were only about half a mile from where she had seen the Devil's Trumpet. Now all she needed was the opportunity to slip away from Tomas for a short while. She thrilled with excitement at how close they were, and tamped down feelings of guilt at her deception.

She got her chance when, after they had eaten a snack of *empanadas* and green plums, Tomas lay back on a tuft of thick grass, his arms crossed underneath his head and his hat tipped over his eyes. 'Join me, *corazon*, for you must surely be tired.'

'I am fine,' Elizabeth replied. 'I wish to sketch a while. The plants here are quite different from the ones in town.'

Tomas grumbled. 'Always drawing, always painting . . .' Though his tone was indulgent.

Elizabeth picked up her pencil and pretended to study a small plant that grew on a rocky outcrop nearby. After waiting several minutes, she judged he was asleep and began a casual stroll in the direction of a large palm tree, the same palm tree that featured in her rough map. If Tomas were to awaken it would be a simple matter of explaining that she was searching for new plants to catalogue.

Hurrying towards the site, her father's vasculum over her shoulder, she almost tripped over a tree root, her large belly sending her off-balance. Her heart pounded and she was breathing heavily from the exertion and the subterfuge. Even though she was married, and carrying Tomas's child, she had kept the promise she had made to her father more than a year before, and had told no one, not even her husband, of her mission. The burden of the secret had begun to weigh on her mind and in quieter moments she wondered whether it might be wise to inform Tomas. This was not the time for hesitation, however, and she stopped and looked carefully about her, consulting her sketch once again. The placement of trees was exactly as she had drawn it, so she walked outward in a circle from where she thought she had first seen the plant.

No luck. Again. Nothing that even looked like the white trumpet-shaped flowers.

She glanced back to see if Tomas had stirred and then, thankful that he was a heavy sleeper, she kept searching.

As the minutes ticked by her heart grew heavy. She turned, about to give up and wake Tomas, for the sun was low in the sky and it was long past time for them to return. It was then that a divine scent reached her nostrils. It was the most alluring fragrance she had ever smelled: sweet but not cloying, with a fresh undertone and a lingering spiciness. Like vanilla and jasmine and sweetbriar and sandalwood, but somehow more than all of those. She inhaled deeply, looking for the source of the intoxicating aroma. Two steps further on and then there it was, partly hidden behind an acacia bush. The most beautiful white flowers, petals striped with purple, bloomed along thick green stems. Drawing closer, she saw that the deep purple–black stamens were topped with orange pollen so vibrant it appeared to almost glow in the fading light.

Her hand shook as she donned her riding gloves – she had no desire to risk any harm to herself or her unborn child by allowing her skin to come in contact with any part of the noxious plant. Taking a quick glance to make certain that Tomas was still asleep, she bent down and snapped off one of the flowers, then placed it carefully in the vasculum.

Further along the plant, she saw a number of seed pods. They were just as her father had described: round and prickly, and one of them had split to reveal several small, kidney-shaped seeds. She plucked those too and placed them in a small drawstring bag that she tucked into a pocket of her dress.

Almost swooning from the heady scent, she was startled as she heard Tomas's call. Straightening up, she waved, gathering up her things and hastening towards him.

'*Querida*,' he said, as she reached him, out of breath. 'I was worried. I woke and couldn't see any sign of you. It is nearly dark.'

'My darling, I was not so far away, but yes, it is late and we should make haste.' Elizabeth quickly stowed her sketchbook and gloves in a leather satchel attached to her horse's saddle and then looked to Tomas to help her up. Her growing belly meant that it was harder for her to keep her balance as Tomas boosted her into the saddle, but once she was astride she was quite comfortable. She checked the strap on the vasculum, making sure it was secure across her shoulder.

'I think this is the last time you should ride,' said Tomas as they travelled back along the trail home. 'I wish only for your safety.'

'You are probably right,' she agreed. Further riding expeditions would no longer be a necessity. She felt a small thrill: she had accomplished the first part of her task.

They returned by nightfall, and Elizabeth excused herself from dinner. 'I am rather weary from our excursion today. I think I should retire for the evening. Perhaps you can have Cook send me some supper later?' she asked.

'Of course, my darling, whatever you wish.'

Once in the small dressing room that adjoined their bedchamber, Elizabeth took out the bag containing the seeds, put on her gloves and withdrew the lily from her father's vasculum. She placed it in a jug and began to sketch, working quickly, for she had little time. Dinner would go on for several hours, but often her drawings could take that time and more, and it was important that she made a precise likeness.

Eventually, she was finished and she removed the flower from the jug and pressed it between two pieces of vellum before placing it and her sketchbook in the metal box. She then burrowed to the bottom and lifted the flap to the hidden compartment. The bag of seeds fitted easily inside, next to her mourning jewellery, her mother's silver-backed mirror and the photograph she had brought with her of her and her father at Trebithick, taken not long before he died.

She hid the box in one of her travelling trunks, knowing that neither Tomas nor Daisy was likely to venture there. She would retrieve the bag containing the seeds when she was certain of being undisturbed and find somewhere to dry them out.

She breathed a sigh of relief when everything was carefully stowed away, but she could not rid herself of the sick feeling in her stomach that she was deceiving her husband.

Chapter Thirty-six

Cornwall, Summer 2017

When Anna regained consciousness, she was lying on a chaise in a corner of a very pretty tearoom. There was a small marble-topped table next to her, on which sat a carafe of water and a glass. She lifted her head and looked out onto a walled garden, its lawn divided by neat gravel paths and a low, immaculately pruned hedge. Pink rose bushes bloomed in circular beds, and she stared, dazed, at a stone fountain that was spurting water several feet into the air. She blinked, not knowing for a moment where she was. 'How . . .'

'It's all right, Jenkins. You fainted not long after we went into the house, and I carried you across here.' Ed, who was sitting at the end of the chaise, indicated the tearoom. 'You gave me quite a fright, not to mention causing a kerfuffle with the tour leader. I think he was more put out by your peacock leggings than seeing you keel over next to the precious porcelain, though,' he grinned at her. 'Take it easy, don't try to move until you're ready.' He placed a reassuring hand on her ankle.

'I didn't . . . I didn't break anything, did I?' said Anna.

He had such a concerned, tender look in his eyes that any embarrassment Anna felt dissolved like mist on a sunny morning. She slowly sat up.

'Neither in the house, nor about your person. Now, I've ordered some tea. It'll make you feel better,' he said firmly. 'I think it was the heat that did it. Being so hot outside and then going into that chilly hallway.'

'I'm so sorry. I don't know what happened. One minute I was looking at the painting of Lady Augusta—' She broke off, remembering what she'd seen.

'It's all right,' he reassured her, 'happens to the best of us. 'You know, there *is* quite a similarity between the portrait and you,' he said casually.

'You thought so too?' she said weakly.

He nodded. 'Here, have a glass of water,' he said, reaching over to the table and passing her one. 'You might be dehydrated.'

But she hadn't fainted because of dehydration. She knew the real reason. That woman in the painting – she had to be related to her. She just knew it.

After they finished their tea, Ed suggested a stroll in the gardens. 'Only if you're up to it,' he said. 'If you prefer, we can go back to the pub and you can lie down.'

Anna insisted that she was fully recovered and unlikely to faint again. Nevertheless, he slipped his hand into hers as they walked, saying nothing. She felt a small thrill at his touch, his concern for her.

The gardens were indeed spectacular: lush, green and blazing with summer colour. Anna particularly loved the path to the stables, which was lined with ancient oak trees, their foliage creating a tunnel of green shade through which to walk.

'Rosa Mundi,' said Ed, pausing at a bush heavy with candy-striped bright pink-and-white blooms. 'One of the oldest roses, introduced to Britain before William the Conqueror.'

Anna was once again reminded of how extraordinarily long some plants had been around for, blooming, dying and blooming again across the centuries, seeds scattered on the wind, seedlings divided and shared, sold and replanted in foreign soil.

Their footsteps eventually led them in a large circle, and they reached the formal garden again, coming upon the sundial, a globe that turned on an axis, etched faintly with the countries of the world. 'It reminds me of one in the Botanic Gardens, in Sydney,' she told Ed. She reached out to touch the metal. It was hot in the afternoon sun. As she ran her fingertips over its raised surface, she noticed that the central ring surrounding the globe bore engravings of different herbs. Mint, rosemary, bay, four-leafed clover. 'It's the same engraving as the box!' She stopped and counted them. Thirty-eight in all.

'The box?' asked Ed, confused.

'The box in which the drawings were locked.'

Comprehension dawned on his face. 'Are you sure?'

Anna nodded emphatically. 'Positive.'

'It all makes sense, doesn't it?' he said. 'I think we need to find out more about John Trebithick and his daughters.'

'Daughters? I didn't know he had more than one.'

'I read about them while you were laid out on the chaise. Elizabeth and Georgiana. Georgiana married a Robert Deverell and they lived at Trebithick Hall after John Trebithick's death. They had two children, George and Penelope. Turns out that Penelope died, unmarried, in 1967 and George had a daughter, Florence Elizabeth, who was born in 1935 and is still alive – that'd be your FE Deverell.'

'Elizabeth!' cried Anna. 'ET – the artist.'

'Correct, Jenkins.'

'Was there any other information about her?'

He shook his head.

'Should we go and find the guide, and see if he knows any more?' Anna was seized with a desire to get to the bottom of the mystery as soon as possible – it was so tantalisingly close.

Ed looked at his watch. 'It's after five, so it'll have to wait till tomorrow, I'm afraid.'

'What do we do now?' Anna said, frustration creeping into her voice.

'Steady on. The mystery has waited this long, I think it can stand another day.'

Reluctantly she followed him back to the car, casting a longing glance at the house as they left. When they passed through Padstow, Ed pulled up outside a small deli. 'Won't be a sec,' he said, and disappeared inside. He returned several minutes later and placed two white shopping bags on the back seat, then without a word edged his way back into the traffic that clogged the narrow, winding streets and drove out of town and along a road that wound along the clifftop.

'Are you going to give me any clues?' said Anna, bemused.

He put a finger to his lips. 'It's a secret. Unless, that is, you've had enough of them for one day?'

'I think I might just be able to take one more.' She turned her attention to the scenery flying past: vertiginous rocky cliffs, emerald-green fields with pathways cut across them and weathered stone cottages huddled into folds in the hills. The landscape must have looked this way for centuries.

A few minutes later, Ed pulled over onto a small farm track and parked. 'I think this is the spot,' he said. 'We used to come here from school at the weekends sometimes. Come on.' He reached in the back for the shopping bags and they set off along the path in front of them. 'This is pretty close to Trevone,' he said.

As they began to walk, Anna noticed the wheat fields were studded with poppies, their fragile petals like the crumpled skirts of a scarlet ball gown. The path soon became steep and rocky, with steps cut into the hillside. 'Ladylove Cove. Also known as Lady Luck Cove,' said Ed. 'A popular spot with smugglers, so legend has it.'

'Smugglers?'

'Contraband – rum, more often than not – from Brittany and the Channel Islands. Centuries ago Cornish miners often supplemented their income with smuggling. Made some of them quite wealthy, too. There were also rich pickings from the shipwrecks along this part of the coastline.'

They had reached the end of the steps, and ahead of them was a narrow golden sand cove. Between the steps and the sand was a fast-running stream, which Ed loped across, but even with his long legs he cleared the bank by only a few centimetres.

'Think you can make it?' he said as Anna stood assessing the distance. 'Don't worry, I'll catch you,' he grinned.

She raised her eyebrows at him.

'I've got this,' she said, waiting for him to move. She took a couple of backward steps and then launched herself across the gap, landing neatly on the far side of the bank with plenty of room to spare.

'Impressive, Jenkins.'

'Year six long-jump record holder, St John's Primary,' she said with a smirk.

The aquamarine water glinted and frothed in the late afternoon sunshine as they walked onto the small, deserted beach.

'Oh, what a lovely spot!' Anna cried.

'We aim to please,' Ed gave her a fleeting wink.

She kicked off her sandals and walked to the water's edge, letting out a yelp as it washed over her ankles. 'Christ it's cold!' she called over her shoulder.

'It's the Atlantic, not the balmy South Pacific,' said Ed, laughing at her.

Anna retreated, discouraged by the freezing temperature from venturing further into the water.

They found a spot near a huge driftwood log that had washed up on the beach and Ed began to unpack the carrier bags. 'Supper: cheese, olives, tomatoes, salami, oh, and a baguette and some chocolate,' he said with a flourish. 'And, of course, not forgetting a cheeky bottle of wine,' he said retrieving a bottle of rosé. He had also carried a covered wicker basket with him, and from this he produced two tumblers, a small chopping board and a couple of plates. 'I thought this would be more fun than dinner in the pub. I don't know about you, but I can never spend enough time outside, especially in summer.'

Anna smiled at his enthusiasm. 'You *were* a boy scout, weren't you?'

'Not for nothing is our motto: "Be Prepared",' he said, pouring them both a glass. 'And you never know when the urge to picnic might come upon you.'

'I can sense that might be fairly often,' she said.

'Weather permitting. Though the company is not always so delightful as today.'

'One has to make do,' she said gravely.

They sat side by side and leant back on the driftwood, gazing out to sea. 'Quite a day, hey?' he said.

'You're not wrong,' she replied, thinking back to their early start in London. More had happened to her in the past few days than in the past few years. Her head spun even thinking about it, and she felt almost as if she had fallen between the pages of a storybook into an adventure that didn't quite belong to her.

'So, who was he?' Ed asked, breaking the silence.

'I'm sorry?'

'The chap who hurt you so badly?'

Anna froze. 'What?' How did he know? What did he know?

'You've got that look,' he said with a sad smile. 'When you think no one's watching. Like you've got the weight of the world on your shoulders. I noticed it when we first met, and then at the party I was sure . . . It's something I'm familiar with.'

'Oh,' Anna said quietly, gazing firmly at the smudged blue horizon.

Ed waited for her to speak. Eventually she did.

'Simon. We'd been together throughout university. Inseparable. Had grand plans to take the trip of a lifetime once we'd graduated. See the great gardens of Europe. We had a whole, wonderful future ahead of us. So much to look forward to.' She took a slug of wine. 'It was a few days after our final exams. I'd stayed over at my sister's – she has three kids, and Fleur, my youngest niece, had croup. My sister was having a tough time of it, so I offered to give her a hand. I went back to the flat the next morning and found him. He'd taken a bottle of pills. There was no note. No warning. He'd been a bit stressed, but I thought it was just the exams. I had no idea.' Her last words came out as a sob. She'd never really spoken to anyone about it – she had barely even discussed it with her mother and her sister – but somehow, so far from home and to someone she barely knew, it was easier to finally unburden herself.

'Oh, Anna. I'm so desperately, desperately sorry.'

'When the results came out, he'd come top of our class. Had everything to live for. I still don't really understand why. Why he didn't talk to me about it, how he was feeling. I wonder if I should have known, did I miss something? Could I have prevented it? Got him some help? Was I a terrible girlfriend?'

'How long ago was it?'

'Nearly six years.'

'Still hurts, huh?'

'It's getting better,' she smiled weakly.

'You're allowed to let it go, you know.'

She stared at the ocean. Was she? Would she ever?

'There's no prize for mourning the longest. Or the hardest. Sooner or later you have to start living again. There's no other way.'

'I suppose you're right,' she said finally, still not convinced.

'Has there been anyone else since?' Anna didn't answer for a moment and he added, 'Stop me if I'm prying.'

She thought fleetingly of Noah, back in Sydney, but she shook her head. There had been no spark of attraction there, lovely and kind as he was. 'No, no one else.'

'Okay, enough sad stories. Do you think you can help me collect some of the wood that's up there?' He pointed to the far end of the beach, which was littered with flotsam washed up by higher tides.

'Sure, why?'

He reached into one of the bags and waved a box of firelighters at her. 'There's nothing quite like a fire on the beach.'

She looked at the box. 'Not exactly Bear Grylls are you, though?'

'Hey,' he said, indignant, 'I'll have you know I was not your common-or-garden scout; I was actually an eagle scout, believe it or not. Got the badges to prove it.'

'Just not the making-fire-from-two-sticks one, hey?' she teased.

'Okay, you've got me there,' he replied. 'You get the kindling and I'll try to find some larger stuff.'

She wedged her tumbler of wine in the sand and got to her feet. 'Okay, I'm on it.'

By the time she returned, dragging a huge branch behind her, a bundle of smaller sticks under the other arm, Ed had gathered a couple of big bits of driftwood and was scrunching up the paper that had been wrapped around the wine bottle, and dotted it with firelighters. 'Whoa! We might be here for a while if we burn that,' he laughed. He took the smaller sticks from Anna and placed them in a teepee shape around the paper. Producing a box of matches, he began to light them and drop them into the teepee, then knelt and blew gently on the tiny flames.

The driftwood was bone dry, and before long the fire was crackling away, sending sparks into the twilight. They sat, companionably, gazing into the red-hot centre of it, watching as the branches flaked and pale ash caught in eddies around the heat of the flames.

Much later, when the picnic had been all but finished, the wine bottle emptied and the embers of the fire were dying down, Ed hauled himself to his feet. 'Come on, let's get you off to bed. You've had a long day.'

For a moment she misunderstood his meaning and felt a bolt of alarm. But she looked into his guileless blue eyes and saw nothing but concern for her and was reassured. She liked him and felt more comfortable with him than she had with anyone in the longest time, there was no doubt about that, but she wasn't ready for anything more. Besides, she would be on her way to Europe in a week's time and in all likelihood never see him again. That didn't stop her being thankful for his presence, or immune to his considerable charm.

'Here,' she said, pulling her mobile out of her pocket and switching on the torch. It had grown dark while they sat by the fire and there was no other light for miles around. The cliffs looked suddenly dark and forbidding.

Ed kicked sand into the fire to extinguish it and then Anna felt him next to her. Her breath caught and goosebumps raised on her arms.

'Lead on, O bearer of the light,' he said, picking up the picnic basket.

Stumbling in the dark, they navigated their way to the steps cut into the cliff and climbed out of the cove. Anna almost fell asleep on the short drive back to the pub, and declined Ed's offer of a nightcap in the bar.

'Not even a hot toddy?' he offered.

'Thanks, but I think I'll head upstairs,' she said.

'Good night, Jenkins,' he said, leaning towards her and kissing her chastely on the cheek. 'Don't let the bed bugs bite.'

As she climbed the back stairs towards her room, Anna found herself chuckling at the expression – she didn't think she'd been told that since she was a little girl.

Chapter Thirty-seven

Valparaiso, 1887

Elizabeth's labour began slowly. A dull ache in the small of her back. A light cramp in her stomach that she did her best to ignore. The last time she had seen the doctor in Valparaiso he had assured her that the birth was still several weeks away, and so she and Tomas had travelled to his family's *estancia* to spend some time there before her pregnancy made the journey more difficult. She loved it: the cool mornings that gave way to warm days, the gentle breezes that ruffled the long grasses and the distant mountains, completely white with snow now, that towered above the flat river valley.

Before they left the city, Elizabeth had made enquiries of the next ship departing for England, but discovered that there were likely to be none headed in that direction for several months. It was imperative that Daisy take the Devil's Trumpet cutting and seeds to Kew as soon as possible, for it could only be a matter of time before Mr Chegwidden, with his resources and knowledge of the area, came across it for himself. She intended to book a passage for her maid on the next available sailing, but decided to wait until closer to the time to ask her to undertake the journey. She also had no intention of informing her husband until it was absolutely necessary, for she did not wish him to raise any objections to her plan. She found herself frustrated both at the delay and the almost bovine slowness of her body. Her rounded stomach was too big to allow her to sit and paint for long periods as she had been used to, so she contented herself with a seat placed in the shade of a cypress tree and watched the hawks that frequented the area glide and swoop high above her.

This was where she was sitting when she got the first indication that the baby might come early. She shifted in her seat, wondering if the pain was from something she had eaten at breakfast. She suffered an almost constant burning in her throat as the baby pressed up on her stomach. Sofia had brewed a viscous, milky concoction that she swore would help, but Elizabeth gagged after one sip of the slimy liquid and chose instead to put up with the dyspepsia.

'Elizabeth!' Sofia was by her side. 'Did you call me?'

'No, I don't believe I did,' replied Elizabeth, knowing that, uncomfortable as she was, she definitely had not made a sound.

'You look tired. May I?' Sofia placed her long brown fingers on Elizabeth's belly, gently pressing on it. Elizabeth closed her eyes and enjoyed the comfort her hands brought. Sofia had inherited her mother's healing touch.

'This baby, he wants to come soon,' said Sofia.

Elizabeth's eyes flew open. 'No!' she cried. 'I am not ready. *Señor* Calabras said it would be weeks yet.'

Sofia gave her a look that seemed to Elizabeth as wise as time itself. 'I doubt that I am wrong. It is written in the sky – the moon is nearly full – I have been watching and waiting.'

Elizabeth was suddenly terrified, thoughts of her mother crowding her mind, a voice in her head reminding her she was miles from a doctor.

'Don't be alarmed now, sweet one,' Sofia soothed. 'I have helped many women have their babies, and all will be fine.'

'But you don't understand,' Elizabeth protested. 'My mother—'

'I know, *mi corazon*, but do not worry. Just do as I say and before you know it you will have a beautiful baby in your arms.'

'*Oof!*' Elizabeth leant back in the chair as another wave of pain, stronger this time, swept through her.

'Come. We should go to your bedchamber. I will send someone to let Tomas know. Lean on me now.'

Elizabeth took her arm and they made their way haltingly back to the house.

~

'Talk to me, Sofia. Tell me a story,' she said much later. 'Anything to take my mind off this . . . this . . .' Elizabeth was lost for words. The pain was unlike anything she had ever known; she felt even more wretched than she had when she was aboard the *Corcovado* and struck down with seasickness. Waves of contractions ripped through her, leaving her panting for breath and every muscle trembling uncontrollably.

Throughout it all, Sofia had only left her side once, to assemble a bizarre collection of objects: a grey feather, what looked like an amethyst that sparkled even in the dim light, and a crude silver figurine. Daisy, coming in to check on her mistress, pursed her lips as she saw the amulets but said nothing.

'Hush now,' Sofia soothed, brushing back the damp gold hair from Elizabeth's forehead. 'I remember the time my mother first took me to a birthing. I was a young girl. Ayee, I was so scared, I imagined the woman was going to be split in half like a melon.'

Elizabeth looked up at her anxiously. The thought of such a thing chilled the sweat that had broken out on her forehead, and she swallowed, her throat dry from the guttural moans she had been unable to silence.

'But she was fine,' Sofia continued. 'A few short pushes and out came this wet, wriggling bundle of arms and legs, covered in a fine, dark hair. It was the most wonderful thing I had ever seen, and I could not hold back my tears of joy. A new life, my mother said, is a sacred thing.'

'Did your mother use her herbs to help the women?' asked Elizabeth.

'Of course,' said Sofia. 'As I will for you.' She walked over to a table on the far side of the room on which stood several small dark glass bottles. 'Here,' she said, returning with one in her hands. 'A few drops of this will help you sleep better than you have in your entire life. You must get some rest, for you will need your strength soon enough.'

'What strange magic is this?'

Sofia gave her a mysterious smile. '*No te preocupes.* Open your mouth.'

Elizabeth, too exhausted to protest or even care what she might be ingesting, opened her mouth like a baby bird as Sofia dispensed a dark, oily liquid that tasted like bitter almonds. She barely had time to recoil at the vile taste before she was dragged into oblivion.

When she woke, it was dark outside and Sofia was by her side. Daisy sat, looking anxious, at the foot of the bed.

'Tomas?' she asked.

'He is waiting outside, do not worry.'

Before she had time to ask to see him, a wave of pain crashed over her. Daisy moved to her side and wiped her brow with a cool cloth. Sofia gripped her hand tightly. 'It is almost over. Be strong now and all will be well,' she promised. 'Daisy, can you fetch me some more water, please?'

'What was in that medicine?' asked Elizabeth after Daisy had gone. 'I cannot believe I slept through this. I had the strangest dreams . . . My mother was there, looking just as she does in a painting at home . . .'

Sofia held her gaze. 'It was a tiny, tiny amount of that herb, the one you asked me about when we first met. *Trompeta del Diablo.*' She said the name in a whisper.

Elizabeth's eyes widened and she gasped, but this time it was not from the pain.

'A sliver from the leaf, no larger than my smallest fingernail. Soaked in oil and then the oil is strained. But you must tell no one of this. Mr Chegwidden is one of several Englishmen who have come to Valparaiso in recent times to search for this plant. Those of us who know how to use it do not want it falling into the wrong hands. It is extremely powerful, but more than that, it is also very dangerous.'

Elizabeth could do no more than nod.

'It is almost impossible to find unless you know exactly where to look,' said Sofia. 'They all think it grows high in the mountains, but I do not know why. In fact, it prefers the warmth of the valley.'

Elizabeth allowed herself a small, secret smile. She relaxed back on her pillow and let the urge to bear down, to push this baby out of her no matter what the cost, take her over completely.

Chapter Thirty-eight

Cornwall, Summer 2017

'Come in. I've been expecting you.'

The woman standing in the doorway spoke with a very precise accent, the vowels clipped and formal. She was small and round, with a cardigan stretched over her ample bosom and floral-print dress. Her shock of white hair was neatly pinned back under a wide-brimmed straw hat. Her skin was liver-spotted and creased with deep lines, but her faded blue eyes held a look of sharp focus.

'I know exactly who you are,' the elderly lady went on. 'You're that girl who wrote to me.'

Anna exhaled the breath she had been holding in. 'Yes, Miss Deverell, I am,' she said with relief. 'Anna Jenkins. But have we caught you at a bad time? You look as if you are about to go out?'

'No dear, I'm just back from church. The flowers this week weren't a patch on mine. Still, you've got to let others have a turn now and again, don't you? And who are you, young man?' she asked, turning her attention to Ed.

'Oh, he's a friend of mine,' said Anna. 'Edwin. Edwin Hammett-Jones.'

'A pleasure to meet you Miss Deverell,' Ed said formally.

She looked him over critically and seemed to approve. 'You'd better both come in, then. I'll put the kettle on. You'll stay for a cup.' They were statements, not questions. She was obviously used to people obeying her orders, thought Anna as she watched her head off down the cottage's dark hallway. Anna and Ed followed, finding themselves in a small sitting room crammed with furniture and books. There was not a spare inch of horizontal surface that didn't have a figurine, towering pile of hardbacks or lamp on it. 'Off you get, Mr Darcy,' Florence barked at a fat ginger cat that had been sunning itself on a chintz sofa. The cat lazily flicked its tail at her but didn't move. 'Have a seat, I shan't be a jiffy.'

Anna caught Ed's eye, which was a mistake as he was trying hard to keep a straight face. 'Mr Darcy?' he said incredulously when Florence had left.

'Shush!' said Anna. 'She might hear you.'

'What? She must be ninety if she's a day. Not a chance.'

'Stop it!' cried Anna, but she couldn't help her lips curving in amusement, both at Ed and the improbably named cat.

There were two old-fashioned wing-backed chairs upholstered in sun-faded rose-patterned chintz, and they took one each, the sofa having been requisitioned by the ginger tom.

'Here you are, then,' Florence bustled back into the room carrying a tray laden with a teapot, cups, saucers, sugar bowl, milk jug and a plate of sugared biscuits.

'Let me get that for you,' Ed sprang up to offer assistance.

She fixed him with a steely glare. 'I'm perfectly capable, thank you.'

Anna was reminded of Granny Gus again. Florence had the same uncompromising look.

Ed sat down once more, but not before flicking a look of amusement at Anna.

'One lump or two?' asked Florence.

'Oh, none for me, thank you.' Anna took the proffered cup and saucer and rested it on her knee.

'Quite right too, dear. People these days eat far too much sugar.'

Anna had been on the point of reaching for a biscuit, but stilled her hand. Ed had no such qualms, however, and helped himself to two.

Florence sat on the sofa, unceremoniously shoving Mr Darcy to its far corner. 'So.' She folded her hands in front of her. 'Exactly why did you wish to see me? It's not very often that I receive such an intriguing letter. You said you had found an old photograph of Trebithick?'

'Yes,' replied Anna. 'As I mentioned in my letter, I was having some work done on my grandmother's house in Sydney – well, actually it's my house now – when the builders found a box. This was one of the things in the box . . .' Anna reached into her bag and pulled out the picture of John Trebithick.

'And you came all this way because of an old photograph?'

'Well, there were a few other things in the box as well . . .' Anna hesitated to reveal more until she was certain about the photograph.

'Such as?' The old lady was not to be fobbed off.

'Some jewellery – nothing particularly valuable; some drawings. There was also a diary.'

The old lady raised her eyebrows. 'All right then, let's take a look at this photograph.' She patted her chest in search of a pair of spectacles that hung from a chain around her neck. Locating them, she put them on the end of her nose and peered at the picture that Anna held up in front of her.

There was silence.

Florence turned the photo over. 'Well, it's definitely Trebithick Hall. You can tell that straightaway.'

'Yes, we went and had a look yesterday,' said Anna. 'Even the rhododendron is still there.'

'It's one of the oldest in all of England,' said Florence, a note of pride in her voice. 'We nearly lost it in the storms of '87.' She put the photograph down next to her cup of tea and went over to a bookshelf on the far side of the room. Rummaging among its contents, she pulled out books seemingly at random, all the while muttering under her breath. With an exhalation of victory, she found what she was looking for and turned to show Anna and Ed. 'A biography of John Trebithick, my great-grandfather.' She turned the pages, coming to rest at the plate section in the middle of the book. She passed it to Anna, handing her the photograph as well.

'It's almost identical!' cried Anna, comparing the two. In the picture in the book, the young girl was looking to the right, as if her attention had been caught by something just out of view. Anna read the caption aloud, '"John Trebithick and his daughter Elizabeth" – Elizabeth. I knew it had to be her.' She continued, '"Sir John had recently returned from a plant-hunting expedition to South America."'

'So, my dear, I wonder quite how almost the exact same photograph came to be – where did you say? Australia?'

'Yes,' said Anna.

'How extraordinary!' Florence flipped to another page in the book. 'There's one more photograph of Elizabeth here, of the mourning party after John Trebithick's death.'

Anna stared at the photograph. It showed a number of black-clad people in a funeral procession; they were following a horse-drawn hearse, the animals festooned with ostrich plumes. Standing in the foreground, by the horses, was the same young woman – Elizabeth. Anna looked closer. She could just make out that Elizabeth was wearing a jet necklace over the bodice of her dress. 'Oh!' she gasped. 'I think I have that necklace! It was in the box. There was a mirror, too. With the initials AH on it. Do you think it might have been her mother's – Augusta's?'

'Oh, my dear,' said Florence, 'I must say, I don't know what to make of all this.'

'What became of Elizabeth?' asked Ed. 'It would seem that that is where we should start to try to unravel this mystery.'

'Yes indeed, young man,' said Florence, looking at him over her glasses with respect. 'I expect we should.'

'Can you tell us any more about her?' asked Anna. 'I'm afraid we missed most of the tour of the house yesterday, so I didn't get the chance to ask the guide.'

'Hm,' snorted Florence. 'Neil? He wouldn't tell you much in any case. Sticks to the script and never wavers. No imagination, that man.' She took a sip of tea and set the cup noisily back on the saucer. Then she leant forward towards them and began to speak. 'I grew up at Trebithick Hall, though my father, George, was forced to turn over the house and what land was left to the National Trust more than fifty years ago. The place was falling down around our ears and there was no money to repair it. He thought that, as he had no son for an heir, it was the best course of action.' Florence gave a derisive sniff. 'I was nearly forty, unmarried, and never likely to be. I was living here,' she indicated the room they sat in, 'in the holidays anyway. I was headmistress at Truro School until I retired. Fifteen years ago this July.'

Anna wasn't surprised to hear this. Florence Deverell might be slightly hard of hearing, but she had a teacher's brusque manner and a mind as keen and precise as a scalpel.

'Do go on,' Ed urged. He looked as anxious to find out what happened to Elizabeth as was Anna.

'Father's parents, Robert and Georgiana, were largely the ones responsible for Trebithick going to rack and ruin. Not that one should speak ill of the dead, particularly when they are one's grandparents,' she broke off. 'But still, it's the truth.'

'Why was that?' asked Anna.

'They cared little for the upkeep of the house and let the plant business founder. By all accounts, they preferred to spend their money indulging in holidays on the Continent and the purchase of fine wines. In fact, the cellar was one of the only things of value that my grandfather managed to accumulate. He certainly didn't have the same luck with the stock market. When my father inherited Trebithick, he also inherited debt like a noose around his neck. Don't get me wrong, it was a wonderful place to grow up, but I've never forgotten the freezing winters in those draughty old rooms. I'm certain that's why my mother died young. Pneumonia.'

'Oh, I'm so sorry to hear that,' said Anna, but Florence waved her concern away.

'Ancient history. Besides, I'm far more comfortable here than I would have been at Trebithick. Though I do miss the gardens.' She sighed, looking out of the window at the patch of lawn stretching towards a field that arced down to the ocean.

'Anyway, where was I?' For a moment Florence looked confused and her eyes clouded over, and Anna suddenly saw her for the old lady that she was, despite the fact that she otherwise managed to give a general impression of sprightliness. 'Oh yes,' she continued, her focus sharpening again. 'Elizabeth. Younger sister of my grandmother Georgiana. Well, she was quite the artist. There are several of her drawings on show at Trebithick. Early work, I think. Neil will be able to show you.'

Anna's eyes met Ed's, and she knew they were both thinking of the sketchbook.

'Did she become famous?' asked Anna excitedly.

Florence paused, and sighed. 'Well, in a way I suppose she did.'

Chapter Thirty-nine

Valparaiso, 1887

'Here she is,' said Elizabeth as she presented the tightly wrapped bundle to Tomas. An unblinking pair of dark blue eyes and rosebud lips were all that could be seen.

'A daughter,' he said, wonder in his voice as a teardrop trembled on his dark eyelashes. 'She is perfect. But so tiny.' Tomas cradled her as if he were carrying the most fragile piece of china, walking over to the window to get a better look at his first-born. 'She has my chin,' he said, edging the blanket down with the tip of his finger.

'Do you wish she had been a boy?' she asked. 'I know how much you desired a son.'

Tomas snorted. 'A beauty such as this? How could I not think she is the most exquisite baby ever born?'

'Are you sure?'

He smiled up at her. 'There is plenty of time for sons.'

After the ordeal of birth, Elizabeth couldn't begin to imagine having more children. The baby's head had got stuck like a cork in a bottle, and it was only Sofia's strong fingers and sure touch that had helped both mother and child to separate and survive. She wasn't sure she ever wanted to repeat the experience, even though she had fallen irrevocably in love with her daughter the moment she had seen her, bloodied and screaming at the top of her lungs at the indignity of her birth.

The baby girl began to mewl again and Tomas reluctantly returned her to Elizabeth's arms. 'The wet nurse I engaged is in Valparaiso. I shall have to suckle her myself,' she said. 'Sofia will show me, for she says she has seen many women feed their babies, that it is the most natural thing in the world.' Elizabeth paused, noticing Tomas's look of discomfort at the subject matter. 'Perhaps you might leave us for a while and come back later?' she said gently.

Elizabeth proved to be a natural mother, and with Sofia's guidance was soon expertly feeding and burping. The baby, in turn, grew round and bonny with every passing day, quickly catching up in size what she had lacked from her premature arrival. They stayed on at the *estancia*, as Tomas did not want them to make the journey back to Valparaiso until both mother and baby were strong and well.

She had her father's easy-going personality, delighting her parents with even the slightest yawn or splay of her tiny fingers. Elizabeth noticed that Daisy loved having a baby to look after – she had told Elizabeth that she had helped her mother with her youngest sister and so she had plenty of experience with newborns. She soon became her de facto nanny, and Elizabeth, seeing how well Daisy cared for her daughter, refused to consider employing anyone else. The wet nurse also proved unnecessary.

When she was feeling stronger, Elizabeth wrote to Georgiana to tell her that she now had a fair-haired niece who looked for all the world exactly like their mother, Augusta; a cousin for George. She longed for a letter in return, for news from home; it had been months since their last communication.

Tomas's father came as soon as news of the birth reached him, and he was as besotted with his first grandchild as her parents were. It was he who insisted on a christening, and did not want to wait until the family returned to the town. He arranged for the priest to make the journey out to the *estancia*, and invited many of his business associates, wanting to share and celebrate his family's good fortune. As she had with her wedding, Elizabeth bowed to the wishes of her husband's family, and the baby girl was baptised a Catholic.

On the day of the christening, Elizabeth, with Tomas by her side, carried her daughter, who was swathed in a lace robe, towards the priest who stood in the main hall. As she looked around the assembled guests, smiling, one in particular caught her eye and she stumbled, staggering with the baby in her arms.

Damien Chegwidden. She couldn't help but be reminded of the tale of the bad fairy at the christening of *Sleeping Beauty*, a story that had fascinated her as a child. She had often wondered what it must be like to sleep for a hundred years and then wake to find a world utterly changed. Was his presence to be a bad omen for her daughter?

Tomas steadied her, supporting her elbow. '*Cariño.* Are you all right? Do you need to sit down?'

She swallowed. 'No, no, I am fine. Please. Let us continue.'

After the ceremony, Elizabeth handed the baby to Tomas. She was now officially named: Violeta Tomasina Augustina; Violeta as a tribute to her old governess, Mam'zelle Violette. He proudly showed her off, revelling in the clucking from the older ladies in the party, while *Señor* Flores and the other gentlemen retired to smoke their pipes. 'To talk about politics and trade, no doubt,' said Sofia as she passed Elizabeth.

Elizabeth was thirsty, and was making her way towards a table laden with food and drinks when Mr Chegwidden accosted her.

'My dear. You are looking well.'

'Thank you, sir, but I cannot say the same for you.' Elizabeth couldn't hide her shock. Chegwidden was thin to the point of emaciation and his eyes burned like coals in the hollows of their sockets. He looked like a ghost of the man she had first met.

He grimaced. 'We were caught in the Andes. Terrible storm. Then robbed by a band of *montoneros.* They stole all of our food and most of our equipment. We didn't eat for weeks. Lucky to survive.'

Elizabeth wished for a moment that he had not survived – it would have made the task of getting samples of the Devil's Trumpet to Kew less of an urgent one. 'Oh goodness,' she said, feigning politeness, 'I had not heard of your troubles.' She had, however, heard of *montoneros*, lawless bandits who roamed the region.

'It was surely worth it, though.' He leant in to whisper to her. 'For I have finally found what we both have been searching for . . . Miss Trebithick.'

Elizabeth felt a roar fill her ears as her mind scrambled to take in the meaning of his words. She swallowed hard, unable to think of a reply. She hadn't been called that name for months. *How did he know?*

Chegwidden gave her a sly wink. 'I beg your pardon. Of course it is *Señora* Flores now, isn't it?'

He pulled her to one side, away from the chatter of the women, and spoke to her in a low voice. 'I think you know very well what it is I am referring to, now don't you?'

She felt like a rabbit caught in the sights of a hunter's gun, and her heart began to thud in her chest so loudly that she wondered if he could hear it.

'I knew I recognised you from somewhere almost as soon as we met, but I couldn't place you. I wondered to myself why a young woman would journey halfway around the world to fiddle about sketching plants. And there was also the fact of your maidservant, who has as broad a Cornish accent as I ever did hear. I knew your father you know. We were friends for a while. But then I came across him in the Himalaya. I had found a rare magnolia and he challenged me for it. I was forced to defend myself.' Chegwidden sucked on his teeth as if reliving the confrontation.

That wasn't the story her father had recounted, thought Elizabeth angrily, remembering the scar on his arm.

'He told me once of his two daughters; his flowers, he called you. I guessed your true identity on the night of the fiesta, when you mentioned your maid wore your sister's gown, but I have kept it to myself until now. Knowledge is power my dear, as you well know.'

'What do you want from me?' Elizabeth hissed, finally finding her voice.

'Don't worry. I came merely to gloat, for I have found that which you sought and I shall be on a ship back to England within the fortnight. The glory of the Devil's Trumpet shall be mine.' His black eyes blazed. 'I shall be rich beyond measure, for I will sell the seeds to the highest bidder, and believe me, there will be plenty of men interested in my find. Your father could never have succeeded where I have done; he had neither the stamina nor the skill and he was doubly a fool to send his daughter on such a mission. A mere slip of a girl cannot outwit a man with my experience.' He gave a victorious smile, the skin so tight on his scalp she could see a vein throbbing at his temple. There was no trace of the urbane gentleman now. 'But of course you surely must care less for such endeavours, now that you have all this . . .' He spread his arm wide to indicate the enormous hall.

'How dare you patronise me, you infuriating man,' Elizabeth retorted. 'And you lie about my dear papa. He was a most honourable gentleman and there are plenty who can attest to that. What makes you so sure you have the right plant anyway?' she spat at him.

'Of course I have the right plant,' he scoffed. 'It is exactly as I have heard it described: large, white turning to orange trumpet flowers with deep rust-coloured stamens, and a sweet scent.'

Elizabeth found herself able to breathe more easily. She was certain that he had not found the Devil's Trumpet. She knew this plant of which Chegwidden spoke – her father had described it as the 'fiery trumpet', a glorious tree that featured bushels of pendulous trumpet-shaped flowers, hanging downwards, 'as if musical instruments left behind by a fairy orchestra' he had said. It was nothing like the real Devil's Trumpet. However, she failed to hide the glint of relief in her eyes.

It was her undoing.

Chapter Forty

Valparaiso, 1887

'You doubt me, *señora*?' Smart as a whip, Damien Chegwidden had caught the expression that flashed across her face.

'Oh no, not at all,' Elizabeth said, wishing she could take back her words. 'But you must admit, there are many such lilies that grow wild in these parts. It is hard to tell one from the other.'

'Indeed, but none that has the particular scent I have smelled with my own nose,' he said, watching her closely.

'What scent would that be?' Elizabeth enquired, her innocent expression belying the pounding of her heart.

'An unholy scent, if ever there was one. One that would tempt even the purest heart.'

Elizabeth arched an eyebrow at his hyperbole, but said nothing.

'I can see you do not believe me,' he said.

'Oh, I do believe you, sir. A scent like that can never be forgotten. But,' she couldn't help but add, 'there is more to the true Devil's Trumpet than its scent. Though I am sure a plant-hunter as clever as you would know that.' There was an edge to her words – she wanted nothing more than to wipe the supercilious expression from his face. Ignoring the warning her father had given her more than a year ago, she continued. 'I hear tell that it bears a black vein, like the blood of Beelzebub himself.'

Mr Chegwidden grasped her by the elbow, pulling her further away from the other guests. 'I see you are rather well informed,' he said quietly but with urgency. 'Though as John Trebithick's daughter, I suppose I should not be surprised. Do, pray, tell me more,' he demanded.

Elizabeth's temper had been stoked by the look of arrogant triumph in Mr Chegwidden's eyes when he spoke and she was unable to stop herself from goading him further. Shaking off his hand, she said, 'If indeed you have seen the Devil's Trumpet for yourself, then you would surely know of that.'

He stroked his wispy moustache slowly. 'Do you not think that your husband would be surprised to hear of your deceit? Your real purpose for being in South America?' His eyes glittered, and Elizabeth wondered if he was quite unhinged; there was a look of a madman about him.

'What is it you want from me?'

'You have it. The Devil's Trumpet. You must have, to describe it so precisely.'

Elizabeth noticed Daisy out of the corner of her eye. 'I most certainly do not!' she cried. 'I have merely heard it talked of by those who are well informed on such matters.'

He gripped Elizabeth by the wrist, leaning in close to her face. 'Know that I will stop at nothing to get that plant for myself. You can bet your husband's and your child's life on it.'

She shuddered at the chilling thread of fanaticism in his voice but replied lightly, 'Really, sir, those are serious words indeed.'

'I am always serious.'

His eyes bored into her but she held his gaze before wresting her arm free and turned, about to leave, when she remembered Daisy hovering nearby.

'Daisy!' she said, trying to calm the thudding of her heart and gather her wits. 'Would you please take Violeta for her nap? I'm sure it is past time. Tomas has her.'

The maid gave her mistress a worried look and then glanced in Mr Chegwidden's direction. 'Are you feeling quite well? Can I get you something? Can I call someone?'

Elizabeth waved her off. 'No, no, really I am fine. If you could find her for me?' she pleaded.

'Of course, miss,' the maid bobbed obediently.

Elizabeth turned back to Mr Chegwidden, but he had vanished like the morning mist. 'Damn and hellfire!' she cursed, though there was no one to hear her. She should have let him think he had been successful in his quest and then he would be gone, away on the first ship to leave port and returned to England believing he would be covered in glory. She had to confess her secret to Tomas before Mr Chegwidden had the chance to tell him. She had to ensure her family was safe.

What had she done? A few ill-chosen words and her whole future was in jeopardy. Would Tomas understand why she had lied to him, lied to his family about who she was and her true purpose in Valparaiso? At that moment she wasn't sure.

One thing was certain: she must find a safer place to hide the box containing the cuttings and seeds. Somewhere no one would ever think to look.

Taking her leave from the christening party with the excuse of seeing to Violeta, she crept into the baby's bedroom, where Daisy was laying her in a sheepskin hammock suspended from the roof poles. Sofia claimed it helped babies to sleep better and so far Elizabeth had no reason to doubt her. Violeta generally only woke once at night and Daisy brought her into Elizabeth's chamber to feed, before returning with her to their rooms.

'Daisy,' she whispered once her daughter was asleep. 'Come with me.'

She led the maid to the other wing of the house, which housed the family's bedchambers.

'I have something I must entrust to you, for I fear that the secret is now too big to be mine alone.' Elizabeth grasped Daisy's hand. 'I made a promise to my dying father to search for a plant. A plant of great power, but one that in the wrong hands could wreak terrible havoc.'

Daisy blinked in silent astonishment.

'It is called the Devil's Trumpet,' Elizabeth continued, 'and is extremely rare. I promised that if I found it, I would return with it to England. It is said to have the power to cure all manner of disease. Daisy,' she implored, 'can you imagine what that might mean? For the sick? To end suffering? I myself experienced its power when I was giving birth, truly I did. I fear I should not have survived if it wasn't for Sofia's knowledge of it.'

Daisy looked even more astounded.

'Mr Chegwidden also seeks it, but unlike my dear papa, his motives are far from pure. He believes it will make his fortune. He thinks he has found it, but I foolishly let it slip that he is mistaken. Damn my stubborn pride. I have the true Devil's Trumpet. Here.' She reached into the trunk and brought out the sketchbook. 'I have the very greatest favour to ask of you. Mr Chegwidden has discovered who I am, and now we are all in danger.'

Daisy caught her breath.

'You never questioned why I insisted on travelling under my mother's name, but now you know. I fear he will do anything to prevent me from getting it back to England. I need you to keep it safe for me. But you must not touch it, I beg you, for it is also deadly poisonous. No one will suspect a maid of having it.'

'Are you not terrified of what he might do?' asked Daisy. 'That he will stop at nothing?'

She nodded. 'I fear he has descended into madness,' said Elizabeth. 'He threatened my life, and Violeta's and Tomas's too. That is even more reason why he must not find this flower and especially not the seeds. You must promise me that if anything happens—' Elizabeth broke off in a sob. 'If anything happens to me or Tomas, you will make sure that Violeta is safe.'

'Of course,' Daisy assured her. 'But it will not come to that.'

'Do not be too sure. He is capable of anything.'

'There is something else.' Daisy hesitated, biting her lip. 'Earlier today I came across Mr Chegwidden and *Señor* Flores at the stables. I had gone out to see if there was any milk and was on my way back when I heard their voices. They . . .' She paused, swallowing. 'They were arguing. Mr Chegwidden was asking *Señor* Flores about a plant.'

'What plant, Daisy?'

'The Devil's Trumpet. I am not mistaken. Those were the words I heard. Today is the first time I've heard of such a plant, and to hear of it twice in one day; well, that is most uncommon, do you not think?'

Elizabeth was confused. 'What could this mean?' she wondered aloud. Had Damien Chegwidden involved Tomas in his search for it? Was Tomas keeping a secret from her? Had she married in a romantic rush, not truly knowing the man who was now her husband? As this thought occurred to her, she saw the irony in it, for she had kept a secret hidden from her husband all this time.

But had Chegwidden told Tomas the truth about Elizabeth, revealed who she really was? No. He could not have. Tomas would have confronted her about it if he had, she was sure of it.

'They did not see me,' Daisy reassured her. 'I am certain.'

'Well, that is something, I suppose,' said Elizabeth, still lost in thought.

'Come now, I know where to conceal it,' said Daisy, urging Elizabeth on. 'There is a cupboard. We can hide it away at the back; there is plenty of space. One would not think to look there, not in a nursery, among a baby's things.'

Chapter Forty-one

Chile, 1887

As Elizabeth returned to the party to farewell the guests returning to Valparaiso or Santiago, she noticed Tomas and Damien Chegwidden in conversation and fear coursed through her like a lightning bolt. Would Tomas forgive her once he found out the truth? She had to tell him first, before the malevolent Chegwidden had the chance to poison her husband against her.

She bade a distracted farewell to Mr and Mrs Campbell, promising that she would be back in Valparaiso before long, and then she watched, clenching her trembling hands in her skirts, as Mr Chegwidden mounted his horse. He locked eyes with Elizabeth, but she stood her ground, staring defiantly back at him.

The group left in a flurry of hooves, and Elizabeth retreated indoors to avoid being covered in the dust they had kicked up.

'*Mi corazon*, you look exhausted,' said Tomas as he saw Elizabeth reclining on a chair. 'It has been too much for you, too soon perhaps.' He went to her side and took her hand.

Elizabeth looked up at him, fear in her heart.

'I shall be fine,' she said, brushing a hand across her eyes. 'You and Mr Chegwidden seemed to have plenty to talk about,' she said.

'We were merely discussing some business.'

'How is that, my darling?'

Tomas sighed. 'Mr Chegwidden seeks a particular plant and I have been helping him with the search. We disagreed over a trifling matter; it is nothing, *mi corazon*. I will resolve things to everyone's satisfaction.'

Elizabeth's blood turned to ice in her veins but she kept silent as Sofia joined them.

'You speak of *Señor* Chegwidden?' her sister-in-law said. 'I do not trust that man. He thinks in lies. He converses in lies. *El es un loco*. A madman.'

'Oh nonsense,' her brother scoffed. 'Do not worry yourselves, either of you. Elizabeth, you need to look after the baby and recover your strength; and Sofia, this is not of your concern.'

Elizabeth felt a small burst of displeasure at being dismissed in this way, and imagined Sofia must too, though her sister-in-law had bowed her head meekly at Tomas's words.

Immediately after the christening, the weather worsened. One particular day, all of the servants had been given leave to attend a wedding some several hours' ride away. Daisy had also been invited but chose at the last moment to stay behind and help with Violeta. She, together with Tomas's father, Sofia, Elizabeth, Tomas and the baby remained at the *estancia*.

As Elizabeth retired for the evening, she was surprised to see that snow had begun to cover the ground. Though a cold wind had been blowing, she had not anticipated snow would fall so late in the season.

'I fear we may be forced to remain here for several days if this continues,' said Tomas as he stood behind her and slid the strap of her chemise from her shoulder. Goosebumps rose on her skin, despite the warmth coming from a fire burning in the grate.

'Will that be so bad?' she asked.

'I had planned for us to return to Valparaiso in the coming days. I have a number of pressing matters to see to.' He shrugged. 'But it can't be helped. We shall see what it looks like in the morning. I hope the servants make it back tomorrow.'

'Tomas . . .' She paused, turning to face him. 'There is something I must speak to you about.' Elizabeth's voice shook. She had rehearsed this speech over and over in her mind, resolved to tell Tomas everything – including that she had found the Devil's Trumpet and planned to send it to England with Daisy – to lay herself bare and suffer the consequences. She wanted no more secrets from him, nothing that would eat away at her until she could find neither rest nor refuge.

'Can it wait until morning?' he said quietly. 'It is late for conversation, but not too late for love.' He smiled at her, his eyes sparkling in the light from the candle flame.

Elizabeth's resolve faltered and she melted into his arms. Her last conscious thought was that she would speak to her husband of the matter that troubled her, just as soon as they woke.

The arrival of snow made it possible for the four *montoneros* to creep across the paddocks of the *estancia* without making a sound. They had left their horses some miles back, to not alert any other animals, and had continued their journey on foot. They had their orders. Normally they answered to no one; plundered what they needed and moved on, living roughly, moving constantly, sleeping high in the mountain passes. But the gentleman had offered them a sum of gold far greater than any they had ever seen. Greed overcame any good sense, and they shook on the deal.

It was done, and done quickly. One man for each victim. They had been told where to find them, and they each opened a bedchamber door as if choreographed in a deadly dance. The glint of a too-sharp blade in the moonlight was all that could be seen.

Señor Flores, *Señorita* Flores, Tomas and Elizabeth – all took their last breath before a slit to the throat silenced them forever.

The job done, the men wiped their bloodied knives on the bed sheets. One of them left, as instructed, several lilies on the covers. Then they began to search.

Chapter Forty-two

Cornwall, Summer 2017

'It was quite a scandal at the time. According to family history, not long after the death of her father, John, Elizabeth travelled by ship – well, of course it was by ship; that was the only way to get there in those days – to Chile. To the port of Valparaiso.' Florence looked at Anna as if making sure she was paying attention. Satisfied, she continued. 'This was in the late 1800s, I believe. My grandmother told me the story only once. I must have been about ten. I remember it as if it were yesterday . . . we were sitting in the yellow drawing room and I had come to see her about some slight or other; I think I was missing my mother, who was confined to bed upstairs . . . anyway, whatever it was I remember asking about the painting of great-grandmother Augusta, the one in the hallway of the house.'

Anna suddenly remembered noticing Augusta's dimples, it was what she'd seen just before she'd fainted. She'd completely forgotten it until then. Florence appeared not to notice Anna's sharp intake of breath, and carried on. 'She said that her mother had died when she had given birth to her younger sister, Elizabeth. I remember being astonished. This was the first I had ever heard of my grandmother having a sister. To begin with, I didn't believe her. I distinctly remember asking, "Well, why doesn't she live here too?" Grandmother Georgiana looked at me sadly. "Oh sweet Florence, I wish that she did. I miss my dear sister terribly, and she is in my prayers every single day. Several months before your father was born, and not long after my father's death, Elizabeth – she was always so headstrong – grew determined to go to South America, to continue the work of our father, discovering and collecting rare plants to bring back and grow here. Elizabeth was a fine artist, with a particular eye for flowers and plants and suchlike."'

Anna held her breath and barely dared blink; she did not want to distract Florence from her story.

'I remember Grandmother Georgiana letting me snuggle next to her – which was a rare treat, let me tell you, she was usually far too busy to spend much time with me – and regaling me with stories about my adventurous and headstrong great-aunt. I was thrilled to hear of her voyage on the high seas. "Of course, letters were few and far between in those days," my grandmother said. "They had to wait for a ship returning to Southampton or Liverpool, and often only found their way to us months later. But we eventually had word that she had met a young man, the son of a local landowner, and that she had fallen in love. I was worried for her being so far away, and him not being an Englishman – imagine! I begged her to return home, but her next letter told of her marriage and then another of a baby. I became taken up with my own family – your father George had been born by then – and her letters sounded happy and were full of stories of an exotic life. I doubted there was anything I could have done to persuade her to return home in any case." I have those letters,' Florence said, coming abruptly back to the present. 'I can look for them, if you like. Though it might take me a day or so to dig them out.' She indicated the general clutter of the living room. 'I know they're here somewhere. I saved them and a few other things when we had to leave Trebithick Hall.' She made as if to look for them there and then.

'Do go on,' Anna urged, wanting to hear more of the story. 'What else did your grandmother tell you about Elizabeth?'

'Well, she said that it was some time before she heard from her sister again, but that it didn't concern her greatly. However, when almost a year went by after her last letter, she was seized with dread. "I suppose you are old enough to know the truth," she told me. "Your grandfather, Robert, engaged a private detective, who travelled to Chile to investigate. He returned with the most catastrophic tale. Elizabeth, her husband, sister-in-law and father-in-law had been violently murdered while they slept in their beds at their farm in the mountains. According to the investigator, bandits were to blame, although the local authorities had had no success in tracking them down. It seems they had simply vanished into the hills." Well, of course I was shocked, but also a tiny bit thrilled by this story. Nothing nearly as exciting ever happened in Cornwall. I have to forgive my ten-year-old self, but I couldn't help but relish the grisly details, and I begged my grandmother to tell me more.' Florence looked apologetically at Anna.

'She was murdered?' repeated Ed, aghast.

'I'm afraid so,' said Florence. 'The story made the London papers – most likely because of my great-grandfather, John Trebithick, who had been a well-known plant collector. Grandma showed me the cutting. It's in a scrapbook somewhere here, I believe.'

'But what about her baby? You said she had a baby?' asked Anna.

'Yes, she did.' Florence's mouth set in a grim line. She faltered, closed her eyes briefly, and then as she opened them she said, 'You will have to excuse me. I am suddenly very tired.'

The sun was streaming in through the bay window, overheating the crowded room. The old lady did look weary, as if the remembering and the telling had taken it out of her. Her face was pale and her hand shook slightly as she lifted her cup to her lips. 'Oh dear,' she said, realising it was empty.

'I'm sorry,' said Anna, 'we've worn you out.'

'Unfortunately we have to return to London this afternoon,' said Ed.

'Actually,' Anna began, surprising herself by making a snap decision, 'I think I might stay on for a few more days. I'd love to spend some more time talking to you, if I may, Miss Deverell.'

'Of course, that would be lovely.' The old lady brightened at the prospect. 'But I could manage a little lie-down now, I think. Stamina isn't what it used to be, I'm afraid.'

Ed looked at Anna questioningly. 'How will you get around?'

'Oh,' she said doubtfully.

'Where are you staying, my dear?'

'In the pub in the next village, the Smugglers Arms.'

'That's not a problem, then,' said Florence decisively. 'I can pick you up tomorrow morning and we can talk some more.'

'You still drive?' asked Ed incredulously.

'I'm not in my grave yet, young man,' she scolded him. 'Though I only potter about the place – just far enough to get my groceries.'

'Thank you,' said Anna. 'I really would appreciate talking to you further.'

'And I shall enjoy the company,' declared Florence. 'Now, if you will excuse me . . .'

'Well, that was all very interesting, wasn't it?' said Ed as they walked to the car.

Anna had paused to admire the frilly purple–blue petals of a bearded iris in the front garden. She looked up at Ed, her eyes shining. 'I know. I can't quite believe it.' She paused. 'Um . . . Do you think we could go back to Trebithick Hall before you go? And you don't mind me staying on a few more days, do you? I mean, I'm really grateful to you for coming here with me, but I don't feel I can leave just yet.'

'Of course not,' said Ed. 'You've only just begun to unravel this mystery.' He winked at her. 'I will expect regular updates, though.'

'Thanks. I mean it. For everything. You've really gone above and beyond, especially for a virtual stranger.'

He looked hurt. 'I wouldn't have said we are exactly strangers any more, Jenkins.'

'I didn't mean it to come out like that. Of course we're not.' She grasped his arm. 'I really, truly am very grateful.'

He looked mollified. 'Come on, then, we've got an hour or so before lunch and then I really will have to get on the road. The traffic back isn't going to be pretty if I leave it too late.'

They drove the few miles to Trebithick Hall, which was packed with Sunday morning visitors enjoying the bright, sunny day. 'I'm going to have a wander round the gardens,' said Ed. 'There are some particularly fine *camellia sinensis* that I'd like to take another look at.'

Anna nodded, smiling. 'Okay,' she agreed, loving that his passion for plants matched her own. 'I'd like to see some more of the house. How about we meet back at the entrance in an hour?'

Anna stepped into the cool, dark hallway again. She stopped at the portrait of Augusta again, feeling another thrill of familiarity. She'd missed the guided tour, but she was happy to wander the rooms, transported into a late-Victorian well-to-do household. It was a beautiful home; unlike any she had seen in Australia. The scale of the rooms was what surprised her most: their soaring ceilings – but as Florence Deverell had stated, they must have been the very devil to heat in winter, especially when one didn't have a full staff to keep the fires blazing in every room.

There was even a nursery, decked out with a doll's house, a rocking horse and a train set. Had they belonged to Elizabeth and Georgiana, she wondered, or were they brought in to add period flavour to the place? It was most likely the latter, but Anna allowed herself to imagine the possibility nonetheless. It was strange to think that these rooms had once echoed to their girlish laughter and quick footsteps.

Having toured the bedrooms, she returned down the grand main staircase and found herself in the library. Hundreds of worn leather-bound tomes lined two of the walls. The third had windows that looked out onto the garden, and the final wall was hung with framed watercolours. She recognised the style immediately, though some were less detailed than the ones in the sketchbook. There was a particularly beautiful study of a scarlet rhododendron flower, the detail of the petals and the stalk finely drawn. In that moment, the reality of what had befallen Elizabeth hit home. How bold and brave she must have been to venture so far from home, and what a tragedy that her life – and her obvious talent – had been so savagely cut short.

'There you are,' said Ed, coming up behind her and putting his hand on her shoulder, making Anna jump at his touch.

'Look at these, Ed.' She pointed to the wall of watercolours.

His eyes followed the direction she indicated. 'Yes, they're definitely the same artist, aren't they?' he said.' Although somewhat earlier works, by the looks of things. You can really see how her skill developed in the later watercolours in your sketchbook. They're still quite stunning, though.'

Anna smiled sadly. 'What a shame she never reached her potential.'

Chapter Forty-three

CHILE, 1887

The *montoneros* searched. Quietly but frantically. Moving through the bedrooms, pulling down blankets, rifling through chests of clothes in the darkness.

They searched in vain, then regrouped and were about to move to the empty servants' quarters when they heard a noise. A baby's cry. Without a word they stopped in their tracks. The leader signalled the others with his eyes. The gentleman had paid them half of the enormous sum when they accepted the commission; it was more money than they would see in a year. The remaining amount was due when they brought him the prize. The leader held up his hand and then pointed to the door. The message was clear. They would not stay to complete the task; they had been unable to find what the gentleman had described and they would not have the blood of an innocent child on their hands. Silently, the men followed their leader down the stairs and out of the house the way they had come, through a window in one of the living areas.

It had all happened within the space of an hour. The *montoneros* galloped away, their foot and hoof prints slowly covered over by the gathering snow, eventually to leave no sign of where they had come from or where they were going.

Daisy, who had risen to bring Violeta to Elizabeth, found the bodies. She didn't notice anything awry at first, for her lamp let out barely a flicker of light. She put her arm out to rouse her mistress and was surprised when her fingers encountered a warm wetness. Looking at her hand, she could not believe her eyes. Blood? So much blood! She lifted the lamp higher and saw Elizabeth, her skin ghostly against the dark blood. Strangely, her face looked peaceful, as if she were merely asleep. And there was *Señor* Flores, blood blooming like a flower against the white of his nightshirt. She let out an unearthly scream, the noise rising unbidden from her throat at the horrible, horrible sight. Violeta, cradled in her arms, began to howl as well, and Daisy pulled her closer, turning to shield the baby's eyes from her parents' bodies. As she did so, she caught sight of flowers, scattered at the end of the bed, glowing in the darkness. Pure white, trumpet-shaped lilies. A chill came over her, and her screams died in her throat. She knew what they meant. She knew who was responsible for this. She ran from room to room, already knowing what she would find. *Señor* Flores. And then Sofia – beautiful Sofia. They too lay lifeless, their throats slit, blood pooling and darkening beneath their still-warm bodies. They were beyond saving, all of them.

Still clutching Violeta to her bosom, she heaved the contents of her stomach into a bowl that sat on a chest in Sofia's room. Then she wiped her mouth with a shaking hand, gathering her thoughts. 'Shush now . . . shush,' she rocked the baby, who was wailing from hunger.

She thought hard. She had to get out of there, had to keep Violeta safe. And Elizabeth's precious plant – the cause of this nightmare. She fled back along the corridor to the baby's room and put her down in her sheepskin hammock. 'Hush now, little one, it's just while I prepare,' she whispered. Miraculously the baby ceased her wailing. Daisy gathered an armful of gowns and underthings and threw them into an old flour sack before returning for Elizabeth's box and the sketchbook. Whoever had murdered her and *Señor* Flores and his family had not found what they sought. It was up to her to make sure that they never did.

She crept along the corridor and as she came down the stairs she felt an icy draught. She nearly jumped out of her skin as the front door creaked on its hinges. She waited several seconds, scarcely daring to breathe. It was only the wind.

She had dressed Violeta as warmly as she was able and took her mistress's heavy cloak for herself, pulling the hood up over her head until she was almost unrecognisable as a woman. It would keep her warm, and incognito as she travelled, but she also remembered helping Elizabeth sew money in there. She might find herself in need of it in the weeks to come.

She stepped outside with the baby strapped to her by means of a thick band of cloth wound around and around her middle and shielded by the cloak. The landscape seemed to glow in the moonlight. The snow was falling lightly now, but she could see several sets of footsteps leading away from the *estancia*, on the path that led further into the mountains. She crossed herself, praying that the murderers would not return. Her only hope of escape was to head along the other path, the one that led to Santiago. To flee to Valparaiso and seek help from the Campbells would be a mistake; they were too connected in the town, and news of her presence would reach the ears of Mr Chegwidden without a doubt. Her only option was to travel to Santiago, where she hoped to find Mr Williamson.

Daisy reached the stables and approached the quietest of all the horses, a chestnut mare, coaxing her into a bridle that she found hanging on the stable wall. She hefted a saddle awkwardly onto its back and then lashed the box and her bags to each side of it. Shuffling along to a hitching post, she hoisted herself up, careful not to disturb the baby nestled against her chest.

The ride to Santiago was slow going. The horse picked her way along in the darkness and Daisy had to resist urging the mare on, trusting her good sense to get them there safely. She tensed at the slightest movement in the grasses beside her, gripping the reins so tightly that they bit into the soft skin on her palms. She barely noticed the pain. Mercifully, Violeta, cocooned in her makeshift papoose, slept, oblivious to her surroundings.

As dawn began to light the sky, she came upon an inn where she could rest her horse and seek refuge for a few hours. Slowing the mare, she approached with caution. She dismounted, careful of the baby bundled around her waist, and untied the saddlebag and box, carrying them with her. Violeta, still strapped to her front, began to whimper. 'Hush, little one. I will get you some food soon, hush now,' she soothed. Daisy went inside and was thankful for her foresight in bringing Tomas's bag of pesos with her. She handed a few notes over, enough for a room for a few hours, speaking only enough Spanish to make her needs known. She kept the baby concealed beneath her cloak and prayed that she would not cry out.

Daisy reached the room and sat heavily on the thin mattress, working her frozen fingers until the feeling began to return to her hands. It sent sharp pains through her but she barely allowed herself to notice. As soon as she was able, she began to fumble with the cloth that bound the baby to her, eventually working it loose and holding the child in her arms. Violeta had begun to wail loudly now. Daisy opened one of the saddlebags and brought out a goatskin of milk. She dribbled a little on her fingers and let the baby suck. 'I know, sweetheart, but it's the best I can do,' she said, rocking her back and forth. Violeta soon quietened as she got a taste of the milk.

As the baby drank, Daisy lay down next to her, spent. Sleep dragged her into its dark embrace before she had a chance to relive even a moment of the horror of the previous hours.

Chapter Forty-four

Cornwall, Summer 2017

Ed drove Anna back to the pub, and they found a spot outside in the sunshine. The beer garden was crowded and their food took a while to arrive, but Ed didn't seem to mind the delay. As they lingered over pints of Doom Bar, Anna felt herself relax, happy in his company. He made her laugh more than she had in years. She found herself noticing his smile and the way it crinkled the corners of his eyes. She became conscious of his legs, so close to hers under the table, his large, square hands as they clasped the beer glass and the way his hair flopped delightfully into his eyes despite his continued efforts to push it back. She didn't want the afternoon to end, and despite his earlier words, Ed seemed in no hurry to make the drive back to London. It was only as the shadows began to lengthen that he noticed the time.

'I really must get going,' he said reluctantly.

'Of course. And thank you again.'

'No, I should thank you for letting me tag along. It's been a breath of fresh air to get out of town. Not to mention getting to know you, Jenkins. You can be as spiky as a *parodia magnifica*, but when you open up you're as beautiful as its flower.'

'Don't you try and sweet-talk me with botanica,' she replied, grinning at him.

They walked outside to the car park and Anna kicked self-consciously at the gravel, not knowing how to say goodbye to him. He surprised her by sweeping her into a bear hug and they remained entwined for some moments. Anna allowed herself to be caught up in the wonderfully comforting feeling of his arms around her.

'Let me know how you get on tomorrow,' he said, eventually releasing her and opening the car door. 'And don't go scaring the locals in those peacock trousers.'

'I'll be doing just that!' Anna called out as he drove off, feeling as if a piece of herself had gone with him.

She abandoned half-made plans to walk off her lunch and instead returned to her bedroom upstairs. It was a small room, with sloping ceilings and a tiny window that overlooked the village rooftops and offered a brief glimpse of the ocean. She flicked on the kettle and pulled out the diary from her bag. Marguerite's journal. She had read more of it, learning of Marguerite's life and details of Lily's development, fascinated to be learning of the early life of her great-grandmother.

It seemed that, after her initial arrival in Sydney, Marguerite only wrote entries every few years. In the part Anna was reading, Lily was five and about to start school. ''Tis good that she will learn her letters, for I have never been so glad as to have mine. I remember Miss Elizabeth—'

Anna broke off in excitement. This was the first mention of Elizabeth, she was sure of it. But what was the connection between them? Anna had first thought that Elizabeth and Marguerite might be the same person, but that theory was now discredited. She looked down at the page again and read on. 'I remember Miss Elizabeth teaching me on the long voyage to South America. I feared I should never see land again; we were tossed about like driftwood for so many days and nights. Having something to occupy my days was a blessing.'

So, Marguerite and Elizabeth had travelled to Chile together. The mystery was unfolding like origami in reverse, each exposed crease revealing a new facet of the story.

She read on. Marguerite kept circling back to the man she was scared of, wondering if he was still at large. There was a name, Anna could just make it out, it looked to be Damien Chegwibben, or possibly Chegwidden. The ink had faded in places and was hard to read.

Anna couldn't wait to speak to Miss Deverell in the morning. Surely she would be able to shed some light on who might have accompanied Elizabeth on that long voyage. She briefly wondered about calling Ed to tell him of this new development, but looked at her watch and reckoned he would still be on the road. It would have to wait.

Anna kept reading, but there were no further references to Elizabeth, and her eyelids grew heavy, eventually fluttering shut as a sudden shower drummed on the roof, lulling her to sleep.

She didn't wake until early evening, when her stomach began to complain that it was time to eat again, so she braved the pub on her own, sitting at the bar and chatting to the publican who had showed them their rooms.

'You're from Australia, then?' he said with a charming Cornish burr.

'Correct,' said Anna. 'Just visiting.'

'And how do you like it here?'

'I like it very much,' she replied. 'Though I've barely had time to explore. We did go to Lady Luck Cove last night – what a pretty spot that is.'

'Aye,' he said, putting a pie and a plate of chips in front of her. 'That's a local favourite. Specially for courting couples.'

Anna reddened as she remembered the feeling of sitting so close to Ed as they watched the flames from the fire flicker and glow.

'And we've been up to the house – Trebithick Hall.'

'Trebithick Hall . . . My family used to work there, oh, many years ago now. My great-grandfather, James Banks, was the stablemaster and my great-grandmother the housekeeper, and then my grandfather thereafter. That were before the family went broke, of course. Then they dismissed all the servants and sold off a lot of the land.'

'Did you ever hear stories of John Trebithick and his daughters – Georgiana and Elizabeth?' asked Anna, her interest sparking at his connection to the house.

'Happen I did. 'Twas quite the scandal when Miss Elizabeth went missing, and Miss Daisy too. I recall my grandfather telling me about it when I was a lad.'

'Miss Daisy?'

'She were the lady's maid who travelled with Miss Elizabeth. What two young women were doing going off virtually on their own halfway around the world in the first place is anyone's guess. Though times have clearly changed, of course,' he added, indicating her.

'Yes, I suppose they have,' she agreed, her mind working furiously. 'I don't suppose you remember the surname of the lady's maid?' she asked, hopefully.

He scratched his head, then shook it. 'Nup. Haven't the faintest, I'm afraid. Your best bet is to speak to Miss Deverell. She lives over Trevone way. She's the last surviving member of the family.'

'Thank you,' said Anna with a smile.

The publican was called away to the other end of the bar to serve other customers, and so Anna finished her pie and drained her glass of Doom Bar – she'd become quite fond of the beer since Ed had introduced her to it.

She wasn't ready to return to her room, so she stepped outside into the soft evening light. A footpath that cut through the patchwork of green and golden fields towards the sea beckoned her. The rain had stopped, though the wild grasses that clogged the lane soon drenched her legs. She breathed in the cool evening air, which was scented with the sweet, soapy smell of Queen Anne's lace and clover. As she climbed a stile dividing two fields, being careful to avoid the stinging nettles that swarmed around its base, she looked up to see a flock of swallows coming in to roost. Bells rang from the village church, a cascading harmony that sounded across the landscape. She followed the sound, venturing into the churchyard where ancient lichen-covered gravestones leant at angles, pushed off-kilter as the ground had settled over the years. She peered at the names, finally coming across the Trebithick family section. There was John Trebithick, buried next to his wife, 'dearly beloved Augusta Rose'. A little further along were the graves of Georgiana and Robert Deverell, then George and Penelope, the surfaces of their much newer stones dark and shiny. A gust of wind blew through the churchyard, rustling the leaves on the horse chestnut and despite the warm evening, she shivered. There wasn't a stone for Elizabeth. Anna imagined her buried perhaps on a Chilean hillside, thousands of kilometres away, but with the man she had loved. Anna lingered until the bells ceased and she heard the sound of chattering voices coming out of the church. Practice was over.

She retraced her steps and turned in the direction of the sea. As she caught sight of its deep, fathomless blue, Anna felt a profound peace descend. She didn't stop to question why it was that she felt such a strong connection to this place where she'd barely spent forty-eight hours. She didn't resist what she would normally have dismissed as a fanciful notion. A notion of coming home.

She clambered down the rocky path to the cove where she and Ed had picnicked the evening before. Now, as then, it was deserted. Anna pulled her hair, sticky from the salt and sweat of her walk, off her face and then yanked her T-shirt over her head. Shucking off her shoes and hurriedly unbuttoning her shorts before she changed her mind, she stripped naked. Taking a deep breath, she ran towards the water, plunging in up to her waist. She ducked under an incoming wave and came up gasping with the cold, but this time she didn't return to shore. Determined, she kept on wading until the water reached her neck and she could only just touch the sandy bottom with the tips of her toes. The chill was exhilarating.

Chapter Forty-five

Cornwall, Summer 2017

Anna returned to her room, damp and sandy but refreshed from her freezing swim. After a warm shower, she settled back on the bed and picked up Marguerite's diary. There were only a final few pages to be deciphered.

'I cannot go to my grave without telling the truth, and so I must unburden myself here . . .' Anna read slowly, stumbling over the fine copperplate. 'Would that my mistress Elizabeth had not perished . . .'

Ah. It was suddenly obvious. *Marguerite was Daisy* – Elizabeth's maidservant. *Of course.* Anna did a mental face-palm. The truth had been hiding in plain sight: a marguerite was a type of daisy.

'. . . for, were she breathing today, Lily would be with her mother as she should be.'

Anna reeled in shock. Lily was *Elizabeth*'s daughter. The daughter that Florence had mentioned. She could scarcely believe it. Lily, Anna's great-grandmother, Granny Gus's mother . . . Anna felt a tingle of adrenalin run right to her toes. Did Marguerite ever tell Lily the truth about her parentage? She couldn't have done, otherwise Granny Gus would have known about it, surely? There was also the fact of Augusta's dimples; Anna knew from high-school biology that they were genetically inherited. But plenty of people had them; they were extremely common . . . both Gus and Anna's nieces had them. She dropped the diary and picked up her phone, scrolling until she reached her mother's number.

No answer. She looked at the time. Three in the afternoon in Sydney.

She tried another number. Again, no answer from her sister. Of course; school pick-up time.

Anna considered calling Ed, but it was nearly midnight and she didn't think it fair to disturb him. She lay on her back on the bed, her mind swirling with the possibilities that this new piece of information had thrown up. If this were true, then it meant that she was related to Florence Deverell. How would Florence take the news? Would she even believe it?

~

The sun was casting bright shafts of light through the open curtains and Anna heard the grating sound of a delivery truck bouncing beer barrels down into the pub's cellars. For a moment she lay there, listening to the soft warble of birds outside her window, feeling a sense of calm and certainty. She blinked as she remembered the diary, and felt for it on the bed.

Two hours later, she sat at a table outside the front of the pub, enjoying the morning sun. She was waiting apprehensively for Florence's car and started as the sound of a motor pierced the village quiet. There was a jaunty toot-toot and the old lady was waving at her through the window of a small vehicle that looked as if it were held together with baling twine and optimism. The front bumper sagged at one end and there was no glass in the passenger window.

'Hello, my dear. Glad to see you're ready on time. Punctuality is a virtue, don't you think?'

'Oh yes,' she agreed with an inward smile.

They were soon whizzing out of the village with Anna clinging on for dear life thinking that though Florence might look like a sweet old lady, she drove like a V8 supercar champion. They narrowly missed several stray sheep on the high-hedged, narrow country lane that led to Trevone.

'I've found them,' Florence shouted over the roar of the engine. 'The letters from Elizabeth Trebithick to her sister – my grandmother. You can read them when we get home.'

'Oh good,' said Anna, her hands gripping the door handle afresh as Florence careened around a blind corner, blithely oblivious to the white line in the middle of the road.

'I'll pop the kettle on,' said Florence as they came to an abrupt stop in front of the house. 'We can sit outside; it's a lovely morning for it.'

Anna shakily followed her up the garden path.

'Now, here we are,' she said, ushering Anna into the back garden, which was a pretty tangle of deep purple pansies, scarlet zinnias, and orange marigolds and nasturtiums. As Anna sat turning the diary over and over in her hands she couldn't help but smile at the thought that Granny Gus would have loved the colours. The two women were so similar – but then they were cousins, Anna reminded herself.

Florence eventually returned with a tray of tea and a buff-coloured envelope. 'We gave a lot of the family's artefacts to the Trust,' she explained. 'But my grandmother couldn't bear to part with these. Be careful, though; I fear they are now quite fragile.'

Anna carefully opened the envelope and extracted several folded sheets of thin paper. 'Oh my goodness,' she said. 'How wonderful that they have survived.'

Florence nodded. 'Indeed. It is the last we ever heard of her. It is some small blessing, I suppose, that they are full of love and joy.'

Anna read the first of the letters and was transported to a fiesta in a Chilean *estancia*, reading of the feasting and the dancing that went on until dawn. In another, Elizabeth wrote warmly of her new husband, reassuring her sister that he was kind as well as handsome and strong. 'I am helpless in the face of it,' she had written. Anna smiled as she looked up from the pages.

'Miss Deverell—'

'Florence, please. "Miss Deverell" sounds like one of my students addressing me.'

'Florence, then,' said Anna. 'There is something that you must also see. I mentioned that one of the things I found was a diary. I finished reading it last night. It was written by a woman named Marguerite, in the 1880s and '90s. It tells the story of her arrival in Sydney by boat to make a new life for herself.'

'But I don't understand,' Florence said, puzzled. 'There's never been a Marguerite in the family, and certainly not at that time.'

'She brought with her a child – I presumed she was her daughter – Lily,' Anna continued. 'I only discovered the final piece of the story yesterday. Here . . .' She opened it at the final few pages. 'The handwriting is a little tricky, but I think you should at least read this.'

Florence looked intrigued as she took the book that Anna offered her, placing her glasses on the end of her nose and peering down at it. 'Oh my dear, I can barely see this, the ink is so faint. Would you mind reading it aloud?'

'Of course,' said Anna. '"My mistress Elizabeth . . ."'

Florence's eyes widened in shock.

'". . . made me swear to take care of Lily should any ill befall her. Of course, I never did imagine that I should have to fulfil this promise."'

'Oh my dear,' Florence interrupted. 'Can this be true?' The old lady's rheumy eyes appeared to water as she wiped them with her sleeve. The two women looked at each other. There were no words.

Anna heard the buzzing of the bees in the flowers and the cry of a bird overhead. Time seemed to stand still.

'Can it really, possibly be true?' Florence repeated.

'I think it must,' said Anna.

Chapter Forty-six

Cornwall, Summer 2017

Anna poured tea for them both and waited for Florence's questions. She had barely taken a sip when they came tumbling forth.

'Your family in Australia? Your grandmother?'

'My grandmother was called Gus – Augusta,' replied Anna. 'Her mother I never knew, but she was called Lily. I am certain that this is the same Lily who came with Marguerite to Australia in the 1880s.'

'Then we are related,' said Florence, a trace of wonder in her voice. 'Branches of the same tree, separated by a hemisphere.'

'Yes, I think we must be,' said Anna.

'Do you have brothers, sisters . . . your mother and father?'

'My mother, Eleanor, was Granny Gus's only child – and I've a sister, Vanessa, she has three children, Fleur, Ivy and Jasmine

. . . I know, the floral thing seems to be a bit of a theme in the family, one way or another,' she laughed. 'My dad isn't around, though – he died when I was little.'

'I'm sorry, Anna. Do you have children yourself? I never thought to ask.'

'No, no I don't.'

'Well, there's plenty of time,' the old lady replied, 'though you may prefer not to. I certainly did, although now I wonder if that was the right choice. And, well, I found I rather preferred my own company. But,' she beamed at Anna, 'how absolutely splendid that I now find I have a cousin. Albeit several times removed.'

'I suppose you do.' It was almost, in a strange way, as if she had a part of Granny Gus back. 'Although it feels as though you should be a kind of great-aunt.'

'You know, you have quite the look of her,' said Florence. 'I meant to mention it earlier, but it seemed like simply the fancy of an old woman.'

'Of who?'

'Augusta. The portrait in the house. You're almost the spitting image of her.'

'You may be right. I thought I was seeing things when first I looked at the painting,' admitted Anna. 'But Ed mentioned it too.'

'Well, I think this calls for something stronger than tea. Will you have a nip of whisky with me, Anna?'

Anna smiled. 'I will indeed.'

Two glasses later, Anna began to feel a little woozy as the sun rose higher in the sky and the heat began to build. There had been something niggling at the back of her mind ever since she'd read the diary and realised that Marguerite/Daisy had brought Lily to Australia. 'I've been wondering,' she said to Florence. 'Who the man was that threatened her, and why she never went back to Cornwall.'

'And never returned Lily to her family?' Florence asked.

'Yes. It seems odd that she didn't. I mean, I know from what her diary says that she feared for her life; but you would have thought that she would one day bring her back, or at least tell Lily.'

'Don't forget what a long way it was to travel in those days – the voyage took months and not everyone survived it. Not like today where you can jump on a plane and be there in a day. Anyway, maybe she loved Lily as if she were her own and after a while couldn't begin to think of letting her go. Did she marry in Sydney?'

'Yes, she did. She mentions a man in the diary that she liked – a carpenter called Joseph Bailey. She married him.'

'Well, maybe that was another reason she didn't want to leave. She'd made a new life for herself. And don't forget, back in England she was a servant and probably always would have been. In Australia she could create a whole new life for herself; there were far fewer boundaries.'

'Yes, but what a secret to take to your grave,' Anna mused. 'It must have been awful.'

'We all have regrets we have to live with, but I agree, this might have weighed very heavily on her conscience.'

'I mean, she lived a lie her whole life,' said Anna.

'What's done is done, my dear, and there's no point in trying to make it otherwise. Now, I think I might need a rest if you don't mind,' said Florence getting unsteadily to her feet. 'Be right as rain after that, though. Would you care to stay to dinner? I've a bit of steak in the fridge and a nice bottle of red I've been saving for a special occasion.'

'I'd love to,' said Anna. 'But perhaps I should leave and give you a chance to nap?'

'Take my car, my dear. In fact,' she said, 'you are welcome to borrow it until tomorrow. I'm not very good after dark.'

Anna breathed a sigh of relief. She wouldn't be subjected to Florence's driving again, especially not after a few glasses of whisky. 'If you're sure, then that would be very kind.'

Anna spent the afternoon exploring some of the local villages, charmed by ancient stone and slate houses that huddled into the landscape, as if sheltering from the wind blowing off the ocean. As she walked she tried to imagine growing up on this rocky, wild coastline; what sort of a person she might have been. All a bit silly really, because she wouldn't exist if Daisy had returned to Cornwall with Lily. She eventually came to the conclusion that Daisy/Marguerite couldn't be all to blame, and that she had at least preserved Elizabeth's sketchbook and her own diary; a trail of crumbs that had led Anna to solve the mystery, and brought her to Cornwall. What was it that Fleur was always belting out at the top of her voice? 'Let it go . . . let it go . . .' Perhaps it was time for her to do some letting go of her own.

Her thoughts turned to Ed and she pulled out her phone to call him. It rang through to his voicemail but she didn't leave a message. She'd try again later. She found herself missing his good-natured teasing, not to mention the lopsided smile that made her stomach somersault whenever he directed it at her.

Florence looked delighted to see her again when she opened the front door, and hugged her warmly. 'Hello, Anna dear,' she said.

'There's something else, something I read in the diary,' Anna said as they took a seat out in the garden again. 'I forgot to mention it earlier.'

'Oh yes?'

'The name of the man who threatened Marguerite – Daisy. His surname was Chegwibben or Chegwidden. She seemed especially concerned about him. She mentions that she feared he would hunt her down and harm her and Lily. That she was concerned about where he might be.'

'Chegwidden, most likely. It's not that uncommon a surname in Cornwall. I know a family of that name. Not far from here. If I recall correctly, I had a couple of the girls go through the school. Wild girls, but likeable nonetheless. I always thought they could have done better than they did.'

'You don't think it could be the same family?'

Florence shrugged. 'More likely than you might think. Come on, why don't we Google it?' She disappeared into the house.

Anna hid her surprise when Florence returned with a slim, silver laptop.

'Now, what was his first name?'

'Damien. With an e.'

Florence's gnarled fingers skipped over the keyboard. 'Computer lessons at the village hall,' she explained, noticing Anna's impressed expression. 'Ah, there's a Reverend Arthur Chegwidden . . . no . . . a Daniel Chegwidden wanted for a pub brawl . . .'

'Why don't you put in a bit more information?' suggested Anna. 'Damien Chegwidden and the word "plants" or "botany" perhaps?'

'Oh yes, that's an idea. Okay, here we go.' She double-clicked and then began to read. 'This is from a historical site, something about botanical scandals of England. Ooh, this could be good . . .'

Anna leant over to read alongside her. 'Damien Chegwidden, born 1852, died 1893, arrested and found guilty of smuggling seeds. Died in Bodmin Gaol of causes unknown.'

'Oh goodness. Is there anything more?'

Anna waited a moment as she read on. 'Nope. That's it. How disappointing.'

'Hm.'

'I know, what if I went to Bodmin Gaol? Surely they'd have records? We might find out some more from those?'

'Anna dear, I hate to disappoint you, but the place is now a ruin. There haven't been prisoners incarcerated there since the 1920s. But hang on a second, I've got an idea.' Florence stomped off back into the house again.

'Here we go,' she said, returning with a battered White Pages. 'Chegwidden C . . . Claire was her name, I'm almost certain of it. Happily it would seem she's not married and taken another surname. It has to be her. Pass me your phone and I'll give her a call.'

Anna was dubious about the plan, but duly handed over her mobile and watched while Florence dialled.

She listened as someone answered and Florence made plans for the following morning. Anna could scarcely believe her ears. Was everything here so intertwined?

'Now, are you hungry, my dear?' Florence asked, handing her back the phone with a look of satisfaction on her face.

'Miss Deverell. I must say I was surprised to get your call last night.' The woman standing in front of Anna and Florence had a baby on one hip and a toddler hiding behind her skirts eyeing them with as much curiosity as his mother. She held a ragged piece of tissue in one hand, wiping the baby's nose, before turning and ushering them in.

'You are very kind to see us, Claire,' said Florence as they walked along the hallway.

'It must be more than fifteen years ago. I can't say I was the best of students,' she said, a note of apology in her round Cornish vowels.

'Yours was my last year. I remember it well.'

'Aye. I'd not much use for school by then.' She led them into a small, bright kitchen and shifted the baby into a highchair, fetching him a sippy cup. The toddler disappeared into what looked to be a sitting room, and soon the sounds of cartoons burbled in the background. 'Perhaps I should have done. Might not have ended up on my own with two little 'uns.'

'There's always time, Claire.' The schoolteacher in Florence was still evident.

Claire shrugged. 'You think? With these two under my feet?' She looked at the baby, who was banging his cup on the tray of the highchair.

'This is my— er, my friend, Anna, from Australia,' said Florence.

Claire raised her eyebrows. 'You've come a long way. Can I get you both some tea? You'll have to have it black, though. Milk's run out.'

Anna and Florence shook their heads.

'We won't keep you long,' said Florence. 'Anna is here doing some research for a history project. I'm helping her out with it.'

'Oh, and what does that have to do with me?'

'Well, she mentioned that one of the people she is researching was a man called Damien Chegwidden.'

The woman's eyebrows lifted even higher at the sound of her own surname.

'He lived in the late 1800s, and it seems he was imprisoned in Bodmin Gaol.'

The woman nodded. 'I know the story well.'

'You do?' asked Anna.

'Aye. The blackest of black sheep in the family. My dad used to like to joke about it. Said if we weren't careful we'd end up no better than Great-great-great Uncle Damien, rotting in prison. Used to scare me silly.'

'So, what happened?' asked Anna.

'From what I know of it, he was a thief.'

'Yes, I gathered that,' said Anna. 'Stealing seeds? It hardly seems such a heinous crime.'

'That's where you're wrong,' said Claire, relishing her story. 'Apparently in those days there was a great deal of money in bringing seeds and plants from across the world back to England. Cornwall was known as a place where rare plants were grown and sold to gardeners throughout the country. Anyway, according to Dad, who heard it from his grandfather, Damien Chegwidden became caught up in a seed-smuggling racket in South America.'

Anna and Florence exchanged the briefest of looks.

'Apparently – though no one knows for sure – he was killed while he was in gaol. What did you say you were looking into him for?'

'Oh, it's a project on plant-hunters in the nineteenth century for . . .' Anna thought quickly. 'For uni. Finding out about Damien Chegwidden is a small piece of the puzzle. But an interesting one nonetheless.'

'Well, I'm pleased I could help . . . oh Christ!' she yelled as the baby tipped water all over himself, soaking his towelling playsuit. 'I've only just changed him.'

'We really shouldn't keep you,' said Florence. 'But here's my number.' She handed Claire a piece of paper. 'I'd be happy to help you with any further study, point you in the right direction. As a thank you, if you like. You showed promise.'

'I did?' Claire seemed pleased with the compliment.

Chapter Forty-seven

Cornwall and London, Summer 2017

'Thank you, Anna,' said Florence as Anna drove them away – after the previous nerve-shredding experience Anna had insisted on it.

'What for?'

'For not telling Claire that Damien Chegwidden was most likely a murderer as well as a thief.'

'I didn't think it would have served any purpose. She might have got defensive. After all, he was a relation of hers, however distant. And it seemed he got his just deserts.'

'You're a perceptive girl, Anna. Sometimes the truth does no one any favours.'

'But it was my search for the truth that brought me to you.'

Florence smiled at her. 'It was, and I'm very glad of that. You have solved a mystery, but, more importantly, given me the satisfaction of knowing that the Trebithick line will carry on after me, even if it is on the other side of the world. It is more comfort than you can know. I have carried the burden of thinking I was the last for so long. It is good to be able to cast it off.'

Anna nodded. She was beginning to understand the relief that came with the throwing off of burdens.

'I suppose I should return to London,' said Anna, feeling sad at the prospect. She had come to love the wild beauty of the Cornish coast, even after such a short stay, and it would be a wrench to leave so soon.

'Your young man will no doubt be missing you,' said Florence.

'My young man? Oh, you mean Ed? He's not my "young man" as you call it. We actually don't really know each other that well.'

'Are you sure about that?' Florence clearly wasn't convinced. 'He certainly looked like he was very keen on you.'

Anna went pink at the suggestion. 'Anyway, I'm only here for a few weeks,' she said quickly. 'I've a home and a business to return to.' All of a sudden her lonely flat didn't seem quite so appealing.

'You never did say what it is you do in Sydney.'

'I'm a gardener. Well, that is, I have my own horticulture business.'

'Now, that doesn't come as too much of a surprise – you come from a long line of those with their hands in the soil one way or another.'

'Yes, I suppose I do. My grandmother taught me the thrill of growing things. You would have liked her, I know it.'

'I'm sure I would have, my dear.'

Anna pulled up in the car park of the Smugglers Arms. 'Lunch. My shout,' she insisted. 'It's the least I can do after all your help.'

'Nonsense,' said Florence, 'it's been absolutely fascinating. Given an old stick like me something to focus on other than the church flowers. Not to mention that I've got a new relative – cousin or great-niece, I don't care which.'

Despite her assertion, she agreed to Anna's invitation and they feasted on sausage rolls and crisp, cold beer, as Anna told Florence all about Vanessa and the girls, even about Harvey, who somehow didn't seem quite so obnoxious from a distance. When they had finished, Anna hugged Florence farewell but she found it hard to let go, not knowing when or if she would see her again.

'Off you go, then. Come on, don't get all sentimental on me. Can't stand that stuff,' said Florence gruffly as Anna released her.

The last Anna saw of the old lady was the back of her head, barely visible over the driver's seat of her car as it careered around a bend in the narrow lane. On the wrong side of the road. The woman must have nine lives thought Anna, smiling in amusement.

Anna returned to her room and swapped her sandals for trainers. She was booked on the London train late that after-noon, but before she left, she wanted to visit Trebithick Hall one final time. She had a plan that was taking shape in her mind, and she wanted to talk to the head gardener to see if, rather than a flight of fancy, it might be a possibility. The house was only a few miles away and she welcomed the exercise.

~

Arriving in Paddington late that evening, tired and travel-weary, she splurged on a taxi to Richmond. It was nearly midnight when she retrieved the key her Airbnb host had left out for her and crept, as quietly as possible, up the stairs to her room. She wanted to call her mum, but she couldn't risk the sound of her voice waking the sleeping household. She'd rung Ed before boarding the train, and had arranged to meet him the following afternoon after work. 'We'll go for a ride through Richmond Park,' he'd suggested and rang off before she had a chance to say that she hadn't ridden a bike since she was a kid. Spin classes didn't really count.

~

'Jenkins!' Ed bounded across the gardens to where Anna stood at the Victoria Gate, its imposing, curlicued wrought iron bearing a royal emblem in gold leaf of a lion and unicorn. Anna felt a thrill of recognition at the sight of his loping stride, the broad shoulders and, as he got closer, the endearing scattering of freckles across his face.

'Jenkins!' he said again, his pleasure at seeing her as evident as her own. He enveloped her in a hug, lifting her clear off her feet. Anna returned his embrace, and for a moment neither of them spoke, each sinking into the other, savouring the closeness.

Then, both at once, they began to talk.

'How are you, Ed?'

'You made it back safely?'

Having reassured each other of their mutual wellbeing, Ed took hold of Anna's hand and they walked towards the main road.

'Do you know, I think they are growing on me,' he remarked, taking in her peacock leggings.

Anna whacked him gently with the bag she was carrying.

'Oof!' he cried, doubling over theatrically. 'I suppose I deserved that.'

As they walked towards the park, Anna told Ed about the rest of her stay in Cornwall. 'So, it turns out Elizabeth was my great-great grandmother,' said Anna. 'If you can believe that.'

'I can,' he said solemnly. 'There had to be a reason for the box being in your grandmother's house.'

They eventually came to a small wooden shed outside which stood a rack of bicycles.

'I . . . er . . . it's been a long time since I've ridden a bike,' Anna said. 'Possibly not since I was a kid.'

'Oh, it'll come back to you,' Ed said confidently. 'You'll find that it's like riding a bike.'

Anna groaned.

After a wobbly start, she soon found her balance and was flying down the path ahead of Ed. It was a million times more fun than being in a dark, sweaty cycle studio. Anna shook her hair loose, loving the feeling of the wind across her body and the scent of cut grass in the air.

'Steady on, Jenkins, it's not the Tour de France!' Ed yelled after her.

Anna slowed slightly, letting him catch her and then grinned like a loon at him as he came alongside.

'I didn't know you were such a speed demon,' he gasped, pedalling hard to keep up with her.

She laughed with glee. 'I'd forgotten. It feels almost like flying.'

Later, Anna having finally slowed down, they meandered back in the direction of the bike rack.

'You know, that's the first time I've seen you so exhilarated,' said Ed. 'I like it.'

'I guess it made me happy,' she said with surprise. It had been a long time since she'd felt she had a right to such a feeling.

They handed back their bikes and walked back towards the park entrance. 'Is it because of Simon?' he asked gently. 'Because I've a feeling there's more to that than you've told me so far.'

Anna's elation vanished, as if the sun had suddenly slipped behind a cloud. But she took a deep breath and began.

It was a relief to finally tell someone.

It all came flooding out. Everything she'd kept hidden, even from her family, from Simon's family.

'I didn't want to go to Europe with him. I said we should take a break from each other, that I was fed up with his irrational behaviour – one minute he was sky high, the next in the depths of despair. That I couldn't put up with his moodiness any more. No matter what I tried to do I couldn't make him happy. I told him we would be better off apart. Two days after that conversation, I found him in the flat, in our bed.'

'Oh Anna, sweetheart.' Ed put an arm around her shoulders as they walked. 'You must stop punishing yourself.'

'But, don't you see? It's all my fault. I told him we were over.'

'That may be, but it doesn't mean you were responsible for his actions.'

'But if I had been more patient, less selfish—'

He stopped her, pulling her to face him. 'It wasn't your fault, Anna.'

'But it was.'

'No, Anna,' he said gently. 'Get this straight: it wasn't. From everything you've said, it certainly wasn't. Anyway, what good has come of blaming yourself? You've got to forgive yourself, as hard as that is. For your own sake.'

She was undone, broken open with the telling of a story she'd kept to herself for so long. She wrung her hands together but she couldn't stop them from trembling. 'I don't know how to.'

'Come here, Jenkins,' he said gently. 'You're shaking like a leaf on the last day of autumn.' Anna fell into his arms, burying her head in his shoulder.

'It's okay; it's okay,' he murmured into her hair. Ed began to tell her the story of manzanita. 'One of the prettiest shrubs I've ever seen. It grows in the desert chaparral of the American southwest and its bark is so shiny, it looks as if it's been polished with beeswax. Some people know it as "mountain driftwood" because its branches dry out to a beautiful grey, smoothness.'

Anna wasn't sure why he was telling her this, but she was intrigued nevertheless. His story had begun to calm her.

'It has some of the hardest seeds of any plant. They can stay dormant for several years, just sitting on the bush, doing nothing. Do you know what it takes to make them germinate?'

Anna shook her head.

'Fire.' He stroked her hair. 'Only after the intense heat of a bushfire will their tough outer covering disintegrate and allow the seed within to grow.'

Finally, after her shakes had subsided to the occasional tremor, he released her, cupping her face in his hands like a flower. 'You'll get there.'

'I will?'

'You will, I know it. You just have to keep walking through the fire. And then you'll bloom.'

His certainty acted like a ballast. Steadied her. Helped her believe she might.

Chapter Forty-eight

Santiago, 1887

Daisy travelled all the next day, growing increasingly weak as her meagre food supplies ran out. She gave all of the milk she had brought to the baby, but it was barely enough, and Violeta grew listless and lethargic, spending many hours asleep. Daisy worried for her, but their only hope was to keep going. The snow had ceased, and the weather during the day became warmer, but she did not dare to remove her cloak for fear of discovery. The road zigzagged through the hills like a staircase and it was all she could do to stay upright. She was thankful for having spent so many hours riding horses along the steep Cornish cliffsides as a girl, for the rough going would have terrified someone with lesser experience.

Wrapped in Elizabeth's cloak, with Violeta strapped beneath, her flame-red hair caught up beneath its hood and a scarf obscuring much of her face, Daisy was, nevertheless, the subject of some curious glances by the few people she passed. Despite her churning nerves, she managed calm nods, occasionally exchanging a few words of Spanish, but never giving a hint of her purpose. She hid her shaking hands in her reins and recited in her head the words, 'Nearly there, nearly there . . .' even though she still had far to go and wasn't at all certain what she would find when she reached her destination.

It was late in the afternoon when the buildings of Santiago eventually came into view. The city appeared before her like a mirage in the desert – steeples and the roofs of houses poked through the dark foliage of fig and olive trees. She crossed a stone bridge over a river – the Maipo River, she remembered Mr Williamson telling her.

She felt her resolve falter. How was she going to find the place she sought? The city looked enormous and overwhelming, but she knew she had to get the baby and the box safely away from Mr Chegwidden, for him never to know of their existence, and she prayed that Mr Williamson would come to her aid. She went over in her head the words she had heard him say when they had celebrated together at Elizabeth's wedding. 'I have found a very agreeable lodging indeed. At the base of San Cristobal, one of the highest hills in the city . . . a large ochre-coloured house with white shutters. It is quite perfect.'

'*Donde esta San Cristobal*?' she asked a passing *chilena*.

The woman appeared to understand. '*Por ahi*,' she said, pointing northwards.

Sometime later, and almost as soon as she turned into the quiet, tree-lined street that circled the base of the hill, Daisy saw the house, a square, dun-coloured building and the only one that she could see with white shutters. Her heart beat faster and Violeta stirred, as if she could feel its thudding.

Pulling up her horse as quietly as she could, Daisy clumsily dismounted. She rapped on a pair of wide doors and then waited, lurching from foot to foot with nervousness and fatigue. There was a movement at an upstairs window. She knocked again, and after what seemed like an eternity but must have only been a minute or so, the doors opened.

For a moment there was silence. Daisy pulled her hood from her head, allowing her curls to escape.

'Mr Williamson?' she asked the maid. 'Is he here?'

There was a call from the shadows of the house. 'Who is it?'

'Mr Williamson!' She cried louder.

'Miss Helyer!' Mr Williamson was now at the door. 'What on earth?'

Daisy was nearly delirious with tiredness and only kept herself upright by sheer force of will. She found that she no longer had the ability to take another step and swayed, collapsing forward and falling into his arms.

When she came to, she found herself lying on a chaise in a light, attractive drawing room, a wall of which was entirely taken up with books, their spines stamped with gold lettering. There was the softness of velvet under her sore palms, and she felt as if she were lying on goose down, which she may well in fact have been, for there were several large pillows under her head. Suddenly she groped about her body, missing the weight of Violeta against her. She began to rise, panic blooming in her chest.

'There, there . . .'

She looked up to see Mr Williamson leaning over her, concern furrowing his brow. 'The infant is well. My maidservant is caring for her. I took the liberty of finding a wet nurse. Rest assured she will be most discreet.'

Daisy felt relief shoot through her. 'Oh, the baby is not mine,' she reassured him. 'But your discretion is very much required.'

'As you wish, my dear. So, tell me, what brings you to my door? I never have been so surprised as to see you here.'

Slowly, haltingly, Daisy began her story. When she got to the part about finding her mistress and her husband drenched in their own blood, she stuttered, barely able to put into words her horror at finding them thus.

'We must inform the police. At once!'

Daisy shook her head vehemently. 'Let me finish. For I have an idea who was behind this, though I doubt it will ever be proven.' She explained about finding the lilies on the bedcovers, about overhearing Mr Chegwidden and *Señor* Flores arguing. About the search for the Devil's Trumpet.

'Oh my dear,' he said, looking at once concerned and outraged. 'What are we to do?'

'I sincerely hope you will help me,' Daisy pleaded. 'Hide me for a while, for Mr Chegwidden believes that everyone at *Estancia Copihue* was murdered that night. And then I must escape. I must leave the country.' She didn't mention that she also had the Devil's Trumpet with her. She couldn't trust anyone, not even him.

'Oh my dear. What a dreadful, dreadful time you have had of it. And to travel all this way on horseback. I can scarcely credit it.'

Daisy barely registered his concern. 'I had no choice,' she said bluntly.

'Your bravery is astounding. I know of not a handful of men who would have made that journey in this weather. Let alone with a baby to tend to.'

Daisy didn't feel terribly brave. She felt scared and tired and very, very hungry. A sudden knock on the door startled her.

'It is fine, my dear,' he said, noticing her concern. 'I asked my cook to make you some food. You look like you have not eaten for days.'

She salivated as the smell of soup wafted towards her. 'Thank you, Mr Williamson, you are most generous.'

'Come now,' he said kindly, 'eat. Regain your strength.'

The maid set a large covered pot on the table and another moved noiselessly about the room, retrieving a plate, spoon and a loaf of bread from a sideboard.

When she had eaten her fill, almost emptying the tureen that sat in front of her, Daisy leant back in her chair. Mr Williamson, who had remained silent but not taken his eyes off her the entire time she had been eating, began to speak.

'It is plain that you must leave here, my dear. I must also inform the authorities.'

Daisy looked up, her eyes wide in alarm.

'As you have said, for the safety of yourself and the baby, you must go.'

'But how? And where? I have but only a little money.' She thought of the small purse of coins and notes that she had brought with her.

'I can arrange it; do not worry. There is a ship leaving for Australia in a month's time; I have some cargo due to be loaded aboard it. I will make it my business to arrange a berth for you.'

'But they cannot find out about me, or Violeta.' Her voice rose in consternation.

'Hush now, my dear. I shall send word to them via my man. Your presence here will remain secret, I can promise you that.'

'Thank you. I do not wish to appear ungrateful, but is there not a ship bound for England?' She had been holding onto the thought of one day returning home to Trebithick like a rope thrown to a drowning sailor.

He shook his head. 'Unfortunately not for some months, and I cannot keep you here for that long, for word would surely get out.'

She steeled herself, accepting her fate. It would only be for a few years, she promised herself. Until she could be sure that there was no longer a threat from that madman. Then she would bring Lily home.

Chapter Forty-nine

London, Summer 2017

Hal Graham looked even more rumpled than the first time Anna had met him, if that were possible. He rose from behind his desk and came around it to shake her hand. 'Anna. Good to see you again.'

'You too, Dr Graham. I'm sorry it is a little later than planned, but I stayed longer in Cornwall than I'd anticipated.'

'Oh yes, well, I'm not surprised. Lovely county.' He returned to his seat and motioned for her to sit on the other side of the desk.

Anna looked at him expectantly, eyeing off Elizabeth's sketchbook on a shelf behind him, wanting the small talk to be over.

He noticed her eyes flick towards the shelf, and turned to retrieve the sketchbook.

'Now, it would appear that you have quite a find on your hands. I can confirm that it is the work of Elizabeth Trebithick.'

Anna nodded.

'But you probably already know that. Edwin mentioned that you had both visited Trebithick Hall.' He shook his head. 'But what is puzzling is, as we suspected, the last watercolour. It is subtly different, but nevertheless significantly, from other examples we have of *Datura*, to safely assume that it is a subspecies. Most excitingly, it is one that we know very little about. There is only one other drawing in existence. If you come with me to the library, I can show you. I took the liberty of arranging its retrieval from our archives especially for your visit.'

When they reached the library and Hal had located the drawing Anna blinked with astonishment. It was exactly as he had said: the two drawings were of an identical plant, from the sepals to the snowy petals with their stripes of velvety black, to the stamen and the stalk.

'*Datura niger*,' Hal whispered in the library hush. 'One and the same. Native to a once-remote valley in central Chile. It's believed to have been extinct for nearly a hundred years. Once upon a time one of the most powerful plants known to humankind. Misused, it causes hallucinations and death, but in the right hands, it has unparalleled healing properties. There are even stories of it being used to treat confusion and memory loss – what we now know as dementia.'

'Alzheimer's?' she said quickly, thinking of Granny Gus.

Hal nodded. 'Not only that, but in certain concentrations it was also a painkiller, similar to laudanum, but non-addictive, according to reports from those times. It was truly a remarkable plant – it had the potential to ease the suffering, perhaps even extend the useful lives of millions, even billions of people. It's no secret that Alzheimer's is one of the biggest concerns of our times.'

Anna knew all too well.

'It's a tragedy that it became extinct. Who knows, it could have led to the development of some of the world's most valuable medicines. This drawing –' he indicated the artwork before them, 'was made by the botanist Alexander Grantham at the beginning of the twentieth century. Unfortunately, the ship that he was travelling back to England on in 1901 sank. All of his samples were lost. He had sent on his drawings ahead of him, and this is why we have this today. In later years, botanists made further expeditions to try to locate the plant but it was never found again.'

They contemplated the drawings as a realisation hit Anna with the force of a lightning strike, illuminating everything.

'It wouldn't still be that powerful if it were around today, would it? Surely developments of other drugs have superseded its potential?'

Hal shook his head. 'We'll never know and that's the tragedy. And although there are promising developments for some drug treatments for the early stages of Alzheimer's, there's still no cure.'

Anna thought of the tragedy of Elizabeth and her husband being murdered for possession of the plant, for the lives that had been affected, and the course of her family forever altered. It made her head spin to think of it, for, had Elizabeth never made the perilous journey, and then Daisy after her, then Anna, her sister, her mother, her grandmother would never have existed. If

Elizabeth had succeeded in her quest, then the world would be a different place again. So much was dependent on a twist of fate.

'You can't change the past. What's done is done,' said Ed, inadvertently echoing Florence's words as they talked later that day. He'd invited Anna to his home for dinner. 'Come and meet Ella. She's dying to find out about my mysterious new Australian friend.'

His house wasn't far from Kew, and was in the middle of a smartly kept terrace of pristine white houses with neat front gardens, each with a dazzling display of summer flowers – in one were rose bushes, heavy with blooms, in another, digitalis rose behind sweet William and delicate white fleabane, and yet another featured scarlet geraniums blooming in terracotta pots. Ed's garden was a scented mass of sage, rosemary and thyme. She also noticed a circular bed of calendula, hyssop and angelica – healing plants, all of them. She rubbed the soft flowering spike of a lavender bush as she passed, inhaling the calming scent, before knocking at the door.

There was a pounding of feet from within, and the door opened to reveal a girl, about eleven or twelve years old Anna guessed, with long, dark hair and her father's blue eyes. Ed appeared behind her in the doorway.

'Anna!' he said welcoming her in. 'Anna, this is Ella.'

'Hello,' the girl said. 'We've been waiting for you. We've been cooking especially.'

Anna sniffed – the unmistakable aroma of a roasting chicken. 'Yum. Are you a good cook, Ella?'

The girl nodded. 'Pretty good. We made pudding too. My favourite.'

'Well, I am in for a treat,' said Anna as Ella took hold of her hand and pulled her along the hallway into the house. Anna's shoulders relaxed in relief that the little girl seemed so pleased to see her. She knew from her own nieces that tween girls could be some of the hardest to figure out: at times caught up in a world of their own creation, yet at others undeniably sweet and sociable.

Ed poured her a glass of wine and they sat in a cosy kitchen at the back of the house. French doors were open onto a strip of back garden, which included a small vegetable patch, and Ella, having quizzed Anna about Australia, soon wandered off to play outside.

'Cheers,' Ed said, clinking his glass to hers. 'So, how did you get on with Hal?'

Anna filled him in.

'Heavens above. Well, what a story.' He shook his head as if regretting the loss of such a powerful plant.

'There's something else.' Anna paused. 'I have a dried specimen. And some seeds. *Datura niger*.'

Ed, who had opened the oven, nearly dropped the roasting dish he was holding. 'What? You're kidding! Really? How?'

'They were in the box with the drawings and the diary. I'm almost certain that's what they are.'

'Oh good lord,' he said. 'Did you bring them with you?'

Anna shook her head. 'No. They're still in Sydney. I wasn't sure whether quarantine rules would even let me bring them, and at the time it didn't seem important. But Ed, there's something else.'

'There is?' he said, putting the roasting dish down on the kitchen benchtop.

'Uh huh.' She paused to let the importance of her words sink in. 'Ed, I planted a few of those seeds. Thought it couldn't hurt.'

'Don't tell me . . .'

'Yup. I spoke to Mum this morning. She's been watering my plants while I'm away. I asked her about the pot of soil on my balcony. I'd particularly asked her to water it as well. She said there were green shoots.'

'You're kidding!'

'Deadly serious.'

'Do you know what you've done, Jenkins?'

She gave him a quick grin. 'Pretty good, huh?'

'I'd say so. I've heard of old seeds being propagated after years, of course, but still . . .'

'I know, right?' Anna, too, was incredulous.

Ed looked thoughtful for a moment. 'Did you plant them all? How many were there?'

'Only about half of them. Hal's going to help me arrange to airfreight the rest over to Kew. It's only taken a hundred and thirty-odd years to get them there, but I'd like to think that Elizabeth Trebithick and her father would be pleased that they're finally going to make it.'

'Good lord,' he said again. 'I can barely believe it.'

An acrid smell of burning emanated from the stovetop. 'Er, Ed,' said Anna, 'I think the vegetables might have boiled dry.'

'Oh Christ.' He took the lid off the saucepan and looked miserably at the contents.

'Why don't I go and pick some lettuce for a salad, with Ella?' Anna suggested.

'I rather think that might be wise.'

Later, after Ella had been dispatched to bed, they lingered over the dregs of the bottle of wine. 'So, what's next for you then, Jenkins?' he asked. 'I expect you'll be off to Europe?' He looked downcast at the prospect.

Anna shook her head. 'Actually, I've had a change of plan. I'm going to go back down to Cornwall. Florence has offered me her spare room and I think she'd like the company. Believe it or not, I've wangled a job for the summer working in the gardens at Trebithick, volunteer basis only. I feel as if I need more time there. And the experience will be useful. I'm keen to learn more about the plants that thrive down there and what's involved in looking after such a large estate.'

Ed brightened. 'So, you're not leaving our shores just yet?'

'Nope,' she replied. 'Think you might want to come down for another visit? Bring Ella with you this time?' Hope that he might say yes thrummed through her and she held her breath, waiting for his answer.

'I think that can certainly be arranged, Jenkins.'

They grinned foolishly at each other.

Chapter Fifty

Sydney, 1888

Marguerite gripped the rail and tried to still the mass of butterflies ready to take flight in her stomach. She could rightly be considered a veteran of ocean travel now, but her nerves were as taut as they had been on her first voyage, nearly two years earlier. The smell of the land reached out to greet her, of earth and industry and growing things and she breathed it in deeply, steadying herself against the ship's railing.

As dawn broke over the horizon the ship sailed into the glorious harbour, the one she'd been told about, had dreamed of during those long days at sea. The ship rolled in the swell as it entered the heads, and then turned to starboard, towards a small crescent of sand. Marguerite could make out several low buildings, the roofs of which were barely visible through the thick vegetation. The quarantine station. Where incoming migrants were screened for disease, their belongings fumigated and their bodies scrupulously cleansed.

As she stepped onto the rickety jetty, she raised the small soft bundle in her arms up to the buildings that hunkered on the water's edge. 'How's that, little Lily, eh? What a sight for sore eyes.' She was sure they had travelled far enough to be safe.

The baby blew bubbles from her Cupid's bow lips and blinked her bright blue eyes at Marguerite. Coffee-brown curls escaped from her bonnet and shone like mahogany in the sunlight. A smile dimpled her cheeks. Marguerite hugged the baby tight to her, humming 'Hush little baby' under her breath. Together, they had survived, and she wasn't about to let her go. They had new names in this new land and they would be safe. No one would find them. Marguerite would make sure of it.

Chapter Fifty-one

CORNWALL, SUMMER 2017

Anna woke early on her first morning at Trevone. It was three miles to Trebithick, and Florence had lent her an old boneshaker of a bicycle to get there and back, but she reckoned that after her experience in Richmond Park, she was capable of wrangling even a recalcitrant steed with wobbly steering.

Before she left London, she'd Skyped her mum and her sister, filling them in on everything that had happened since she'd been in England. 'I can't believe you've solved the mystery,' Vanessa had said. 'Well done, you.'

'Congratulations darling,' her mother had said. 'I'm really proud of you for seeing it through. What an extraordinary story. Without your persistence we might never have known that part of our history.'

'Not to mention the fact of bringing a plant back from extinction – and one with such potential,' added Vanessa. 'That's just amazing.'

Anna told them of her plans to stay on for a few months and work at Trebithick, the excitement clear in her voice.

'Sounds like a terrific idea. You sound almost like your old self,' said her mum.

There had even been a 'Good on you' in the background from Harvey. 'Are you sure he's feeling all right?' Anna asked.

'Oh, him?' Vanessa had answered. 'He's on his second glass of shiraz and the Wallabies look like they might finally beat the All Blacks.'

'Right.'

She'd called them again on arriving in Cornwall, only to discover that they had some news of their own.

'We're coming over to see you!' said Vanessa. 'Me, Mum, Harvey and the girls. End of August. It's all organised. We've booked a place in Port Isaac – it's really close to where you are, at least I think it is.'

Anna nodded. 'It is. But what about school?' she asked. 'And their activities? Fleur's ballet?'

'Oh, I think a few weeks off might be good for all of us,' replied Vanessa. 'Besides, I want them to know about this part of their history.'

Anna couldn't wait to see them, to introduce them to Florence, and perhaps also to Ed, who was coming to visit in a few weeks' time.

As she sailed along the narrow lane towards the house in the cool of the early morning, she smiled to herself. The wind rushed through her hair and she revelled in the smell of the salt air and the sounds of the sea and the sharp cries of seagulls as they hovered over the cliffs. The lane was thick with grasses, nettles and brambles, and wind-bent trees formed a green tunnel over her head. At one point she was forced to throw herself onto the tall hedge on the side of the road as a truck passed her with an insistent beep of its horn.

She made it to Trebithick Hall in one piece, if rather flustered, and parked her bicycle around the back of the old stables next to a number of others, some even more decrepit than her own. She walked towards the gardens, stopping to run her hands over the sundial, its familiar raised relief of herbs worn by more than a hundred winters.

'Ah, Anna, there you are.' It was Richard Allen, the head gardener. When she'd returned to Trebithick on her last visit, she'd sought him out and on discovering her love and knowledge of plants, he'd kindly given her a personal tour of the estate. She hadn't mentioned her connection to the Hall, but he had joked that if she ever wanted a job, she could contact him. It was exactly what she'd had in mind.

'Hello!' she called out. 'Beautiful day, isn't it?' And it was. The sun was already warming the air and the sky was a cloudless periwinkle blue.

'Ready to get stuck in?' he said, handing her a pair of gloves.

She nodded happily.

'I've paired you up with Jamie. He'll show you the ropes. Jamie!' he called, putting a hand to his mouth.

Anna looked in the direction of his shout as a man emerged from the greenhouse.

'Jamie. This is Anna. I'd like you to help her out today.'

'Anna. Jamie Chegwidden.'

Anna stumbled backwards, looking up into a pair of the blackest eyes she had ever seen.

Acknowledgements

The story told in this book came to me as the result of a couple of events: a sultry afternoon in Sydney's Royal Botanic Garden, long a favourite place, where I ran my hands along the beautiful sundial there and was suddenly transported to an English walled garden, imagining where a similar such sundial might be fixed. Then, several months later, I visited Kew Gardens, and the wonderful Marianne North Gallery, hung from floor to ceiling with her extraordinary oils, depicting the flora of the many countries to which she travelled. I began to wonder what the life of an adventurous lady botanist must have been like, and so my story began. Two years later, I was at Kew again, and found the exhibition of botanical art from Dr Shirley Sherwood's collection, together with an exhibition of the work and letters of Joseph Hooker. It was also instructive to read the transcripts of his letters and of his travels and travails as a nineteenth-century plant-hunter.

Any errors in imagining late-nineteenth century Cornwall and Chile are my own. I found Maria Graham's, a sea captain's widow, *Journal of a Residence in Chile, During the Year 1822* invaluable and drew heavily upon her accounts and descriptions of Valparaiso in the nineteenth century. Kate Forsyth, a historical fiction author and whom I very much admire, very generously gave me advice on tackling a dual timeline story. I am also very grateful to Varuna, The Writers' House, in the New South Wales Blue Mountains, for the chance to spend a precious, uninterrupted week stitching the two narratives together.

Thanks also go to my agent, Margaret Connolly, for her continual encouragement and belief in my writing, and without whom I would not be writing these words or all of the others that make up this story. To Richard, for his fearless driving along the winding Cornish lanes. To Andy, Becky and Mercedes for being such positive early readers and to Taryn the most honest critique partner I could wish for. Finally, I could not be luckier to have such a thoughtful, intelligent and enthusiastic publisher in Rebecca Saunders. Indeed, the entire team at Hachette Australia, including Fiona, Justin, Louise, Karen and Alana, have been so incredibly supportive and generous and I am very lucky to have found a home there.

Read on for an extract from Kayte Nunn's next transporting novel

1951. Esther Durrant, a young mother, is committed to an isolated mental asylum by her husband. The hospital is at first Esther's prison but soon becomes her refuge.

2018. Free-spirited marine scientist Rachel Parker discovers a collection of hidden love letters, and is determined to track down the intended recipient.

2018. Meanwhile Eve is helping her grandmother, a renowned mountaineer, write her memoirs. When Rachel contacts her, secrets kept buried for more than sixty years resurface . . .

A gothic, impossible love story full of intrigue – perfect for fans of Elizabeth Gilbert and Kate Morton.

CHAPTER ONE

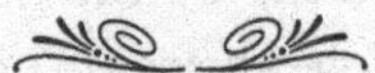

London and Little Embers, Autumn 1951

It wasn't their usual destination for a holiday and the timing was hardly ideal. John and Esther Durrant generally took a week in Eastbourne or Brighton in the final week of August, so the far south-west tip of England was an odd choice, even more so considering it was early November. John, however, had been adamant. 'It'll do you good,' he said to his wife, in a tone of false jollity, when he suggested – no, *insisted* on – the trip. 'Put some colour back in your cheeks. Sea air.' Never mind that a bitter cold gripped the nation with the kind of weather that you wouldn't put the cat out in and Esther couldn't have felt less like a week away even had she spent the previous year down a coal mine. She also didn't understand why they were leaving Teddy behind with the nanny, but she couldn't begin to summon the necessary enthusiasm for an argument.

Before catching the train south, they dined at a restaurant near Paddington station. Esther wasn't hungry, but she allowed

John to decide for her nonetheless. After a brief perusal of the menu and dispatching their order to the black-clad, white-aproned waitress, he unfurled his *Telegraph* and spent the time before the arrival of their food absorbed in its pages. Winston Churchill and the Conservative Party had been returned to power she saw, noticing the headline on the front page. John was pleased, although privately she believed Mr Churchill terribly old and probably not up to the job. They didn't discuss politics anymore, for they saw the world quite differently, she had come to realise.

Esther managed a little of the soup that arrived in due course, and half a bread roll, while John cleared his dish and several glasses of claret. Then Dover sole and tiny turned vegetables, all of which he ate with gusto while she pushed the peas and batons of carrot around on her plate, pretending to eat. Her husband made no comment.

Esther declined dessert but John, it appeared, had appetite enough for both of them and polished off a slice of steamed pudding made with precious rationed sugar and a generous dollop of custard. He glanced at his watch. 'Shall we make our way to the train, my dear?' he asked, wiping the bristles of his moustache on a starched napkin. She couldn't help but be reminded of an otter who'd just had a fish supper: sleek, replete and satisfied with himself. He was wearing the dark suit – his favourite – and the tie she'd given him several birthdays ago, when she had been expecting Teddy and the future felt as if it were the merest outline, a sketch, waiting for them to paint it in bold and vivid colours. Something to look forward to, not to fear.

She nodded and he rose and reached for her hand, helping her to her feet. It was a short walk from the restaurant to the station, but Esther was glad of her thick coat and gloves. She'd not ventured from the house in weeks – the November weather had been simply ghastly – and she shivered as she felt the wind slice through her outer garments and numb the tip of her nose and lips.

They entered the cavernous terminal and Esther was almost overwhelmed by the bustle and noise, the hissing of the giant steam engines and the raucous cries of porters as they effortlessly manoeuvred unwieldy barrows top-heavy with luggage. It was as if they were part of the opening scene of a play, the moments before the main characters take the stage. She might once have enjoyed the spectacle, found the purposeful activity invigorating, but today she gripped John's arm as he steered her towards Platform One. 'We'll be there in a jiffy,' he said, reassuring her.

Everywhere she looked, lapels were splashed with poppies, blood-red against dark suits. A brief frown creased the pale skin of her forehead as it took her a moment to place them. Then she remembered: it would soon be Armistice Day. The terror, uncertainty and deprivations of the recent war were a scarlet tattoo on every Englishman and woman's breast.

Eventually, the train was located, tickets checked and they were ushered to their carriage by a porter. She took careful steps along a narrow corridor and they found their cabin: two slim berths made up with crisp cotton sheets and wool blankets the colour of smoke.

She breathed a quiet sigh of relief that they would not be expected to lie together. In recent months John had taken to sleeping in his dressing room and she was still not ready for him to return to the marital bed. 'I confess I am rather tired,' she said, pulling off her gloves. 'I might settle in.' She opened a small cupboard, put her hat on the shelf inside and hung her coat on a hook that was conveniently placed underneath.

'I shall take a nightcap in the Lounge Car. That is if you don't mind, darling,' John replied.

He had taken the hint. So much between them went unsaid these days. Esther turned around and inclined her head. 'Not at all, you go. I shall be perfectly fine here.'

'Very well.' He left in a hurry, likely in pursuit of a dram or two of single malt.

She sat heavily on the bed, suddenly too exhausted to do more than kick off her shoes and lie back upon the blankets. She stared up at the roof of the cabin as it curved above her, feeling like a sardine in a tin. It wasn't unpleasant: if anything, she was cocooned from the activity going on outside and wouldn't be bothered by it.

Before long, a whistle sounded and, with a series of sudden jerks, the train began to move away from the station, shuddering as it gathered speed. After a few minutes it settled into a swaying rhythm and Esther's eyelids grew heavy. She fought to stay awake. Summoning the little determination she still possessed, she rallied and found her night things. It would not do to fall asleep still fully clothed, only to be roused by her husband on his return from the lounge.

John had asked their daily woman, Mary, to pack for them both, telling Esther that she needn't lift a finger. Normally she wouldn't have countenanced anyone else going through her things, but it had been easier not to object, to let them take over, as she had with so much recently. She had, however, added her own essentials to the cardigans, skirts and stockings, and tucked away among her smalls was a small enamelled box that resembled a miniature jewellery case. She found it, flipped the catch and the little red pills inside gleamed at her like gemstones, beckoning. As she fished one out, she noticed her ragged nails and reddened cuticles. A different version of herself would have minded, but she barely gave them a second thought, intent as she was on the contents of the box. Without hesitating, she placed the pill on her tongue, swallowing it dry.

She put the box in her handbag, drew the window shades and changed quickly, removing her tweed skirt and blouse and placing them in the cupboard with her hat and coat before pulling a fine lawn nightgown over her head. After a brief wash at the tiny corner basin, she dried her face on the towel provided and ran a brush through her hair before tucking herself between the starched sheets like a piece of paper in an envelope. She was lost to sleep hours before John returned.

~

On their arrival in Penzance the next morning he escorted her from the train, handling her once more as if she were his mother's best bone china. She didn't object, for she knew he meant well. His concern for her would have been touching had she been able to focus her mind on it – or anything else for that matter – for more than a few minutes, but it was as if there were a thick pane of glass, rather like the ones in the train windows, separating her from him, the world and everything in it.

In Penzance harbour, John engaged a small fishing dinghy – 'hang the expense' he had said when Esther looked at him with a question in her eyes. 'There is a ferry – the *Scillonian* – but there was a nasty accident last month, she hit the rocks in heavy fog by all accounts, and anyway it doesn't call at the island we want to reach. I looked into the possibility of a flight – there's an outfit that flies Dragon Rapides from Land's End, which could have been awfully thrilling, but they only operate in fine weather.'

Esther had no idea what a 'Dragon Rapide' might be, but thought that a boat was probably the safer option. As he spoke, she glanced upwards. The sky was low and leaden, the grey of a pigeon's breast, and the air damp with the kind of light mist that softened the edges of things but didn't soak you, at least not to begin with. She huddled further into her coat, hands deep in her pockets. What on earth were they doing here? The boat looked as though it would scarcely survive a strong breeze. The hull was patched and its paintwork faded; translucent scales flecked its wooden rails and it reeked of fish.

'Shall we embark?' His face was hopeful.

Esther did as she was bid and climbed aboard, doing her best to avoid stepping on the purple-red slime that stained the decking. It was definitely the guts of some sea creature or other.

They huddled on a bench in the dinghy's small cabin as the captain got them underway. Beneath a pewter sky and afloat an even darker sea, she was reminded of Charon, the ferryman of Hades, transporting newly dead souls across the Acheron and the Styx. The air was undoubtedly fresh here though. Sharply scented. Briny. Far more pleasant than the filmy London fog, which coated your hair, your skin, even your teeth with a fine layer of dirt. It roused her a little from her somnambulant state and she glanced about the cabin, seeing a dirty yellow sou'-wester, a length of oily rope acting as a paperweight on a creased and frayed shipping chart.

'Look!' John called out as they puttered out of Penzance's sheltering quay. 'St Michael's Mount. Centuries ago the English saw off the Spanish Armada from its battlements. At low tide you can walk across the causeway. Shame we didn't have time for it.'

'Perhaps on our return?' she offered, her voice almost drowned out by the roar of the engine and the sound of the water slapping against the hull of the boat.

John didn't reply, looking out to sea instead. Had he even heard her?

'Oh look! Kittiwakes.'

Esther raised her eyes towards the horizon; there were several grey and white gulls wheeling above them, their shrieks rending the air. To the left, a trio of torpedo-shaped birds whipped past. 'And puffins!' he cried. The new sights and sounds had invigorated him, while she was already feeling queasy as the dinghy pitched and rolled. She registered their fat cheeks and bright orange bills and was reminded briefly of a portly professor friend of her father's. She tried but failed to match John's enthusiasm, pasting what felt like a smile on her face and swallowing hard to prevent herself from retching.

The captain cheerfully pointed out the site of several shipwrecks but Esther did her best not to pay too much heed to his story of a naval disaster in the early eighteenth century, where more than fifteen hundred sailors lost their lives. 'One of the worst wrecks in the whole British Isles,' he said with a kind of proud awe. As he spoke, a lighthouse, tall and glowing white against the grey sky, came into view. It hadn't done its job then. But then perhaps it had been built afterwards, to prevent such a tragedy happening again.

They motored on as the rain thickened and soon a curtain of fog erased the horizon completely. Esther's stomach churned and bile rose in her throat. Even John's high spirits seemed dampened and they sat, saying nothing, as Esther fumbled in her pocket for a handkerchief and pressed it to her mouth, hoping that she was not going to empty the contents of her stomach onto the decking. She tried not to think about them mingling with the fish guts and salt water that sloshed just beyond the cabin. She gritted her teeth against the spasms of nausea while her insides roiled and twisted as if she had swallowed a serpent.

The boat pitched and heaved in the rising swell as the waves frothed whitecaps beside them. 'It's getting a bit lumpy,' said the captain with a grin. 'Thick as a bog out there too.' John hadn't mentioned the name of the particular godforsaken speck of land that they were headed for and Esther didn't have the energy to ask. She tried to think of something else, anything but this purgatory of a voyage, but there were darker shapes in the yawning wasteland of her mind, so she forced herself instead to stare at the varnished walls of the cabin, counting to five hundred and then back again to take her mind off her predicament. She was only vaguely aware now of John next to her and the captain, mere inches away at the helm. Outside, the sea appeared to be at boiling point, white and angry, as if all hell had been let loose, and she gripped a nearby handhold until her fingers lost all feeling. She no longer had any confidence that they would reach their destination. She had ceased caring about anything very much months ago, so it hardly mattered either way.

Eventually, however, an island hove into view, and then another, grey smudges on the choppy seascape. Almost as soon as they had appeared they disappeared again into the mist, leaving nothing but the grey chop of the water. The captain's expression changed from sunny to serious as he concentrated on steering them clear of hidden shoals and shelves. 'They'd hole a boat if you don't pay attention. Splinter it like balsa,' he said, not lifting his eyes from the horizon.

All at once the wind and rain eased a fraction, the fog lifted, and they puttered alongside a small wooden jetty that stuck out from a sickle curve of bleached-sand beach. Like an arrow lodged in the side of a corpse, Esther imagined.

The bloated carcass of a sea bird, larger than a gull, but smaller than an albatross, snagged her attention. Death had followed her to the beach. Her thoughts were so dark these days; she couldn't seem to chase them away. There was, however, some slight relief at having arrived, that the particular nightmare of the journey might soon be ended. For now that would have to be enough. 'Small mercies,' she whispered. She tried to be grateful for that.

The captain made the boat fast, then helped them and their luggage ashore, even as the boat bobbed dangerously up and down next to the jetty, its hull grinding, wood on wood, leaving behind flecks of paint. An ill-judged transfer and they would end up in the water. Esther stepped carefully onto the slippery boards, willing her shaky legs to hold her up.

Once they were both safely on land, the captain slung several large brown-paper-wrapped parcels after them. 'Pop them under the shelter and when you get there, let the doc know that these are for him – he can send someone down for them before they get too wet. The house is up thataway. A bit of a walk, mind and none too pleasant in this weather. There's not many that care to come this far.'

The pelting rain had begun to fall again, blown sideways at them by the wind and Esther silently agreed with him; she couldn't see the point of this wearisome journey, but John hefted their suitcases, looking at her with anticipation. 'Think you can manage it, darling?'

Some small part of her didn't want to disappoint him and she nodded faintly, still no clearer as to exactly where they were.

The walk wasn't long, but the wind buffeted them this way and that and Esther was obliged to hold onto her hat, a small-brimmed, dull felt affair that did little to keep off the rain. She faltered as she almost tripped on an object on the path and stopped to see what it was.

The doll lay on its back. Naked. China limbs splayed at unnatural angles. Eyes open, staring vacantly at the sky. A tangled mat of dirty yellow hair strewn with leaves and feathers. Esther stepped over it, feeling as she did, a tingling in her breasts and a spreading warmth at odds with the blustery, chilled air. It was a moment before she realised what it was, bewildered that her body still had the ability to nurture, in spite of everything.

John strode ahead, his steps unfaltering. He didn't appear to have noticed the abandoned toy, or if he had, had paid it no heed. Angling her chin down, Esther drew her coat in closer, its astrakhan collar soft against her cheeks, her grip tight on the handbag at her elbow.

As if sensing she'd stopped, John turned to look back at her. 'Not far now.' His expression coaxed her forward.

She gave him a curt nod and continued on, leaving the doll where it lay. The path ahead wound steeply upwards and was pockmarked with shallow pools the colour of dishwater. Esther had to watch her step to avoid them. Her shoes were new, barely worn-in, not that she cared particularly about getting them wet. The avoidance of the puddles was an automatic action, a force of long habit, like so many were for her now.

A few steps further on she glanced up, seeing the grasses either side of them rippling and swaying, pummelled by the unrelenting gusts blowing off the ocean. Westwards, cliffs like fresh scars marked where the land ended, rising abruptly as if forced upwards from the earth's bowels. Huge boulders lay scattered at their base, a giant's playthings. It was a wholly foreign landscape for someone used to red brick, stone, tarmacadam and wrought iron.

'Nearly there, darling.' John's tone was meant to encourage her, but it sounded a false note. Ersatz, her mother would have called it. And she would have been right.

CHAPTER TWO

Aitutaki, South Pacific, February 2018

Rachel eased herself from the arms of her lover, sliding from beneath the thin sheet, being careful not to wake him. It was not yet dawn, but a waxing moon cast a glow through the uncurtained window. She located her shift, tossed on the tiled floor the night before, and shimmied it over her shoulders, down onto her torso, smoothing it over her thighs. She twisted her long hair into a knot and worked a kink out of her back, twisting and rolling the stiffness from her shoulders. Picking up her sandals, she tiptoed towards the door.

As she laid her hand on the latch, she allowed herself a single backward glance. He was beautiful: Adonis-like, with skin the colour of scorched caramel, dark lustrous hair that she loved to curl around her fingers and full, curving, skilful lips. Young, as always.

Closing the door gently so as not to wake him, she stood outside the straw-roofed bungalow and gazed across to the lagoon. The moon glistened on the water, and a faint light was visible on the horizon. On a clear night here, the sky was a sea of stars, with the Milky Way a wide belt arcing across the heavens. She would miss these skies more than the man she had just left behind. She checked her watch. Only three hours until her flight.

'Rachel!' The Adonis stood in the doorway. He had woken and found her missing. Damn. She'd lingered too long, taking in the beauty before dawn one last time.

She turned, meeting his gaze. 'You knew I was leaving.'

'Yes, but like this? No chance to say goodbye?'

'I thought it would be easier.'

'On you perhaps.' He looked sulky, his lower lip jutting out.

She tried, but couldn't feel sorry for him. He was young and gorgeous and would soon find someone else. Eager female research assistants would be falling over themselves to take her place. 'You'll be fine,' she said.

The sultry climate of the islands, where a permanent sheen of perspiration covered the skin, together with their remoteness, meant that relationships sprang up as quickly as the plants that flourished here. Generally their roots were as shallow, too.

'Come here?' It was more a question than a statement.

Rachel steeled herself against the pleading tone even as her footsteps led her back to him. Taller and broader than her, he easily enveloped her in his arms. 'I'll miss you,' he murmured into her hair.

'You too.' Her voice was brusque, hiding anything softer.

'Somehow I doubt that,' he laughed. 'You have the blood of a lizard.' He released her and placed his palm below her collarbone. 'There is a stone where a heart should be.'

They weren't entirely unfair comments and she didn't have time to argue with him.

'Stay in touch, eh?'

She gave a noncommittal shrug.

He kissed her forehead and hugged her once more before releasing her. 'Au revoir Rachel. Travel well.'

She almost raced along the path to her bungalow in her haste to get away.

~

An hour later, she burst through the doors of the tiny airport and dumped her backpack at the check-in counter. '*Kia orana* LeiLei,' she greeted the woman waiting to take her ticket.

'*Kia orana* Rachel.' She gave her a smile that split her face. The island – atoll to be precise – was small enough that Rachel had got to know most of its permanent inhabitants in the time she'd spent there. LeiLei, who did double-duty checking in passengers on Air Pacific and mixing fresh coconut piña coladas at Crusher Bar – both with equal enthusiasm – was a favourite.

LeiLei examined her ticket. 'Flying home?'

'Something like that.' The real answer was a complicated one. Growing up in a military family, Rachel had been to six different schools by the time she was twelve, moving from place to place, leaving friends behind and being forced to make new ones almost every year. She still remembered the name of her best friend when she was five. Erin. Could still recall the curly hair that never stayed in its pigtails and the swarm of freckles across her face. The two of them had been inseparable from their first day in Mrs Norman's kindergarten class, sitting next to each other, spending every recess and lunchtime together. Rachel had cried as though her heart would break when her parents told her they were moving away. The next time it happened, she made a deliberate decision not to give her heart to people or places again. It was undoubtedly part of the reason she was still a rolling stone.

Home had, for a few years in her teens, been Pittwater, at the northern tip of Sydney. Accessible only by boat. She'd loved those years living with the rhythm of the tides, never more than footsteps away from salt water, so it came as no surprise that after graduation she sought research postings on islands or waterways.

It was on Pittwater that she learned to drive a small aluminium boat powered by an outboard motor that passed for transport in that corner of the world. At fifteen, she was part of the tinny tribe, ferrying herself and her younger brother to and from the high school on the mainland and racing their friends across the sheltered waters, something they'd been expressly forbidden to do. She learned to pilot the tiny boat through pouring rain and bustling gales, as well as on days where barely a breath of wind rippled the water's glassy surface and none of them hurried to lessons.

She'd learned where to find the plumpest oysters and when to harvest them; where the shoals were shallowest and likely to ground the tinny. To appreciate the beauty of the pearly light of dawn during the solitary joy of a morning kayak, her paddle pleating the water into ripples that stretched out in her wake. It had been hard to leave and go to university in the city.

When her dad had retired, he and her mother had returned to Pittwater, to a house built into the side of a hill and surrounded by gum trees and overrun with lantana.

She planned to squeeze in a week or so with them on her way through Australia, but hadn't rung. Wanted to surprise them. Her mouth watered at the thought of her mum's scones, warm and spread thick with homemade jam. They'd be disappointed she wouldn't stay longer, but she couldn't help that.

Rachel shed lives as easily as a snake its skin, starting afresh somewhere new every couple of years, never stopping to look back. The new posting, to a group of islands off the coast of southern

England, was an interesting one – to her anyway. She would be studying the unattractively named *Venus verrucosa*, or warty venus clam. Another bivalve, if rather smaller than her beloved pa'ua. Clams, it seemed, had become her thing.

She was to survey the islands, estimating the *verrucosa* population to determine changes and their correlation to ambient and sea temperatures. She would be entirely on her own, not part of a group as she had been previously, and it was this, as much as the actual project, that most appealed to her.

The irony that she studied sessile sea creatures, ones that barely moved once they fixed themselves to the ocean floor, when she drifted through the world like weed on the current, was not lost on her. Unlike the clams that cemented themselves to the seabed with sticky byssal threads, she never became attached, to anything, anywhere or anyone.

'Safe travels,' said LeiLei, coming around the counter to engulf her in a plump, sweetly scented hug and handing back her passport. 'Come and see us again soon.'

She smiled at her friend, turned and didn't look back.